One Real McCoy

By Anne Harper

ISBN: 1-4196-9628-9
ISBN-13: 9781419696282

Visit www.booksurge.com to order additional copies.

AUTHORS' NOTE

ACKNOWLEDGEMENTS

I'd like to thank my editor, Von Gadd, for the insightful way she reshaped this book, for sound boarding ideas and laughing at my jokes, and for recognizing the process; John Sutherland for reading and re-reading countless drafts, for never losing his patience and for offering editorial encouragement; Alex Heredon of International Mining Associates for sharing his lifetime knowledge of the mining industry; USN Captain George Harley for his insights into the military and his advice about aviation; Jenny Graham of Radisson Hotels for introducing me to the world of the hospitality industry; my parents for my 'creative' genes, and my American family for opening their home and their hearts to me.

And, finally, the very helpful and talented team at BookSurge (in the order in which they got involved in this process): Stefan Markey, Richard Riley, Mabry Morrison, Lauren Woolley, Sarah Southerland and Angela Johnson.

Dublin, Ireland, May last year

<u>Reasons to marry Sean:</u>
1) He asked me
2) Mum and Dad love him
3) I'd be a future politician's wife

<u>Reasons NOT to marry Sean:</u>
1) He asked me (only one I've been with – I'm settling)
2) Mum and Dad love him (~~I don't~~) (I like him as a friend!) (with benefits!!!) (such as they are)
3) I'd be a politician's wife (LOLOLOL!!!)

She fiddled with her necklace and looked over her list.

Jaysus! Get a grip! She thought. *It's a solid relationship. No one will ever love me like he does. I've known him forever. Oooh! Those should go on the list! Good!*

She added to her list:
4) He's crazy about me, & treats me well
5) It's safe
6) Broccoli, chicken fillets, milk, potatoes

Well, at least I got something constructive done today. Better do some shopping to clear me head.

She gathered her unopened books, shoved them in her backpack and looked around the study hall. She could see the tops of the heads of her dedicated fellow students, their noses deep in their study material, and felt a pang of guilt.

Broccoli, chicken, milk, potatoes ... Oooh! Soap! And then I'll finish this chapter. Now, where the bloody hell did I leave me purse this time? Jaysus! It'd better be at the flat!

With a heavy sigh, she left the study hall.

Tomorrow! I'll have a nutritious dinner tonight, get a good night's sleep ... Sean'll have to spend the night elsewhere ... put in ten or twelve solid study hours tomorrow... Hmmm? Better change broccoli to asparagus... and ace the exam Friday. Good plan. Tomorrow! ... Asparagus, chicken, milk, potatoes, soap.

She arrived at her apartment, opened the heavy front door and located her purse behind the hallway table.

Asparagus, chicken, milk...

The sound from the living room made her stop cold.

... potatoes ...?

Curiosity fuelled by adrenaline and fear got the upper hand and she quietly pushed the living room door open.

Whatta bloody FOCK?!?

Chicago, Illinois, May this year
1

Jaysus! The sun comes out, and the freckles won't be wanting to be outdone. Look at me! Me face looks like a bloody connect-the-dots puzzle!

Kelly McCoy was washing asparagus in the Russell kitchen and caught a reflection of herself in the window above the kitchen sink.

She'd arrived at the Russell household in the previous July. A fresh-faced, slender girl with glasses, Kelly appeared shy, timid and reticent. She turned out to be the complete opposite. She was the Energizer Bunny the Russell family had so desperately needed.

Susan Russell had been very close to giving birth to her third child, and when they met Kelly at O'Hare that hot, humid July afternoon, she was so utterly uncomfortable that Kelly assumed responsibility immediately. Two weeks later, Jonathan Edward Russell Jr. was born, and life, as Kelly knew it, would never be the same again.

She smiled absent-mindedly at her reflection in the window.

Well, I guess that's the whole point of this au pair business. Pick a young, inexperienced girl up from the boonies, drop her right smack in the mayhem of changing poopy nappies, cleaning a home big enough to house a small Irish village, cooking for kids who think ketchup is one of the main food groups, and 'poof!' a year later, she'll return to Ireland to start a family of her own.

Kelly paused in her thoughts and frowned at the window.

Naah, scratch that. In a year's time she'll have sworn off ever having children, taken an oath of celibacy and become a nun…

"I still hate you!" a child's voice defiantly interrupted Kelly's thoughts.

"And I still love you, Pudge!" Kelly responded.

"You promised you were gonna stop calling me that!"

"And you promised to stick to your diet!"

She heard a door slam upstairs and rolled her eyes at her reflection.

…a nun in a silent *order.*

The image of a penguin appeared next to hers in the window. "Holy Bat, Shiteman! It's James Bond!" Kelly exclaimed as she saw Jonathan Russell's reflection.

"I'll have my martini shaken, not stirred," Jon said, striking his hallmark James Bond pose.

For a slightly beer-bellied, prematurely graying thirty-seven year-old father of three, Jon Russell looked very handsome in a tuxedo. Kelly turned from her vegetables to face him.

"Has she called?" Jon said, looking worried.

"Afraid not," Kelly wiped her hands on a kitchen towel. "I don't think she'll make it. Her last message was over an hour ago, and she did say for you to go and make her apologies."

Sighing deeply, Jon ran his fingers through his hair. This was not good. Even though Parker MacIntyre III was an egocentric womanizer, he did have a sense of social decorum and especially wanted the young executives with attractive wives to appear at social functions. Susan certainly fell into that category.

Jon looked up at Kelly. "So, how are the kids?" Just then he noticed that the under-the-cabinet TV was broadcasting about the upcoming summit to be held in Dublin in June. "Kelly?" Jon said. "Is everything alright?"

Kelly almost had to tear herself from the tiny screen. "Huh?" she said, turning her attention back to Jon. "I'm sorry, yes. Eddie has had his bottle, and is now working off the calories."

She nodded to the floor by her feet. Jon looked across the kitchen island to see his ten month-old son crawling across the tiled floor with a face as determined as if he intended his tiny body to break the sound barrier. Eddie heard his name being spoken, stopped crawling and looked up at

Kelly, who winked at him and pointed in the direction of Jon. Eddie's gaze followed her pointed finger, and he saw his father.

"Awffaghawwedbadda!" Eddie drooled happily and clapped his hands on his knees.

Jon and Kelly laughed out loud. "I believe that's Kurdish for 'Daddy, where have you been all day? I missed you'." Kelly said.

Jon walked around the kitchen island and picked up his son.

Kelly sneaked a peek at the tiny TV screen. Commercials. "Emma is at Amber's. Tammy will bring her home for dinner. And Abby is upstairs in her room. Sulking." Kelly sighed that last word. She rolled her eyes. Jon raised an inquisitive eyebrow at her while cooing at his baby son. "She tried to sneak a cookie by me, and I caught her and gave her an apple instead," Kelly said matter-of-factly.

"So, that's what the door-slamming was about. Heard it, didn't want to get involved," Jon said, and raised an arm in resignation. "Did she relinquish her loot, though?"

"Aye. What choice did she have?" Kelly said with a wink, as she turned her attention back to the TV. The BBC cable channel was again on the subject of Condoleezza Rice, Gordon Brown and Gerry Adams meeting in Dublin. Kelly was absent-mindedly fiddling with her necklace. "I can't believe they're broadcasting this meeting like this," Kelly said with worry written all over her face. "It's…like…it's like they're sending out invitations for trouble," she said.

"Hoping to catch a glimpse of Sean?" Jon said with a smirk.

Busted!

"No, it's just so rare for news from Ireland," Kelly lied. "I can't believe they're negotiating with Sinn Fein. Not all terrorists are hide-in-a-hole Arabs, you know." But Sean was involved in the summit, so naturally Kelly was curious.

"Heard from him lately?" Jon read her mind.

Kelly sighed. "Got an e-mail this morning." She turned away from Jon. She couldn't handle his inquisitive eyes.

"Aaaand?"

"Oh, you know," Kelly tried to sound casual, while giving the asparagus a disproportionate amount of attention, moving them to the steamer. "Nothing of consequence, really."

"Let me guess. 'I'm so sorry.' 'I made a huge mistake.' 'She meant nothing to me.' 'It'll never happen again.' 'You're the only one I've ever loved.' 'Ever will love.' 'Please forgive me.' 'I love you.' 'I want you back.' 'I can't live without you.' 'If I can't have you I'll do something drastic … I'll … I'll … switch to decaf!'" Jon ranted like a broken-hearted teenager.

It was all too familiar to everyone in the Russell household. Kelly's former fiancé had left messages for her with the Russells while she was still on the plane from Dublin nearly a year ago. How he had gotten their phone number was a mystery.

The cheating Muppet was the uncrowned King of Blarney and probably got the number by sweet-talking the au pair agency. Or else, they gave it to him just to shut him up.

So, Kelly had no choice but to share the story of her sad love life. She had never talked about it to anyone, and sharing it with (then) strangers, astonishingly, helped. Sean had become the butt of many jokes over the past months.

Kelly laughed and turned to Jon.

"Any of the above?" Jon mused.

She heaved a sigh. "All of the above. And he still wants to marry me. Can you believe the nerve of that yoke?!" She was idly fiddling with her necklace again.

"What can I tell you, hon? We are the shallow and empty creatures we appear to be," Jon said absent-mindedly, while making faces at Eddie.

"But you're not," Kelly insisted. "You're like the picture perfect husband and father."

Yikes! Sounded a bit like tacky Tammy, the two-tonne trailer tramp, just then.

"What I mean is, it's obvious you and Susan love each other very much. You never quarrel. I've seen men flirt mercilessly with Susan and women literally going goo-gaah over you. And it never ruffles a jealous feather! What's your secret?"

"Women go goo-gaah over me? Who?!" Jon said, intrigued.

Tacky Tammy, the two-tonne trailer tramp for starters.

Kelly decided to remain silent.

Jon shrugged. "I dunno. I guess our secret is the fact that we both work long hours, and we're always away on business. When we finally do have some time to spend together, we'd better make the best of it."

Kelly raised an eyebrow. *Not buying it, macho-man. You're grand in spite of being apart, not because of it!*

Jon set Eddie gingerly on the floor and emerged from behind the kitchen island, striking his Arnold Schwarzenegger pose. "Owa, it could be," he said and pushed his hands in the air as if pumping a shotgun. "Shee vudn't dawe cheet on me. Ewe vanna cheet on me? Aye vill cheet on ewe fuast."

Jon's imitations always had Kelly and the girls in stitches. Kelly was wiping the tears from her eyes as Tammy Martin, Emma's friend Amber's young, single mother walked through the back door with the two three year-olds in tow. Jon, always the entertainer, continued his Arnold impressions for the girls, to the point of hysteria.

"Tami! Ewe are blont tooday!" Jon pointed at Tammy's new hair color.

Tammy giggled and twirled around for Jon. "You like?" she said.

"Aye luuuf!" Jon responded and pecked a quick kiss on her cheek.

Tammy looked disappointed. Just then the phone rang. Kelly hurried to answer it.

"Kelly? … you? It's Susan! Can you hear me?" The connection was awful.

"Yeah, barely. Where are you?"

"… Phoenix. … flight … ..layed. … too hot to take off, … sitting here, … cool down. … Jon home …?" Susan sounded frustrated.

Kelly handed the phone over to Jon mouthing, 'Susan'. Jon took the phone and walked into the dining room.

"What's fo dinnew?" Emma asked Kelly. "Can Ambew and huh Mom stay?"

"Of course they can," Kelly said, knowing full well that Tammy had only volunteered to look after Emma that afternoon in hopes for a dinner invitation. Life was not easy for a single mom in an upscale suburban Chicago neighborhood.

"Come on Ambew, wet's go watch Spwingy!"

"Halt!" Kelly commanded. The two three year-olds froze. "First you set the table, then we eat, then maybe you'll get to watch Springy."

With exaggerated sighs Emma and Amber turned toward the dining room, and did as they were told. Kelly didn't much care for the way the children set the table, but would much rather have them do that than watch Springy. Or anything currently on children's television, for that matter.

Teletubbies had been a horrifying experience of foamy, formless aliens with zero educational value. Sponge Bob was a washcloth wearing a tie, shorts with a belt and suspenders and living under the sea. And Disney! Evil is always ugly and good is always beautiful? What kinda bizarre message does that send the future genera-

tions? And did anyone in that corporation know the real meaning of the word 'classic'? And now Springy, a mattress spring, meant to keep the Boogey man away,… I guess… yet so disturbed it was a wonder any child in America ever slept at all. What were the producers of children's television thinking of? And whatever happened to little girls playing dress-up and serving air to their dollies?

"Sooo, Kelly," Tammy said, taking a seat by the kitchen island. "When is it you're leaving again?" she asked for the umpteenth time.

Not soon enough for you, since you've asked me that same question every day for the past two weeks, ya daft cow!

Kelly smiled at Tammy and said, "Friday a week is my last day. My parents are coming over and we'll do some traveling together, and I'll go home with them. Back to Dublin, where I'll finish graduate school. Business Management." Having answered the same questions from Tammy so often, she volunteered the information, knowing what the progression of questions was going to be.

Write it down already!

Kelly both disliked and pitied Tammy. The Irish Catholic upbringing in her taught her to 'pray for those less fortunate'. So she had. The Russells had taken Tammy, a recovering alcoholic, under their wing, after her husband abandoned her while pregnant with Amber. They told Kelly that she used to be quite attractive once, but on the wagon, she had piled on the pounds.

Kelly's thoughts were interrupted by Jon walking back into the kitchen.

"That was Susan. Her plane is on the ramp now, so she probably won't make it, or will have to rush there directly from the plane," he said, and the disappointment was obvious on his face. He turned to Tammy, whose face lit up like a Christmas tree. "Tammy, I have a huge favor to ask."

Tammy turned her face to his and looked as if she were ready to be kissed. Kelly felt nauseous, and turned her attention to the stove.

"Tammy, I really shouldn't go to this thing by myself tonight," Jon started, looking very sincere. "You know how MacIntyre can be."

Tammy nodded, moving closer to Jon. Kelly made a conscious effort to avoid looking at their reflection in the kitchen window. She tried to concentrate on spooning the vegetables on the plates for the children.

"Even though he's difficult at times..." Jon said, "...he is my boss, and expects me to show up with my wife."

"Of course, Jonathan. I understand," Tammy whispered, looking deep into Jon's pale blue eyes.

Gag me with a spoon Kelly thought, while picking a bubbly Eddie up and squaring him on her hip.

"So, as Susan can't make it," Jon said, "I was wondering..."

"Yeees?"

"...if you'd watch the kids tonight so I can take Kelly?" Jon finished with a triumphant smile and a wink to Kelly's dumbfounded reflection in the kitchen window.

* * *

"But what will I wear?" Kelly asked Jon with a genuine concern. "This is a cocktail party. I have nothing that's even remotely appropriate."

A very upset Tammy had packed up all the food and taken the children, including a still sulking Abby, to her house.

"What's wrong with what you've got on now?" Jon said.

Kelly looked down on her torn jeans, and oversized T-shirt.

He's kidding, right…?

"So, you'll borrow something of Susan's. What's the big deal? She's got plenty of clothes, and she won't mind you borrowing something," Jon said. "Oh, and I probably should mention that we need to leave in less than fifteen minutes", he continued, glancing at his watch. "We have a company car picking us up."

Men! Have you ever even looked at yer wife? Do you know how petite she is compared to me? I'm an Irish peasant raised on meat and bloody potatoes. Anything of hers I'll rip apart just looking at it! And fifteen minutes? Are ya kidding?

Kelly could feel the heat rise at the back of her neck. She had been working all day. It being Friday, she had cleaned the entire house, all three floors of it, run after the children, fed them and bathed them. She was actually looking forward to an evening of soaking in the tub, reading a good book and falling asleep after a good meal and watching some mindless cable show, knowing that the kids had been fed, were in bed, and that the parents would be at this MacIntyre-do until way past midnight. Now, instead, she had to ready herself in fifteen minutes to represent the family at the very do.

"Jon, I'd love to go with you to this thing. I can be ready in fifteen minutes, and seeing as you're ready, I'll need your help."

How to put this in a man's terms?

"I'm going to take a quick shower. Please go through Susan's closet and find me a black, long dress," she said.

Let's hope that a 'long' dress for Susan's five-three will cover some of my five-eleven virtues. Virtues? Whatever made me think that?!

Kelly sped through the shower, running the razor over her legs and armpits.

Sooo not worth it for a bunch of old fart miners and their too-rich-for-their-own-good wives, Kelly thought, careful not to nick herself.

She was done in less than ten minutes, and exited the bathroom just to bump into Jon holding up two black cocktail dresses, looking slightly uncomfortable at the sight of Kelly wrapped in a towel. He cleared his throat and held up one of the dresses.

"This one... I'm pretty sure Susan wore at the company Christmas party." Jon was clearly trying to keep his focus on the dresses rather than a wet Kelly in a towel. He was blushing slightly. He held up the other dress. "This one, I don't think she's ever worn. Look - the price tag's still on it. This one's longer, but lower cut. The label says Ralph ..."

Jaysus, Jon! Making a wee puddle on the hardwood floor, here...

"They look great. Let me try both," Kelly said, grabbing the dresses and vanishing into her room. She eyed the dresses while pinning up her long red hair. Short, high neck line versus long, low cut.

Eeenie meenie miney moe, one of you has got to go!

Two minutes later Kelly emerged in a fabulously skin tight Ralph Lauren sheath. Low cut.

"Two more minutes, Jon, I'll just slap on some make-up," she told an astonished Jon, as she was pulling on a pair of black sandals.

"Wow", Jon said and gave a low whistle. "You look really good. Somehow, not quite what I'd expected from that dress. Forget the make-up. The car's here," he took Kelly by the elbow and walked her down the stairs to the company limo.

The party, hosted by Jon's boss Parker MacIntyre III, but undoubtedly organized by his fourth wife, was being held at the renowned Albany Hotel, one of Chicago's oldest landmarks. Verna-Jean, Parker's fourth wife, had been adamant about booking the biggest ballroom for their first anniversary. She'd also insisted on being in charge of everything herself. Verna-Jean, although a sweet girl, had no sense of taste, no education, and no place in high society. She had been an exotic dancer when she met Parker, and he 'rescued' her from that life. The marriage shot Verna-Jean to instant fame, and she loved every minute of it. You could rarely open a tabloid without finding at least one spread of her in it.

"Ohmygod! It's Barbie on acid!" Kelly gasped as she and Jon walked into the ballroom.

They both stopped dead in their tracks. The entire room was draped in pink chiffon. The floor was covered in pink sheepskin. The waiters wore glitzy pink tuxedo jackets over pink kilts, and served pink champagne. The band was actually sitting enclosed in what looked like a Formica castle. Pink. Jon and Kelly looked at each other and burst out laughing.

"Where did she go to design school? The renowned Pepto Bismol Institute?" Kelly said, laughing. "I sure hope Susan makes it. She'll never believe me when I tell her." A pink waiter appeared, and both Jon and Kelly took a glass of pink champagne. "I rest my case! Pepto Bismol in a champagne glass. How very appropriate. Making us nauseous and providing the remedy."

Kelly was wiping tears from her eyes and didn't notice Jon poking an elbow in her side.

"I mean, really!" Kelly continued, still giggling, "where did she find all this shite? Pink Craps 'R' Us?" Kelly looked up at Jon while still laughing at her little joke. Jon looked very somber, and was fixated on something behind Kelly.

"Parker! Great party!" he said.

Kelly spun around and was eye to eye with Parker MacIntyre, Jon's boss, and one of the Fortune 500's wealthiest men on the planet.

Oh, holy Mother...

His steel gray eyes bore into Kelly, and the sheer iciness of his stare stopped her cold. She could feel the blood rushing to her cheeks, and was, uncharacteristically, at a loss for words. Jon stepped between them.

"Parker, may I introduce Kelly McCoy, our Irish au pair? Kelly, this is my boss, Parker MacIntyre, owner, president and CEO of MacIntyre Industries," Jon said ceremoniously.

Should I curtsy? Kiss his ring? What?

Kelly extended her hand to shake Parker MacIntyre's. He did likewise. Just then, a spark of static electricity shocked them both.

"Son of a ..." Kelly said instinctively, but refrained herself.

Bitch.

She looked up at Jon, who was stone faced, then over at Parker, who had a twitch in the corner of his mouth. More blood rushed to Kelly's cheeks.

Is he mocking me? All right, stand up straight, things can't get any worse. Mustn't embarrass Jon in front of his boss.

"Feisty little thing, aren't ya? It's the false sheepskin. Been shocking me all night," Parker said, his eyes still piercing in on Kelly. "McCoy, huh? And are you the *real* McCoy?"

Yeah, original! Never heard that one before! Kelly thought sarcastically, but managed to smile politely at him.

"Susan not here, Terry?" This was directed to Jon, although he was still looking at Kelly.

"She might be a bit late. Stuck at the airport in Phoenix," Jon said.

"Hope she makes it. She'd get a kick outta this," Parker said waving an arm around the pink room. "Can't believe I'm paying for all this. But then again," his amused glare returned to Kelly, "can't have cost much at the... what was it? Pink Crap for Less."

Focketyfockfock!

"Anyway, divorce papers will be filed before the last of this pink stuff has made it to the dumpsters," his face was suddenly serious and he turned to face Jon again. "Doesn't even know it yet, poor simple-minded Verna." He saw her across the room and waved his glass at her. "Happy Anniversary, sweetheart!" he shouted. Then added quietly, "Enjoy it while it lasts."

Kelly followed his gaze and saw a blonde bombshell blowing kisses to Parker. Verna-Jean. She was clad in a shiny, sequined pink sheath that made her already huge bosom appear as though independent from her body.

"Two great assets, all there is to Verna," Parker mumbled to himself.

Another waiter appeared with a tray of pink champagne. Kelly helped herself to another glass and took a long sip. She could feel Parker's cold steel eyes boring into her again.

"How old are you, Irish?" he said, eyeing her up and down.

"She'll be twenty-six in June," Jon said.

"In that case, you may have had enough," Parker mused, taking her champagne glass from her and replacing it on the tray. "Bring her a Coke." His gaze stopped on Kelly's cleavage. "Better yet, make that a tall glass of milk." Parker smirked at Kelly, nodded to Jon, and left.

Kelly was flabbergasted. Jon put his hands on her shoulders and turned her to face him.

"Don't mind him, Kelly. I guess it's the prerogative of the very wealthy that they can say whatever they want. But he's right, though. About the champagne, I mean," he added hastily, with a slight blush. "You alright?"

Kelly's eyes were following Parker. She was breathing heavily.

"Kelly?" Jon said worried. "Are you okay?"

Kelly slowly dragged her eyes from Parker MacIntyre's muscular back and broad shoulders and looked at Jon. "Yuuummy!" she said. "He looks much better in person than he does on telly."

Jon chuckled. "Do we have a little crush on the Bill Gates of the mining industry?"

Kelly blushed to the roots of her hair.

Ohmygod, he's gorgeous! Well, for an old fart, anyway.

"Of course not!" Kelly huffed. "He really is a royal pain in the neck, isn't he? How can you stand working with him?"

"He's a sharp business man, and I admire and respect him. The private Parker MacIntyre can be a bit of a pain, I suppose. I've gotten used to that. Sorry I didn't warn you."

"What in the world is this? Revenge of Cotton Candies everywhere?" Susan appeared behind them, astonished by the tackiness of the decorations.

Jon leaned over to kiss her. "I'm so glad you could make it, dear. I owe you a hundred bucks. Although they just barely made it a year," he said. "How was the flight?"

Susan hugged Kelly. "The flight was fine, once we were airborne," she said with a flick of her hand, her usual sign to drop the subject. "Any adult beverages in this puke puce palace of poor taste?" She looked around, and her gaze fell on Kelly's dress. "Kelly, honey! What are you wearing?"

Kelly looked down on the dress Jon had found for her in Susan's closet.

What's wrong with it? This is what one would wear to a black-tie do, no?

"It's yours. I-I didn't have anything appropriate to wear, so … I hope you don't mind?"

"Of course not," Susan said with another flick of her hand. "Jon, please excuse us, we'll just pop in the powder room. Back before you miss us!" She took Kelly by the hand and hurried her to the ladies' room. Safely inside, Susan turned Kelly to face the mirror, and a big smile spread across her face. "Didn't give you much time to prepare, did he, the love of my life?" Susan said to Kelly's reflection in the mirror, while pulling out an assortment of make-up essentials from her purse. She started giggling. "Only you could get away with this, hon!"

Susan was laughing now. Kelly looked at herself in the mirror.

What's so funny? So I could have done something about my hair. Sure. No make-up. Going au naturale today. I'm twenty-five and gorgeous! The dress fits, although me chest is straining to stay inside. A bit snug over me rump, but so what? Kelly looked at Susan, perplexed.

"Honey, you're wearing it backwards!" Susan hiccupped.

2

Parker MacIntyre III was born into money. His great-great-grandfather founded MacIntyre Mining Corporation shortly after the California gold rush. The company, one of the few that had survived the rush, did quite nicely for generations, until Parker MacIntyre's father's untimely death twelve years ago. In a few years Parker had nearly quadrupled the net worth of his inheritance.

Parker's first act as CEO was to move the headquarters from Denver to Chicago. As the company now owned properties all around the globe, he felt that he should be closer to a central hub that he could fly into and out of easily. So, he bought the 77th and 78th floors in the Sears Tower, the upper for offices and the lower for his private condo.

His two children, Jack and Victoria, were from his first marriage. He married Sara, his high-school sweetheart, while they were both still in college. She had been the love of his life, and he had been hers. They were exceptionally well matched; emotionally, economically and physically each other's equals.

When Jack was eight years old and Victoria three the perfect family picture was shattered. Sara was killed in a head-on collision. Victoria was sitting in the back of the car, safely bundled into her car seat, and although covered in her mother's blood, she survived without any physical injuries.

Sitting in the leather chair at his office, Parker took off his reading glasses and pinched the bridge of his nose, trying to shake off the memory of his dead wife. He poured himself a Scotch. He finished the drink in one long gulp and hoped that the liquid would drain away the painful memory. It didn't. It never did. After the accident Parker had thrown himself into work, putting in long hours seven days a week, and eventually, at night, when he had to return to his empty bedroom, he started drinking. A lot.

By grace of divine intervention the phone on his desk rang, and distracted his thoughts. He looked at the display. His son's cell phone number.

"Jack, my boy! How are you?" Parker answered, happy about the distraction.

"Now, we've been over this, Daddy, I go by Jackie now. That's spelled J-a-c-q-u-i. Anyway, just calling to see if you'll make it to Vicky's graduation on Friday. No biggie if you can't. I *think* she'll totally understand."

Parker cursed silently. He'd forgotten. "Of course I'll be there," he said a bit too enthusiastically. "Where and when again?"

"Fabulous!" Jacqui shrieked. "Noon at Allstate Arena." The line went silent for a while, then Jacqui said hesitantly "Do you think you'll be bringing Verna-Jean?" Jacqui didn't mind her, but knew that his sister despised her intensely.

Parker poured himself another Scotch and took a sip before answering. "Verna got her divorce papers served this morning," he said solemnly.

"Way to go big papa! Mazel Tov!" Jacqui screamed over the line. "So what now, back to the trailer park, baring her boobies for bread?"

Parker sighed deeply, and took another sip. "Jack, we're Scottish. If you insist on me calling you *Jacqui*," he said with disdain, "I must insist that you drop the use of Jewish expressions."

"Saawree... My bad! So, where is Verna-Jean headed?"

"Don't know, don't much care."

"Sorry big papa, I must dash, got to prepare for a big interview! Get this – with Alman. Yay!"

His son sounded so excited that Parker couldn't help but smile into the phone. He knew of Alman Interiors of course, mainly from the financial papers, rather than the home and garden ones.

"I'm proud of you, son. Break a leg."

"Thanks. Oh, hey, almost forgot. If you're getting a divorce, did you still have that massive splash on Friday?"

Parker laughed. "Oh, yes, and you can read all about it in glossy print tomorrow."

"The tabloids were there? Eeesch!" Jacqui gasped. "Which ones?"

"All of them! Specially invited by Verna herself. She really wanted to make the most of her fifteen minutes of fame." Had she ever. Parker thought with great regret of the day he married her. He should have known better. But he had been caught at a weak moment. A large-breasted woman was to Parker MacIntyre what kryptonite was to Superman. "Anyway, let me know what Vicky wants for a graduation present, and also, if you guys want the house for a party."

"Oh, Daddy!" Jacqui let a valley-girlish laugh, "graduation parties are like sooo last century. Gotta run. See you Friday. Bye-eeee!"

"Bye, um … er … Jacqui," Parker said, but the line had gone dead.

Parker replaced the receiver and shook his head. Victoria was graduating. He couldn't believe it. She had been in the gossip papers every week since the age of sixteen, partying with the 'rich and fabulous' as Jack put it. And what about his son? Had 'Jacqui' had too little male influence in his life? Granted, Parker himself had never been around much, and his wife had pampered him, so he had become something of a 'mama's boy', but still? Aren't most boys closer to their mothers? Was that enough reason to make the boy so effeminate? There had been no warning signs that Parker had seen, and then out of the blue, he announces that he wants everyone to call him Jacqui and that he's going to design school.

Parker loved his son, but getting a degree in interior design was not something he was particularly proud of. The mining industry was a very masculine business, but the only interest Jack had ever shown in precious metals or gemstones was when they were cut, polished, and wearable.

Parker had agreed with his son that after Jack graduated from college, he'd intern a year with MacIntyre Industries, to give the family business a fair shot. That year was now almost over. Parker had long since given up hope that his son would some day take over the business.

3

Susan and Jon were sitting at the breakfast table reading the morning papers. It was early Tuesday morning, and sunshine was streaming through the windows in the breakfast room. They could hear Kelly in the kitchen, preparing the children's breakfast and listening to the BBC on the tiny kitchen TV.

Susan turned to her husband. "I'm really gonna miss her," she said, and felt a lump forming in her throat. It would not be the first time she'd cried at the prospect of losing the best help the household had ever had, not to mention a great friend and confidante. "She'll be impossible to replace."

"I know," Jon said, without looking up from his paper. "We were just talking about it during our jog. Kelly's made her peace with the fact that she's leaving when her visa expires. But how do we break it to the girls? They'll be devastated."

"That's uncharacteristically pessimistic of her," Susan said, surprised.

Jon still didn't look up from his paper. "She's neither an optimist, nor a pessimist, dear. She's a realist. She's playing the odds. Either way, she still intends to be in the marathon again this year."

"Good," Susan sighed. "Any news from Kate?"

Jon shook his head.

"I'll call her today," Susan said resolutely, and typed in a reminder to herself in her PDA.

Months ago, the Russells hired an immigration lawyer, to see if Kelly's current alien status could be extended another year. They had loved Kelly from the moment they read her application, and she hadn't needed much persuasion to agree to stay on with the Russells. Kate Fleming, their lawyer, was referred to them by Parker MacIntyre, who'd hired her himself on several occasions to bring foreign mining engineers to the US.

"I wish we could keep her here," Susan said silently, and looked at Kelly's slender silhouette in the kitchen. Susan burst out laughing. "Maybe Parker can marry her!"

Jon nearly choked on his coffee. "What?!" he said. "Have you lost your mind?"

"Oh, come on! He dates women half his age all the time, and often marries them. And you said yourself that he was coming on to her at the party."

"For crying out loud, Susan! She's only twenty-five! Even Parker MacIntyre has some scruples. Besides, he comes on to every single woman he meets."

"He's never come on to me," Susan said teasingly.

"Every *single* woman, Susan. Like I said, even Parker has *some* scruples."

Kelly walked into the breakfast room, carrying Eddie. She sat down at the table and started giving him his bottle. "What's up?" she looked at Susan and Jon.

Susan put down her paper. "Kelly, what did you think of Mr. MacIntyre at the party Friday?" she asked conspiratorially.

Kelly smiled like a little schoolgirl. "He's hot," she said, eyes twinkling.

Dreamy. Dangerously attractive in a tux. Wonder what he looks like naked…in bed…with me… post-coital? Mmmm…

"Total pain of course," Kelly added quickly, when she saw Jon's horrified expression. "Why?"

"No reason, just Jon told me that he came on to you," Susan said.

"Really?" Kelly blushed. "Oh, you mean that little milk comment he made. Oh, that wasn't a come-on! He just suggested I drink some milk to build up me bosom, that's all.

Thinks me too flat chested. Well, anyone would be compared to … what was her name? Vernon? Bit of a chauvinist, he is."

Susan and Jon exchanged glances. Jon folded his paper and said with careful consideration "Kelly, honey, please take this the right way. First of all, you don't need to 'build up your bosom'. Trust me. Second, when a man looks at a woman's chest and says 'milk', believe me; it's a come-on."

Kelly let his words sink in for a moment.

Ohmygodohmygodohmygod! There I was standing in a dress I wore backwards, with me chest straining to stay inside it, and Mr. Hot Billionaire came on to me?

"Hey, why does he call you Terry?" Kelly asked Jon hoping to change the subject.

"Another guy thing. We sometimes work with highly confidential materials, and have to create code names for each other," Jon said.

Not very confidential if he calls you that in public, now is it?

"Terry's a play on words on my name, that's all," Jon said.

How do you get Terry from Jonathan Edward Russell? Maybe it's some sort of an anagram, or something. I don't get it.

"I don't get it," Kelly said.

"In America," Jon said, while finishing the last of his toast and licking the jelly off his fingers, "Johns are sometimes nicknamed Jack." Jon didn't volunteer any more information, and watched amused as Kelly tried to figure it out.

Jack Terry? Terry Jack? Jack Ru…

"Jack Russell terrier!" Kelly exclaimed so loudly, that even Eddie momentarily stopped playing with her necklace. "Du-uh! Terry the Terrier. Very clever!"

Jon winked at Kelly. "Parker's one of a select few who gets away with it, so don't go getting any ideas."

Wonder what Parker MacIntyre's code name is? Ritchie Rich? Naah… With a man like him it's gotta be something below the belt, like … Dick Steele, or … Rod Long or … Rock Hard … Well, he is a geologist, so that last one's not necessarily dirty.

Susan and Jon got up from the table and scrambled to get ready to go to work. "Don't worry about Mr. MacIntyre's little flirt. Believe me, he'll not have thought once about you. Like you said, the man's a chauvinist," Susan said, and grabbed her purse and briefcase. She kissed her husband. "See you Thursday night. Call me when you get there, okay?" She ran to her car and drove off to work.

Kelly turned toward Jon. "Thursday? Where you going?"

Jon was looking for his car keys on the kitchen counter. "Yeah, early morning call from da boss man. He's sending Jack MacIntyre and me up to the U.P. today to try to negotiate with Nick the dick Delaney. Again." Jon sighed.

Kelly hastily covered Eddie's ears. "Hush, Jon, you won't be wanting your son's first word to be *dick*, now would you?" she whispered.

"You're right, sorry. Just … negotiating with that man is like negotiating with Hitler. 'So, Austria was easy, now give me Czechoslovakia, and while you're at it, throw in Poland as well, and for good measure, how about Hungary and Norway, too'." Jon heaved a deep sigh. "The man is always nicking for a little bit more. I keep telling Parker that we're wasting our time with Delaney. Nickel is abundant in the U.P., and we're the first ones on the scene. We don't need his mineral rights that badly. You haven't seen my keys, have you?"

Kelly pointed to the kitchen island.

Jon located his keys and pointed them at Kelly. "Do you know what Delaney's asking for now?" Knowing what a sore subject the Delaney mineral rights had been for months now, Kelly shook her head quickly. "Three million and royalties! Three million *and* royalties!" Jon nearly shrieked.

So? Three million is probably pocket change for a man like MacIntyre.

"So why would Mr. MacIntyre care? He's a bloody multi-billionaire."

"He's not a *multi*-billionaire, Kelly," Jon corrected her. "Very few people are multi-billionaires. The Sultan of Brunei and Bill Gates possibly. Oh, and that Richard Branson guy, too, I think. But not Parker MacIntyre."

"So he's only a … what? … Single billionaire? Hundred millionaire?"

"Well, yeah. I don't know. Ask him."

Yeah, right. Great pick up line for hot rich guy. 'Excuse me, sir? Just what is yer net worth?'

Kelly could see that Jon was growing frustrated and tried to appear supportive. "So, what are these mineral rights worth, then?"

Jon looked at her as though abruptly awoken from a deep sleep. "Not three million and royalties, that's for shit sure."

The Russells were going to miss Kelly. Susan vowed to contact the President himself, if that's what it took to get her another visa. She had been such an inspiration to the whole family when she arrived. The youngest of five, Kelly was the aunt of four nieces and two nephews ranging in ages from newborn to ten, and was certainly no stranger to childcare. She definitely was not the usual 'fresh out of high-school, dying to come to the States' unsuitable au pair that prompted host families to invest in nanny-cams.

The kids all adored Kelly and she loved them as if they were her own flesh and blood. Abby, although sometimes still a bit sulky about it, had managed to lose weight, and was getting into really good shape. Hide it though she might, she enjoyed all the physical activity she was getting with Kelly. And Emma, who hadn't uttered a sound for the first three years of her life, now would not shut up. Although she couldn't pronounce her R's or some of her L's yet, she certainly had lots to say nevertheless. The girls now sounded more Irish than Kelly, who had started adopting more American expressions. By now Kelly could pull off an 'aw, man!' better than many Americans. And Eddie regarded Kelly as his mother. Susan realized that that was the price you have to pay to return to work three weeks after giving birth.

The Americanization of Kelly McCoy over the past few months was nothing short of astonishing. The Kelly McCoy who got off the plane from Ireland was tall and lanky, opinionated and outspoken to a fault. She wore glasses and would never expose any skin. Now, she wore contacts, and, although smart about not exposing too much skin in the sun, with her fair Irish-red complexion, her wardrobe was much more feminine. Susan secretly wished that Kelly would let someone cut her hair just once. Her red, thick pony-tail, although gorgeous, could be shaped into something Hollywood would want to copy, if done right. And although Kelly was still opinionated, she now thought before she spoke, and insulted far fewer people than she initially had. The Kelly McCoy who got off the plane from Ireland hadn't eaten beef in years, but one of Jon's grilled hamburgers got her hooked again. And suddenly she wasn't lanky anymore, but had started filling out, something she herself had not realized yet, or else she wouldn't be wearing a designer sheath backwards. Try as they might, the Russells had not managed to convince Kelly how beautiful she was. She turned heads everywhere she went. She wasn't glamorous, by any definition of the word, but she had a look and an aura that exuded confidence. She was very comfortable in her own skin. Men admired it, women envied it.

Susan pulled her car up by the front entrance of the soon-to-be J Hotel in downtown Chicago still in awe about landing this client. The Chicago property was only the third to open in what the financial papers already projected to be the next gold mine in the international hotel industry. The owners were young, hip, self-made millionaires, who'd made their fortunes on Jim, the 24-hour gym chain. They fell for Susan the minute they met, and Susan's near-term financial future was secured. She was under contract for five more properties, scheduled to open over the next three years. Landing the J Corporation as a client had earned Susan a partnership in her firm and put her name on the stationery.

Alen and Bryce bought the property dirt-cheap from the previous owner, the estate of a deceased lawyer, who had originally bought the hotel as a nest egg, but was clueless about the hotel business, and never invested in it. The estate obviously had no idea what it was sitting on, and how it could quickly generate lots of revenue with a little bit of renovation. The partners laughed all the way to the bank.

Susan could now see the partners in their glass-enclosed office in the corner of the lobby as she entered the hotel. They were fluttering around like humming birds. Susan tugged at the front of her pastel-blue suit jacket, and frowned. Her professional attire was far more conservative than pastels, and up until she met the new partners, had consisted solely of grays, blacks and pin-stripes of the two. Today she was wearing a pale blue two-piece suit over a navy blouse, and for good measure she had thrown a long navy and lime Dior scarf over her throat, floating in her wake as she strode through the hotel lobby.

She could see Bryce Hart, the senior partner, rubbing a piece of white cloth over his face. Susan realized that the long elusive Egyptian sheets had finally been delivered. She made a mental note to discipline her assistant for not informing her about that fact. Alen Marshall, the junior partner, saw Susan through the glass wall, and started jumping toward the office door.

"Suzy Q, you God's gorgeous creature, you," he said air-kissing Susan on both sides of her face. "Guess what?" He looked like a child at Christmas.

Susan almost felt guilty spoiling his enthusiasm, but she had to retain her professionalism. "The bedding has finally been delivered?" she said.

"Mon Dieu! You're good!" Alen said in awe. "Come see! They're to die for! Just like you said they would be, you goddess, you."

The bedding had been an issue between Susan and the two partners. Having done her homework, and having stayed in many a luxury hotel recently, she knew that bedding was the new selling point in upscale hotels. The sheets she practically forced Bryce and Alen to agree on were

400-thread count Egyptian cotton, and actually spun in a mill in Egypt. The duvets were all full down, not feather, as were the pillows. Susan had insisted on six pillows per bed, and had nearly torn her hair out in aggravation during the endless weeks of tug-of-war over the bedding. To add insult to injury, when she finally had the partners agreeing on the quality and amount required, the mill in Egypt started giving her a hard time about the cost and delivery date. Susan was no stranger to playing hardball, and after weeks of ungodly early morning phone calls, the bedding had now finally been delivered within budget.

Alen practically dragged Susan into the office.

"Susan, darling, don't you look adorable! Love the scarf. Dior? Come, feel this fabulous fabric! Couldn't you just feel yourself falling in love with it? Or between it?" Bryce thrust the piece of fabric he had been rubbing over his face toward Susan and she rolled it between her fingers.

"Oh, yeah, that's the stuff," she said.

"How's everything with the Phoenix property?" Bryce asked.

"On schedule and budget," Susan feigned nonchalance. "My presence there will be unnecessary for the next few weeks. Do a walkabout with me?" Susan knew that her presence on the premises was merely a formality. The pre-opening phases of the J, as far as she was concerned, were a well-oiled machine, but she did enjoy the company of the two partners. They made her feel young, fabulous and beautiful.

"I'd love to, oh, how I'd love to," Alen the drama queen said. "But I have a nine o'clock meeting with the ice biatch," he said melodramatically.

Susan looked at her watch. "It's ten past," she said, then caught herself. "Never mind."

The Ice Bitch, also known as Gina Lombardi, the very brassy, very divorced, newly appointed Managing Director of the soon-to-be J Hotel Chicago, lived in a time zone all her own. Nine a.m. could just as easily mean eight a.m. or noon.

"Why don't the two of you go?" Alen said. "I'll see you later."

Bryce took Susan on a tour of the property. This was something she did at least once a week, always appearing unannounced, to keep her staff and contractors on their toes. The two bars and the restaurant were done, and ready to open as soon as the liquor license cleared. Jim the gym was already operational. The ballroom was being painted. The guest suites were waiting for the bedding. All that needed doing was the lobby, and that was another one of the partners' and Susan's great headaches. To open on schedule they would have to come up with a golden compromise or they could kiss the 4th of July rush goodbye. So far, including the elusive bedding, they had been on schedule and on budget, but the lobby had proven to be a sore spot that there seemed no way around.

Susan and Bryce finished their walkabout in less than two hours and returned to the partners' office. Alen was on the phone.

"No? Thanks, Kristin. Let me know, okay? You're a gem, doll." He hung up the phone. "I've checked InnTime, just got off the phone with Kristin, and still no sign of the Ice Bitch." Alen looked up at Susan. "You've met Kristin, haven't you, Susan? Best thing the Ice Bitch ever did, hiring her. Fabulous creature."

Susan had met Kristin, Gina's assistant. She was a forty-something rabbit on acid. Before anyone had the chance to voice his thoughts, Kristin would have the memo typed. Susan wanted to clone her and hire the original, too.

Alen's PDA rang. He answered, said a quick 'okay' and hung up. He shrugged and turned towards Susan and Bryce. "The iceberg is moving south, children," he said gravely. "Better take cover."

Moments later the three of them saw Gina Lombardi slowly make her way through the lobby. All three of them shrugged. Gina was short, not breaking five feet barefoot, and showed the signs of post-menopausal flab. It was obvious that she had been attractive once, but years of heavy smoking had left her face a road map of wrinkles and creases. Her hair was always coiffed in a perfect china-doll bob, and was immaculately colored raven black, in sharp contrast to her ivory white skin. Susan and the partners had bonded on many levels, but their common dislike of Gina was on top of the list.

She walked leisurely into Alen and Bryce's office. "Good morning!" she said in a tone that was far too cheery and didn't reflect the words themselves. "Susan?!" she said in feigned delight. "Didn't expect to see you today. Don't you look lovely in powder blue. Or is this robin's egg blue? Alen, my office in five minutes." She left the partners' office, with a trail of disgust lingering after her.

Susan, Alen and Bryce all shrugged as if touched by a leper.

Susan couldn't hold it in any longer. "Pardon me, if I'm out of line here," she started, "but why, in the name of all that's good, did you ever hire that woman? She's horrid. She's like … evil personified."

"She came with the property," Alen said with a sigh. "Part of the deal. My guess is that she had some kind of pull with the previous owners. But she presented an excellent bottom line, and we were impressed by the numbers. You remember what this place used to look like, don't you, Susan? For someone to pull off a profit from that pile of bricks is pretty remarkable."

"From now on, we'll spend way more time on interviews and background checks," Bryce said. Looking at each other, as if sharing a secret, a smile spread across Bryce's face, and Alen started clapping his hands. Bryce took Susan's hands in his. "You *have* to meet this hunk we just hired yesterday for our Assistant Manager," he said, eyes gleaming.

"Hitched, unfortunately. Way straight, of course, but Gawd, how hot!" Alen added, nearly drooling.

Bryce huffed. "Not hot, like … Who's hot this week? Jude Law?"

"Jake Gyllenhaal!" Alen winked.

"Still?" Bryce said incredulously. "Anyway, he's not Gyllen-hot, but more like cute, in a Brad Pitt-esque, boy-next-door-non-threatening kind of cute."

"Pre-Angelina, of course," Alen added quickly.

"Of course," Bryce huffed. "Sandy blond. Tall. Tight little tushie. Zero body fat, and the most adorable eyes." He paused, and looked at Susan's suit. "Baby blue, like your Donna Karan here. Or is this robin's egg blue?"

Susan smiled. "And where did you find this hunk of meat?"

"We were at the Drake Saturday night, and there he was in the lobby, all 'spread me on a cracker' delicious. I gave him my card, and asked him to call me if he was ever interested at all in leaving his position at the Drake. And first thing Monday morning he called. We met with him that afternoon, and he'll be ours next week. Yay!"

Susan could barely refrain from laughing. "And how did you manage to hire him, without consent from the Ice Bitch?"

"We just reminded her …" Alen started.

"In just so many words …" Bryce cut in.

"…who signs her paychecks," Alen finished.

"Besides," Bryce continued, "I think we can totally trust Mattie, that's *him*, to do most of the hiring from now on. He's already said something about bringing his maintenance man and head housekeeper from the Drake with him."

Anne Harper

"And, one of them's a former Navy something or other!" Alen said excitedly.

"So when's the big day?" Susan asked, hoping to get the conversation back to business.

"Wee-eell," Alen started, looking over at Bryce. Bryce gave him an encouraging wink "We're still on target for opening for July 4th. But…" he took a long pause, during which both he and Bryce edged toward Susan, until their faces were only inches from each other's. "…we have to have a great something-to-do first to get the word out. Granted, our marketing team, fabulous people that they are, are working red hot, but still, we need to get the word out that it's the J, he's gay, come play! And we need to do it with the rich and beautiful, because those are the kind of people we want to come and play with J."

"So," Bryce filled in, while Alen was drawing for breath, "we want to know how strong your pull is with Parker MacIntyre?" Both men were looking at Susan expectantly.

Susan thought fast, wondering what they were after. She and Parker were on good terms, but only because Jon was his number one guy. To ask for personal favors could be a bit iffy. Then she got it.

"Are you boys asking me to ask Parker MacIntyre, one of the Fortune 500's most powerful people in the world, the sexiest man alive as voted by People Magazine three times, and my husband's boss, to host his daughter's twenty-first birthday party at the new and fabulous J Hotel?"

Susan eyed the two men who were nodding in unison. "Alright, boys, if, and I do mean *if,* I pull this off - wiifm?"

Alen and Bryce pulled away from her, then looked at each other perplexed. Alen was first to regain the ability to speak. "Whiff 'em?"

Susan smiled, and knew she had them in the palm of her hand. "Not whiff 'em, darling Alen. W-I-I-F-M, as in 'What's In It For Me'?"

Suddenly both Bryce and Alen were a flurry of activity.

"Anything you want, darling."

"Name your price, sweetheart."

"Sky's the limit."

"Money's no object." they shrieked simultaneously.

Susan couldn't help but smile. It was never going to happen. Never in a million years would she ask Parker MacIntyre for a favor for two clients. Two openly gay clients, at that. No way, no how.

"I'm not making any promises, but I'll see what I can do," was all she offered. The partners seemed pleased with that. "Do you boys have any plans for dinner tonight?" Susan asked as she was gathering her purse and briefcase. "It's just that my girls are invited for a sleep-over, Jon's out of town again, and I just don't think I can handle being by myself with our au pair."

"Oooh," Alen said, hoping for juicy gossip. "Do we not like the help?"

"No. We adore the help. It's just that she's leaving next week, unless our immigration lawyer pulls a rabbit out of the hat, and we've all grown to love her, and if I spend any time alone with her, I'll go to pieces. Kelly's become like an oldest daughter or a younger sister I never had. I can't stand the thought of her leaving." Susan could feel the now-too-familiar lump starting to form in her throat again. She took her time arranging the scarf around her neck.

The partners got the message. "We've nothing planned that can't be changed," Bryce said.

"We'll be there," Alen agreed. "Bring some wine?"

The phone rang again. Alen leaned over to look at the display. He turned toward Bryce, and made a face. "Ice Bitch," he whispered as though Gina could hear her, through a concrete floor. "You answer it, tell her I'm on my way." He grabbed a few folios, pecked a kiss on Susan's cheek "Love you, sweetums," and started for the door.

"Seven o'clock, my house!" Susan said. Kisses all around, and she was out the door.

At the Russell house Kelly was packing the girls' overnight bags. She was looking for Abby's bag, and raised the bed skirt to look under the bed.

Whatta fock?

"Pudge!" Kelly yelled at the top of her voice. "Get yer big, fat bottom in here RIGHT NOW!" Kelly was so upset she was visibly shaking.

Abby entered the room. "I'm not fat anymore and you *promised* to stop calling me that!"

Kelly was too distraught to speak. She pointed at the bed. The floor beneath was covered with candy, doughnut and cookie wrappers, and a frozen pizza. Kelly was so disappointed she could feel the tears welling up behind her eyelids.

"That's not mine! I didn't do it!" Abby's reply came a bit too quickly. "This is my room. What are you doing going through my stuff!?"

Kelly raised an eyebrow. "So, this is yours then?" A silence fell over the room while both girls were fighting to hold back tears. "Abigail Alaina Russell, I vacuumed under this bed on Friday. It's now Tuesday. I'll give you one minute to explain how enough food to feed a small Irish village appeared and then disappeared from under your bed in less than four days. Time starts now."

"I was hungry," was all Abby could say before the tears started gushing down her face. She was looking at Kelly apologetically.

"Oh, stop the waterworks, Abby. I know that game. I invented that game."

"I'm sorry," Abby sobbed. "Everyone was so proud of me for getting thin, but it's so hard. I miss all the foods I used to eat, so I stole some and hid it there. It's only happened this once, I promise, Kelly. Please, don't hate me!"

Kelly swallowed hard. She was trying not to look directly at Abby, for if she did she knew she would break down herself. "Abby, I don't hate you. I'm just going to ask you this

once, so the answer better be something I believe. How…"
Kelly took a deep breath for theatrical effect, "…did you
plan to cook the pizza?"

"Wha…?" Abby wasn't sure she had heard the question
right. When Kelly made eye contact with her again, she
knew she was forgiven. Both girls started laughing. They
sat on the floor, hugging each other, laughing and crying
simultaneously.

After a while Kelly sat up straight and looked at Abby at
arms length. "Don't feel bad, pet. I know it's tough. You've
worked so hard, and you've done so well. And you're so close!
Just remember – you're not doing this for beauty, you're doing
it for health. But if you're lying about the foods you eat, you're
only lying to yourself," Kelly looked Abby squarely in the eye.
She had a point to make, and wanted to make sure the nine
year-old got it. "Do you understand what I'm saying?"

Abby nodded. "Yeah, like you and Mom and Dad care
and stuff, but it's really my life and my body, and what I do
to it, is really up to me. Right?"

"Well, … yeah. It's up to you once you know what's good
for you and what's not, once you've learned your limits. I
don't want you going to bed hungry. Ever. You'll just get
sick. If that happens again, will you please speak to me?"

A new onset of tears was falling down Abby's face. "I-I-I
kinda already did get sick," she hiccupped. "From Mom's
chocolates."

"Your Mum doesn…"

Oh. My. Gawd!

Barely able to keep a straight face Kelly held Abby's chin in one hand and with the hem of her T-shirt wiped away her tears. "So, I guess you've learnt your lesson, then?" She kissed Abby on her nose. "Looks like we've got about fifteen gazillion calories to burn off here. What's your poison? Grounding, and not going to cheerleading school *or* Amber's tonight, a five-mile jog or an hour of tennis? Choose wisely, young Jedi," Kelly said and made the Darth Vader breathing sound.

Finger on lips, as if thinking very hard, Abby made her decision. "Tennis," she said with resonance.

"You have chosen wisely," Kelly said, again with the breathing. "And I'll quit calling you Pudge," she said in her normal voice.

A horrid thing to be calling a child anyway. Like bullying, really.

They sat on the floor and hugged each other silently for a while. Abby was the first to break the silence. "I love you, Kelly. Promise you'll stay with us forever."

If it were September 10th, 2001 I could make that promise, but as it isn't…

"I'm working on it, pet," Kelly kissed Abby's hair. "I'm working on it."

* * *

In his office on the 78th floor of the Sears tower, Parker was pacing up and down, occasionally sending a glance to the pile of tabloid magazines that lay open on his desk. He had become accustomed to the media bashing by now, but this was crossing the line. It was one thing to take a shot at him, quite another to aim for his children. Parker read every gossip magazine published in the US. Sadly, this was often the only way he knew what Victoria had been up to. Save from locking her in her room, or hiring a professional chaperone, there was very little Parker felt he could do to tame her. And he wasn't quite ready to do either yet.

Victoria was the tabloids' current sweetheart, and to their defense, they had never said anything too offensive about her. Her weight had been an issue, until about this time last year, when she was admitted to rehab for her eating disorder. Parker paid all the major tabloids hush money to leave her alone while she regained a healthy weight. Then Victoria overdosed on laxatives, in her quest for perfection, in her words, but in the words of her psychiatrist, to get attention. She certainly got it from the press, when she returned from rehab the second time and became the new wild child. Until then, she had only appeared in the magazines entering premieres or other well-chaperoned society events. After her second trip to rehab, she had started smoking, and what's worse, drinking. Still, nothing too mean from the media. So Parker hadn't worried.

Until now. He ran his fingers through his hair and sat down at his desk. As soon as the papers had been delivered he asked not to be disturbed. All the tabloids featured the Anniversary party last Friday. Most of them made snide remarks on his marriage to Verna-Jean, and some of them even mentioned the divorce proceedings. Parker didn't care about them. The three rags that he did care about, though, reported that his son, an openly homosexual man, had been turned down by every renowned interior design firm in the greater Chicagoland area. One even suggested that the reason for the blatant refusals, was that he had decorated the ballroom in the Albany Hotel, and with that kind of taste, would never be hired anywhere. To make their point, the magazines adorned the pages with an overabundance of pink pictures.

Parker cursed loudly, got up and walked toward his bar and poured himself a stiff drink. To Parker, Jacqui was just a kid. Although he disapproved of both his choice of profession and his choice of lifestyle, Parker loved his son, and did not want to see him get hurt. The media had no right to out him. Besides, Parker wasn't absolutely certain his son was gay. He had actually never said it in so many words, nor had Victoria, who was much closer to him than Parker could ever hope to be. After all, the boy had practically raised his sister. Parker hoped that Jacqui was just naturally feminine, as a result of growing up without a mother. Still, he had nothing to do with that bash on Friday, and to kill his career before it had even started, was just low, in Parker's opinion.

Parker needed to get his mind back to his business and called Jon on his cell phone to get a progress report on the Delaney negotiations.

"What's the scoop?" Parker barked into the phone before Jon had had a chance to answer.

"You would be very proud of your son, Parker. Get this - Jack stepped up to the plate and almost got phony-Delaney to agree to half-a-mil at signing and drop the royalties, but now he's excused himself to go and make a phone call," Jon whispered into the phone. "It's not looking good. The man won't negotiate with me. He feels insulted that you didn't fly up here to talk to him in person. That's how bigheaded he is. Parker, I say we drop this. Walk out now, concentrate on what we already have, and stop wasting my time and your money on this loser."

Parker was contemplating. "I trust your judgment, Terry," he finally let out. "You know that. Jerk him around for a bit. You know the limit. I bet he's on his phone right now talking to his wife, telling her she can't have that new Mercedes, or the pool or whatever, and she's telling him she'd better. Stick in there, Terry. You're doing good." he hung up.

Hiring Jon Russell had been the best thing that had happened to both MacIntyre Industries and Parker MacIntyre. Jon was young, energetic and intelligent, and reminded Parker of a younger version of himself. Parker laughed at they way Jon had been convinced to join MacIntyre Industries. He was fresh and eager, still wet behind the ears, just out of Northwestern University. He had written his thesis on the trail of indicators to the Campo Verde emerald deposit, and Parker's old Duke roommate, Don Duncan, was his field mentor in Colombia. The thesis had been sent anonymously to Parker, and he sent his own field crew to investigate the site. It had proven very profitable, just like Jon's thesis suggested, and Parker bought the rights to mine it. The mine produced a profit in its first quarter, and Jon was hired fresh out of grad school. Parker never regretted either acquisition. Second only to Duncan, Jon was the nation's foremost expert in emeralds, and under Parker's mentoring, quickly became his number one man. Parker admired and envied Jon. Jon had the life that was Parker's once. A beautiful, devoted wife, great kids and a passion for his job.

4

Back at her office in the Loop, Susan went through her mail, voicemail and e-mail and found nothing of interest or urgency. She sat back and listened to the hustle of activity outside her door. She glanced at her watch. It was nearly one and she hadn't heard from Jon yet. The flying conditions, as far as a layman could tell, were perfect. Clear skies, slight breeze. The corporate jet was due to take off at eight-thirty this morning, so surely they should be there by now. Susan felt worried.

She picked up one of the photos on her desk. It was taken that February in Disney World. The entire family, including Kelly, was looking back at her from the frame, smiling behind sunburned faces and under Mickey Mouse ears. Kelly blended well into their family. Although Kelly's were more pronounced, all the girls had fair hair and freckles, as did Jon. Only Eddie looked like Susan, with her brown hair and brown eyes.

She picked up the phone and dialed her home number. Kelly answered after the third ring.

"Kelly, honey, it's Susan. How's everything?"

"Grand. Just about to wake Eddie and Emma up from their naps. Abby's helping me fold laundry. Haley's Mom will pick her up in an hour for cheerleading school. What's up?"

Susan never called home just to check in, and Kelly knew it, so Susan got straight to the point. "We're having company for dinner tonight, you and I. One vegetarian, one lacto-ovo vegetarian. Could you please call and ask Mario to deliver something that meets the criteria? They'll be over at seven, so with drinks, we'll be eating at eight."

"No prob. Just one thing, though. What's a lacto-ovo?"

"It means that he eats no meat but does eat dairy and eggs," Susan said. She paused for a moment, then laughed. "Or maybe he eats no dairy and no eggs but does eat meat. I really don't know. Just tell Mario lacto-ovo, and he'll know."

"Will do. Who are these people, anyway?"

"The jays."

"The partners from the J? Gotcha," Kelly said. "Been dying to meet them."

"Kelly, I don't think I've ever asked you this, but how do you feel about openly homosexuals?" Susan asked carefully.

"Couldn't care less," Kelly shrugged. "As a matter of fact, Evan, one of my best mates in Dublin, is gay, and he's the funnest person I know. So long as they don't share any details, I don't much care."

Really don't want heteros to share any details, either.

"Thanks, Kel," Susan said and they hung up.

Kelly had really been looking forward to an evening alone with Susan, something that hadn't happened since Kelly first arrived, during Susan's five weeks of maternity leave. Two weeks before and three weeks after Eddie was born. Kelly missed those days. Although she *was* curious about Susan's clients. Susan had been so excited about landing this account, and spoke about them daily since, so Kelly could hardly wait to meet them.

Wonder if they're funny, Cher-adoring, concealer-wearing, great shopping advice gays? Or militant, just outed, 'the world owes me', gays?

Kelly had told the girls they could have Jell-O for an afternoon snack, if they were good, made it themselves and Emma took a nice long nap.

Yadda-yadda-yadda. What a load of dung. Sometimes I don't even believe meself anymore.

But somehow Abby and Emma bought it and were on their best behavior all day. It was only the second day of summer vacation, and Kelly was anxious to see how much longer the two girls would get along.

She organized everything in military fashion on the kitchen island, and as soon as Emma wandered downstairs, she and Abby were to start making the Jell-O together while Eddie was getting his bottle.

Abby was rapidly growing bored, and decided to get started on the snacks by herself. Kelly was busy with Eddie, and when a groggy Emma appeared at the kitchen door all hell broke loose. Abby insisted on doing everything herself, Emma was screaming at the top of her lungs for not having been woken up to share in the cooking, and Eddie, sensing his sisters' anxiety, left a comforting pile in his diaper, looking diabolically proud of his accomplishment. So, as Kelly was trying to wrestle the bowl of Jell-O mix from the girls, who at that time were both screaming, while holding a stinky Eddie at arms length, also screaming, the phone rang.

Kelly answered the phone in a hasty "Russell residence."

"Who's this?" a husky voice demanded.

"… me! I wanna do it!" Emma yelled.

"No!" Abby retorted.

"Keui said I could!"

"She lied!"

Trying to separate the screaming girls with her foot, as one hand was holding the phone and the other holding Eddie, Kelly said acidly "Who's asking?"

"You're that Irish chick. McCoy, right? Gimme Susan's office number."

With that, Kelly's patience reached its limits. "You're the clever one, aren't you, recognizing an accent. Now do your mammy proud and introduce yourself." Kelly could have sworn she heard a gasp at the other end of the line, but it was hard to tell with all the ruckus going on in the kitchen.

"This is Parker MacIntyre."

Kelly froze in mid-air, and somewhere in the back of her mind her old Sunday school teacher's voice came back to haunt her repeating 'Respect you elders.'

Why didn't I let the voicemail kick in? Better to have let people think we'd all been abducted in our sleep by flesh-eating aliens, than to answer the phone and talk to Parker 'I've had a plethora of women, none of whom can spell plethora' MacIntyre.

"Aaah! Let me, Abby!" Emma was shrieking.

"No!"

"I want to!"

"NO!"

"Poopoohead!"

"You're the poopoohead!"

"Am not!"

"Are too!"

"Keuiii! Abby won't shea-ow!" Emma was near hysterics.

This was followed by a spray of Jell-O mix thrown by Abby, barely missing Emma, hitting Eddie square in the back of his head.

"Oooh," Emma laughed, pointing at Abby. "You in trouble!"

"Shut up, poopoohead!"

"Would you hold for one moment, please, Mr. MacIntyre," Kelly said with all the politeness she was able to muster. She held the mouthpiece of the phone to her chest and yelled to the girls. "SHURRUP!" They both froze in mid fight. "I'm on the phone with yer Dad's boss. Now, very quietly clean this mess up, grab an apple and go to the playroom. NOW!" To her astonishment, the girls obeyed. "Mr. MacIntyre, how may I help you?"

I don't have the energy, so don't fock with me.

"What's going on there? You slaughtering a pig?"

I'm holding a twenty-pound baby, who just dropped half his body-weight into his nappy, while fighting one barely awake and one malnourished child. You know what that can be like, having kids of yer own, Mr. Billionaire? No, probably not. Probably had an army of nannies erase the scent of poopy nappies in yer mansion before you came back from a hard day's work of counting yer money.

"Minor domestic crisis. Now, what do you want?" Kelly didn't have the energy to be polite any more.

"Gimme Susan's office number."

Please? Thank you? You're welcome?

"She is listed, you know. Ever heard of the Yellow pages? Or how about all the small people that jump at your every command? You know, the ones you pay minimum wages and call assistants. They could probably look her number up for you. Or, you know what? Check her website. Her address is bite me dot com."

"Are you always this much trouble, Irish?"

Ya think this is trouble? You should see me thought bubbles!

"Just gimme Susan's damn office number!" Parker barked into the receiver.

Kelly relented. Without so much as a thank you, Parker hung up. Kelly stared at the dead phone.

What an arrogant arse. No wonder he can't hold on to a woman! Who'd want him for more than a quick fix? A quick snog, buy me a Corvette for the good time I've shown you, and please don't ever talk to me again.

Kelly shrugged with disgust.

I can't believe I once quite fancied him. Was that only four days ago? I guess the line between Adonis and Arsehole really is a fine one. … What a Muppet! Even in Ireland, where we're poor, we know that a thank you costs ya nothing.

'Respect yer elders' the voice kept repeating in the back of her mind.

Oh, shut up, ya old Muppet.

"Muppet", Eddie burped.

Jaysus, Mary and Joseph! It's his first word! Ohmygod, he spoke! Wait a minute, what did he just say? Muppet? No, better not copy that for the baby book. Maybe it was a one-off.

"Muppet," Eddie repeated.

Kelly was cleaning Eddie up, when the phone rang again.

Why does the phone always ring when you're in the crapper? Someone ought to do a study on that. 'The Calling Habits of People with Regular Bowel Movements.' Naah. Need to work on that title.

Kelly decided to let it go to voicemail.

Susan sat silent, staring through her windows at the Chicago skyline for a long time while she let her thoughts wander. She knew she had to call Kate Fleming, and see how things were proceeding with Kelly's visa application, but she needed some time to prepare. Kate was a pit bull, and she would chew Susan's head off, if pushed. But she was a straight shooter, and Susan respected that. She also knew that if Kate set out to do something, she would not give up until it was done. Susan picked up the phone again and dialed Kate's office number. The call was answered immediately by Kate's paralegal.

"Good afternoon, Kate Fleming's office," a very professional voice came over the line.

"Good afternoon. Susan Russell for Kate Fleming, please."

"Please hold, while I see if Ms. Fleming is out of her meeting," came the reply.

Susan chuckled while she was listening to elevator music. Did all assistants say that to callers while they checked if the boss wanted to talk to them? Susan knew that her own assistant, Patrick, said things to the same effect. She should have just e-mailed, she thought, as she saw the light on her phone blinking, indicating a caller on the other line. Susan was enjoying the elevator music, and decided to let her voicemail take the other line.

"Mrs. Russell?" The assistant was back. "Ms. Fleming is currently not available. Would you like to hold, or may I connect you with her voicemail?"

Susan looked at her phone. The caller on the other line had hung up. "How long do you think she'll be?"

"No more than a few minutes."

"I'll hold, thanks."

Back to elevator music. There was a knock on her office door, and Patrick opened it and quietly poked his head in. He made the hand signal for telephone call. Susan waved him away. Patrick shook his head.

Susan put her hand over the mouthpiece. "What?!" she hissed.

"Parker MacIntyre on line two. Says it's urgent," Patrick said somberly.

Susan felt like someone had thrown a bucket of ice water down her neck. Parker never called her. The only time he called the mining wives was to let them know that there had been a cave-in and that their husbands were dead. Susan was still staring at poor Patrick.

"What shall I tell him?"

"Kate Fleming, speaking," Susan heard a voice through the receiver as if spoken at a great distance.

"I'll call you back," Susan said, hung up, and signaled to Patrick to put Parker's call through.

She was staring at the phone as if it were the bell of doom, and she willed it not to ring. The sound of the ringing phone cut through her like glass shards. Susan jumped, and with clammy hands picked up the receiver. Her throat was dry and she could hear how small she sounded.

"Susan, this is Parker MacIntyre. Can you hear me all right? Seems to be a bad line." Parker greeted her with his typical staccato voice.

Susan cleared her throat. "What can I do for you, Parker?" She managed to sound professional, almost upbeat.

"That's what I like about you, Susan," Parker said, and slapped his desk. "Short, sweet and to the point," Parker said and then caught himself, "No offense," he added hastily.

"None taken. Seriously, though, what's the purpose of this call?" Susan decided to overlook Parker's gaffe.

"Can you meet me in my office in, say, half an hour?"

Susan could not make herself ask the inevitable. She knew. Parker would not deliver bad news over the phone. Jon was dead. Perished in a plane crash. Fighting back the tears, she was barely audible on the phone. "On my way," she managed and hung up.

She was distressed. She picked up her purse, got her PDA out and checked for messages. None from Jon. She called Kelly, and got her own voice on the voicemail. She quickly asked if Kelly had heard from Jon, and if so, to call her immediately. Then, with shaky hands, she hit the speed dial for Jon's cell phone. It also went immediately to voicemail. A tear made its way down Susan's cheek as she heard her husband's recording.

"If you're alive, call me!" she said, close to hysteria. She was breathing heavily. Jon could be in a meeting with that Delaney, and shut his phone off. Or, the phone could have melted in the crash. Susan made herself not think about it, grabbed her purse, and left her office.

"Back before you miss me, Patrick," she said over her shoulder, as she headed for the elevators.

Out in the busy Loop afternoon traffic Susan easily hailed a cab. She knew she was in no condition to drive. Barely in the cab, she started typing an e-mail to Kate Fleming on her PDA.

> To: kdf@alienimport.com
> From: Susan.Russell@Byrne-Russell.com
> Subject: Update
> Kate- What's the stat on Kelly McCoy's application? –Susan

She had just sent the message when the PDA rang. The word "Home" appeared on the little screen, and her heart skipped a beat.

"Kelly? Has Jon called?" Susan answered.

"No, I'm sorry, but Mr. MacIntyre called to ask for your office number, and then you left that message, and I thought it was all bizarre, so what's going on?"

"When Mr. MacIntyre rang, how did he sound?" Susan heard the all too familiar digital beeps on her cell, letting her know that her battery was low.

"Dunno," Kelly shrugged. "I don't know him that well. You know, rude, arrogant, bossy. What's going on?"

Susan felt extreme relief talking to Kelly. Before realizing it, she blurted out her fears. "I think Jon's dead."

"No, he's not!" Kelly snorted in her usual laid back 'believe it when I see it' fashion. "What's making you say that?"

"I have been summoned to the Tower to meet with Mr. MacIntyre. That can only mean one thing."

"Yeah, and what's that one thing? Did he say what he wanted to see you about?"

"Noo-oo…" Susan started.

"So, you don't know that it's about Jon. Could be about you. Let's see. Oh, I know! He wants to buy your first-born and raise ostriches with her in Bermuda. Or,… okay, he's now single and wants to declare his undying love and admiration for you, so the two of you can run away and raise dolphins in Arizona. Or… yeah, he's divorced, the voluptuous Vernon decorated their bedroom suite, and he won't enter it before it's been totally redone by a professional. Insert name of Chicago's most prominent interior designer here, please…"

Susan felt calmer now and laughed. "Susan Russell," she said, and then realized she was talking to dead air. The battery had died. She rummaged through her purse and realized that in her haste out of the office she had grabbed her chargers, but not her spare battery. She leaned toward the driver and knocked on the glass partition. The driver met her eyes in the rear-view mirror. "Excuse me," Susan looked at the driver's identification card on the dash board, "Um, Vashi… ah, Vasyr … er… Mr. Singh? My battery died," she said waving her PDA and charger to the mirror. "Mind if I charge it?"

The driver was smiling at her in the mirror. "Yeez, yeez, berry nice. Blackberee. I like. How much you sell me?"

Susan was puzzled. "No, no, I'm not trying to sell you my phone, I'm trying to get the battery charged," she said still waving both charger and phone.

"Yeez, yeez. Laydee, my ship oba pie oglock tonigh. You come see me, yeez? I pay top dollah." He has handing her a card with the name and address of a shady south-side bar printed on it. Susan didn't accept it. She just shook her head, waved him away and sat back. She couldn't comprehend how this man, who barely spoke and obviously didn't understand any English, could get a work permit, yet it was so difficult for someone like Kelly.

* * *

In a small café in the middle of nowhere outside Marquette, Michigan, Jon looked out the window at Nick Delaney. Nick was yelling into the phone and gesticulating passionately. Jon was sitting too far away from the windows to hear the conversation. He looked at his cell phone. A missed call from Susan. He felt guilty about not having called his wife, but they had been late leaving Chicago, and had to rush to meet Delaney. The corporate pilot had 'overslept'. He dialed Susan's number. He got her voicemail.

"I'm alive," Jon said. "Tag your voicemail." He hung up and turned to Jack MacIntyre. "Look, man," he said, and pointed to the maps on the table in front of them. "Your offer was appealing to him, I've dealt with the man long enough to know what he's thinking. He's going to come back and ask for more. He's almost agreed to drop the royalties, and we won't offer them again. He can either have the land we've already surveyed west of the county road," Jon pointed to the map with a pen, "that proved unprofitable to us, or he can have the half-a-mil at signing. Now, he's going to come back asking for both, you watch."

Delaney reappeared. "Okay, I know my mineral rights are worth more than what you're offering, so I think it would be fair for me to have the original three million, and the land west of the county road."

Jack could barely maintain a straight face.

Jon took a deep breath. "The offer is the eighty acres west of the road, or one half million dollars US cash at signing. Your choice. No negotiation."

Delaney's cell phone rang. Without excusing himself he went outside again.

Jon turned toward Jack. "I bet you he's asked someone to call him every few minutes, to make us believe he's actually got a life."

Delaney was back. "An emergency has come up, and I have to go to Green Bay," he said, grabbing his coat, and his copies of the maps on the table between them.

Jon had had it with him. "Listen! There's a narrow window of opportunity in mineral exploration. If you don't get on the train, you'll be left alone at the station. And believe me, even if another train came along, your ticket won't be valid. Not after trying to screw Parker MacIntyre! The offer's on the table for the next twenty-four hours. Call us when you have something intelligent to say," Jon frothed. "Come on Jack, we're wasting our time with this loser." With that, Jon and Jack stormed out the door.

In the rental car en route to Marquette, Jack turned to Jon. "Do you think he'll bite?"

"Honestly, Jack, right now I couldn't give a rat's ass if he does or doesn't. He's trying to mess with us, and quite frankly, I've had it with him jerking us around like we were some puppets on a string."

"I thought you handled him very well," Jack said with admiration. "Kinda reminded me of Dad."

Jon laughed. "Don't ever say that, not even as a joke, man!" he huffed. "Seriously, though, I broke the cardinal rule in negotiations. Want to remind me?"

"Never lose your temper while negotiating; the other party will think you're weak," they both chanted as if reading from a book of prayers.

They laughed. "You know," Jon said, "I think you did really well in there today. Almost had him accept your offer. Your Dad would've been proud. I wish you'd reconsider this business, you have a knack for it, kid."

"Gee, thanks. Sooo not my cup of tea. I promised the old man one year, and the love for dirty mines just didn't rub off on me in that time."

"There's more to this business than mines, you know."

"Yeah, I know. And you've been a really great mentor and all, but it's kinda like Dad's forcing his calling on me. I've found my own calling, and it certainly isn't mining."

"You'll still come to the barbecue, won't you?"

"Miss a Russell barbecue? Moi? Ne-vah!"

"Bring Vicky, too, won't you. We haven't seen her since…, man, I don't even know how long it's been."

"Since the barbecue a few summers ago. The case of the missing liquor, and coincidentally Vicky's first stomach-pump incident."

"You're right! Well, since then we have supervised activities for the children. And by supervised, I mean we've hired professionals."

"You're not making that poor au pair of yours work during the barbecue? That's way cruel, Jon!"

"No, she'll be joining the party, she's part of the family now. Besides, Friday's her last day of work, so it'll sort of be a going away party for her, too. No, Susan's hired an army of professional nannies and entertainers."

Stepping out of the elevator and into Parker MacIntyre's newly decorated reception area, Susan stopped cold in her tracks. A sense of admiration and envy rushed through her. She hadn't seen Parker's offices since they had been redone, and was astonished by the outcome. The style was very much Parker's and exactly what, had she been asked to do it, Susan would have pitched herself. She remembered reading an article on Parker about a year ago. In one of the pictures Parker was sitting in his boardroom, another winning design, and the article had revealed that the interior designer had been ... something ... Ashford ... maybe Ashton. Susan couldn't think of her name now, but for months had thought of it often, as she had relentlessly and unsuccessfully searched all of Chicago, in hopes of finding more of her work.

Susan asked Parker's receptionist to announce her.

"Yes, Mrs. Russell," the elderly woman said. "Mr. MacIntyre said to go right ahead in as soon as you arrived. Right through that door," she smiled and pointed to the heavy double doors at the end of the hallway to her left.

"Look, here's my charger, and my PDA. Could you charge my battery for me, please? It died in the middle of an important conversation." Susan felt almost embarrassed asking the older person to do this.

The receptionist smiled. "Happens to me all the time," she offered sympathetically and took the PDA and the charger and plugged them in. "Would you like me to let you know once it's charged?" she offered helpfully.

"No, thanks, that won't be necessary. I'll pick it up on my way out."

The fear of Parker's bad news had vanished after Susan spoke to Kelly, but as she opened the door to Parker's office and saw the worry on his face, the fear overcame her again. Parker rarely expressed any emotion on his face, and to see him this worried, made Susan's stomach turn.

"It's Jon isn't it?" Susan said as she shook Parker's hand. "How did it happen? Cave-in? Plane crash? Give it to me straight." She tried to be strong, and fought the tears welling up behind her eyes.

Parker looked perplexed. "What the hell are you talking about, woman? Jon's fine. Just got off the phone with him."

Susan felt slightly better. "But he didn't call," she insisted. "I hate to be one of those wives, but he always calls."

Anne Harper

"The plane was late taking off," Parker offered, but left out the fact that the corporate pilot had spent the night in his bed, and had 'overslept' because she surprised him in the shower, and offered a re-run of the previous night's endeavors.

"And then I get your call," Susan continued, "and you never call the mining wives, unless there's been an accident."

"Yeah, um, sorry about that. This is kind of personal, and I didn't want to get anyone else involved." Parker offered her a seat by his big desk, and walked to the opposite side of it. "Do you read the tabloids?"

Susan smiled. "I guess I should say that I read the head-lines in the line at the grocery store, but the truth is that I find it a guilty pleasure and relish them at the hairdressers and the nail salon."

Parker smirked. "I like you, Susan Russell. You're my kind gal. Call 'em as you see 'em. I guess that's where that firecracker nanny of yours gets it from, huh?"

"Kelly? Oh, no. I get it from her. She's a no nonsense, shoot from the hip, opinionated, outspoken, squared away kind of gal. But she was much, much worse when she first got here, believe me. She used to offend everyone. We had to actually make her stop and think before she spoke. Oh, God! She didn't offend you, did she? I apologize on her behalf."

"No need for that. Nothing I didn't deserve." Parker thrust three national tabloids across his big desk. "These are today's. You seen them?"

Susan picked them up, and glanced at the pictures of Parker's Friday night anniversary party. "Oh, look! There's Kelly …" She smiled at the picture and kept skimming the text. She looked up at Parker. "Oh, no, Parker, they didn't," she whispered.

Parker sighed deeply. "They did," he said, picking up one of the magazines. "And it's probably going to get much worse than this."

"Has Jack seen any of this?"

"Doubt it. He's in the U.P. with your husband." Parker got up and walked to his bar in the corner of the office. "Drink?"

"Christ, no, Parker, it's not even three yet!"

"It's cocktail hour somewhere," Parker said as he poured himself a Scotch. "Jack will never work in interior design, thanks to this crap. I should be overjoyed, since I was hoping he'd take over MacIntyre Industries one day, but this can't be good for his already fragile ego. And to out him like that! Damn it! He's just a kid!"

"Parker, Jack's not gay," Susan said. "He's worked with Jon for a year now, and Jon's never mentioned anything about it. Besides, Jon thinks Jack's really good, and would do a great job running the business one day."

Parker walked slowly to the windows and looked out. "If Jack is any good at something he hates doing, it's only because he's been shadowing one of the best in the business. Jack's smart. He watches and listens carefully and every thought, every act of excellence is memorized and later copied in the suitable situation. It's all an act for him. He hates it. It's a dirty business for a little queen." He took a long sip of his Scotch without turning around.

Susan felt uncomfortable about Parker's remark, but sensed the need for encouragement, one parent to another. "Even if he were gay," she insisted, "would you love him any less? I don't think so. Besides, Jack's not gay, Parker. He was a jock, wasn't he? Homosexuals aren't into sports, except for the ice-capades," Susan added, hating herself for the cliché. She was searching Parker's face for clues to his reaction. "What sport was it again that Jack lettered in?"

Turning away from the windows, Parker sighed. "Fencing." He walked back to his desk, sat down and looked Susan square in the face. "I need a favor," he said.

"Name it."

"I want you to take Jack on, give him a start in the business, show him the ropes."

Susan sat silently for a while, absorbing the words. "I can't afford it."

"I'll pay you." The pain in Parker's face was sincere.

"Is he any good?" Susan was hoping for a way out. "Have you seen anything he's done? A school project, maybe? Some sketches?"

Parked leaned back in his chair and threw his muscular arm out. "He did this," he said indicating his office. "And one of the boardrooms and the reception area."

Awestruck, Susan had to physically hold her jaw from dropping. "Jack did this?" she asked mesmerized. "*Jack* did *this?*"

Parker nodded, looking around the room. "Turned out nicely too."

Susan was searching her brain. "No, wait a minute. I explicitly remember reading about the designer not a year ago. I remember admiring her work, because it was so, you know, *you*. I remember thinking that it was exactly what I would've done, had I been offered the job..." She nearly bit her tongue. Parker let it slide. "The article raved about her work. I can't think of her name now, something Ash..."

"Jacqui Ashton?" Parker offered.

"Yes! That's her!"

"That's my son," Parker said disheartened. He looked at Susan's puzzled face. "My son, John Parker MacIntyre IV, graduated last year from the Chicago School of Interior Design, and in his new professional role is to be known as Jacqui Ashton." Susan still looked baffled. "He didn't want any favors that might come his way from being related to me. Ashton was Sara's maiden name," Parker concluded.

They sat staring at each other for a while.

"So, what do you think, Susan? Can you do this for me?"

As if snapping out of a trance, Susan was all business. "He's really talented."

"I hate to admit it, but yeah, he is."

Susan leaned forward, to make a point. "No, Parker, he's *really* talented. How much direction did you give him to do this?" she asked.

Parker shrugged. "None. Gave him a budget, a deadline and pretty much a free hand."

"And are you contented with the results?"

"Very! It's as if the kid had read my mind."

Trying to hide her excitement, Susan took her time re-arranging her scarf. She tried to sound casual. "Have Jack … I mean Jacqui give me a call, and I'll see what we can do."

"No! I don't want him to know of my involvement," Parker said, and pulled a card out of his rolodex. "Here's his number. You call him. Make it sound like you've seen something of his, I don't know, make something up, just don't let him know I asked you to do this." Visibly embarrassed, Parker handed Susan Jacqui Ashton's prissy business card. "E-mail me a copy of your expenses, and Jack's salary every Friday, and I'll reimburse you."

Susan inched toward Parker and stared him square in the eye to make a point. "And if I do do this, Parker? Wiifm?"

"What's in it for you? Damn, you drive a hard bargain, woman! I've already offered to pay," Parker laughed, then relented. "What do you want? New SUV? College funds for the kids?"

Susan leaned back and studied her French manicure in silence for a long while. Coyly she looked up at Parker.

"I want you to host Vicky's twenty-first birthday party at the new J Hotel," she said slowly.

"Done," Parker leaned over his desk, and vigorously shook Susan's hand "But how will that benefit you?"

"You know what, Parker? Somehow, I think it might just."

5

"Come on, Kelly," Abby was whining. "I just heard Mom's car. Let's *go* already!" Abby was clad in a black tennis skort that her parents had given her for Christmas, and that she had fit into for the first time that very afternoon.

Kelly looked at her, smiling proudly. "I need to talk to your Mum first. Go get your blanket, and your bag, and put them in the hall, because Amber and her Mum will be here as soon as we're done with tennis."

"Aaawright," Abby said sulkily. "Where are they?"

"Your bag's in your room, and your blanket's in the dryer," Kelly said waiting for the words to sink in.

"What's my blanky doing in the dryer?" Abby asked anxiously.

I'm washing away nine years of germs. That thing had a life of its own. No almost-ten-year-old should have a snuggle blanky anyway.

"I washed it. It was covered in peanut butter. Care to explain?"

"Aw, come on Kelly! Do you always have to be the food police? It was my one *allowed* junk food day last week at Haley's," Abby put her hands defiantly to her hips. "And you know it! Don't you trust me?"

Why should I? After all those wrappers I found under yer bed just this morning? You're a spoiled little kid and you'll die of morbid obesity. … Maybe I'm being too strict. She's only a kid, after all. A kid who's doing remarkably well.

"Of course, I trust you. Now go!" Kelly said, and ushered Abby towards the laundry room just as Susan entered the house.

"Hi, Mom!" Abby hollered without turning around.

Emma bounced down the staircase and threw herself at her mother. "Guess what, Mom? You nevah guess! Guess what?" she kept repeating like a parrot while Susan was trying to unbutton her jacket and kick her shoes off.

She kissed her daughter on the forehead. "What, darling?"

"Eddie said his fiwst woad!" Emma announced proudly as Kelly walked into the hall carrying Eddie. She handed him to his mother who kissed him on the cheek and beamed with pride.

"You said your first word? You're such a big boy. What did you say? Mam-ma?"

"Hiddlesteggheddalabba," Eddie said in a rain of drool.

"Naah, that wasn't it. It was some Iwish woad, I fowget," Emma said, turning to Kelly. "What was it, Keui?"

Muppet.

Susan looked excitedly at Kelly.

"It wasn't a word, I think it was gas," Kelly said.

"When's Ambew coming?" Emma turned back to her mother.

Thank God the child has the attention span of a fruit fly.

"In an hour, darling. Right after Abby and Kelly's tennis game, I should say." Abby entered the hall. "Sweetie, you look so adorable in that outfit! Really fit." She bent over to plant a kiss on Abby's head.

"Aw, Mom!" Abby whined, but smiled. "Come on, Kelly, let's go!"

"Girls, why don't you take Eddie to the playroom, while I talk to Kelly for a minute, okay?" Susan said, as she handed Eddie to Abby.

As soon as the girls left them Kelly said "Jon called. He's fine." She couldn't wait to tell Susan, knowing how worried she had been. "Said he got your message, and had tried to call, but kept getting your voicemail."

Susan flicked her wrist.

Uh-oh. Change of subject coming up.

"I know," Susan said, "my battery died, and I couldn't get it recharged until I got to Parker MacIntyre's office.

"So, what did he want? Mr. MacIntyre, I mean."

"You were right. Well sort of," Susan said while walking into the kitchen. She laid her purse, keys and PDA on the kitchen counter and opened the refrigerator. "What a day. Dying for a drink. Would you like one? Oh, that's right, you've got tennis yet," she said as she poured herself a glass of white wine. "Anything interesting in the mail?"

She's avoiding the subject. Wonder what's up?

"What did Mr. MacIntyre want?" Kelly asked patiently. "What had I been right about?"

Ohmygod! MacIntyre and Susan are moving to Arizona to raise penguins!

"It did concern interior design," Susan answered curtly. "Did you get hold of Mario?"

Kelly nodded. "They're delivering at seven forty-five tonight. And he did know what lacto-ovo meant. Made me look like a right fool for not knowing."

Susan was leisurely sipping her wine, while going through the mail. She turned slowly, and eyed Kelly from top to bottom. "Why don't you wear that cute little outfit we got you for Christmas?"

That slutty Serena Williams thing? I'll freeze me bum off!

"I think it may be a bit cold for that yet," Kelly said trying to find a plausible excuse.

"Nonsense! It's positively lovely outside," Susan waved her hand toward the windows. "And I see Abigail's all dressed up. Who knows, this might be your last chance for tennis in a long while. And then, once you and Abby are done, you could maybe wear one of your new sun dresses for dinner, huh?"

Okay, something's up. I'm being put on display here.

"Let me just go get out of this suit, and then you and Abby can go, okay?" Susan grabbed her wine and started toward the stairs, peeling clothing off as she went.

Kelly was turning to go to her room to change, when she spotted Susan's PDA on the counter.

I shouldn't. I should! Could I? Wonder if I'll find anything there anyway? Too bad for Susan leaving it lying there. … I really shouldn't!

Kelly's curiosity took the upper hand, and after a quick glance toward the playroom and the staircase to make sure she wouldn't be detected, she scrolled down Susan's inbox.

Boring, boring, work related, work, more work, Jon, boring, her brother, boring, boring…Hello!

She stopped cold, as she saw the name of her immigration lawyer in the senders' column. Kelly could feel the hairs on the back of her neck rising as she read the message.

> To: Susan.Russell@Byrne-Russell.com
> From: kdf@alienimport.com
> Subject: Re: Update
> Susan-
> It's a no-go for Kelly McCoy. This type of visa
> cannot be extended or renewed. Call me.
> - Kate

So, that's what this is about. She got the news this afternoon, and now I'm to be paraded like a show pony for two gays. No, wait, that makes no sense. Where's the logic in that? I don't get it. But, hey - if she wants to show me off as a hottie in that tarty outfit, then I'll make her proud. You want hot? I'll give you smokin'!

Gingerly she replaced the PDA, and went to her room to change into her tennis outfit. She brushed her long red hair vigorously until it shone, then braided it loosely a la Anna Kournikova down her neck. She grabbed her racket, and ran down the stairs to the playroom.

"You ready, Abby?" Kelly poked her head around the door.

Abby and Emma were playing monkey in the middle around Eddie, who was clapping his hands on his knees and drooling happily at them. When the girls saw Kelly, they stopped.

"Wow, Keui! You look like a weal tennis playa," Emma said and bounced toward Kelly, tugging at her dress. "I see England, I see Fwance, I see Keui's undeapants!" Emma chanted, skipping around Kelly.

Yeah, you can see Germany and Belgium, too, I'm afraid. I feel like an eejit.

Kelly tried to pull the hem of the skirt down.

"Stop that, Emma Elizabeth, that's not nice," Susan appeared behind them. She was wearing a loose yellow silk dress. "Kelly, honey, you look really nice. Off you go, girls."

Abby and Kelly walked up the hill in the back of the Russell lot, toward the tennis court. The house was old, and the grounds extensive. The tennis court was there when the Russells bought the lot, but had been neglected for years. When Kelly arrived and realized there was a tennis court on the premises, she took it upon herself to fix it up. She spent all of her spare time for weeks pulling weeds, pouring mortar into cracks and painting the court. When the Russells saw how passionate Kelly was about it, they had a roof built on the court and installed heating and air-conditioning. This is how Kelly and Abby were able to play tennis all year round in Chicago weather.

Kelly turned to Abby. "So, how was cheerleading today?"

"We-ell," Abby started, and Kelly knew that this rendition could take hours, and she was left to her own thoughts.

Wonder why Susan didn't tell me she'd gotten an e-mail from Kate? Wonder why Kate didn't e-mail me? She's my attorney after all. Well, the Russells are paying, so I guess she thinks she's got to buck for the buck. ... So now what? This visa can't be renewed. Is there another one we can try for? Will it be worth it? I sure think so... I really would like to stay here for a while. I love these people. And besides, I'm not ready to go home, get married and start a family of my own quite yet. Am I? And who would I start a family with? Sean? Hah!

They were at the court, and Kelly opened the glass door.

"And then Antwon said..."

"Antwon, is that your boyfriend?" Kelly teased.

"Kelly! No! Yuck!"

"But you kissed him."

They were inside the enclosed tennis court. Abby looked baffled. "How'd you know that?"

"Haley told me he was your boyfriend and she saw you kissing at lunch one day," Kelly sounded like a tattletale nine year-old.

"Yeah, well, that's just 'cause he said I could have his pudding if I kissed him."

"And did you?"

"Yeah, but I didn't like it…"

They took their places on the court and started volleying. "What?" Kelly asked hitting the ball, "the pudding or the kiss?"

"The kiss. But that was when I was fat. I don't do that anymore."

"What? Eat pudding or kiss boys?"

"And this is my daughter Abigail at Christmas," Susan pointed at a picture on the fridge. Abby, still quite heavy then, was sitting on a very uncomfortable Santa's lap. "You'll meet her soon, and see the changes Kelly's no-nonsense diet regime has done for her. It's quite amazing."

Susan had intentionally removed all pictures of Kelly. Alen Marshall leaned forward to study the picture. He could have sworn that Santa was mouthing 'Help!' from behind his fake beard.

"And is there anything she *can't* do, this Mary Poppins of yours?" Alen turned to Susan. "I mean from what you've told us so far, she sounds practically perfect in every way. Seriously, Susan, it's all quite cute and PG-rated, and making me want to bust into a verse of Kumba-ya, but why are you telling us all this?"

Susan had been waiting for this, and had let the momentum grow. She had been building Kelly up in their minds, knowing full well that the info would be of no interest to them until she'd present them with the real deal.

"Parker MacIntyre will have his daughter's birthday at the J," she said conspiratorially. The jays flurried around Susan, hugging her, kissing her on both cheeks. "On one condition," Susan continued somberly.

"Anything, darling."

"You name it, goddess."

Taking a long breath, Susan walked around the kitchen island, so the jays were between her and the kitchen window, so she could see the girls coming down the hill from the tennis court. She filled all three wine glasses. "I want you to hire Kelly," she said solemnly.

The excitement on the jays' faces vanished quickly. They both stared at Susan.

"What would we want with a nanny?" Bryce asked in disbelief.

Susan sipped her wine, and looked out the window. Just as she had calculated, she saw Kelly and Abby walking slowly down the hill toward the house. Abby was talking and gesticulating wildly with her tennis racket and Kelly was laughing. Susan smiled at their images in the long shadows.

"The way I see it, gentlemen, is that you know the young and the hip, the players and the international shakers," Susan started. "Kelly's an alien. Her current visa can't be extended or renewed, and she needs a new one. I've run out of ideas, and really don't want her to leave. You help me with this, and I'll give you Victoria MacIntyre's birthday bash."

Both Alen and Bryce looked perplexed at Susan, then at each other. The images of old mammies flashed through Alen's mind, and Bryce was picturing a militant Julie Andrews flying in on an umbrella while bursting into song on an alp top.

Smiling, Susan felt as though she could read their minds. "She's twenty-five. She has a BA in Marketing from Trinity College in Dublin. She's only a thesis away from her MBA. And quite frankly, she's more than a little bit fabulous."

"So, what's a twenty-five year-old with a college degree doing being a nanny?" Bryce asked.

Susan looked out the window. The girls had stopped half way down the hill for no apparent reason. Susan was mentally willing them to hurry up. She had given the cue for Kelly to enter.

"You'd better ask her that yourselves," was all she volunteered.

A car pulled up to the front door. Susan cursed silently that Tammy had picked this particular day to arrive on time to pick the children up. Through the window, she could see Abby running down the hill toward the car.

"Will you excuse me a moment," Susan said, grabbing her purse. "Emma? Amber and her Mom are here!" she yelled toward the staircase, only to find her daughter at the front door, overnight bag in one hand her blanket in the other.

"I heard, Mom. Bye!" Emma said as the door closed behind her.

Kelly entered the house through the back door, turned the corner to the kitchen and bumped right into Bryce Hart's turquoise polo shirt. "Oh," she said hastily, "I beg your pardon."

Bryce was holding her by her shoulders, eyeing her from top to bottom, and then made her spin around. "My God!" he exclaimed. "You *are* more than a little gorgeous. Love the hair, the skin and the freckles."

Alen Marshall joined them. "And the legs!"

Who are you?

"Very Cameron Diaz meets Rita Hayworth meets Li-Lo," Bryce cooed.

"In a movie about Maria Sharapova."

What kinds of movies have you been watching? Imagine that mix? Crikey. Oh, probably Lindsay Lohan rather than Lilo from Lilo and Stich… I would be that mix? Alright, then!

"Please tell us you're Kelly?" Bryce said, and extended his hand. "I'm Bryce Hart, and this," he pointed at Alen, "is Alen Marshall, my partner."

Aaah, the jays! But partner? As in bed partner? Susan had never said they were partners.

"Kelly McCoy," Kelly said shaking their hands.

"I know what you're thinking," Alen said. "We're partners in business only."

"We don't mix business with pleasure," Bryce said. "Besides, he's not at all my type…"

"Nor is he mine," Alen filled in.

Kelly smiled and nodded appropriately.

Yeah, for the two of you to be bed partners, you'd have to be lesbians.

"Bye Kelly!" Emma and Abby appeared to hug her by her waist and disappeared just as quickly.

Before Kelly had time to react, the girls were through the front door, where she saw Susan talking to Tammy. Susan was holding Eddie in his baby seat, and was handing it to Tammy.

Oh, no! She's taking Eddie! He was going to be my excuse to leave the party when it got too … happy. God, I'm thinking PC now.

Kelly hadn't noticed that the jays were still fluttering about her.

"How tall are you, Kelly? Five foot ten? Eleven?" Bryce asked, while unloosening her long braid.

"Yeah."

Are these clowns for real? Who behaves like this? They're Susan's clients, they're Susan's clients, they're Susan's clients, must be on best behavior.

"And you weigh about, what, one twelve, one fifteen?" Alen was saying.

"Sure."

Closer to one-thirty, really. Okay, probably one-thirty-five by now, but who's counting? If you think I can pass for one twelve, then who am I to burst yer bubble? I like you! One twelve! Really!

"What gorgeous red hair! Naturally red, of course, you're Irish." Bryce stared her in the eye. "To *die* for green and gold eyes! Like burning emeralds! Very feline! Colored contacts?"

I'm Irish! Know yer stereotypes? Red hair – green eyes, hello?

"No."

"My darling girl, what are you doing hiding as a nanny? You should be a model. You've got that whole wholesome girl-next-door look about you," Bryce exclaimed and turned excitedly toward Alen. "Are you thinking what I'm thinking? She and Mattie! What a gorgeous couple-next-door!"

Maddy? As in short for Madeline? What's going on here?! Susan, please save me, please save me, please save me...

"So, I see you've met?" Susan walked in the kitchen, and with amusement watched the jays examine Kelly. "What did I tell you, boys, isn't she fabulous?"

"She's beyond fabulous, she's got gorgeous coloring, cheekbones to die for and a body that could make a gay man straight. Well, almost." Bryce turned to Kelly. "No offence, sweetums."

"None taken," Kelly said. *Fersure.* "Will you please excuse me, while I go shower and change?" Without waiting for a reply, Kelly bolted up the stairs for the sanctity of her room.

What just happened? Susan better come up with something really good really fast, because this is humiliating. Although quite flattering, too. They seem nice. Harmless. Funny! Like Evan, split in two. And I'm beyond fabulous. Cute!

6

In the hotel bar in Marquette, Jon and Jack were quietly enjoying a pre-dinner drink. The bar was empty apart from them and the bartender, so they felt comfortable talking business.

"Do you think he'll call?" Jack asked nervously glancing at the clock behind the bar.

"He will. Just give him time. This is by far not over yet."

The bartender placed a bowl of salad in front of Jack and a plate of deep fried jalapenos in front of Jon. Jack looked over at Jon's plate, and made a face. "Eeeuw, how can you eat that? Have you any idea how many calories there are in each one of those? Have you no respect for your body? I thought, between me and that Irish nanny slash dietician of yours, that we got you on the right track."

"Yup. You both did. And this is my reward," Jon said popping a jalapeno popper in his mouth.

"Yuck!" Jack said, digging into his salad.

A blonde entered the bar.

"Uh-oh," Jack said from the corner of his mouth. "Jumpsuit Barbie- alert."

Jon followed Jack's glance and saw Candi Jones, Parker's corporate pilot, make her way toward them.

"Oh, shit," Jon said under his breath.

"How's it hanging, boys?" Candi said, lighting a cigarette.

"Would you mind taking that stick of cancer elsewhere?" Jack said waving the smoke in front of his face.

Candi drew in a long breath of smoke and blew it right in Jack's face. "You're in the smoking section, fairy queen."

Jon stood up, and pressed his face to Candi's. "Listen, Captain Jones. Do yourself a favor and fly *Parker's* plane back to Chicago, give *Parker* his well deserved blow-job and meet us here at eight tomorrow morning, not forgetting whose *father* signs your paycheck, and apologize to him," he said between clinched teeth.

Candi eyed Jon for a moment, blew a ring of smoke in his face, got up and walked out the door.

On the bar, Jon's cell phone rang. He looked at the display.

"That him?" Jack asked, forking his salad like there was no tomorrow.

"Yup," Jon answered, a mouth full of jalapeno poppers.

"Aren't you gonna get it?"

"Nope."

"Why not?"

"I want to see what he wants first."

The cell phone went quiet. Both Jon and Jack were staring at it, hoping for it to beep, indicating that the caller had left a message. Jon popped another popper. No beep. He popped another. Still nothing. Suddenly Jack's cell phone lying on the bar rang. Startled, both men looked at the display.

"It's the dick Delaney," Jack whispered. "What do I do? What do I do!" Scared, he looked at Jon, who was popping the last popper, and slowly licking his fingers.

"Answer it," Jon said. "See what he wants. But remember, he knows you're the heir apparent."

"Jack MacIntyre," Jack said struggling to hold his voice steady.

Jon was studying Jack on the phone. He was doing a lot of 'Uh-huh's and 'I see's and rolling his eyes at Jon. He had come a long way, this kid, and Jon was going to miss him. He wished there was something, anything, he could do to keep Jack with the company. A thought flashed his mind. He finally realized that this is how Susan must feel about losing Kelly. Jon's thought process was interrupted by Jack's hand on the bar forming a fist.

"What part of *no* do you not understand, Mr. Delaney?" Jack was saying, very calmly on the phone. "We mutually agreed to no royalties. You know that. I know you know that. I was there in person when you agreed to that. Now, we might consider stock options, but to no greater a value than the half a million cash on signing Mr. Russell offered this morning."

Jon was impressed with Jack's patience and professionalism. He was enjoying watching his protégé fly the coop.

"You know what, Mr. Delaney? We've quite had it with your unreasonable demands. I wish I could say it has been a pleasure doing business with you, but my mama taught me not to lie. Good day, sir." With that, Jack hung up.

In her room, Kelly was brushing her hair. She could hear Susan giving Alen and Bryce a tour of the house. While she and Abby were playing tennis, Susan had laid out two summer dresses on Kelly's bed. Both were short, slinky and showed lots of skin. Kelly chose the green one. Through her open window, facing the driveway, she saw Mario's delivery van pull up to the front door. She pondered her reflection in the full-length mirror.

Okay, hair loose, as they seem to prefer it so. Dress accentuates my no-colored-contacts eyes. Hmmm. Some lipgloss mightn't hurt.

Kelly brushed some nude gloss on her lips.

Why do I bother? They're gay. But they're Susan's clients, and this is as close as I'll get to a girls' night in, so here goes.

Kelly joined Susan and the jays in the sun room, where they were enjoying the sun setting over the little pond to the west of the Russell lot. Kelly surveyed Susan's two clients.

Christ! We look like a bag of Skittles.

Bryce was wearing a turquoise polo shirt over a pair of peach colored khakis that were so crisply ironed, you could cut yourself on the crease. Alen sported navy khakis and a pink-and-yellow pinstripe button-down shirt. For good measure he wore a yellow sweater over his shoulders, tied around his neck.

Huh? They actually do wear the sweaters around their necks, I thought it was some old cliché.

Kelly looked down at her lime-green dress.

Well, I know now why Susan insisted I wear this thing, I'd blend into the furniture in anything else.

Susan heard Kelly enter, and slowly tore her eyes from the yellow-and-mauve sky.

"There you are, hon. Don't you look lovely. Some wine?" she said, waving a glass in Kelly's direction. She took it. "Mario's just delivered. They're setting up in the dining room. Hope you boys are hungry, because you're in for a Chicago treat!"

The jays were licking their lips and making yummy noises, while Kelly carefully sat herself down on the sofa opposite them.

What's the proper social etiquette in this situation? Legs crossed? Ankles crossed? Left leg over right knee or right leg over left knee? ... Why should I care? I'm in a room with a married woman who's practically me second Mum and two gay guys, I'm going to sit the way I bloody well feel comfortable.

She sank into the cushions.

Bryce leaned toward Kelly. "I hope we didn't overwhelm you when we first met..."

You did.

"...and I hope you'll take this the way it was meant to be taken..."

I won't.

"...I don't know how much Susan has told you about our little endeavor..."

Not enough.

"...Alen and I are just about to open a hotel in downtown Chicago..."

That I know.

"...and we'd love it if you'd come work for us."

... ??? ... I have no response to that ...

A deadly silence fell over the little room. Kelly stared in awe at Bryce. Then at Alen. Then at Susan.

"Um, Mr. Hart..." she started.

"Oh, call me Bryce, please," Bryce said. "Mr. Hart makes me sound like I should be sitting in a boardroom, wearing a navy pinstripe three-piece suit." He made the gesture for gagging.

Kelly cleared her throat. "Okay, Bryce, thank you. Ah, I don't know how much Susan has told you, but I'm not legal to work in this country without a visa, and the visa I'm currently on expires soon, and apparently cannot be renewed." The last part of her sentence, Kelly shot at Susan, who avoided her glance by pouring everyone more wine.

"Yes," Alen said. "Susan has explained all of that, but you see, we're offering you a chance to stay here, in the US, for another eighteen months. Wouldn't that be fabulous?"

Why does every American think that every non-American is living and dying for the opportunity to come work in America? Oh, yeah, millions of illegal Latinos jumping the border daily. Right. Of course.

"Well, that's very generous of you. I just have a couple of questions. First, how are you proposing to do that? No offence, but the Russells have hired an immigration lawyer to work my case, and if she can't get me in, how could you?" She could see Alen drawing a breath, but held up her hand. "Please let me finish. Second, I know nothing about the hotel industry, so how do you suppose the INS," *or whatever they call themselves nowadays,* "will grant me a visa to do something I know nothing about, when they wouldn't extend a work permit allowing me to continue what I've been doing for the past year?" This was meant as a jab at Susan, who excused herself to go and pay the caterers. Kelly turned back to Alen and Bryce. "And lastly, what's in it for you?"

Alen and Bryce stared at Kelly in disbelief for a moment, then looked at each other. Both broke out laughing simultaneously.

"The Ice Bitch!" they both shouted.

"Won't she have a challenge with this one?" Bryce said, looking inquisitively at Alen. "Oh, I love it! The Irish volcano melts the Italian iceberg. I could sell tickets! And make a profit!"

"Oh, stop!" Alen said. "My foundation is running."

Could I see myself working for these two? Easily. And enjoy every minute of it. They're funny. And kinda cute. But what would I be doing in a hotel? What do I know about the hotel business? You check in, you get yer key, you spend a night or two, you check out, you pay, they make money. ... Huh? I do know something about the hotel business!

Bryce and Alen were both trying to appear serious, as they were wiping tears from the corners of their eyes.

"In all seriousness," Alen said, "we know of this lovely little company based in Charlotte, North Carolina that specializes in the exchange of hospitality staff. They arrange for everything. Visas, insurance, host properties..."

"In fact," Bryce chimed in, "most of our front desk staff at our San Fran hotel are recruits from this program. And we're interviewing candidates for the Phoenix property, too. Gorgeous creatures. And we want you, because we think you're simply gorgeous, and we only hire gorgeous people," he limp-wristed.

"Well, gorgeous and young, of course," Alen corrected him.

"Gorgeous, young and talented." Bryce continued.

"I get to tell the best part! I get to tell the best part!" Alen was clapping his hands in excitement. "Guess what the visa, or rather, the training program, is called? You'll never guess!"

The multi-national 'Have you been serviced' program?

"I give up."

In unison, Bryce and Alen said "The J-1 Visitor Exchange Program!"

So?

"J-1? Isn't that absolutely marvelous?" Alen said.

"Aaah, J-1" Kelly said. "Very fitting."

I'm an eejit. J Hotel won! … They must think me a retard!

Susan walked into the sunroom. "My friends, dinner, if you're ready, is served." The four of them walked into the dining room, where the caterers had set up a feast.

Susan became all business. "Bryce, why don't you sit over here, and Alen, you take this seat. Kelly, how about you sit there…"

Yadda-yadda-yadda. Let's see. I'm in the best possible lighting. I'm facing Bryce, so he must be the most important to impress tonight. Okay, watch me work it. Although it would help me to know where we were going with this, it can't be all about a visa. Could it? I'm young, gorgeous and … well don't know how talented until I've tried it out. Me in a hotel? Brilliant!

Why not?! I'll try anything once! ... Well, within reason, of course...

They helped themselves to salads and hors d'oevres while chit-chatting about the hotel and the progress they'd made and the budget and deadline they were facing. Kelly was trying to stifle a yawn.

Good thing the food is good and that there's plenty of it, or else they'd find me face-down in the soup, trying to drown myself from boredom. Although, better look interested. These could be my future bosses, after all.

"So, Kelly, tell me a little bit about yourself," Bryce said out of the blue.

"What do you want to know?"

"Well, for starters, what's a gorgeous twenty-five year-old with a college degree doing as a nanny?"

Kelly looked at Susan, who raised her eyebrows. 'Your call' her expression seemed to say.

"I needed some time away," Kelly said.

"From?" Alen jumped at the gun.

Kelly sighed. "From Sean. My fiancé."

Oh, God! Can has been opened, worms are taking over!

Bryce and Alen both dropped their utensils, giving Kelly their full attention. "Do tell," Bryce urged.

Oh, what the hell.

"We were engaged for a about year. We were going to get married right after I graduated from business school. One day I arrived home early from study hall and found him ... um ... *doing* someone on the floor of my living room."

"We're going to need more details," Alen said, wiping his mouth on the napkin.

"Picture it," Kelly said, and made rectangle with her hands, as a camera screen. "I walked right into an x-rated picture. They were at it like a rabbits on Viagra."

"And what did you do?" Alen asked.

"I sat down and told them to please finish. She gathered her clothes and left. I called him every vile name in the book. Threw some cookware at him. When I ran out of things to throw, he packed his bags and left." Absentmindedly Kelly was fiddling with her necklace.

"Do you know who she was?" Alen asked excitedly.

He's hoping for drama, here, I suppose. Okay, let's see. Who was she? My sister? No, too day-time drama. The neighbors' eight year-old son? No, too Michael Jackson. My dog? Plain too sick.

"Never seen her before or since," Kelly said.

"Then what did you do?" Bryce asked.

"I applied for a year's extension on my thesis. Got it. Then went to visit my aunt in Galway. ...Um, that's western Ireland. She raises horses. Good place to get your mind off anything. Found this ad for au pairing and applied for a position."

"Tell me about Sean. What does he look like?" Alen prompted.

"About average. Average height, build, hair and eye color," Kelly said, looking into the horizon, playing with her necklace.

"What about his character?" Alen asked.

Loyal? Trustworthy? Honest? Who am I kidding? Well hung, well hung, well hung.

"Average. Kinda bla-ha until he started screwing around. He was kind of … you know … well endowed," Kelly volunteered with a blush.

"Well! That explains it then!" Alen said. "It's a well-known fact, that men with large testicles are more likely to get you pregnant, and less likely to be faithful."

"Ever hear from him again?" Bryce asked.

"Daily for about three months, then every other day, and as of about two weeks ago, just once a week," Kelly said.

"Do you still love him?" Alen asked.

"I'm not sure I ever did. Sad, really. I thought the relationship safe. My back-up plan. Little did I know," sighing involuntarily she dropped the necklace.

"Is he worth going back to? What does he do for a living?" Bryce asked.

"He's with the Irish Government. External affairs."

"How was the sex?" Alen asked bluntly.

Whoa! Change of subject? I'm going to hell admitting that I've had …pre-marital relations. Hah! I'm going to hell for having had pre-marital relations!

"It was, you know, sex," Kelly said, and could feel her cheeks heating up. She took a long sip of her wine, to hide her face.

"Were you making love, fucking or having sex?" Bryce asked.

"I didn't know there was a difference," Kelly said looking from one face to the other.

"Oh, you sweet, innocent girl," Bryce said and reached across the table and patted Kelly's hand. "You make love when you're in a committed relationship or when you're trying to make a baby, you fuck someone you pick up at the bar and never see again, and you have sex with your secret, possibly married, lover. So, which one was it?"

Jaysus! They don't beat about the bush, do they? Oh, hah-ha, that's right, they're gay, they wouldn't. Kelly McCoy, you naughty girl you – 'Hic'- you're drunk!

Kelly shrugged.

"Clothes off?" Bryce asked.

"Yes. Well, sometimes he'd leave his socks on. He had very cold feet, you see."

"In bed? Under the covers?"

"Yes. Always."

"Lights off?"

"Yes."

"Him on top?"

"Always."

"Girl, you haven't lived, much less had sex! Forget him!" Bryce exclaimed.

Alen raised his glass at Kelly. "Are you trying to tell me that a gorgeous creature like you has never had toe-curling, shock waves up your spine, breath-stopping, sweaty sex? Girlfriend! Have you wasted your time on this loser! There are men out there who are dying to be with someone like you!"

"And if Sean walked into this room right now, what would you say?" Susan asked.

I forgive you.

Kelly shrugged, finished her glass of wine and started fiddling with her necklace again.

7

Early the following morning, Susan and Kelly were driving to meet with Bryce and Alen and iron out the details about Kelly's possible future traineeship with the J Hotel. Kelly had no recollection of them having set up this meeting the previous evening, and had been sound asleep, looking forward to a morning off, when Susan woke her up, looking crisp and bright-eyed.

"Would it be something you'd consider?" Susan asked.

"Dunno, it's all happening too quickly for comfort. I was preparing to go back to Dublin, finish graduate school. I had a plan. Now I don't know anymore. I'm tempted, of course, but the pull to go home is strong as well." Kelly was pulling her yellow cardigan closer around her. She was wearing gray slacks and a yellow cotton tank top under the cardigan. Apparently Alen and Bryce had told her to dress casual. She remembered nothing.

"Well, I suggest that you enjoy your two weeks with your parents, think about it, get your parents' input. But if all else fails, what does your gut tell you?"

My gut? That I had too much to drink last night, that you're driving too fast, and that I really need to hurl.

"What do you think?" Kelly asked.

"I don't want to influence your decision."

"You won't."

"Well, then. I think it's a great idea. Personally I'd love for you to stay here. Professionally, well, it's a growing company, they're offering you a traineeship on their marketing team, which, from the little I've seen of their work, is very fast-paced and on the wire. You'll meet all kinds of interesting people, work with the best in the industry, and they'll pay you competitive wages. Since they're offering you room and board, you can probably save most of the money. You can always finish grad school after you've finished your training. Or, start working on your thesis now, while you wait for the paperwork to be processed."

That was a lot of information in very little time. God, my head hurts. What was the gist of what she just said?

"Think about it, at least." Susan was hoping that Kelly might change her mind once she saw the property first hand. "Any word from your parents?"

"Yeah. All systems still go. Be here Monday. Dad says it's safest time to travel. Security tightened in city and airport." Kelly tried to use as few words as possible without sounding rude.

Must not talk. Hurts.

"Hung over?" Susan asked with a smile.

Kelly nodded.

Ayayay! Very bad idea. Must not move head. Try blinking in Morse code. … Not much better. Don't know Morse code.

"Susan, you're smaller than I am, and you had loads more to drink. How do you do it?"

Susan smiled smugly. "Oh, there are lots of remedies, I guess. Someone will tell you to take aspirin, someone else will tell you to drink gallons of strong coffee, and then there are those who believe in sweating it out in a sauna, or the gym."

Uh-huh. Aspirin - check. Hot shower - check. Black coffee - check. Didn't work.

"My secret weapon," Susan stuck a hand in her purse and produced a banana. "Potassium. Sucks the alcohol right out of your blood. Well, I don't know really what it does, but it works for me. Here, have one. And once you've eaten that, drink this." Susan produced a water bottle from her purse. "You're dehydrated."

Whatcha got in there? A mini fridge?

They arrived at the soon-to-be J Hotel, and through the glass windows of the jays' office they could see the backs of Alen and Bryce, and opposite them, a tall, blond, young man in a gray suit. Kelly stopped and took Susan's hand.

"Who's the hunk?" she whispered.

Susan smiled at her. "Feeling better?" she teased.

Kelly unbuttoned her cardigan, adjusted her cleavage, and shook out her hair. "Let's go introduce ourselves!"

Susan knocked on the open door, and smiled at Bryce and Alen. "Is this a private party, or can anyone join in?"

"Suzy Q, and her sidekick, the Irish emerald on fire! Come in, come in, have a seat. There's a gorgeous creature here you absolutely have to meet," Bryce said, waving them in.

Kelly found herself staring at the most amazing blue eyes she had ever seen. The tall young man stood up. His smile sent shock waves through her entire body.

Am I still drunk, or is this the most gorgeous man I've ever seen? Oh, please don't be gay! Not that I'd mind, but we'd have loads more fun if you weren't.

Bryce did the introductions. "Susan, Kelly, I'd like you to meet our newest addition, Matthew Bradshaw, the future Assistant Manager of the J Hotel Chicago. Matthew, this is Susan Russell, our fabulous designer, and Kelly ...," Bryce looked at Kelly for clues, but her eyes were glued to Matthew's.

"Kelly, sweetie, I've completely forgotten your last name. I am so sorry, precious. I'm such a ditz."

Bradshaw. Kelly Bradshaw. Mrs. Matthew Bradshaw.

"Ah, um McCoy," Kelly said hastily. "Kelly McCoy."

"Yes, of course! Matthew, this is Kelly McCoy, whom we hope we can persuade today to join our team as a J-1 trainee.

Kelly, should you accept our offer for the training program, you'd be reporting directly to Matthew," Bryce continued.

You'd be my boss? You *would be my boss!*

Kelly was still shaking hands with Matthew. He smiled at her, and she could feel the color on her face rising to the roots of her hair. As if she were looking into a mirror, Matthew was blushing as well.

"So, Kelly, how can we convince you to join the J team?" Kelly could hear Bryce's voice in the very far distance.

"Oh, um, no convincing required," she finally let go of Matthew's hand, and slowly tore her eyes from his. "If the visa people say it's a go, then I'm here, ready to play with J."

They sat for a while outlining the training program. Alen, always impatient, wanted Kelly to start immediately.

"I have an idea. You said your current visa status allows you to stay in the country until, what, end of June? I suggest that we don't put you on the payroll, but you move in, you appear at all the happenings, especially the ones with lots of media, we work out the details with the visa agency in Charlotte and the INS, and if all goes well, by end of June, you'll have your visa, and we'll reimburse you. And so, J won! Really, it's a win-win situation. Am I right?"

Kelly was eyeing Matthew under her brow, and slyly moved her left foot, so it was just inches away from his right foot.

He's so cute. And he blushed like a little boy. … Ohmygod! He's a life-size Ken-doll! I just want to pick him up and put him in me pocket and take him with me everywhere, bathe him and change his clothes and have him sleep on my pillow and ... what? Who said what just then?

"No objections," she blurted out.

"Good," Alen said, taken aback. "Here's the contact information for the company in Charlotte, I suggest that you make an appointment for an interview ASAP, so we can get the ball rolling. And Mattie, we're hoping to add more international flair to our front line staff. You'll do the hiring, or course, but we would like a foreign man god on every shift."

"At least," Bryce added.

"Ahem, sure. And, with all due respect, I prefer Matthew," Matthew said firmly.

"Ooopsee. My bad," Alen said.

Good for you Mattie! Nip it in the bud. Oooh! Bud. Butt. I'd like to nip you in the butt, Mattie.

Kelly's sandaled foot coyly brushed against Matthew's leg. He bounced out of his seat, face crimson.

"I got to go, sorry, I've taken up enough of your time already. Nice meeting you, ladies." He was gone before he had finished the sentence.

Bryce winked at Susan. "What did I tell you? Dreamy, huh? Too bad he's straight."

"And married," Susan added as if reading Kelly's thoughts.

He's married? Damn! Well, maybe he wasn't all that cute after all.

"Kelly? Any questions so far?" Bryce said.

"Yeah, I've got one."

"We're here to answer it."

"Why J? What does it stand for?"

Can't be because J rhymes with gay? Although cute, not very original.

Bryce sat up straight in his chair. "Wee-eell, Alen and I found that among other things we have in common, is an abnormal admiration for the same people. And, oddly enough, all their names start with the letter J!"

"Such as?" Kelly asked, intrigued.

"Such as... well, let's see, ...James Dean, Julie Newmar, Joni Mitchell, Judy Garland ..."

... Jack Kevorkian, Jeffrey Dahmer, Josef Mengele... Oooh! James Joyce, Jonathan Swift, Javier Perez de Cuellar, ... Oooh-oooh! Jose Cuervo, Jack Daniels, Johnny Walker! Man! J is a really popular letter!

"...Jude Law, Johnny Depp. Anyway," Bryce waved his hand, "the list goes on and on. I'm sure you'd like a tour, huh?" He handed her his master key. "Would you mind, darling, if we borrow Susan while you look around. This key lets you in everywhere except the offices. We've put fingerprint locks on those. Have fun, little one. We'll see you here in, say, half an hour?"

"Oh, and while you're touring, pick a suite for yourself, since you'll be staying here for the next eighteen months. Anything but the Penthouse, obviously," Alen added.

* * *

Kelly took the elevator to the second floor and used the key to open the door to the room closest to the elevators. The room was very Spartan. It was decorated in various shades of white, no art on any of the walls, except the wall facing the bed, where she saw a gigantic plasma screen TV and tiny speakers in all the corners of the room.

This is what they're raving about? I don't get it. It's white-on-white-on-white. I could have done this!

The bed was huge, and sported a massive amount of pure white linen. Kelly sat down on the bed and looked around the room.

Oh, I get it now! Susan Russell, you're a genius! White-on-white-on-white. Who would've thought? Hmmm... This bed is really comfortable. Soft and cushiony. Oh, no! This isn't one of those cheesy vibrating beds, is it?

Kelly saw a remote lying on the pillows and reached for it.

Do I dare? Oh, who's to know?

Curiosity got the better of her and she lay down on the bed and pushed the red 'on' button on the remote. Suddenly loud music emanated from all corners of the room. ABBA was singing *Dancing Queen*.

Jaysus Christ! How do I turn this off?

Kelly tried pushing every button on the remote, but nothing worked.

Where's it coming from?!

Kelly frantically pointed the remote at all the speakers.

Christ, it is a vibrating bed. Vibrating from the decibel level.

The door opened with a jerk, and a stern-looking older woman walked in. She grabbed Kelly's remote and silenced the noise.

Wait! I thought the hotel wasn't operational yet. Am I in her room?

"And just what are you doing in here?" the stone-faced woman asked.

Kelly jumped off the bed, and noticed that she was almost a foot taller than the other woman.

"I was just looking around," Kelly said apologetically. "Ma'am," she added. "What are *you* doing here?"

"How did you get in?" the woman said ignoring Kelly's question.

Kelly waved Bryce's master key.

"Where did you get that!?"

"Bryce gave it to me," Kelly said.

Why am I telling you this?

"Bryce Hart? How do you know Bryce?"

"He and Alen just hired me."

"I beg your pardon?!"

She's really rude!

"Hi, I'm Kelly McCoy," Kelly said trying to break the ice. She smiled and extended her hand. The other woman didn't smile back nor did she shake Kelly's hand.

And you are?

"If this is some sort of joke, it's in extremely poor taste," she said and turned to the door. "I think you need to leave now."

Who are you telling me what I need to do?

"I don't think I need to. You see, I'm selecting my room. I'll be living here for the next eighteen months."

Take that ya dwarf!

"You can ask Bryce or Alen if you don't believe me," Kelly added. The other lady was about to leave the room. "By the way, who are you to come in here, without knocking and telling me what I need to do?" Kelly called after her.

"If you're such chums with the owners, why don't you ask them?" she said and left the room.

Kelly, you just got frost bitten by the infamous Ice Bitch.

"I'm so sorry to have to drag you with me, Kelly, I didn't realize we'd be that long at the J," Susan said as she was driving them toward her office in the Loop. "I promise, this interview won't take very long, and then I'll drive you home."

Kelly waved her hand. "Nonsense. I'll take the El. Just, if it would be okay, I would really need to use the bathroom in your office. I had all that coffee earlier."

"Of course," Susan said as she pulled into the parking structure in her office building. "So, I hear you met Gina Lombardi?"

"God, I see now why you call her the Ice Bitch!" Kelly exclaimed. "Suits her better than Gina Lombardi! Way too glamorous a name for … *that* …"

"She might've made it up," Susan said. "It's more common than you think. Bryce Hart was actually born Bruce Haapa... nen... lainen...something... . And Alen's birth certificate spells it A-l-l-a-n."

"Why do they do that?"

Susan shrugged. "To appear exotic. To pretend they're someone they're not. To cover personal insecurities. Hide their heritage. Who knows? You ever find out – please tell me."

Hmmph? I'm exotic, aren't I? And I'm just good old generic Kelly McCoy.

"So, which room were you in when she came barging in?" Susan asked.

"One of your white ones. On the second floor? Just off the elevator?"

"Ah, yes, room 205. No wonder. Her office is unit 206. Well, for now, anyway. She'll probably move into Bryce's office once he and Alen move to their next property," Susan said. "Don't take her too seriously. Nobody does. She's got issues. Plus, you'd be reporting to Matthew."

"What an interesting mix of people they got at that hotel. I mean, Bryce and Alen are grand! I'd really enjoy working with them. And Matthew! Mmmm. He's dreamy!"

"He's mar-ried!" Susan singsonged.

"I know, I know! A girl can still have some eye-candy, right? I mean, no harm in looking," Kelly said smiling.

"And that's all you'd better be doing. Don't get too attached to Bryce and Alen. They're about to wrap things up here in Chicago since they are already in due diligence in Asheville."

"Oh, no! I don't know if I want this job, then," Kelly said heart-broken.

They arrived at Susan's office, and said their goodbyes. Susan headed for her office to prepare for her interview and Kelly headed for the ladies' room.

Where's me purse? Oh, no! I left it in the car! And it's locked. And Susan's got the key. And she's in an interview. Aw, man!

Kelly took a seat in the small waiting area outside Susan's office. Susan's assistant, Patrick, was on the phone, speaking in a language Kelly didn't understand. He hung up and smiled at Kelly.

"What language was that, Patrick?"

"Korean," he said. "You weren't eavesdropping were you? Because I was just telling my brother how much hotter you've become since I last saw you," Patrick winked at her.

Kelly blushed and decided to change the subject to get her natural color back. "You speak Korean? I thought you were, like, third generation Korean-American, or something."

"Fourth," Patrick admitted proudly. "We live in a small Korean community on the south side, and everyone in our family is bi-lingual."

A young man carrying a sketch case approached Patrick. "Excuse me," he said. "Would you please tell Mrs. Russell that Jacqui Ashton is here for his eleven o'clock appointment?"

"Of course, Mr. Ashton, would you please take a seat?" Patrick motioned to the sofas and announced him to Susan.

Jacqui took a seat by Kelly. "Jacqui Ashton," he said, trying out his name, and extending his hand.

Kelly shook it. "Kelly McCoy, nice to meet you."

I know you! Where do I know you from?

"You here for the interview?"

"Yes," Jacqui said and nervously started tapping his hands on the sketch case on his lap.

"Nervous?"

Might I have snogged you after a pub-crawl?

"Yes," Jacqui admitted and let out a small nervous laughter. "You here for the interview as well?"

I know those eyes and that smile.

"Just had what you might call an interview. It was decided well before I even got there, though," Kelly said.

This is really bugging me now. Ashton? No, doesn't ring any bells.

"How was she?" Jacqui asked nervously.

This is really going to irritate me. I know I know you!

"Total bitch, but what could be expected? The job was mine, luckily, before I even met her," Kelly said. "Although, I don't know if I want the job now."

Susan opened the door to her office, and saw an ashen-faced Jacqui talking to an inquisitive Kelly. "Jack …ee! How wonderful to see you!" Susan said and extended both arms.

Jacqui took them and air kissed her on both sides of her face. "It's been ages! Have you met Kelly? Kelly, this is ..."

"Jacqui Ashton, yes, we just met," Jacqui interrupted her hastily.

"What are you still doing here, Kel?"

"Forgot me purse in yer car."

"You know? I just got off the phone with Tammy, and she's taking the kids to Six Flags, so they won't be home until supper. After I'm done here with ... Jacqui..., how about lunch?" Susan said excitedly as she ushered Jacqui into her office.

"The Grill?" Kelly said, licking her lips.

"Where else?" Susan replied, and closed the office door behind her. She offered Jacqui a seat, and sat down behind her desk. "So, Jack, how've you been?"

"Fine, thank you. And I really appreciate you calling me Jacqui in public," he said nervously. "I must say I was surprised by your call.".

"And I must say I was offended that you hadn't called me," Susan teased. "I knew your year with your Dad was over, and I had hoped to snag you before anyone else did."

"Wha...?"

"I am ready to offer you an internship on a trial basis, if you're interested."

"Oh, I'm interested!"

"So why didn't you send me your resume? Why did *I* have to call *you*?"

Jacqui shifted uneasily. "Well … you know … I've known you and Jon since, like, junior high, and having worked with Jon this last year … well … I didn't want you to feel like you were doing me a favor, just because your husband works for Dad …"

Susan flicked her hand. "I know what you did to your Dad's office. Maybe it was a lucky fluke, maybe you're really talented, I don't know. But I'd love to see what you're made of."

Outside Susan's office Kelly was fascinated by Patrick's computer. "So, you can actually get it to display in Korean. That's brilliant! Can you make it do that in any language? Say Arabic? Or Russian?"

"Sure," Patrick said excitedly. "I can make it do it ancient Aramaic, if I want to. Of course, I have no frame of reference whether it's correct."

"Can you type in Korean as well?" she said and sat down on the corner of his desk.

"Yeah, check this out," Patrick said and typed a few symbols. He turned his display toward Kelly. "Whatcha think?"

"Very clever. What's it say?"

"This symbol here makes up 'Che', this one here 'Li'. It spells your name. Well, sort of."

"Brilliant! Can you print that out for me, please? I find it so absurd when westerners go and get Asian symbols tattooed on their arses thinking it says 'Love' or 'Peace' or something, and for all they know it really says things like 'I've got a teeny weenie'. She looked at the printout of the name in Korean. "This doesn't mean I've got a teeny weenie, does it?"

Patrick laughed. "No. Very loosely translated it means 'Style Star'."

Oh, yeah! That's me alright! ... Not!

"However," Patrick continued, "make the slightest changes, and you've got 'Winter Gold'."

"Better!"

In her office Susan pulled out a thick folder of sketches, blueprints and architects' drawings. "Here's a challenge for you, Jacqui. You pull this off, and I'm ready to offer you a full-time position," Susan said spreading the papers across her desk.

Jacqui was perplexed. "That's what you call an inter-view?"

Susan laughed. "Pretty much. I've seen your work and would like to see more, before I offer you anything perma-nent. And like you said, I've known you for longer than I care to remind myself, " she laughed. "Don't tell anyone how far back we go, please, it just reminds me of how old I am!"

"Oh, shush!" Jacqui waved away her argument. "You look fabulous for a twenty-five year-old mother of three!"

Susan laughed and walked around her desk. She planted a soft little kiss on Jacqui's forehead. "*Twenty*-five!? God bless you, child. Look at you, all grown up! To me, you'll always be the pre-pubescent boy who peed in my pool." She turned back to face her desk. "Let's see what you can do with this bit of challenge," she was pulling rolls of paper out of tubes. She looked back at Jacqui, who still looked worried. "What?"

Jacqui was visibly uncomfortable. "Well, … just that girl, Kelly, outside, said that she'd gotten the job, and that … well … you'd been a real biatch … That's your nanny, isn't it?"

Susan laughed heartily and opened the door. "Kelly, come here a sec, would you?"

"What?" Kelly said looking up from Patrick's computer.

"Please tell Jacqui that you didn't interview with me and I wasn't the one being a bitch to you today."

"Right," Kelly said. "I think I already told him that."

"Thank you, Kelly," Susan laughed, and closed the door. "I think I know what happened. Kelly thinks faster than she talks, and although we're really grateful for that, she can be a bit difficult to decipher at times."

"Not that that makes any sense, but okay," Jacqui said, and turned his attention to the papers on Susan's desk. He was rubbing his hands together. "What fabulous project do you have for me?"

"A new J Hotel is about to open, hopefully by 4th of July, right here, downtown, and we still haven't agreed on a lobby." She pulled out a thick folio. "These are some of the rejected ideas," she said, and handed the folio to Jacqui. "Here's the budget. These are the blueprints and the architectural drawings," she gave the rolled-up papers to Jacqui.

"And this is a list of what the owners want." She gave Jacqui a long, hand-written list. "We have yet to see eye-to-eye on anything, and I'm, quite frankly, out of ideas. Your challenge is to come up with an idea that meets the budget, the owners' wishes and the deadline. If you pull this off, I'll offer you a permanent position."

Susan leaned against her desk and eyed Jacqui. His eyes were gleaming with excitement, and he was gathering all the papers and shoving them quickly into his sketch case.

"Thank you, Susan," he said smiling ear to ear. "You won't be disappointed." He pumped Susan's hand enthusiastically and headed for the door. "I'll make you proud," he said as he was opening the door. "Thanks again."

"Wait!" Susan called out after him. "Won't you join us for lunch? We're going to The Grill."

Jacqui was so excited, he could hardly stand still. "I'd really love to, you know, get started on this project. I'm like, *dying* to see the property! Get the vibe, you know. My head is, like, positively exploding with all these fabulous ideas, and if I don't put them on paper immediately, I think I'll need to be institutionalized!" he exclaimed as he headed toward the elevators. "Lovely to have met you Kelly! Love you Susan! Talk soon!"

"Will you be at the barbecue Saturday?" Susan shouted after him.

"Wouldn't miss it for the world, darling!" Jacqui replied as the elevator doors were closing.

Kelly turned to Susan. "Who *is* that?"

Susan smiled. "Quite possibly the best thing that's about to happen in interior design," she said with a sigh, and reached for her PDA.

> To: bhart@jhotels.com, amarshall@jhotels.com
> From: Susan.Russell@Byrne-Russell.com
> Subject: Lobby design
> Be prepared! My new intern, Jacqui, is headed
> your way, and will be sketching the lobby
> momentarily. – Susan

"Not that is matters to me, but is he gay?" Kelly asked after Susan sent her message.

Susan smiled and raised an eyebrow. "The jury's still out, hon."

Is that what they call a hung jury?

"You ready?" Susan said to Kelly. "Let's go eat. I'm starving."

Susan's PDA beeped as they were walking down the street toward the restaurant.

> To: Susan.Russell@Byrne-Russell.com
> From: bhart@jhotels.com
> Subject: Re: Lobby design
> Susan- Met him. Love him! Trying to keep the
> ice biatch away from him.
> B

"What, did he fly there?"

* * *

Susan and Kelly had just been served their lunch at The Grill when Jacqui stormed toward them. "Ohmygod, Susan, I've seen the property. Fabulous! About the lobby - I can't wait to run some ideas by you. See, I was thinking, we burst through this wall, it's not a bearing wall...," he looked up from his drawings. "Oh, ... sorry... you're having lunch." He looked at Kelly's monster size burger, which she was devouring. "Oh, honey, how can you eat that? Have you any idea how many cows had to die for that burger?"

About one one millionth?

"Don't care."

"How can a skinny girl like you eat like that?" Jacqui said in disgust.

"Ketchup opportunity," Kelly said, and dunked her burger in a glob of ketchup. "Wanna bite?" she pointed the burger in Jacqui's direction. "Loads of Lycopene. Good for you."

"Jacqui, honey, would you like to join us?" Susan pulled out a chair. "Tell me about the J."

Jacqui took a seat. "Ohmygosh! It's, like, sooo gorgeous! Love what you did with the bar! So I thought we'd continue that theme into the lobby ...," he ranted while pulling out some preliminary sketches from his case.

What's it that guy on the radio says ketchup contains? Some mellowing agent? This Jacqui could sure use some! Look at him! He's as giddy as a priest in Neverland!

"...oh, and I met the biatch, and she was all 'you really need to clear your presence with me'..." Jacqui went on like a typewriter.

Where do I know him from? This is really bugging me now. Could I have met him in Dublin?

"... and then Bryce tells the ice biatch to unclench. Unclench! She nearly threw a fit!"

"Jacqui, where do I know you from?" Kelly abruptly interrupted Jacqui's rendition.

Susan smiled, and rubbed Jacqui's shoulder. "Honey, Jacqui is ..."

"An old family friend," Jacqui filled in. "I met you at the hospital when Susan was giving birth to Eddie." Jacqui shot Susan a quick glance.

An old family friend, huh? Is that what they call it? So that's the secret of a happy marriage, the wife has a younger lover. No way, not Susan! And not with this Jacqui. Besides, he's a bit ... gay... Ohmygod! Jon was having an affair with him when Susan was pregnant with Eddie! Naah! Maybe he reminds me of someone famous. Eyes are sort of Mel Gibson's only grayer, and smile close to Robert Redford's only not as wide... Yeah, that's got to be it...

"Yeah, sorry. I met so many people when I first arrived, that names and faces just run into each other."

I know that's not it! Did I meet him at one of the Russells' parties last year? That's probably it, seeing as he's an old family friend. He has the aura of those very privileged, so definitely better suited as a friend of the Russells' than hanging around my lot ... Man! Why am I always drunk at the Russell events? Because alcohol is always readily available? Okay, on Saturday I'll stick to ice tea! Or possibly just beer. That's it! Good plan!

8

The Russell barbeques were the highlight of the summer for anyone even remotely connected to the family. Invitations were never sent out, as there were never causes for rsvp. Everyone always showed up.

Parker pulled up at the Russells', and parked his Land Rover right outside the garage. There were already several cars parked up and down the driveway, but Parker spotted a vacant spot, and took it. He was collecting the papers strewn across the passenger seat, and looked up at the long, sloping lawn, set up for the party. There were easily fifty people there, but his glance immediately spotted an attractive, long-limbed figure. She was sitting on the grass, wearing short, cut off blue jeans, and a bright red halter top. Parker was enjoying the image immensely. Her hair, loosely pulled back in a ponytail, with curly tendrils around her face and neck, shone in the sun like burnt umber. She was on her knees in the grass, facing him, but not looking at him. She was tugging at a thick piece of rope holding down a peg for the tent covering the catering. Parker's imagination immediately fled to an image of her in that very same position facing him. He tried to think of more unpleasant things. 'Nick Delaney,' he kept repeating to himself.

Kelly had a huge mallet in her hands, and by the time Parker reached her from his car, she was pounding a tent peg into the ground with all her might.

"What did that poor peg ever do to you?" he asked.

Kelly didn't look up. "The eejit caterers backed their sorry excuse of a van on the peg, nearly knocking over the bloody tent," she muttered.

She gave the peg one more hit, gave the rope a hard yank, brushed the grass of her knees and stood up. "You?!"

Kelly had risen too fast, and got a blood rush, which made her stumble. Parker quickly grabbed her by her arms, and gently held her against him. "Weak in the knees, huh? Do all men have that effect on you Irish, or is it just me?" Parker said with a smirk.

God, you smell delicious. And those are some awesome pecks, under that dark polo.

Kelly pushed Parker away from her. "What are you doing here?"

"I was invited. It's a party isn't it? Where's your party spirit?" Parker was still smirking.

Kelly was about to say something poignant, but when she opened her mouth the only sound emanating was a loud hiccup.

Oh, Holy Mary, mother of God, let me die now!

Parker laughed. "Whoa! Very graceful and ladylike. What's this you're drinking?" He picked up the plastic sports bottle on the grass behind Kelly. "So, what do we have here?"

Milk.

Parker sniffed the bottle. "This is Long Island Iced Tea!"

Yeah, ice tea. I know that.

"This stuff is about eighty-proof, you know. You do know, right?" Parker raised his eyebrows at her.

No way! Way! Aw man! So, that's what LIIT meant on the pitcher. I thought it was meant to say 'light'. Du-uh.

"So, how may I be of service today, Mr. MacIntyre?" Kelly said icily. "Need a copy of the phone directory?"

Putting down Kelly's bottle, while examining her legs, Parker smiled. "Came for the party, didn't I just say that? Where's Terry?"

Kelly pointed up the hill at the back of the property. "Cleaning the pool."

Parker winked and started walking. "Catch ya later, Red."

"You awake?" Jacqui kicked a sunbathing Vicky's foot. She was lying by the pool at the MacIntyre mansion outside Chicago. "You sober?"

Vicky opened a squinted eye, and looked at her brother. "You're in my sun, butt-face." Jacqui moved, and made his shadow cover her entirely. "What's your problem, dog breath?" Vicky whined.

"What time did you come in last night?"

"I don't know. What time does Daddy leave?"

"Let's see, it's Saturday, Candi's in town... As early as his morning glory woke him up, I would say. About six a.m."

Vicky shrugged. "So, I came home at about six a.m."

"You're still drunk, aren't you?"

Vicky was getting mad. "What's it to you? Daddy didn't give me a hard time, so why should you? I graduated college yesterday, fuck you very much! Oh, and thanks for reminding Daddy to come," she said sarcastically, "it was really great being there in that hideous polyester cap and gown, for no reason! Where were you, anyway?"

"Preparing for a new job. Tell you all about it when you're sober. What're you drinking?"

"Tomato juice. Now, get the hell out of my sun!"

Jacqui picked up the tall glass on the table and sniffed it. "This is a Bloody Mary, you biatch! Okay, I'm going to make you some coffee, you're going to get dressed, and we're going to go to the Russell's barbecue."

"Yeah, like a kids' party in the suburbs is something I want to do today. Get real." Vicky tried to kick Jacqui out of her sun.

"Kids are being chaperoned now, thanks to you. Let's go. Plus, I want you to meet Kelly. I think the two of you would really hit it off," Jacqui said impatiently.

"Kelly? Is that your new girl *friend?*" Vicky singsonged. "Oh, sorry, forgot your gate doesn't swing that way," she teased her brother and stood up. "Daddy's not gonna be there, is he?"

"With Candi in town? Yeah, right!"

"Alright, let's go. But you have to drive, and the minute I want to go home, we leave, understood?"

"Sir, yes sir!" Jack stood in a mock salute and started toward the patio doors.

"What is it with gays and the love of the military? Don't ask, don't tell." Vicky mumbled under her breath as she followed Jacqui. Then, shouting at her brother "You know that you've been publicly outed, right?"

Jacqui walked right into the sliding glass patio door. "What?! By who?"

Vicky waved her hand at a pile of gossip magazines by her lounge chair. "Take your pick. *Smile!* and *Eye Spy* called today for a comment on what *Rumor* had written about you on Tuesday, so I bought all of 'em."

"And what did you tell *Smile!* and *Eye Spy?*" Jacqui asked rubbing his head.

"That you're a flaming queen, who enjoys being spanked by spandex-wearing middle-aged men in the steam room," Vicky said matter-of-factly.

"You didn't?"

"Of course I didn't, you moron! I told them 'no comment' and blocked their numbers," Vicky said walking in the house. "God, I hate those rags. Did you know that Lexi was paid fifty grand for that picture she took of me and ... what was his name? That drummer?"

"Buzz?"

"Yeah, Buzz! That picture with his hand up my skirt? God, it seems like everyone with a camera phone is a paparazzi now."

"You still friends with Lexi?" Jacqui asked, skimming through the magazines.

"God no! You kidding me? She's blacklisted and blocked. Besides, she doesn't need to be my friend anymore, she's got her own money now," Vicky said, grabbing her cell phone and her purse. "Let's go."

"Terry, my Main Man! Boy, do I have news for you!" Parker walked up the hill to the pool and waved a folder of papers at Jon.

Jon looked up from cleaning the pool.

"That was going to be my opener! I'm so glad you could come today. I've got some unbelievable news for you! But age before beauty," Jon bowed gracefully.

"You sorry son of a…" Parker smiled. "Nick Delaney called me this morning."

"Oh, no! What now?"

"He's agreed to half a mil in stock options. He's dropped the royalties and the eighty acres west of the county road," Parker said, smiling.

"Seriously?!"

"Seriously."

"Half a million shares or shares worth half a mil?" Jon asked.

"Shares worth half a mil," Parker said, and the crooked smirk reappeared on his face.

"Which company?" Jon was suspicious.

"National Nickel."

Jon could barely contain himself. "It closed at twenty-eight yesterday! How'd you do it?"

"I didn't. You did. You drive a hard bargain, Terry, and the man finally relented. Remind me to give you a nice bonus."

"Although I'd love to take credit for this, I can't. This was all Jack's doing."

"So, what's *your* big news?" Parker asked, before Jon could turn the conversation back to his son.

"Don Duncan's left Kensington," Jon said with a conspiratory smile.

"No!" Parker whispered.

"Yup."

"To do what?"

"To become an independent consultant."

"Shit! We need to get to him before somebody else does. He's the best damn emerald guy in the business!"

Jon held up a hand. "Called him this morning. Said he'd think about it."

"Good job, Terry. Stay on him." Parker shook Jon's hand. "I brought the revised purchase agreement for the Delaney lands, I was hoping once you're done here, we could go through them, so I could FedEx them to his lawyer before he has a change of heart."

"Purchase agreement? He's now selling us the land, not just the mineral rights? Wonder what he knows that we don't."

"Delaney's call was preceded by a call from Mike Finn at Greenwich, telling me that Delaney had offered his mineral rights to him for three million and royalties. Mike laughed his ass off!" Both men snickered.

They didn't notice Kelly walking up behind them. "Jon? Susan says we need to set up the bar. Could you help me carry it out of the garage?" she said.

"Why don't you let the caterers take care of it?" Parker said to Jon.

"These are Mario's people. Remember what happened last summer at the 4th of July party? The wait staff got so drunk, we found some of them sleeping it off in the pool house here the next morning. No, this year me and some of the guys are taking care of the bar."

"Yeah, I remember that party last year. Went home with one of the staff. Hot blonde, with these enormous melons…"

God, you really are the shallow and empty creature you appear to be!

"Anyway, Jon, can you help me?" Kelly interrupted Parker's rendition.

"I'll help you, sugar," Parker offered with a sly smirk. "The bar has always been my favorite place at a party, and especially so when sharing it with a pretty girl."

"I'd rather Jon helped me."

"I can't, Kelly. I need to finish this. Mr. MacIntyre will help you," Jon said and went back to cleaning the pool.

Kelly heaved a sigh. "Come on, then, let's get this over with."

So I can go get drunk. So much for my plan!

They walked back down the hill toward the garage in silence, while Parker was studying her intently.

He's looking at me. I can feel it. Walk tall, look proud. … and hopefully will not fall on me face … literally.

In the garage, Kelly pointed out the wrought iron bar table and chairs.

"You take this end, I'll take the other," she said as she grabbed her end of the bar table. It was heavier than she had anticipated, and the hard material was digging into her bare hands.

No way am I letting him see this is too heavy for me.

Parker grabbed his end and started backing out of the garage.

"Where to?"

"Under the big oak."

Where all the liquor is, du-uh.

"You don't like me, do you, Irish?"

Like? Nope. Lust? Oh, Gawd, yesss!!

"What have I ever done to offend you?"

You're a conceited, arrogant, male chauvinist pain in the arse!

"Nothing," Kelly said without looking at him.

"So why are you being so difficult with me?"

Because I keep imagining toe-curling sex with you.

"Didn't know I was."

"I'm not a bad guy, you know. Just give me a chance, and you'll find out," Parker said, studying her. "I find you very attractive, Irish. And sexy as hell. What do you say, I take you out for dinner and drinks one night, and we'll see what happens."

Kelly dropped her side of the bar table. It was so heavy that Parker's grip slipped and he nearly dropped his end on his foot.

"This is where this goes," Kelly said, and turned around to go back to the garage to get the chairs.

Ohmygodohmygodohmygod! Easy. Breathe in – breathe out. Don't get excited. Absolutely, positively, certifiably, one hundred percent wrong for me. Way too old, and... and what? I'm still re- bounding? Hardly, after a year. ... But he's sooo hot. And he just asked me out. Well, sort of. God, he's gorgeous! He's totally coming on to me! Never gonna happen!

Back in the dimly lit garage, Kelly picked up two of the four chairs, and nodded at the other two.

"Those need to go up too," she said to Parker.

He walked past Kelly, brushed lightly against her and whispered in her ear. "Think about it, Red. You want it - I want it." Parker grabbed one chair in each hand and walked out.

Did he just brush up against me, or was that just wishful thinking? Those are some fine biceps under there. We both want it! Oooh, right, never gonna happen. Right, …right … Too old and all that…

Kelly was trying to get her mind off Parker's insinuation and found herself bored. There were children at the party and there were married couples, but no one her age. The Russells had told her to relax and enjoy the party, but she felt like she needed to do something. But there was nothing to do. The children had planned programming all day, the bar was being tended and the food was being catered and served.

Maybe I'll have another one of these 'light' teas and go lounge by the pool.

In the Russell kitchen Susan and the jays had congregated to gossip with some of the mining wives. Kelly was going to join them, when she spotted Jacqui and a young girl walking up the driveway. She opened the front door for them.

"Kelly, doll, how gorgeous you look in cut-offs and halter! Very Mary Ann!" Jacqui singsonged air-kissing Kelly on both sides of her face.

Mary Ann who?

"Kelly, I'd like you to meet my sister, Vicky," Jacqui said and pulled the young girl toward him. "Vicky, this is Kelly."

My God! These kids' parents really screwed them up royally. A frou-frou son and a hologram daughter. Well, Jacqui's sweet, how bad can his sister be?

Kelly eyed Vicky as she let them in the house. She was dangerously thin. In a pair of low-rise denim shorts her hip bones were poking through her skin like razors through plastic. Her short, brown hair was cropped in a fashionable do, and she wore huge designer sunglasses on her head. She was a classic beauty, but much too thin. Her cheeks were hollow and her eyes red-rimmed. Over a blue bikini top she wore a loosely knit white cardigan, and Kelly could see that her collarbones were in close competition to her hipbones in piercing the skin. Her expression looked bored.

"So, where's everybody?" Jacqui asked.

"Jon's in his study in a business meeting behind closed doors, and Susan's in the kitchen with the jays and other wives," Kelly said.

Vicky's cell phone rang. She and Jacqui exchanged a quick glance. Jacqui mouthed 'Dad?'. Vicky nodded and answered. "Hi, Daddy. I'm alive, I'm sober, I'm with Jacqui. Talk to you when you check in again." She hung up and rolled her eyes at Jacqui. "Must be three o'clock."

"He cares, really," Jacqui said, over-protectedly.

Vicky turned to Kelly. "So, now that that's over with, are there any adult beverages around?"

"Sure, there's beer and wine at the bar outside, as well as mixed drinks." She looked at Vicky's expressionless face. "Do you like Iced Tea?"

"Only if it's Long Island."

"Only kind around, come on," Kelly said, and took Vicky by the hand.

"This party is starting to look up already," Vicky whispered to Jacqui as she passed him.

Kelly and Vicky confiscated a pitcher of Long Island Iced Tea and two glasses, and headed for the pool. Jacqui joined Susan in the kitchen.

The children had their swim and were now being entertained. None of the adults were drunk enough to go in yet, so the girls had the pool all to themselves for the better part of the afternoon. Kelly had located two inflated pool chairs, and they had been drinking, talking and bonding while floating on the water. After an hour they had covered each other's childhoods, school, guys they had dated, guys they wished they had dated, and had found out that, despite very different backgrounds and upbringing, they had a lot in common.

"So, what do you do in your free time?" Vicky was asking.

"Well, I jog every morning, I play tennis in the evenings, and on the weekends Jon and I usually fit in a round or two of golf," Kelly said.

"No, what I meant was, what do you do for fun?"

"I jog, play tennis and golf."

Didn't I just say that out loud?

"No, no honey. What do you do to *relax*?" Vicky insisted.

Jog, golf, tennis! Am I not speaking English?

"Like, where do you and your girlfriends go to hang out, have a drink, pick up guys and go wild?" Vicky said.

"Do you know what? This is the first time I've actually had time for something like that since I've been here. Sad, really," Kelly said, taking another sip.

"You have got to come to my birthday party!" Vicky exclaimed so loudly, that she nearly fell over in her seat.

"Love to. When is it?"

"Saturday , June 30th."

"Oh, no." Kelly said discouraged.

"What?"

"My parents are flying in on Monday, and we're traveling around the US. Then I'm going home with them. I can't. I'm sorry."

"Me too. Let me see if I can't change the date," Vicky said.

"For me? Why would you do that?"

"I like you. I'd like for you to be at my party."

"I like you too. And I'd like to be there."

"I liked you first."

"I'll like you last," Kelly giggled. "Although there is a chance I might get this visa …"

"Take it!" Vicky interrupted.

"… but prubly not by then."

Still would like to go home … see Sean … avoid Sean … make up my mind about Sean…

Vicky finished off her drink. "Waiter person! Mas vino!" she yelled.

"The waiters aren't allowed near the liquor," Kelly hissed.

"Why not?"

"Well," Kelly said, as she was trying to get out of her chair, without falling into the pool, "apparently one of them got drunk and ended up in Parker MacIntyre's bed last year." She laughed. "Gimme your glass." She refilled both their glasses, and finished up the pitcher. A waiter appeared behind her.

"Yes, ma'am?"

Jaysus, where'd you come from?!

"Right, ahem, we'd like something to eat. Can you please bring us two plates of everything. Thang you," Kelly said and dismissed the waiter. "Oh, one more thing."

"Ma'am?"

"Could you please ask Mr. Ashton to come up 'ere? You'll prubly find him somewhere near Mrs. Russell."

"My pleasure, ma'am."

Kelly handed Vicky her glass. "Whaddaya want with Jacqui?"

"The pitcher sempty. He can bring us some more of this most eggcellent tea!" Kelly said and raised her glass.

Vicky giggled. "You said 'eggcellent'!"

"Well it is, isn't it?" Kelly said trying to climb back into the floating chair.

"You're dru-unk."

"That I am, and I feel pretty good, and I intend to get even drunker. I'm celebrating. I've changed the lass diaper I'm gwana change, till iss me own baby's," Kelly said and raised her glass. She spotted Jacqui. "Jacqui, dahling, right on cue. Be a dear and fetch ush a refill, will ya?"

Jacqui mumbled something under his breath, and before he left he shot a glance at Vicky, who stuck her tongue out at him.

"Your food's here," she said.

Two waiters appeared carrying two plates each, filled with everything from burgers to cake. They set the plates down on the edge of the pool and excused themselves. Kelly floated toward the food.

"Yum!" she said and dug in. "I'm schtarving." She turned to Vicky. "Aren't you gwana have any? There splenty here."

"I don't eat," Vicky said matter-of-factly.

"Ever?"

"If I eat, I have to hurl, and my ephosagus can't take it anymore," Vicky said, then started giggling, looking at her glass. "Whoa, these things are potent! I can't even say epho-sagus anymore. Egophasus." The girls were both laughing.

"What are you trying to say? Sarcophagus?"

"Asparagus!" Vicky was giggling hard and trying to pull herself toward the edge of the pool.

Laughing, Kelly picked up a grilled asparagus off a plate, and handed it to Vicky. "Here, have a grilled esophagus." Both girls roared with laughter. "It's really not even funny!" Kelly screamed among tears.

Scrambling to get out of the pool, Vicky looked at Kelly. "I like you, Kelly. Takes a lotta guts to make fun of an eating disorder."

"I'm sorry, I didn't mean to make fun…"

Vicky held up her hand. "Most people won't even talk about it, just sweep it under the rug. Thanks." She hugged Kelly. "Girl! Those real?" She poked a drunken finger on Kelly's chest.

"Aye," Kelly said, blushing.

"How can a skinny, athletic girl like yusself have boobs like that?"

"It'sh gotta do with genes, I'm sure," Kelly said carrying the plates of food to the picnic table.

"Jeans? What do jeans have to do with the size of your boobs?" Vicky was wobbling behind her.

"Well, pretty much everything in my case. Both me Mum and Gran were big chested, so…"

Vicky was roaring with laughter again. "You meant genes? Not *jeans*!"

"Yeah, genes, wharr I say?"

"I thought you were talking about, like, Guess or Calvin Kleins!" They sat down at the poolside table, and laughed heartily.

After their laughter had settled, Kelly turned to Vicky. "So, why do you do it? It's obviously not to lose weight, 'cause you're already very skinny."

Vicky patted her bare, hollow stomach. "You think so? Thanks!"

"No, Vicky, you're dangerously thin. Almost emaciated."

"I know. Burr it's like this. Like, all my life's been controlled by other people. Daddy, nannies, teachers, my Mom's trust fund executors, doctors, shrinks. My brother! This is the one thing *I* control. So I was bulimic first and really screwed up my esophagus. Hey! I said it! So then I started taking laxatives instead. But then I OD'd on them."

"What sat like?" Kelly asked between mouthfuls of potato salad.

"Well, you get wrrreally dizzy, and faint, and nauseous. Then you wake up in the ER wirr a drip in your arm, your brother crying and your Dad cussing you out. But that's not even the wors part. The wors parts that you're in the bathroom all the time. Like All. The. Time. And your butt hole really burns."

"Eeeuw, too much information!"

"Sorry. Okay, so you find out that you've done to your anus what puking did to your ephosagus. Egosaphus. You know wharr I mean. And you look down the bowl, and's all runny and bloody and really foul-smelling."

Huh? And here I thought that rich people's shit didn't stink.

"So now I jus don eat. The way I see it – there sa pork chop in every shot," she raised her glass, "less eat!"

"Do you know what goes wrreally well with pork chops? Asparagus. If you're fascinated by your bowel odors, wait'ill you see what asparagus does to your pee."

Kelly handed a spear of asparagus to Vicky. She took it gingerly and twirled it between her fingers. She looked up at Kelly with a dismal expression. "It doesn't work like that, you know. You can't just make me eat and *shazam!* the problem's gone," she said and waved the asparagus like a magic wand.

"Admitting that you have a problem issa fir schtep," Kelly said while shoveling more potato salad in her mouth.

Vicky staggered on her feet. "Hi! I'm Vicky, and I have an eating disorder," she said and stuck the asparagus into her belly button and chewed air. "Whassa nex tep?"

"Now you eat it."

"What'll it do to my pee?" Vicky asked looking suspiciously at the asparagus.

"Eat it, and find out."

Kelly started on her second burger. Vicky took a bite. She could feel her stomach growling. "Not bad, actually. How many calories, d'ya think in this?"

"In that bite you just took? You probably burnt off more calories chewing it, that you did taking in."

Vicky gingerly placed the rest of the asparagus back on the plate. "I'll finish this later."

Jacqui walked toward the pool carrying two cans of Coke.

"Where se liquor?" Vicky asked.

"You've had enough. Dad's about to check in anyway. Try sobering up," Jacqui said solemnly.

Wobbling, Vicky grabbed Jacqui's hand, and reached for her cell phone on the picnic table. "Kelly, watch me sober rup," she slurred while she dialed her dad's number. "Daddy, it's me. I'm alive, I'm sober, I'm still with Jacqui, talk to you when you check in again," she said and hung up. She let go of her brother's hand. "You may go now."

"Stay off the booze," Jacqui said as he turned to walk back down the hill to join the rest of the party.

"Fucking fascist," Vicky said under her breath. "God! My brother is so anal, that … that…"

That he can't sit down, for fear of sucking up the furniture?

More guests were arriving by the pool. One of them had brought a pitcher of Margaritas. Vicky returned to her floating seat, and Kelly sat on the edge of the pool, dipping her feet in the water. A group of people was walking up the hill toward them.

"Oh, no, we'd better go," Kelly said to Vicky.

"Why?" Vicky was unable to see over the edge of the pool and down the hill.

"They're bringing in the net, and will set the pool up for volleyball. Or we can just stay here in the deep end."

"I vote for stayinere. I also vote for having another chork pop," she slurred and downed her drink. "Pour me anutherrun."

Kelly got up on very unsteady legs, poured herself and Vicky another drink and looked down the hill. She saw Parker's massive shape approach them. A group of men were following a few steps behind him.

Like Prince Phillip to Queen Elizabeth.

Parker had noticed Kelly and was smirking.

God, he's hot!

"Coverrup ladies, the walking erection is forthcoming!" Kelly was pointing her glass toward Parker.

Vicky was straining to see whom Kelly was talking about, and kept slipping on the wet plastic seat. "Whossit?" she slurred while trying to stand up in the seat.

"Parkhur MacIntre. Park Her Mac Entirely," Kelly giggled and turned back toward Parker. "Found a bed mate yet?"

They heard a big splash from the pool. Vicky had slipped off her seat and fallen in the pool. Parker was smiling at Kelly as he was almost at the top of the hill.

"Who's your friend?" he smiled at Kelly.

"Oy, Vicky! Get out and meet Pfarkhur MacIntyre!" Kelly laughed.

The pool area got deadly quiet. Parker's eyes darkened. Vicky's head emerged from under the water.

"Anna Victoria MacIntyre, get out of that pool this instant!" Parker bellowed.

Kelly was dumbfounded.

Victoria MacIntyre? No way! That's Vicky Ashton.

"Yes, Daddy," Vicky mumbled and climbed out of the pool. "Sorry, Daddy." Vicky stood in front of Parker, her tiny frame looking even smaller, as she was dripping water on the tiles. She peeked up at her father from under her brow.

Parker pointed a finger in her face. "You're grounded! Now, go get some dry clothes on! Find Jack! Have him drive you home and sober the hell up!" he yelled in her face, then turned to Kelly. "And *you* will help her!" he barked pointing a finger in her face.

Who do you think I am? I'm not one of yer 'yes sir' men.

She saw the fire in Parker's eyes. "Yes, sir," she mumbled, wrapped Vicky in a towel, and together they wobbled down the hill toward the house.

Upstairs in Kelly's room, wearing Kelly's jeans and T-shirt, Vicky was sobbing. "I hate him! I hate him so much! Why did he have to humiliate me like that?"

Jacqui brought her some coffee. She took the cup, and wrapped her bony fingers around it, but didn't drink it.

"I'm sorry you had to see that, Kelly. He's such an ass," Jacqui said.

Kelly was drying Vicky's hair with a towel. "He's your father? Parker MacIntyre's your father? You're Victoria MacIntyre?" she said in disbelief.

Vicky turned to look Kelly in the eye. "You didn't know that?"

Kelly was stunned. "But then you're his son?" she pointed at Jacqui, who nodded. "But you're Jacqui Ashton."

That's why he looks so familiar! I'm an eejit! He's like a knock-off of the original. Although with a fresher expiration date.

"You really didn't know?" Vicky repeated.

Kelly shrugged. "How could I have known?"

"You never read the gossip magazines?" Vicky asked.

"Or watch *TMZ?*" Jacqui added.

Kelly waved her hand. "Not interested. Pack of lies, exaggerations and innuendoes about people I don't know."

Vicky and Jacqui exchanged a quick look. "And you liked me not knowing who I was?" Vicky said.

"Of course! Well, seeing who your Dad is certainly explains a lot. Look, I'm sorry about that remark I made about him."

"Pssch! Nothing we haven't heard a million times before. Or said ourselves, for that matter," Vicky said. "He's such a jerk. I wish he'd stop humiliating me in public like that. I hate him. Jacqui? Drive me home?"

Kelly could feel her blood starting to boil. She took off her top and shook out her hair.

"Hey, hey, hey! What are you doing?" Vicky cried out.

"Damage control. I need to slip into something a little less comfortable." Bare-chested, Kelly was pulling out a very constricting top from her dresser.

"Jacqui's still in the room," Vicky hissed.

Still topless, Kelly turned around and saw Jacqui eyeing her. "This doesn't bother you, does it, Jacqui?"

Jacqui limp-wristed. "Oh, precious, you can do whatever you want in front of me."

Vicky rose to her feet and pulled Jacqui out of the room. "We'd better get going."

It was getting late. Dressed to kill, Kelly walked back up the hill toward the pool. The sun was setting, and she could see that Parker MacIntyre was sitting alone by the pool, slowly sucking on a cigar. Kelly could hear steel drum music emanating from the tennis court, and deduced that the limbo-contest had started.

Less fun, without an audience, but nevertheless…

Parker spotted Kelly walking up the hill toward him. He admired her guts. She had not taken her eyes off him once since she left the house. Parker hoped she had changed her mind about his proposal, as the sight of her in her very revealing outfit made his crotch tingle.

"Damn, you're sexy in that getup, Red," Parker greeted Kelly as she made it to the pool.

Adonis to Arsehole to Adonis and back to Arsehole.

"Thank you," she said casually as she slowly walked past him, and started moving furniture, lifting pillows and shaking towels.

Watch me work it.

She bent over, exposing her rear in his direction.

"Looking mighty rugged in the business end, there, Irish," Parker said.

Looking at him between her legs, Kelly could see a very distinct swelling on his crotch.

It's working. You sorry son of a bitch.

Parker got out of his chair and walked over to Kelly. "Whatcha looking for?" he said, grabbing her butt.

Kelly stood up with a jerk. "Your daughter, if you care, is fine. She's lost a bracelet, and she and Jacqui are looking for it in house. I thought she might have left it here. Help me look?" Kelly smiled her most innocent schoolgirl smile.

"What?!" Parker exploded. "Not her mother's diamond bracelet? That thing's irreplaceable!" He tossed the cigar and started throwing towels around.

Kelly moved toward the pool and looked over the edge. "I think I see it," she said. "Is that it?" Parker leaned over to look where Kelly was pointing. "This is from Vicky," Kelly said, and with a well placed foot, kicked Parker MacIntyre in the deep end.

He surfaced. He was spitting water and looked at Kelly at the side of the pool. She wasn't laughing. She wasn't cursing him out. She wasn't yelling at him. She just stood there, arms crossed, and stared at him. Parker started laughing and pulled himself out of the pool.

"I got to hand it to you, Irish, you've got guts." He stood next to Kelly and wrung his shirt out. "I guess I had it coming." He held out his hand. "Friends?"

Kelly took his hand to shake it, but before she knew it, Parker was tossing her in the pool. Kelly would not let go of his hand, and pulled him into the pool with her. They landed in the water side-by-side, neither letting go of the other's hand. Submerged, Kelly could feel Parker pulling her toward him. She was kicking water fiercely to try to surface, but he was stronger.

You sick pervert! ... And there goes one of me contacts!

She pressed her eyes shut, so as not to lose the other contact as well. She let go of Parker's hand and tried to push him away. Parker put both hands around her and pulled her close to him under water. Kelly felt his body pressing against hers, and stopped fighting him.

Mmmm... A hard man is good to find ... If he doesn't kiss me now, I'll kiss him. Or die trying. ... And he's back to Adonis! Yesss!

Parker expertly undid Kelly's top, and slowly cupped his hand on one of her bare breasts.

Oh, my God, me lungs are about to burst. Kiss me! Kiss me now!

Kelly started kicking and got away from his hold. She surfaced, gasping for air. Parker surfaced dangerously close to her. He was smiling as he pulled her body close to his again. His steel gray eyes were dark in the dusk. Kelly could hear her heart pounding in her ears. Parker's hands were slowly moving up and down her back as they were treading water.

I think I'm going to explode with ... He's a bit blurry ... Oooh! So not the thing to concentrate on now!

Kelly pressed her body against Parker's and could feel herself giving in.

This is it. I'm going to kiss him.

"Cannonball!" someone shouted, and before Parker and Kelly realized what had happened, a huge wave had separated them, and suddenly the pool was becoming populated again.

Damn, damn, damn, damn, damn! So close!

Kelly quickly tied her top and got out of the pool. She looked over at Parker, who was already out and drying himself on a towel. He paid no attention to her.

Did that just happen? ... I need a drink. And quite possibly a cold shower.

9

The early morning sun rose on a devastating scene in the Russells' back yard. The caterers were due to arrive at eight to clean up and remove the tent. Susan was in the kitchen eating a banana and making a pot of strong coffee, looking out the window at the back hill. The emergency services hadn't been called this time, a sure sign of a successful party. Sighing deeply, she turned her back at the scene and poured herself a cup of coffee. She turned on the TV, and the lead story in the news made her drop her coffee cup, splintering it on the Spanish tile floor.

In her bed upstairs Kelly was sleeping the deep sleep of those heavily intoxicated. She was dreaming that she was falling slowly in water, deep, clear water, until she landed, gently as a feather on the sandy bottom of the ocean. The sand formed a mold around her body, bedding it, and the current was gently rocking her. She realized that she could breathe under water.

La-de-dah. I'm a mermaid. … Funny, how voices sound so muffled under water.

She could feel her head nesting comfortably on the sand at the bottom of the ocean.

Okay, now that's becoming really irritating. Could that Kelly just answer when she's being called, so I can enjoy …

"Kelly, honey, wake up!" Susan was gently shaking her.

That's me *they're talking to. Who knows I'm at the bottom of the ocean?*

Susan shook Kelly harder. "Come on Kelly, wake up. Something terrible has happened."

Kelly forced herself to open her eyes. She was unable to focus, but recognized Susan's multicolored robe.

Jaysus! Way too early for bright colors!

She shut her eyes again.

"Kelly, honey, are you awake?"

No.

"You've got to see this. Sit up."

I can't. Me head's melting and is dissolving into the pillows. … Oy! Who put a hairy sardine in my mouth while I was sleeping? Oh, is me tongue.

Susan turned on the little TV in the corner of Kelly's bedroom. A female news anchor's voice boomed across the room.

Less volume, please!

"…just happened less that an hour ago. No one has claimed responsibility as of yet, and the accurate number of casualties has not been released. According to eye witnesses, however, an estimated twenty people, all civilians, have been injured, and have been taken to a nearby hospital."

Casualties? Injured? Hospital?

Eyes still crudded shut, Kelly was trying to make her mind focus.

"…We now go over to our Dublin correspondent, Peter Markovic, live at the scene of the bombing for an update…"

Dublin bombing?

Kelly bolted up.

Ayayayayay! Me head! What did she just say? Dublin bombing?

"Did she just say Dublin bombing?" Kelly tried to get her eyes and her mind to focus.

God, my eyes feel like what raw oysters must feel when you squirt lemon on them. Slept with me contacts in again, didn't I?

"Shhh! Listen!" Susan was gently rubbing Kelly's back.

"…at the scene of the suicide bombing that shook downtown Dublin a little less than an hour ago local time." The solemn male reporter announced, and suddenly Kelly was sober. "As you can see behind me, the entire block has been evacuated. The bomb left a huge crater in the pavement, killing the driver of the first car of the motorcade of the US delegation, a motorcycle policeman and a plain-clothes law enforcement officer. We have reason to believe, that the plain clothes law enforcement officer had spotted the suicide bomber and was trying to wrestle him as the bomb detonated. It is still uncertain how many civilians have been killed or are injured, and no group has claimed responsibility. We are waiting on an update from the US delegation here for peace talks ..." The reported paused, and put a finger to his earpiece.

Do I know anyone who would be in the city on a ... what day is it today? Sunday? ...on a Sunday morning? Oh, dear God...

The reporter was back. "We have just been told that this was a decoy motorcade. I repeat, the bomb that detonated in Dublin, Ireland early this morning Eastern Standard Time, hit a decoy motorcade. No one from the US delegation has been injured. We are waiting for news from the Secretary of State. Back to you, Leslie."

"Thank you, Peter. And in our other top stories this morning..."

Kelly hit mute. "I've got to call home!" She reached for her cell phone on her nightstand and hit her parents' home phone number.

A digital recording answered "I'm sorry. Your call cannot be completed at this time. Please try again later."

Kelly turned to Susan. "They're sorry. My call cannot be completed at this time. Please try again later. What does that mean?"

Susan was still rubbing Kelly's back. "The phone lines to Ireland are probably jammed. Everyone is calling to see if their loved ones are alright. Happened on September

11th too. The lines were down for quite a while." Susan took Kelly's face in her hands. "Are you worried? Do you know anyone who would have been in downtown Dublin at eleven on a Sunday morning?"

"I was just thinking that meself. Me family would've been in church. Not in the city. College is out, so all me mates have gone home. I hope! Gran has a flat in the city. But she would have been in church, too..." Kelly was fiddling with her necklace.

"What about Sean? He was, after all working with the summit."

Kelly flicked her hand. "Naah, he made that sound more fabulous that it was. He's an intern! He makes copies and brings coffee."

I hope!

Kelly tried her cell again. Same digital recording gave her the same digital response.

Emma, whose room shared a wall with Kelly's, appeared yawning and rubbing her eyes at the door. "What ah you doing?" she said.

Kelly waved her over and helped her climb into her bed. "Some very bad people did a very bad thing to some very good people, in a place far, far away. Nothing to worry about, pet," she said.

God, I hope!

Kelly, Susan and Jon took turns in trying to call Ireland all day. No luck. Kelly sent a mass e-mail to all her Irish

friends and family members, but doubted the outcome of
that. She kept trying sending a text message, and finally,
after dinner that night she received a reply.

> Sender: Mum Mobile
> Got ur msg. Don wry. Evryl ok. Phlines
> V. Apts clsd. Flites cxld. WCF US Mon.
> Must resch. RU ok? Txt bk asap.
> CUL8R. xM

*God luv ya, Mum! Bless yer heart for trying to catch up with
the 21st century.*

"Who's it from? Ireland? What does it say?" Jon and
Susan were asking simultaneously.

"I have absolutely no idea. I wish me Mum wouldn't
think that they charge text messages by the character, and
just type out the word."

*Oh, but it must be good news. No one in their right mind
would send bad news over a text message, would they?* Everyl ok.
Everyone is fine. Good.

"I can't make it all out. Help me decipher?"

After a while, they had decided that the message read

Got your message. Don't worry. Everyone is fine.
The airports are closed. The flights are cancelled.
Are you alright? Text back as soon as possible. See
you later. Kiss. Mum

The only parts they hadn't been able to make out was
'Phlines V. WCF US Mon. Must resch.'

Jon stretched and yawned. "Well, girls, this has been a blast, but tomorrow's Monday, and some of us have to work. At least we know your family is fine."

Susan rose to go to bed as well. "Why don't you send them a text message asking them to explain this message?" Susan kissed her on the head. "Let us know if you hear anything. Good night."

Kelly tried calling her parents again. No luck. The digital recording was still playing. She tried sending them a text message reading

> To: Mum Mobile
> Gr8 2 hear u ok. Don get msg. Pls txt bk.
> No abbr!. xK

The message wouldn't send.

How had Mum's message come through with the phone lines down? Phone lines? Phlines! Kelly, you eejit! It's not Mr. Phlies the fifth! The letter V is an arrow pointing down! Mum's telling me the phone lines are down! Aw, man! Thanks a million Mum, there's an hour of my life I'll never get back! Mobiles are meant to make our lives easier. Well, I guess they would if everyone followed the same standard for abbreviations. Jaysus! I wish mobiles had an abbreviations check, like computers have spell check. Maybe I'll contact the Nokia people about that... ... So that just leaves me with WCF US Mon then. 'WC' traditionally means Water Closet. Is Mum telling me the water closets are full? Prubly not. US Mon, I'm guessing means USA tomorrow, as they are due to arrive at O'Hare... Of course! The airports are closed, the flights have been cancelled, Must resch. *means must reschedule. They're not flying to Chicago tomorrow, so they're flying to ... where's WCF?*

Kelly ran to the computer in the little loft area that had been made into an office, but that neither Susan nor Jon ever used, so it had become Kelly's little retreat. Her initial excitement over deciphering her mother's message soon vanished, as she found out that there were no airports with the code WCF.

Maybe it's a typo. Mum's always complaining about how difficult it is for her to hit the right key, when her fingers are so big and the keys are so small. And she can never find her glasses. Of course, she's too vain to wear them in a string around her neck. Oh, well, God luv ya for trying, Mum. Better try texting again. ... Aaarghh!

The text message would not send, so Kelly rearranged the letters, and googled each letter combination. Nothing.

Okay, so maybe Mum, with her big fingers, no glasses and small keys, pressed the key too many times and got the wrong letter. Or not enough times and got the wrong letter. How many letter combinations can there be? Let's see ... The button for W is the same for X, Y and Z... Ohmygod, the possibilities are endless! I'll be here all night. Better try calling again. Okay, okay, miss digital recording. Are ya really sorry? ... Try texting. Aw, come on!

The message would still not send. Kelly started playing with the letter combinations, her left thumb absentmindedly still hitting the 'send' button on her cell phone. She could barely keep her eyes focused, and before she knew it she had passed out cold on the computer desk. She slept restlessly. She kept dreaming of her mother, with giant baseball mitts for hands being chased by mosquito-sized letters. Her mother was yelling in a digital voice: 'Must txt R dghtr. Wrid ab us in us. ASAP. CU nxt Mon.'

Kelly's cell phone rang, and woke her up with a start. "Hello, pet! It's Dad. Finally got through on the land line."

Landline? As opposed to what? Water line?

"Are you alright, darling? You've sent us about half a dozen copies of the same message."

Kelly looked at her cell phone. She must have compulsively been hitting 'send' in her sleep.

"I'm fine, Dad. Just couldn't figure out Mum's message."

"Well, so far, everyone we know is fine."

Check.

"The phone lines have been rung down since the bombing…"

Check.

"…all the airports are closed, including Belfast, Edinburgh, Galway and London…"

Check.

"…and all the flights have been cancelled."

Check

"Dad, I got that from Mum's message. What I didn't get was 'WCF US Mon'. Where are you flying to?" Kelly asked irritated.

"We're not flying at all, pet. WCF, according to yer Mum, means we can't fly. We can't make it Monday. I'm sorry, pet."

Must resch.

10

The McCoys were able to get a full refund and decided not to make the trip at all. The Russells had arranged for Tammy to baby-sit until their new au pair arrived, so by the following Friday Kelly was utterly bored, with nothing to do.

"Since my parents aren't coming over, I guess I'll be able to attend your birthday party," Kelly woke Vicky up with the news.

"Yay! I'm so excited! Hey, what are you doing right now," Vicky shrieked over the phone.

"I'm on the phone with you," Kelly said sarcastically.

"Hah-haa. No, I meant, do you have any plans for today? I could be there in, like, an hour to pick you up. I need to go downtown. Wanna go with?"

"Sure, I've got nothing better to do but wait to hear back from Charlotte," Kelly said with a shrug. "And they've only got my mobile number anyway, so yeah, let's do Chicago."

"What's in Charlotte?"

"Remember, I told you that Susan's clients are offering me a training position, and the company that organizes the visa is located in Charlotte?"

"So, will you be going there?"

"Possibly, yeah, for an interview. Why?"

"If you do, I'm going with you! Charlotte has, like, one of the hottest clubs in the *world*. Like, the owner's sorta an ex of mine. I told you about him? Smilax?"

"Oh, right! Your supplier. Bizarre name, that."

Sounds like a brand name for a laxative. ... Or a character in a Batman-movie. Evil Dr. Smilax, whose superhuman power is to relieve you from constipation but gives you diarrhea instead.

"That's not his real name, silly, he made it up. His real name is ... Eugene ... something. Huh? Know what? I never knew his last name."

"And you really think it's a good idea hooking up with him again?"

"Hey, his stuff got me through college, and if I'm going to, like, even survive Stanford, I need a fresh stash of Soberrup!"

"Or, you could just quit drinking."

Vicky laughed. "Yeah, good luck with that one! That's like telling a dog to stop licking himself!"

Dogs can be trained ...

"We gotta go," Vicky continued. "Yay! Road trip!" A sharp beeping sound interrupted Vicky's rambling. "I have another call, can you hang on, Kel?" without waiting for a response, she put Kelly on hold.

Kelly walked into the kitchen, and saw Susan and Jon. "You still here?" she said.

They turned to look at her. "You on the phone or talking to us?" Jon said.

"I'm on hold. Why aren't you at work?"

"We wanted to have a little chat with you this morning," Susan said.

Kelly was unable to read her expression.

Uh-oh. What did I do? Ohmygod, Parker MacIntyre in the pool! Am I in trouble?

"I'm still here," Kelly said.

"Still on the phone, or still with us?" Jon said amused.

Kelly pointed to the phone. Vicky was back on the line and was talking a mile a minute. "So, like, that was Daddy, and he goes 'I need to see you right now', so, like, can I call you right back?"

"Come pick me up when you're done with your Dad, okay?" Kelly hung up her cell phone and turned to Jon and Susan. "Let's chat."

Bring it on! I'm ready for battle. I've done nothing to be shamed of. Well, almost... Anyway, he's the one who should be ashamed, taking advantage of me like that! Although he didn't really take advantage of me, and I kinda wanted him to...

They sat down around the breakfast table. Both Jon and Susan looked sincere. Jon cleared his throat.

"Kelly, you know we all love you very much..." he started.

"And I love you very much," Kelly interrupted quickly.

"...and we understand if you're worried or home-sick and want to go home. We'll do everything we can, obviously, to help you get your status changed, so you can stay here, but if you decide that you'd rather go home, we'll help you with that, too, but you'll need to make a decision pretty soon," Jon said without drawing for breath, and seemed relieved to have gotten it off his chest.

Stealth chat! Did not see this coming.

"Thank you. I've decided to ..."

Go back home and marry Sean? Kelly casually played with her necklace.

"Yes?" Susan said.

Go back home, forgive Sean, come back, do the J-1 thing and go back home and marry Sean?

"I think I've decided to ..." Kelly looked at both Jon and Susan's expectant faces.

I love these people so much. I wish I could stay here. But I need to tell Sean ... something...

"...I've decided to give the J-1 visa training a shot," Kelly said smiling.

Huh? Who knew that's what I'd decided?

Relief washed over both Jon and Susan's faces. Susan's eyes started welling up and she pecked a kiss on Kelly's cheek.

Jon became all business. "First thing we've got to do is call your attorney, Kate Fleming, and see what this J-1 visa really entails, and if this company down in North Carolina is legit."

"Of course it is! Alen and Bryce have used them for another property..." Susan started arguing.

Wonder why it's always 'Yer attorney, Kate Fleming'? Parker MacIntyre is always just Parker, Tiger Woods is always just Tiger. But it's always 'Swedish golfer, Annika Sorenstam' or 'Secretary of state, Condoleezza Rice', ... like there's two famous Condoleezzas... or really two Condoleezzas even ... Oooh, important conversation, must concentrate. Oooh-Oooh, Madonna's always just Madonna. She broke the mold. Good for her! You go girl! ... I really can't get away with that expression... Now, concentrate...

"... gave her the contact information. Maybe you should start thinking about contacting them in Charlotte," Susan was saying.

"Already did. They had an online application form, which I filled out, and I'm having my Dad fax them copies of my diploma and transcripts. Just waiting to hear back from them," Kelly said.

Guess I did know I had decided...

"Atta girl!" Jon beamed. "Very Jenny on the spot."

Who?

"I wish we could give you some work to do, but we've already made arrangements with Tammy, since you were going to be out of town anyway," Susan said apologetically. "I guess you could start at the J when they open."

"Vicky's picking me up, and we're going downtown. I might as well see if they have anything for me to do while I'm there. I guess I could move in. The suites are ready," Kelly reflected.

"There's no rush with that," Susan said hastily. "You're always welcome to stay here as long as you like, you know that. Incidentally, did you pick yourself a suite?"

"I like the eleven tier. Do you think they'll let me have one of those?"

"I don't see why not. They're the smaller suites. The hotel would be making more revenue selling the bigger ones, and letting you stay in one of the smaller ones for free," Susan said. "Good thinking."

Kelly was worried. "I just don't understand what it is they want me to do? Appear and look fabulous? And get paid to do that?"

Susan laughed. "Now, remember, you won't be getting paid until your visa comes through, so until then, you're just a like any other young and gorgeous guest at the hotel. And get this – you're not the only one. Alen and Bryce own a modeling agency on Michigan Avenue, and they've hired models to appear strategically at the hotel."

"Why?"

"To attract the media, and the young, rich and famous, of course," Susan said.

But of course!

Vicky was sitting alone in the MacIntyre kitchen. She was holding a cup of coffee between both hands, and was trying hard to stop shaking as Jacqui walked in.

"Did you just get home?" he said looking surprised at seeing her that early in the morning. He poured himself a glass of orange juice.

"Dressed like this?" Vicky looked down at her flannel pajamas. "Yeah, wild night at Club Jammy. Moron."

Jacqui leaned over and sniffed the air around his sister. "You're sober! What are you smiling about?" He took a sip of his juice.

Vicky felt smug. "Daddy apologized," she said.

"What?!" Juice squirted out of Jacqui's nose. "Sorry," he said hastily and wiped his face and the countertop. "How'd you get him to do that?"

Vicky looked baffled. "I didn't. Thought you did."

Jacqui shook his head and reached for the cereal and poured himself a bowl. "I haven't even seen him since the Russell barbeque, and really barely even there," he said and then stopped cold. "Bet Kelly did something! Remember, she talked about damage control in a bikini, or something?! So, what happened? What's an apology from Dad like?"

Vicky got on her feet and gesticulating excitedly, started recounting her rendezvous with their father. "So, okay, I'm in my room. It's like really early, and I'm on the phone with Kelly, and Daddy beeps in and he's all, like, 'Are you sober? Where are you?' Blah-blah-blah… and I'm like 'du-uh, I'm on the phone' and he goes 'I gotta see you in the kitchen right now', so I come down and see him and he goes 'sorry I embarrassed you at the Russells' and, like, 'I was way out of line', and guess what? Ohmygosh! He hugged me! And then he gets like all serious again, you know, and he goes, why hadn't I told him I was an A student and blah-blah-blah and why hadn't I told him I graduated with honors and I'm like, I *did* and why doesn't he ever pay attention to me, then he like hugs me again, you know, and he's all 'I'm so sorry and I'm so proud of you, and I promise to be more involved' and then he leaves and then you came in."

"And now you're eating?" Jacqui said, smiling, as he noticed that while Vicky was ranting, she had been picking at his cereal with her fingers. "Granted, that amount couldn't keep a goldfish alive, but it's a start."

Vicky looked astonished at the bowl between them. "I know! It's like so weird!"

"How do you feel? Like barfing?"

Vicky paused to feel the effect of the pieces of cereal she had just consumed. "No. Huh? You know what? I think I'll take a shower, get dressed, and have, you know, … break-fast." She started toward the stairs.

Jacqui called out after her "Just one thing, Vicky? How can a drunk airhead like you be an A student?"

Vicky smiled smugly without turning around. "We all have our little secrets, Jacqui. You just worry about yours and let me worry about mine, okay?"

Kelly and Vicky were driving down the Interstate toward downtown Chicago. The sun was already beating on their bare shoulders, and the roar of the traffic made any conversation impossible in Vicky's Mustang convertible.

"I thought we'd stop by the hotel first, and see about the plans for my birthday party, then grab a drink somewhere, and then go see Daddy at his office!" Vicky yelled as she turned her car on the off ramp. "He wants to see you. What did you do to him at the barbeque?"

Ohmygod! I very nearly had sex with him! ... Fucked him? Made love to him?

"Nothing," she said, glad that Vicky was paying attention to the traffic, and couldn't see her face. "Just... well, ... I kicked him into the pool."

"You what?! You go, girl! So that's why..." Vicky held her cigarette between her teeth and pulled a shiny new platinum card from her back pocket. "Look! He gave me this this morning. Said he was sorry he embarrassed me. Told me to go spend it and wants to see you." She was smiling widely.

Kelly felt increasingly more uncomfortable.

I must have been very drunk. Never, ever in a million years would I have ever let myself feel what I felt in that pool with that man had I been sober. Christ! How much had I had to drink? I get tipsy from two pints of Guinness, and Saturday I had been pouring down Long Island Ice Teas! I do remember wanting him, though, that's how drunk I must have been! But he's an arrogant arse! Wonder why he wants to see me? Finish what we started? Mmmmm... Oh, God no!

"What does he need to see me about?" Kelly asked anxiously.

"Didn't say," Vicky said, and threw out her cigarette butt. She pulled up in front of the J Hotel and a valet attendant hurried to assist her.

"This is where you're having your party?" Kelly asked as they got out of the car.

Vicky shrugged. "Well, depends on their plans first. We do have other properties that are interested. Let's go see."

She took Kelly's hand and pulled her inside.

"You know, I've been offered a training position here, and a suite," Kelly said nonchalantly.

"No way!"

"So way!"

"Get out! These are the visa people? I thought you said they were the gay clients of Susan's," Vicky said in disbelief.

"Brace yourself, Vicky," Kelly said with a smile, as she saw Bryce and Alen heading toward them. "They're *beyond* gay."

Bryce and Alen were looking very rugged that morning, dressed in blue jeans and polo shirts. No pastels in sight. Kelly decided that she was the bridge between them and made the introductions.

While shaking hands with Vicky, Bryce exclaimed "The two of you know each other? This is fabulous! Let's go to the milk bar and discuss the party details, shall we?"

"The *milk* bar?" Vicky said and creased her nose. "You mean you only serve *milk*?"

Bryce and Alen laughed. "No, sweetie, we just call it that, because the liquor license hasn't cleared yet. We can drum you up a drink, I'm sure, if you'd like."

"I'd like," Vicky stated and let Bryce lead her to the bar.

Bryce whispered to Alen over his shoulder "Get Matthew to come open the bar."

Matthew? Too-cute-for-his-own-good, Matthew? Brilliant! My diet doesn't prevent me from having eye-candy... Serve me a Matthew! ... Oh, right... Married *Matthew ...*

They seated themselves in one of the booths in the retro-inspired bar. Kelly had seen some of Susan's original drawings for the bar, but had never seen the finished product, and was impressed with the results. This was Susan Russell at her best.

Bryce and Alen brought legal pads, and pens poised, were looking expectantly at Vicky.

"Okay," she started and lit a cigarette. "I want it simple, and this setting I think will do. Here's a preliminary guest list," she pulled out a piece of paper from her purse, "only fifty people or so right now, but there will be more. Count on it to double. At least. I don't want a theme, I'm sick of themed parties. And I want you to remember that I'm paying for this party, not my father, so don't listen to him, although he'll offer his two cents' worth. I want an open bar, plenty of champagne and some snacks, nothing too rich. Light finger-food. And I want a live band," Vicky pulled another piece of paper from her purse, "any one of the ones in black, none of the ones in red. I understand if you want the media to attend, but there are a couple of rags that dissed my brother, and I don't want them here," Vicky pulled one more piece of paper from her purse. She handed all her notes to the jays, crossed her arms on the table and looked at Alen and Bryce, who were scribbling away on their legal pads.

Well, she's obviously done this before. Sounded quite professional, and strong. Determined. Not as spoiled as I had expected. What happened to the rich airhead? Where'd she go?

"That's it?" Bryce said in disbelief.

Vicky nodded. "Have your party planner work out the details…" Vicky paused. "You *do* have a party planner, don't you?"

"Stuck on the Kennedy Expressway, I'm afraid," Alen offered apologetically.

"Anyway, have him work out the details, and contact me with a cost estimate," Vicky concluded.

Why is the I-90 called the I-90 across the entire United States, except in Chicago? Surely it's easier to say I-90 than 'thekennedy-expressway'?... Suppose it could be worse. It could be 'thejohnfken-nedyexpressway' ... or 'presidentjohnfitzgeraldkennedyexpressway' ... Oooh-oooh! Or 'reverenddoctormartinlutherkingjuniormemori-alexpresswayandtollbridge'! ... Okay, I'm ranting... Wonder what I missed of the conversation?

"Fabulous! Date still June 30th?" Bryce was saying. Vicky nodded again. More scribbling.

"We'll get together with our events coordinator, who'll be contacting you shortly with details and budget," Alen concluded.

Matthew Bradshaw appeared behind the bar.

"One more thing," Vicky said slowly, eyeing Matthew. "I want him," she said pointing at Matthew.

The bar was close enough so Matthew could hear her, but he pretended not to.

Ooow, he's blushing, and trying to hide his face. How cute is he?

"He could manage the bar, but other than that, he's off limits," Alen whispered to Vicky.

"Why? He yours?"

"I wish! No, he's hitched, unfortunately," Alen said and heaved a sigh.

There's not a single pair of dry knickers at this table, Kelly thought as all four of them watched Matthew in silence for a while.

Vicky rose. "I'll go get a drink. You want anything?" she asked Kelly.

I'll have a Matthew with whipped cream, please.

"Ice tea would be nice," Kelly said. "The regular kind."

"You're sooo boring. Come on! It's summer, you're not working, live a little!" Vicky said as she made her way to the bar.

Back at the booth Bryce turned to Kelly. "When can you move in?"

Kelly was watching Vicky at the bar with Matthew.

She's touching him! Oh, shaking hands, okay. He's blushing! What did Bryce just say? Move in? Right…

"The sooner the better."

"Fabulous!" Bryce and Alen exclaimed in unison.

"Now, our grand opening will be July 4th, and we're already nearly fully booked…"

"You're taking reservations? For a hotel that's not open yet?"

"Of course! We're looking at some very busy weeks coming up with the pre-opening, and all. The sooner you're established, the better. You'll notice a wave of people on property in the next few weeks, as we're interviewing and training those who've already been hired. How are you doing with Charlotte? Anything you need from us?"

"I'm waiting to hear back from them. I do need an offer letter, outlining the training," Kelly said.

"Matthew will get that for you. Sit down with him this afternoon, if you're free. He'll get you a set of keys, and help you with what you need."

Bryce and Alen got out of the booth. They looked uneasily at Kelly's jeans and tank top. "Now, about your wardrobe," Alen started. "How to say this subtly…? You're in desperate need of a make over."

Whoa! That's about as subtle as a bullet in the head!

"Don't get us wrong, darling. You have the look we want, just a tad … unpolished," Bryce continued. "And we understand from Susan that you're not quite comfortable in designer wear."

Ohmygod! Susan told them about the backwards dress?

Kelly blushed up to her hairline.

"Oh, precious, it's no big deal. I know the dress. It's an easy mistake to make. And I bet you looked absolutely adorable in it!" Alen fussed.

And how did you look in it? Oh, God I'm naughty! He's not a cross-dresser. Looks really kinda hunky today.

"So, take some advice from Victoria MacIntyre. Go get a mani-pedi, a facial, a haircut, maybe a few subtle highlights, and go shopping. Copy her style, and hang out with her at the hotel a lot," Alen concluded.

I can't afford it. This is a lifestyle for the rich and famous, not the hungry, huddled masses.

"And that's basically your job description until you get your visa approved," Bryce said and kissed Kelly on both cheeks.

"Door's always open, even if you're just popping in to say hi."

Alen and Bryce left Kelly at the booth, shook hands with Vicky and exchanged a few words with Matthew.

They're looking and pointing at me! Oh, right, keys and that. Right. Better join them.

Alen and Bryce left the bar and Kelly walked over to join Matthew and Vicky.

And he's blushing again. Teasing him will be fun!

"Iced tea?" Matthew offered her a tall glass. "Vicky told me how you like them," he said with a wink and a smile.

Kelly blushed.

Man! You could roast a marshmallow between his face and mine.

Matthew started stocking the refrigerator at the other end of the bar.

I guess I must be over Sean to be this attracted to Matthew today and Parker in the pool, Kelly thought, as her fingers automatically went to her necklace.

Vicky leaned over to examine it. "Girl, is that a genuine Tanzanite?"

"Huh? Oh, yeah, I think so. I mean, I don't know. Jon said it was. Why?"

"Tanzanites are probably, like, the rarest precious stones on earth. You can only find them in Tanzania. They get this incredible purple color from the radioactivity in the ground there. You were smart to get a necklace, and not a ring, because they're not hard like, say, emeralds or diamonds or corundum. See, they're this zoisite variety of pyroxene that exhibits strong pleochroism," Vicky said, sounding as if she were reading from the glossary of geology.

Huh? … Any of that English?

"Where'd you get it?" Vicky was still examining the necklace.

"Sean gave it to me, when we got engaged," Kelly said. "I offered to give it back when we broke up, but he insisted I keep it."

"Have you had it examined for authenticity?"

"I didn't think I needed to," Kelly put a protective hand over her necklace. "I didn't know it was worth anything. Sean's Dad was with Doctors Without Borders in Africa. In fact, Sean was born there. I think that's where they got it. Anyway, I just thought it was a darling little necklace."

"Girl, if you're ever in need of cash, you could sell that rock and retire. Comfortably," Vicky said leaning back. "Well, for a while anyway."

"How do you know so much about Tanzanites?"

Vicky crushed her cigarette in the ashtray. "Thought I was just a poor little rich airhead, didn't you? I'm not as shallow as people accuse me of being. Precious gems are my passion, the one thing I really care about. Why do you think I'm going to Stanford? Best economic geology school in the country, that's why!"

Matthew joined them. "So, how do you like the bar, ladies?" he asked, leaning on it.

Vicky lit another cigarette and offered Kelly and Matthew one. Both declined.

"I like it," Kelly said. "Very retro. Have you decided on a name yet?"

"The marketing team is working on that. There are a few good ones on the table, but nothing that stands out."

Kelly was looking around. "I think they should just go with the Milk Bar. I mean, look around. It's very fifties inspired you know, kinda like that bar in Pulp Fiction, where Uma Thurman has that big milk shake. And you could probably get the … what's it called … the Dairy Association, or whatever, to sponsor you with those 'got milk?' T-shirts for the staff…" Kelly stopped as she saw Matthew's astonished face. "What?" she said irritated.

Matthew laughed. "Did you just come up with that on the spot? It's awesome! Run it by Alen and Bryce!"

"And you could serve those big retro milkshakes that are really laced with rum, and call them rum shakes. And you could have vodka shakes, and tequila shakes and …" Vicky said and took a sip of her drink. "And Pina Coladas!"

Matthew was typing away on his PDA. "So, Kelly, if you're free this afternoon, swing by my office, and we'll get you settled in," he said without looking up. "I'm on the second floor. Take the grand staircase to the top, first door on your left across the hallway from the ballroom. Unit 211."

That's it then. If I get an eleven unit, I'll be right on top of Matthew. Mmmm. On top of Matthew… Married *Matthew!* Married Matthew! Right!

"… and Kahlua and cream, and Bailey's," Vicky was still ranting. "And Irish coffees… Hey, do you call them *Irish* coffees in Ireland?"

Kelly laughed. "Like Italian food is only called *food* in Italy? Okay, Irish coffee…"

The beep from Matthew's PDA interrupted Kelly. Matthew read the message quickly and, smiling, handed the PDA to Kelly.

> To: mbradshaw@jhotels.com
> From: bhart@jhotels.com
> Subject: Re: Milk Bar
> Luv it! Told u she's fab! Legal on it str8 away.
> Tell K thx & gr8 job!
> B

Boys and their toys. Why are they sending electronic messages to each other, when they're close enough to whisper?

"Thanks K. Great job," Matthew winked at Kelly again.

Is he flirting with me or is that a nervous tick? Oh, right, married. Nervous tick, then. Right.

"Ready to go?" Vicky said to Kelly. Getting up from her, bar stool Vicky let out a loud belch that resonated across the empty bar. All three laughed. "Excuu-uuse me!" Vicky said, covering her mouth.

"Jaysus, Vicky!" Kelly said. "Had that come from any deeper, you'd have sucked up a fart!"

Vicky laughed. "Un eructo, segun el doctor Angulo, es un pedo que falta llegar al culo."

Matthew tried to hide a laugh bubbling up. Kelly was perplexed. "Umm, ... What?!" she said.

"A belch, according to Dr. Angle," Vicky smiled, "is a fart that fails to arrive at the colon. It rhymes way better in Spanish."

I served, she returned, and now I'm unable to hit a passing shot! I guess I asked for it...

The girls collected their purses and started for the door. Vicky turned and waved at Matthew. "Nice meeting you Matt!"

"See you soon!" Matthew shouted back. "And it's Matthew!"

"Saawree!" Vicky's voice trailed out the door.

Outside the hotel, waiting for the valet attendant to bring her car around, Vicky lit another cigarette. "You don't mind do you, Kelly?" she said, already puffing it.

"No, but you should."

Vicky shrugged, dismissing the thought. "So, Matthew, huh? And he's gonna be your boss? How will the two of you ever get any work done?"

"What do you mean?" Kelly said.

"Aw, come on! Have you *seen* your boss?" Vicky's expression turned dreamy. "He's gorgeous! Not my type at all, obviously, but the two of you are like meant to be!"

Kelly blushed. "Oh, stop it..."

Please go on! Say more things like that!

"Seriously," Vicky insisted. "You're both tall and good looking. Fair skinned. You both blush! At the drop of a hat!

You would have, like, really beautiful children," Vicky concluded thoughtfully.

"He's married."

"So? A wife's only an inconvenience, not an obstacle," Vicky said.

The car appeared from the underground garage. Vicky gave the attendant a hefty tip and the girls got in. "Besides, what the wife doesn't know won't hurt her, right? Tell me you're not turned on by him," Vicky teased, as she turned the car toward Michigan Avenue and headed south.

I wanted to stick my tongue in his ear just talking to him.

"I'm not turned on by him."

Vicky poked a bony elbow in her side. "You lie! When was the last time you had a good fuck?"

Never.

"Dunno," Kelly said, hoping they weren't overheard. She sunk down low in the passenger seat.

"Okay, so that'd be never. No wonder you're mentally undressing every man in sight! Girl, you need to get *laid*! And that boss of yours might just be the one to do the trick. Now, let's go see what Daddy wants, and then go do some shopping, how's that grab ya?"

"Apparently I need a makeover," Kelly said sulkily.

"Excellent! I was hoping you'd see the light. You've come to the right girl," Vicky said and pulled out her cell phone. "Gimme a sec." She hit a speed dial. "Hi, this is Victoria MacIntyre. Is Roberto available? ... Roberto, darling, it's Vicky. I need an emergency everything. ... Absolutely a mani-pedi, too. Didn't I just say *everything*? When can I come by? … Fabulous! See you then, doll!" She hung up. "You're on with Roberto Leon in five minutes."

"Not *the* Roberto Leon?"

Not the guy Susan says the stars have fly across the country to do their award ceremony hair. Not the salon that you can't pass on the Mag Mile because of all the photographers milling outside? And I haven't even washed my hair this morning! Or yesterday for that matter!

"How'd you manage that?"

"Honey, Daddy's name and credit card open all doors."

I couldn't possibly afford him.

Vicky swirled the Mustang and did a U-turn. Kelly's heart was in her throat and her ears screamed in tune with the car horns honking. "Are you nuts!? You can't do a U'e on Michigan Avenue!"

"I think I just did!" Vicky smiled, and waved at the honking drivers.

That's it. I'm going to die with dirty hair on me way to a mani-pedi. Whatever the hell that is…

The Roberto Leon experience turned out to be less traumatic than Kelly had anticipated. There were a few cameramen outside the salon, but none of them paid Kelly any attention. Inside the salon, Kelly was surrounded by Roberto's staff, and they were plucking, massaging, adding goo, removing goo, washing, rinsing and in general making a big fuss over her. Kelly enjoyed every minute of it. She was checking Roberto out through the mirror.

Roberto Leon my arse! More like Robert Lewis! Why does every-one have to pretend... Oh, who cares! This is kinda fun!

Occasionally she saw Vicky come by, with a glass of champagne, to inspect the progress. Vicky and Roberto would have a dialog that went in the direction of 'Spun gold, rather than morning sun', 'Heavy layers', 'Soft around the face', 'Jaw-line for the flip', 'Soo last season', 'Locks of love'. Kelly had no idea what any of it meant, and didn't much care.

It's only hair, it'll grow back.

But once an assortment of scissors and razors were brought around, and strands of her long, red hair started hitting the salon floor, she started to panic.

It's only hair, it'll grow back! It's only hair, it'll grow back! IT'S ONLY HAIR, IT'LL GROW BACK! ... What I really should worry about, is what they'll do when they find out I can't possibly afford this. They gonna glue me hair back on? Pour the impurities back into me pores? ... Yuck!

Two hours later, Kelly was sitting in a mirrorless workstation, having Roberto examine the final touches, when Vicky poured her a glass of champagne.

"How're you doing?" she said.

"How am I going to look, once this is all done?" Kelly retorted and took a long sip.

"In a word - gorgeous," Vicky replied. "Roberto is not the best of the best for nothing."

"Ta-daah!" Roberto said ceremoniously, and swiveled Kelly's chair around so she could see her reflection in the full-length mirror on the opposite wall.

It's only hair, it'll grow back, Kelly recited to herself, with her eyes closed.

11

"Could you give us a minute, Victoria?" Parker asked when the girls arrived in his office after the make-over. "I'd like to talk to Kelly alone for a moment."

"Sure, I'll wait in the little conference room. I really need to use the bathroom in there anyway," Vicky said heading toward the door.

"Better not be inducing vomit, young lady!"

"Sir, no sir!" Vicky said in a mock salute. "But I really havta go-oo." She left the office with crossed legs.

Parker turned to Kelly and pointed at one of the chairs opposite his desk. Kelly sat down gingerly at the edge of the big leather chair.

Why am I here?

"You're wondering why I asked to see you?" Parker said, looking Kelly square in the face.

Did I just say that out loud?

"I wanted to give you this," he said and slid a platinum card across the desk. "It's a debit card, so don't get excited. It's in your name, with ten grand on it."

Kelly was dumbstruck.

Ohmygod! He's trying to buy me!

"I'm not for sale, Mr. MacIntyre. Anyway, there's not enough money on the planet to make me take me knickers off for you. Just because you're rich and powerful and better than average looking, doesn't mean that you can just buy me services. And anyway, they're not for sale."

Parker held up a hand. "Save your preaching, Irish. If I wanted a date, believe me, I know of some companies that can provide me with an escort, much more experienced and much less of a hassle."

Take a deep breath, Kelly, you'll not want to be blushing in front of him again. So, why is he offering me money then? As a thank you for the touch and feel in the pool?

"I'm no good with words. This is my way of saying thank you," Parker said.

Ah-huh! I knew it!

"You were a loyal friend to my daughter, which in itself is rare, and she tells me you liked her without knowing who she was, which is even rarer. But most importantly, you really opened my eyes about her. Most people wouldn't have dared do what you did. Took a lot of guts, I must admit."

Huh?

"I would very much like for you to have this card. Spend some time with my daughter. Go out, have fun. Keep an eye on her. See who she's with. Keep her on the straight and narrow. Make her eat."

You've got to be kidding me?!

Kelly sprung to her feet. "You're asking me to spy on your daughter? Ya think? That's so low. She's a friend, and friends don't do that…"

Man, I should have turned the mobile off. Or at least turned the vibrating mode off. Or at least not keep it in me jeans' pocket with the vibrator on…

The smile on Parker's face widened as he watched Kelly squirm, trying to ignore her phone. He shook his head slowly. "Not that I mind watching you please yourself, but would you just answer that? That ring tone is really annoying," he said.

Flustered, Kelly answered her phone. There was a rasping noise on the line.

"Good evening. This is Kathleen O'Brien with the Bureau of External Affairs, in Dublin, Ireland. May I speak to Ms. Kelly McCoy, please," a prudish Irish dialect came across the line.

Still looking at Parker, Kelly retorted at the caller "How'd you get my number?"

"Ms. McCoy?"

"Speaking."

"Yer number was listed as one of the emergency contacts fer a Mr. Sean Molloy," Kathleen O'Brien said.

Kelly felt deflated, and sat heavily back down on the chair.

Emergency contact? Don't say it, please don't say it.

"Seeing as yer in the States, I don't know if you've heard ..."

"I've heard," Kelly whispered. Her throat felt paper dry. She hung her forehead in the palm of her hand.

"I'm sorry to be the bearer of bad news Ms. McCoy," the voice continued across the Atlantic, "but Mr. Molloy perished in Sunday's bombing."

Nooooo!

"We're led to believe there was no pain. Death was instantaneous," Kathleen O'Brien said awkwardly in an effort to comfort Kelly. The rasping on the line continued. "Ms. McCoy? Are you still there?"

"Aye," Kelly whispered. "Thank you fer calling. Have a nice day," she said robotically and disconnected. She sat breathing heavily and stared at the phone in her hand.

Sean is dead. He's dead! I never got to tell him I forgave him. And now he's dead. I can't believe this. This isn't happening! Twenty-six year-olds don't die. What business did he have dying before I got to tell him ... something ... anything ... ?

"Kelly?" Parker walked around his desk and looked at her with a worried expression.

Kelly looked up at him. "Sean's dead. Bomb in Dublin. Sunday."

I feel like I should cry. Why can't I cry? Am I not supposed to?

Parker put his arms around her, and led her to the sofa in the corner of his office. He sat her down, and poured her a shot of whisky. "Drink this," he commanded and held the glass to her lips.

She obeyed silently. The liquor burned her throat. "Thank you," she said hoarsely.

He sat on the sofa next to her, and put his arm around her shoulders. "Who's Sean?"

"He's … was… my fiancé. We were meant to get married after I graduated. And now he's dead," Kelly said staring into space.

"I'm so sorry," Parker whispered.

Kelly went limp and leaned her head against Parker's chest. She could hear his heart thumping in her ear. Parker was stroking her hair.

Got new goo in me hair.

"There, there," Parker whispered. "It's okay to cry. It hurts, believe me, I know this hurt, and it's going to hurt for a long time, but then suddenly you wake up one morning and you hurt a little less, and you cry a little less, and you notice that life goes on."

Kelly turned her head and looked up at Parker. "You lost your wife in an accident, didn't you?" she said.

Parker's gray eyes were clouded.

He really is human under that steel exterior. Scratch a billionaire and you'll find a wounded soul.

He nodded slowly. "Car crash, nearly eighteen years ago. I was in the car behind hers. She never had a chance to react to the other car making a turn in the wrong lane. It was a head-on collision. This was a time before air bags. She died instantly."

"I'm so sorry," Kelly whispered. "How'd you get over the pain?"

"I didn't. I learned to live with it. I threw myself into my work. Avoided the kids. Sometimes when I look at Victoria I see Sara, and the pain comes back," he said solemnly.

They sat silently for a while, Kelly's head on Parker's chest, Parker's arms around her, rocking her softly.

"How do you feel?" Parker finally broke the silence.

Like I should cry, but the tears won't come.

"Numb."

"Yes, the numbness comes first, then denial and then the pain."

Kelly could see the pain in Parker's eyes. Their eyes locked for a long time. Their faces were very close. Kelly could feel Parker's breath on her lips. Parker leaned in to kiss Kelly. There was a knock on the door.

I can't believe this! Every time I'm about to bloody kiss him!

"Daddy?" Vicky opened the door to the office. Parker and Kelly separated. "What's going on?" Vicky said as she saw them sitting on the sofa with solemn faces.

Parker got on his feet. "Kelly just got some bad news. Her fiancé died. Why don't you take her downstairs?"

Vicky hurried to Kelly's side, wrapped her gaunt arms around her and led her out the door, murmuring comforting words to her. They were walking toward the lobby.

"I forgot me purse," Kelly said, and rushed back towards Parker's office. "I'll be right back! Call us an elevator!"

"We're an elevator!" Vicky shouted behind Kelly laughing at her little joke.

Kelly didn't hear it. She tiptoed into Parker's office, and found him standing by the bar with his back to the door.

Now or never, Kelly McCoy.

She walked softly over to Parker until she was only inches away from him. "Mr. MacIntyre?" she whispered.

Parker turned around. Kelly recognized the look on his face. She'd seen it in the Russells' pool. She pressed her body, full-length, against Parker's and crossed her hands behind his head. She planted a slow, long kiss on his lips.

"Thank you for being here, Mr. MacIntyre," she whispered.

Parker looked deep into Kelly's eyes. "I think it's time you started calling me Parker."

12

"I really don't have time for this right now. You need to set up an appointment with my assistant," Gina said acidly and walked out the front entrance of the hotel.

Matthew and the jays watched her incredulously. The jays had tried to catch her to introduce her to Matthew, but she hadn't even stopped long enough to look at him.

"Is that woman for real?" Matthew said as he sat down in the jays' office. "How does she fit through the door with that big head of hers? She doesn't have time for what? Shake my hand?"

Alen rolled his eyes. "That was nothing," he said. "You've caught her on a good day! We've seen her way worse than that! Unfortunately we inherited her. And now it seems that we're stuck with her. She was the manager of the old hotel on this site, and we signed her on. Had to. Part of the deal."

"She reminds me a bit of a GM I once had back in Florida," Matthew said, and a smile appeared on his face. "Steel Cojones, we called him behind his back." Matthew chuckled at the memory.

"I think that translates into Ice Bitch for a woman," Alen said. "Especially this particular woman."

"I wouldn't count on her being here much," Bryce said. "So far we've only seen her a total of maybe an hour a day. If that. So you'll pretty much have to run this show for yourself. Are you ready for that?"

"Absolutely," Matthew said enthusiastically. "This is the opportunity I've been waiting for since I was a bellboy! … Looks like I'm gonna need a strong ally, though."

"Or two," Alen chimed in.

"Speaking of allies," Bryce said, "how are you looking at getting the head of housekeeping and that Navy hunk from the Drake?"

"Mitch and Dan?" Matthew laughed. "They'll start next Monday. Although *hunk* maybe stretching it a bit for Dan! He's my Dad's age!"

"But you have a solid working relationship together?" Bryce asked. "We're totally trusting your judgment of them."

"Oh, yeah! We go way back," Matthew said. "Mitch and I used to work together in Florida. For a while he was my manager. I was a senior in high school, I think, when I was in housekeeping. While I was in college he relocated to Chicago and then, when an opening became available at the Drake, he recommended me. So in a sense I'm paying him back by bringing him here. And Dan is a real salt-of-the-earth kinda guy. Runs everything with military precision. Literally."

"Fabulous," Bryce said. "And how are we doing with EUSA, and all our future foreign hard-bodies for the guest services?"

"So far, I've interviewed about a dozen or so…" Matthew started.

"From?" Alen shot in.

"Oh, everywhere. France, Austria, Greece, Sweden … take your pick."

"Anyone that stands out?" Bryce asked.

Matthew laughed. "All of them! I wish I'd known about this company when I was hiring at the Drake! You should have seen the parade of losers I had to interview! Anyway, we'll be fully staffed by opening."

"They're really that good?" Bryce asked.

"Well, they're no Kelly McCoy," Matthew winked.

The jays both sighed. "No, they wouldn't be. There's only *one* Kelly McCoy," Alen said.

"He was a cheating bastard and I wanted bad things to happen to him, but I never wanted him to *die*!" Kelly was sitting in Vicky's hot tub in the MacIntyre condo. Vicky had made them strong Irish coffees, which, when drunk in the hot tub, was the only way she knew to get over bad news. She expected Kelly to start crying soon.

"So, like, had you forgiven him?"

"Yeah, but I never got to tell him," Kelly said feeling a pang of guilt.

"Were you still gonna marry him?"

"I could never have married him."

"But you said you'd forgiven him for cheating on you."

"Yeah, but imagine it – I would've been Kelly Molloy. There's enough L's there for four names."

"Not necessarily. You can keep your own name. I'm going to. Or you could hyphenate! Kelly McCoy-Molloy!"

"McCoy-Molloy? That sounds like an Australian disease. 'I'm sorry, sir, we have to amputate your penis. You have a severe case of McCoy-Molloy'," Kelly said. "Well, it's not going to be Molloy now anyway." She took another sip of her drink.

"How do you feel now?"

"Like I should cry, but can't," Kelly said. "Is that terribly selfish of me?"

"It hasn't hit you yet," Vicky said, finishing her drink. "We must take advantage of the fact that it hasn't. Get your mind off it. Come on. Let's go." She got out of the tub.

"Where are we going?"

"Shopping. You need a new wardrobe. You're starting a new chapter in your life. Might as well look fabulous doing it," Vicky said.

So much for my mourning period.

"By the way," Vicky said, as they were getting dressed. "What did Daddy want from you?"

I'm hoping the same I want from him...

"Oh, he wanted to thank me for ... how did he put it? ... Seeing the error of his ways, or something to that effect."

There was a knock on the door. "Victoria? It's Dad. You decent?" Parker said through the closed door.

"Yeah, Daddy. Come on in!"

Parker entered Vicky's bedroom, looking worried. "I just wanted to see how you were doing, Kelly," he said with genuine concern.

Kelly nodded, and felt a lump in her throat. "Better, thank you," she said quietly.

Now I feel like crying! Although not for Sean. I feel like crying because I want to be with this man so badly and on the day I hear about the death of a former loved one. Oh, I'm going to hell. Fersure.

Parker put a hand on Kelly's shoulder and looked her deep in the eye. "If ever you need someone to talk to, a shoulder to cry on, anything, you know where to find me," he said sincerely and took Kelly's hand. He pressed the debit card in it. "I'd really like for you to have this," he added softly.

Kelly looked at him, and felt the warmth of his presence. She attempted a smile and nodded again. "Thank you," she whispered and took the card.

Would it be immoral of me to take it? I sure could use it. I'd still be a friend to Vicky, had he asked me to or not, and it's not like I'm under obligation to Parker, or anything. I'm going to hell anyway, might as well go looking good.

"Let's go shopping!" Vicky said and pulled Kelly with her. "Later, Daddy!"

Parker found himself oddly disturbed as he returned to his office. He stood by the bar in the corner, pouring himself a drink. He placed the cap on the bottle and smiled to himself at the thought of Kelly's body pressed against his. He raised the glass to his lips, and with a shrug, threw the liquor down the drain.

There was a knock on his door and Jon entered. "Got a minute, Commander?" Jon asked waving that week's issue of the *Northern Miner*. Parker waved him in. "Read today's *Minero Norteno* yet?" Jon said as both men took their seats on opposite sides of Parker's desk.

Parker shook his head and Jon slid his copy across the desk. It was folded open on the Diamond Page. Parker quickly skimmed the text and looked up at Jon with narrow eyes.

"The Aussies are moving into Argentina? In the dead of winter?" he whispered in disbelief. "How did we not know about it before the media?"

"That's not the point right now," Jon said anxiously. "The more pressing issue is, do we want to move in?"

"Ken A we want to move in!" Parker exclaimed. He got out of his seat and started pacing in front of his windows. "Last time I didn't get on board with the Aussies I lost van der Klippe to DeBeers. I'll never live that one down." The

permanent crease between his eyebrows was more prominent than usual. He turned to Jon. "Who do we have in
Argentina? Anyone we can trust on the QT?"

"Mendoza and Nordin are good," Jon started hesitantly.
"And there's always Duncan..." Jon nearly bit his tongue
off. Since the news about Duncan's retirement broke, he
had not been seen or heard from by anyone in the industry.
Jon had been unable to contact him again.

"*Duncan?*! We don't have damn Duncan! If we had
Duncan the Aussies wouldn't stand a chance and I wouldn't
have to read about them in the damn *Northern Miner*! Anyone
know what the hell Duncan's doing or where the fuck he's
now?" Parker barked.

"I'm working on it," Jon said, and rose to leave. He knew
that when Parker started using profanities, it was time to
disappear.

"Well, work harder, damn it! I want Duncan on the
next flight! And in the meantime, get Mendoza and Nordin
snooping. I'm not going to lose to the damn Aussies again,
damn it!"

"And just when would you wear something like this?"
Kelly asked Vicky as she looked at her reflection in the
dressing room mirror in an upscale North Michigan Avenue
store.

"Club openings, premieres," Vicky said and lit a cigarette. "My birthday party."

"I don't think you're supposed to smoke here," Kelly whispered.

"You're right, but what're they gonna do? Throw me out? Puh-lease! I give them loads of business and publicity. Betcha anything, there'll be paparazzi outside the door waiting for us when we leave, you know?" She waved away the smoke in front of her face and walked over to Kelly. "Ever heard 'if you got it – flaunt it'?" she said as she hooked Kelly's dress in the back.

"Yeah, but I don't like advertising," Kelly squirmed uncomfortably and tried pulling the top of the dress higher.

"I thought you majored in marketing?" Vicky said and pulled it further down. "Look," she started patiently, "clothes make a person. You can dress up or dress down, depending on who you want people to think you are. Look at you now! Just a few hours ago you were some sad Irish peasant, and now you could pass for a Hollywood starlet!"

What's wrong with being an Irish peasant if you are *an Irish peasant?*

"Why is it so important to pretend that you're something you're not?" Kelly was growing frustrated.

"Look - do you know how I got Roberto Leon to do your makeover for free?"

Kelly shook her head and pulled her top higher.
Just glad he did.

Vicky pulled the top back down. "I told him that you were in town starring in a movie opposite Julia Roberts,"

Vicky said matter-of-factly and crushed her cigarette on the carpet.

Kelly was pulling her top up again, but stopped amazed and stared at Vicky's reflection in the mirror. "You didn't!?"

"I so did."

"And he bought it?"

"Look, it's as simple as you scratch my back and I'll scratch yours, you know. You got a fabulous makeover and Roberto got the publicity of me entering his establishment and exiting with my new gal-pal. The mysterious red-head. You watch, you'll be in like four or five rags by Thursday. Try this one next."

Vicky was holding up a tank top. It was identical to what Kelly had been wearing entering the store. Kelly looked at the price tag.

Holy Mother of God! How can this little fabric cost this much? What's it made of? Crude oil?

Mechanically her hands went to the label. 'Flammable. Keep away from heat and open flame.'

Well, that settles that, then.

"Now how's this different from the top I had on?" she said as she held both of them up for Vicky.

"This one," Vicky pointed at Kelly's, "you probably got three for nine-ninety-nine, right?"

Close. Five for ten. Various colors, though.

Vicky picked up the other one. "Whereas this one's designer wear. It's to die for!"

It's flammable! It's to die from!

"You'll feel more confident, you'll look like you own a diamond mine, and trust me, people will believe it, too, you know," Vicky continued. "Okay, like, I don't have a problem with bargain shopping. It's great if you're in desperate need for, I don't know, a ten-gallon jug of mayonnaise. But clothes are different. They can make you or break you. Please, just trust me on this, okay?"

Feel more confident? I feel worried that I'll spill that ten-gallon jug of mayo on this cover-nothing, flammable constrictor that costs me one month's wages and that I can't breathe in.

Kelly felt faint. She discarded the top and pulled out a dress instead. As she was wriggling into it, her cell phone rang. The zipper of the dress got caught in her hair.

"Could you see who that is, please," she said to Vicky from inside the dress.

Vicky looked at the display. "Says 'Ireland'."

Kelly sighed. "Would you reject it, please. I can't handle that right now. It's just another condolence call. My voicemail will be very appreciative."

All day friends and family from Ireland had been calling Kelly as the news about Sean's death spread. Finally Kelly had changed her voicemail to saying that she had received the news, and was currently not taking any calls.

I don't want to spend my expensive airtime minutes on pretending that I mourn someone I just can't feel that sad about. ... I am a horrible person. A horrible person, who looks like a slut, she thought as she looked at herself in the mirror in the next outfit that Vicky had picked out for her.

"Now this dress is more conservative…" Vicky started.

Conservative?! Does she know the meaning of the word?

"…wear this one to work, and you'll be promoted in no time."

Promoted to what? Where do you go from slut? Oh, only way is up, I suppose.

"Now, then, leave that one on. We'll go ring these up, get a drink and then go buy some shoes," Vicky said as she lit another cigarette.

"Isn't it a bit early to be drinking?"

"I don't smoke dry," Vicky said and blew a perfect smoke ring toward the ceiling.

13

Susan was trying to hide her enthusiasm while studying Jacqui's plans for the J lobby. She had given him a small drafting table in the corner of her office, and he'd poured all his energy into the plans since she gave him the assignment. Every time she offered to help, he became anxious, so finally she gave up and let him be.

Susan slowly let her hand run over the fabric swatches. Jacqui let out an almost inaudible groan and turned his back to her.

"Okay, Jack," Susan finally said as she straightened her back. "Pitch me."

"I beg your pardon!?" Jacqui said looking Susan over.

"Pretend that I'm the jays, ... um ... Bryce and Alen, and you're selling them this concept."

Jacqui panicked. "No, no, no wait a minute! I thought you were going to do that!"

"Take credit for someone else's work?" Susan said with raised eyebrows. "That's not how I operate, Jack. Now pitch it to me."

Jacqui was nervously picking at a cuticle. "Well, what did *you* think of it?"

"I'm Bryce and Alen," Susan leaned back and crossed her legs. "I don't read blueprints. Now pitch already. You're wasting precious time."

Becoming all business, Jacqui grabbed a pen from Susan's desk and pointed at the first of his drawings. "I went with the theme that you started in the Milk Bar and … what do they call the restaurant?"

"They've settled on My Kinda Town Grill."

"Hmmm? They got away with that?"

"Why?"

"Well, I think there's a My Kind of Towne Grille on Navy Pier," Jacqui replied. "Anyway. The bar and restaurant are very Chicago, very rat pack meets prohibition meets the twenty-first century," he started and looked at Susan.

Her face was expressionless.

"Okay, so I suggest that we bust through these walls," he pointed at the walls between the bar and the lobby and the restaurant and the lobby. "They're not bearing walls. In fact, I'm bringing back the original extended lobby from the twenties' blueprints. With an open floor plan the patrons will walk into a more welcoming setting. 'Is it a bar? Is it a movie set? Is it Capone's living room? Who cares! I've had a long flight and I'm ready for a drink!' or 'I'm too drunk to drive home, I want a room!' More revenue, is what I'm thinking."

He looked up at Susan again. She was nodding slowly, encouraging him.

"The color scheme carries over from the bar. Oh, and P.S. Marble? No good for heavy traffic areas. Beautiful, yes, but it only has the hardness of three on the Moh's scale. So I recommend granite, which is not only cheaper, but also way more durable and more readily available. I moved the bell closet and the reception desk to this corner, which only makes practical sense for guests, as well as staff. I put a tiny Manager's office behind it. Basically everything is turned one-eighty, and the glass enclosed office will no longer be the centerpiece of the lobby, but it's still going to be there, because that's what they wanted."

He stopped to draw breath. Susan's face was still expressionless. She continued nodding.

"Oooh, and the most fab-a-*licious* component," Jacqui said and pulled out four sketches of the same wall. Each with a different background color. "I got us *Day and Night* lights. Yay me! You know the kind that changes color depending on the time of day, or the brightness outside. You know, you install them behind the crown moldings around the room and you get surround-good-feel... anyway... the creator claims that these lights are a traveler's best friend in getting over jet-lag and they create a more relaxing working environment. Whatcha think?"

"Very retro-techno-chic," Susan said slowly.

"That's what I'm calling it, too!" Jacqui exclaimed. "Great minds do think alike, darling... I mean, boss-lady," Jacqui caught himself.

"The only problem is," Susan said ignoring his gaffe and pulled the drawings with the lights closer. "Our budget can't handle these lights. In fact, our budget could probably handle these lights, but not much else."

She crossed her hands under her chin and examined Jacqui's face. He was smiling broadly. He leaned in closer to Susan.

"I got them for free," he whispered with a wink.

"How?"

Jacqui's smile broadened. "Do you like them?"

"I love them!"

"Do you like the lobby design?"

"Love it!"

"Do you think Bryce and Alen will like it?"

"They'll eat it up with a spoon. Now, tell me how you got us the lights!" She rose from her chair.

"Do I have a full-time position with Byrne-Russell?"

"If you tell me how you got us those lights for free," Susan said impatiently.

"I can get us these lights for free for every Byrne-Russell design that I'm involved with."

"How?"

"I own the company."

Susan sat down and let out a long breath. "What?"

"I went to school with the guy who invented them, and he needed some cash for his venture, so I …"

Susan's laughter interrupted him.

"The apple really doesn't fall far from the pear tree! You truly are your father's son!" She got up again and shook Jacqui's hand. "Welcome to Byrne-Russell, Jack!"

Jacqui pecked a quick kiss on the back of Susan's hand. His eyes were moist.

"Thank you," he whispered.

"Get your stuff, we're going to pitch this to the jays," she said, reaching for the phone.

"Now?!"

"Now," Susan said, dialing Bryce's number.

Matthew let out a long whistle as Kelly entered his office much later in the afternoon of her Roberto Leon experience.

"Wow! You look amazing!" he said. "Not that you ever looked anything short of gorgeous, but this is beyond … beyond!" He laughed uncomfortably. "Listen to me! You've made me speechless!"

Kelly giggled. "Thang you," she said and set her shopping bags down. "I's wundrin if I courrave a room now, please?"

Hope he can't tell I'm not entirely sober.

"Gerrin late, and's got more shoppin to do. And Vicky need sapee."

Matthew looked at her, and his smile vanished. "Is everything alright?"

Kelly pressed both index fingers to her mouth and giggled again. "Had a wee liquid lunch," she whispered.

Matthew was still studying her. "There's something else different about you, too." He eyed her for a moment, then shrugged. "Maybe it's the make-up. Anyway, I've blocked suite 2211 for you. It has a nice view of the lake," he said, and pulled out a small box from his desk drawer.

"Your master key, your PDA, your password to InnTime, our clock-in system, your password to Aaria, our operating system," he said as he handed the box to her. "All of which I'll teach you how to use, of course." He still looked worried. "Maybe we should do all that tomorrow."

"Prubly best," Kelly giggled. She pointed at a door in Matthew's office. "Whassin ere?"

"These offices used to be connecting guest rooms," Matthew said as he rose and walked across his office. He opened the connecting doors. "It was meant to be the office of the new Director of Housekeeping ."

Kelly looked into an empty room. "But you haven't hired un yet, my right?"

Matthew closed the doors. "We have. He starts Monday. But he preferred to be closer to the action, which I agree with, so we'll build him an office of sorts by the laundry in the basement," he said as he sat down on the edge of his desk. He was still eyeing Kelly.

Kelly took her little box and was about to leave, when her cell phone rang. She looked at the display. "Where sarea code 704?" she slurred.

"Charlotte, North Carolina," Matthew said. "It's the visa people!" The smile reappeared on his face.

Kelly thrust the phone at him. "You gerrit!"

"It's you they want to talk to."

"I can't! I'm a lirre drunk."

"How badly do you want this visa?"

Hmmph! … Okay, Vicky sobered up at the Russell barbecue talking to her Dad. How'd she dun it? Oh, yeah. Stand up straight, and use short sentences.

Kelly stood up, took a wide stance, cleared her throat and answered.

"Haih Callie!" a very up-beat young man's southern drawl said. "This is Mawrriss fruhm EUSA in Charlotte! How're you today?"

Maawris? Oh, Morris! Maybe Maurice. Oooh! So not the thing to concentrate on right now!

"Grand. You?"

"Doin' just fine, thank you! We've received yore application and yore transcripts fruhm Ahreland, an' understand that you've a training position lined up with thuh Jaay in Chicagoh startin' Jew-lie. 'S that correct?"

"Yes."

Thank God he speaks so slowly!

"An' we also understand that yore currently in thuh US. 'S that right?"

Du-uh! Ya just called me on an American phone number! Ya Muppet!

"Yes."

Cripes, I hope he won't think me rude. Try a wee longer sentence.

"An' what's yore current status, ma'am?"

"Au Pair. Expires July 1st."

Good! Looong sentence!

"Awrighty then. We understand fruhm thuh ravin' letter of recommendation fruhm, ... lemme see 'ere ... Mr. Bradshaw an' them, that they want you ta start as soon as."

Wonder who the 'and them' are?

"Who san um?"

Good! Slip in a question! Clever!

"Um, jest 'im," Mawrriss said.

Huh? 'Mr. Bradshaw and them' is only one person? What a waste of breath.

"Now, when's thuh hotel due ta open?" Mawrriss continued.

"Opening is set fer force a July."

Excellent! Doing well.

"That sure don't give us much time," he said and paused for thought. "Now, would you be willing ta pay an additional thousand for premium processing, an' have thuh visa approved in two maybe three weeks?"

What? That's it? No interview? No going to North Carolina? No 'yay road trip'?

"Could you hold, please?" Kelly said. She covered the mouthpiece and looked at Matthew. "Would I be willing to pay an additional thousand to get the visa in two weeks?" she whispered.

"Of course! Go for it!"

"I don't have an additional thousand."

"We'll work something out. Don't worry about it. Do it! Do it!"

Kelly was back on the phone. "Do it, do it!"

"Excellent!" Mawrriss said. "Now, normally we would ask you ta come ta one of our field offices in Ewerope for an interview, 'cause we actually have ta meet with you in person. Comp'ny policy. Ahm sawrry. But seein' as yore in thuh States…"

"I'll come to Charlotte!" Kelly shrieked enthusiastically.

"Ah sure 'nuff wuz hopin' you'd say that! I'm fixin' ta FedEx thuh forms an that to you right quick 'ere, care of Jaay an' them. All we need fruhm you is a signature, an' bring 'em with you to thuh interview. An' then get ready ta go ta Duuhblin in a few weeks!"

"Why wourr I go to Dublin?"

"Well, you need ta get thuh visa isself from thuh US Embassy in Duuhblin, then re-enter thuh US, with that visa, so thuh border officer kin stamp yore passport. 'S all splained in thuh papers ahm fixin' ta send. Y'all call me now if you have eeney questions."

"Thanks," Kelly said and hung up. She looked excited at Matthew. "Wheels are in motion! Ahm fixin' ta go ta Charlotte!"

Yay! Road trip!

* * *

To: bhart@jhotels.com, amarshall@jhotels.com
From: Susan.Russell@Byrne-Russell.com
Subject: My Kinda Town Grill
Forgot to tell you over the phone. Jacqui says there
already is a 'my kind of towne grille' on navy
pier. My assistant just confirmed it. Got a backup?
We're enroute to J. Be there in a few. – Susan

Susan sent the message and looked over at Jacqui. He was nervously tapping his hands on his sketch case, which he had laid on his lap. Susan put a soft hand on his.

"Nervous?" she said and smiled. He nodded and swallowed hard. "Don't be. I keep telling you, they'll love it. And I'll be with you the whole time."

Jacqui gave her hand a light, albeit clammy, squeeze. "Thanks," he said.

They rode in silence for a while. The traffic downtown was heavy, and Susan was happy that she decided to take a cab rather than drive there herself. A beep from her PDA interrupted her thoughts.

To: Susan.Russell@Byrne-Russell.com
From: bhart@jhotels.com
Subject: Re: My Kinda Town Grill

Thanks for the heads-up. What's Kelly's
e-mail, I'd like to pick her brains again, and
she's not answering her cell phone.

B

To: bhart@jhotels.com
From: Susan.Russell@Byrne-Russell.com
Subject: Re: My Kinda Town Grill
one_real_mccoy@yahoo.co.uk
She only has limited access to e-mail, though.
Try texting her cell.

"I thought she was Irish?" Jacqui was reading over
Susan's shoulder.

"She is," Susan sent her message. "Why?"

"Her e-mail address says UK."

"Oh, that," Susan laughed. "Don't ever mention it to
her. Extremely sore subject. Jon used to call her our 'obligatory Brit', and she sure didn't like that."

"What's an obligatory Brit?"

"Haven't you noticed lately that all TV shows and many
commercials have a British character? That character's your
obligatory Brit. Jon's term."

"You're right! I hadn't thought of that. Even that one
Navy show has a British person on staff. Huh? I didn't think
non-citizens could enlist."

"I don't think they can," Susan said. "Say! Is your uncle
still in the Army? Oh, it wouldn't matter, he'd still know,
wouldn't he?!"

"Yeah! He just made … something … What rank do you make after twenty years of active service? Admiral?"

Susan laughed. "Don't think me unpatriotic for not knowing. But I do know that you won't make admiral in the Army. Ever."

Jacqui started tapping his hands on his sketch case again.

"Is he about to retire?" Susan asked, putting a hand on Jacqui's to stop the tapping.

"This summer. I'm hoping he can make it to Vicky's party, but I doubt it. It'd mean the world to her. He's the only one who can set her straight."

"Why don't you have *E!* or *VH1* or *Entertainment Tonight* or one of those shows fly him in and do an exclusive re-union interview with them. Those shows love that kind of stuff!"

"Fabulous idea!" Jacqui said, then hesitated. "I didn't know you knew him."

"He was at my wedding," Susan said. "Your Dad was between wives as he likes to put it, so he brought your uncle as a date."

"Oh, yeah," Jacqui sighed. "I remember your wedding. I cried…"

The beeping from Susan's PDA interrupted him.

> To: Susan.Russell@Byrne-Russell.com
> From: bhart@jhotels.com
> Subject: Re: My Kinda Town Grill
> She's here. You know her fiancé died? Please
> hurry.

B

Cold chills ran down Susan's back as she read the message. She quickly got out of the cab that had stopped at a red light three blocks from the hotel.

"Jack, please pay the driver, I'm gonna run the rest of the way."

Kelly was sitting in the jays' office, and they were hovering over her.

"Really, I'm fine," she said. "You know the story. I was over him before I even got to the States. Sure I'm sorry he's dead, but I just can't seem to be able to bring myself to mourn him."

Alen handed her a handkerchief. "Just in case."

Matthew entered the office. "What's going on?" he said.

"She'll be fine," Bryce said. "I asked you to come down to program Kelly's PDA. Give her a j-mail account."

"Done," Matthew said. "We were meant to go over it tomorrow, as she didn't seem fit to do it today," he continued and eyed Kelly, whose eyes were fixated on a spot on the floor.

She had checked into her room, force-fed herself two bananas, accepted one of Vicky's Soberup pills and left

Vicky napping on her bed. She was now slowly sipping coffee from a large Thermos cup.

"Good," Bryce said. "We need a new name for the restaurant, and we need it fast. Apparently there already is a My Kind of Towne Grille in Chicago."

'My kind of town Chicago is…' Then how does it go? Oh, no! Now that song's going to be on me mind fer the rest of the day and I don't even know it! Man! How annoying! … 'My kind of town Chicago is …'

"How about Blue Jay's?" Matthew said. "Our signature color being blue, and Jay, you know, for J."

"Hmmm?" Alen pondered the idea. "Isn't there a sports team called the Blue Jays?"

"New England," Bryce said. "Boston hockey team."

'My kind of town Chicago is…' Isn't Blue Jays a baseball team? '… Chicago is…' Kelly thought, her eyes still on the spot on the floor.

"Toronto Blue Jays," Matthew said. "Baseball."

Thank you!

"I don't like it," Bryce said. "Sounds too much like a sports bar, which we sooo are not."

'My kind of town, Chicago is…' Man! That's like a broken record in me brain, now. '… Chi-cago is…'

"Ohmygod! I got it!" Alen exclaimed, clapping his hands in excitement. "Milk Bar! Stockyards! The great Chicago fire caused by Bessie the cow! Let's continue the cow theme!"

Matthew frowned. "And call the restaurant … what? … Holstein's?"

"Luuurve it!" Alen said, eyes gleaming.

"I don't," Bryce grimaced. "It sounds like a Beer Garden. Patrons will be expecting a brass band, yodeling and dirndls."

'... *My kind of town Chi-*cago *is!* ...'

"Oy!" Kelly's head perked up. "Chicago's also known as Chi town, right? Is that something that's known outside of Chicago or is it only used by Chicagoans?"

"Common knowledge," Matthew said.

"Well, how about Shy Town Grill? Chi spelled s-h-y. A little play on words, as well as a jab at Chicago's darker past," Kelly offered.

"Shy Town Grill," the men tried the name out.

"Shy Town Grill and the Milk Bar," Bryce said. "I like it. Let's get legal on it," he said and reached for the phone.

"Um, Bryce? I have to ask," Kelly said feeling uncomfortable, "not that it matters to me either way, after all, my best friend in life is gay..."

"Male or female?" Alen interrupted.

"Male. Anyway, the point I'm trying to make is, will the J be a lifestyle hotel?"

"No! Absolutely not," Bryce responded quickly. "It was at first, but it's been done ad nauseam. It's like, 'we're here, we're queer, so what else is new?' ... Why do you ask? I sense concern."

"Well, you were so quick to jump on that whole Milk Bar idea."

"We loved it. We're working on the rights for it and the ADA will sponsor us with T-shirts for the staff," Bryce announced proudly.

That was quick! I'm impressed!

"Do you foresee a problem with it?" Alen asked.

"Well, it's just that a few years ago, I saw this T-shirt that had a picture of Monica Lewinsky with a milk moustache on it, and the caption beneath her picture read 'Not Milk', and I was just worried that Milk Bar might be misinterpreted."

"That's really funny! And so what if it's taken the wrong way. The wrong way for some often proves to be the right way for others," Bryce said. "We're sticking with it!"

"Well, in that case you might like Vicky's idea for the gift shop," Kelly said and pulled a piece of paper and a pen from Bryce's desk. All three men noticed how her hands were shaking.

"I don't get it, but Vicky thinks it's hysterical. Print this on T-shirts," Kelly said and showed the men her drawing.

I

'got milk'ed

at

J

The men were laughing.

"Would you wear a T-shirt with that logo?" Matthew said, smiling.

"No way!"

"Why not?"

Cause I'm not a bloody Holstein!

"Vicky would, and she fits your demography better anyway," Kelly huffed.

Outside the hotel Susan arrived at precisely the same time as the cab carrying Jacqui. Susan was panting and red-faced and shook her head at him as he was paying the driver.

"One sly remark out of you, young man, and you'll be singing in the girls' choir," she panted.

Jacqui made the sign for locking his mouth and throwing away the key. They entered the hotel together. Jacqui leaned toward Susan. "Who's the hot redhead?" he whispered looking at the jays' glass enclosed office. The look of astonishment on Susan's face made him catch himself. "I mean, who's the gorgeous creature in this summer's Donatella?" he flopped his hand to his chest. He squinted his eyes and looked puzzled. "Wh... Is that *Kelly*?"

Susan followed his gaze. Her breath got caught in her throat. "Oh, my God! That's ... that's our obligatory Brit!" They entered the office. Susan went straight to Kelly and put her arms around her. "Are you alright, hon?" she said, stroking Kelly's hair.

Kelly nodded. "You heard?"

"I'm so sorry. Will you be going to the funeral?"

Funeral?! Oh, my God! He really is dead! There'll be a funeral and he'll be put in the ground ...

Kelly started crying uncontrollably.

Oh, my God! It's hitting me!

Susan was rocking her. She turned to Matthew. "Do you have a suite for her yet?"

"2211," he said, and helped Susan lead Kelly toward the elevators.

Kelly felt as though the room were spinning and she was walking through a hazy tunnel. The last thing she remembered was falling into a strong pair of arms that effortlessly picked her up, and hearing Susan's muffled voice calling her name.

14

Where am I? Am I dead? Oh. My. God. I've died and heaven is a Ralph Lauren catalogue. Or quite possibly hell...

Groggily, Kelly looked around a large, expensively decorated bedroom. The walls were painted a rich green and the chair rails and furniture were mahogany. The enormous four-poster bed was the most comfortable Kelly had ever experienced. On the walls hung pictures of hunting dogs, horses and old manor houses. The first rays of the early morning sun were shining through heavy plantation shutters, casting a striped glow across the ceiling.

She could hear water running through a door that she assumed led to the bathroom. Just then the water stopped running and the door opened. Parker MacIntyre walked in the room, wearing only a towel around his waist.

Wow! Adonis resurrected!

Parker's upper torso was a mass of bulging muscles. The obvious, high-expense result of years of working out with a personal trainer.

Who undoubtedly goes by the name of Sven or Hans or Günter, and speaks with an accent but is really from Schaumburg.

Parker noticed Kelly's admiring look, and puffed out his chest. He walked over to her and sat, smiling, on the edge of the bed. Kelly pulled the covers up to her chin, and realized that she was stark naked underneath them.

"Good morning, sleeping beauty," Parker said and pecked a small kiss on Kelly's forehead. "How are you feeling?"

"Where am I?" Kelly whispered with a dry throat.

"My bedroom. My condo downtown."

"We… didn't…? You know…?"

Parker's smile widened. "Twice. You were fantastic!" He studied her for a while in silence and then laughed. "I'm only joking. If we'd done it, you'd remember it! Besides, I don't take advantage of unconscious women, no matter how hot they are."

"What happened? How did I get here?"

"How much do you remember?"

"Not much. I was at the hotel. I got dizzy," Kelly started. "A really big woman kept asking me really dumb things."

"That's my housekeeper. She's a certified nurse. She kept asking you who the president was, what day it was, your zip code, how you spell your name and things like that, right?"

Who has a certified nurse on staff, and why was she asking me all that?

"She needed to know that you were coming through your stomach-pump all right. She's nursed Vicky through several of them."

"My stomach was pumped?" Instinctively Kelly put a hand to her stomach.

Does feel nice and flat. Huh?

"Why was my stomach pumped?"

"Mixture of alcohol and illegal Mexican drugs," Parker said and ran his hand through his wet hair. "Vicky gave you something, didn't she?"

Kelly shrugged. "I don't remember."

Like I'm gonna rat on Vicky! Ya think!?

Parker laughed and twirled a lock of her hair between two fingers. "You're a loyal friend, even if it kills you, aren't you? It's all right. You remembered plenty last night," he said with a wink. "Nice to finally know how you really feel about me."

Ohmygodohmygodohmygod!

Suddenly Kelly was painfully aware that she was naked under the covers and felt blood rushing to her cheeks. "Please tell me what happened," she managed in a small voice.

Parker sighed and dropped the lock of hair he'd been playing with. "It hit you. And it all got too much, I guess. Everyone copes with the pain of loss in their own way. After you were released from Northwestern, we brought you here, because it's closer than the Russells' and because I have a full-time nurse on staff. Last night you seemed fine. Conscious. Coherent. You sneaked past the nurse, came to my bedroom and undressed. You told me you needed to be held. So I did. Hold you. You fell asleep, and I moved to one of the guest rooms. Didn't take any of my stuff with me though, so I came in here to shower and shave this morning. And that's the short version. The longer version includes projectile vomiting and passing out in public, and I really don't think you're ready to hear it, judging by the lack of color in your face."

"Thank you," Kelly nodded. "How long was I out?"

"From the last thing you remember to just now? I'd say about thirty-six hours, give or take." Parker was studying her. "How do you feel now?"

Kelly sat up in bed and leaned against the pillows. She smiled at him. "Rested," she said. She ran her fingers through her hair and the covers started slipping off her. Quickly she pulled them back up to her chin.

Parker laughed. "Don't play prudish with me, Irish! I've seen the real McCoy already, and judging from what you told me last night, I don't think you'll mind showing me a whole lot more, am I right?"

Yes!

"That was the drugs talking!"

Parker leaned closer to Kelly and gingerly brushed a hair off her forehead. His touch sent shock waves through her body. He leaned in even closer and started kissing her neck. Small, gentle kisses. He whispered throatily in her ear "Then you *do* mind me doing this, Red?"

Slowly he traced his tongue along her collarbone. With one hand he moved the covers off Kelly and with the other he untied his towel. "You can tell me to stop any time, and I will," he said.

His mouth reached her breasts, and his tongue was playing with one of her nipples. "Tell me you don't like this," he whispered, and climbed into bed.

Will you jest quit talking already! ... Slow down! Hurry up! ... Oh, yeah! Adonis! Most definitely Adonis! ... Yesss!!

15

"No! No! And NO!" Parker was barking into the receiver of his office phone. "I will *not* negotiate with that cabron! I don't care what Duncan did. He could sell sand to Bedouins, and I'm sure he had some hold on these cabrones, too." He was listening to the argument at the other end of the line. "I know it's ice to Eskimos, you half-wit! You think I'm stupid? ... I don't have damn Duncan! If I did, I wouldn't have this conversation with you! ... You go tell that damn cabron and the putas he's got working for him, that I won't negotiate. Don't bother me with this again!"

Parker slammed the receiver down, let out a loud groan and sunk into his chair. Jon knocked on the door and entered.

"What do you want?" Parker said irritated. "I'm in the middle of something. Make it quick."

Jon looked at Parker's empty desk, but decided to ignore it. "Your line was busy..." he said with a confident smile. "I found Duncan."

Parker straightened up and pulled his chair closer to the desk. "Ow... How?" he winced.

"Real estate purchases are public information," Jon said. "Duncan just closed on a house in Georgetown, South Carolina! Taking possession a week from Monday."

"A week from Monday!" Parker exclaimed. "You and I are going to South Carolina! Good job, Terry!"

"Thanks," Jon smiled, then got serious. "How's Kelly?"

Parker grunted. "Fully recovered."

"The girls still planning on going to Charlotte? Maybe they could fly down with us?"

"I think they're set on a road trip. Besides, I don't think they have a date yet. I'll ask," Parker grunted again. "Now go call Candi about the plane!"

Jon winked. "Wouldn't *you* rather call Candi?"

"Just do it!" Parker said impatiently.

Jon started toward the door.

"Hey Terry!" Parker yelled out after him. "Really. Good job finding Duncan."

Jon left the office and closed the heavy double doors behind him. He could hear Parker scream a loud 'Yeaaah!' as he was walking away from the office.

Parker's elderly receptionist smiled at Jon, as he was passing her. "Good news, I hear," she said, nodding toward Parker's closed office doors.

Jon smiled proudly. "We've found Duncan," he said.

"Oh, young Donny!" the receptionist cooed. "How is he?"

"You'll be able to ask him that yourself, pretty soon, I hope," Jon said. "He'll be joining MacIntyre!"

Kelly got out from under Parker's desk. She rested her chin on his knee, smiling from ear to ear. Parker took her face in both hands.

"You were really cutting it close that time, my little vixen," he whispered softly and pulled her onto his lap. "Is it your turn now?" he said reaching a hand into her blouse.

Kelly stuck her tongue in his ear. He groaned.

"I gotta go to the hotel. I've been gone too long already, and they'll be wondering. I haven't exactly made a good first impression," she whispered. "But I'll come by tonight, and we can do that thing you like." She was nibbling softly on his ear lobe. "I'll make it worth your while." She had to tear herself from his grip, and left his office smiling happily.

It had been days since Kelly passed out at the J and although the woman in her would much rather have stayed with Parker, the professional in her ached to get to work. She decided to walk to the J, while listening to her voice-mail messages. It was still early in the morning, but the sun was already high, and the pavement under her feet felt hot. She could tell it was going to be a humid day. She felt like singing and dancing and couldn't stop smiling. A few fellow pedestrians shot her awkward looks, but she didn't notice.

I'm shagging Parker MacIntyre! I've finally had toe-curling sex! A lot! The sexiest man alive made me feel like a woman! She sang to herself as she skipped down the sidewalk.

Her cell phone had been turned off when she was admitted to the hospital, and she hadn't turned it on once since.

Too busy shagging.

"You have. Six. Teen. New messages," the recording announced.

Sixteen!? Kelly gasped.

She started playing them. "Hi Kelly! It's Matthew... Um, Bradshaw... Ah, from work... The J? Anyway, I was worried about you and just wanted to see how you were doing. Hope you're feeling better. Okay... Er, bye."

How sweet.

"Miss McCoy, this is Gina Lombardi, Managing Director of the J Chicago."

Oh, no!

"I know about your little escapade. The J Corporation has a strict zero tolerance policy and as soon as you see fit to return to work, you'll be sent to a drug test. You need to know that your future employment with the J is in serious jeopardy."

Bitch!

"Message deleted."

"Hiya pet! It's Mum!"

God luv ya, Mum!

"Happy birthday!"

Birthday?! Have I really been that euphorically shagged that I forgot me own birthday? He really did shag me brains out like he said he would. Hah-haa... Oooh, Mum's still talking.

"... told me what happened. Hope you're better. They've finally released Sean's body. Well, what's left of it, anyway. That poor Mrs. Molloy, she's so distraught, God love her. She won't have her son's entire body to put in the ground. The funeral's this Friday. That's Friday this week. Friday, June 8th. Susan said you probably won't be able to make it, but Dad and I'll go. Would you like us to lay a wreath ..."

"Message saved for. Five. Days."

Sorry Mum. Can't deal with that just now.

"Hi precious! It's Bryce. I just spoke to Susan and she says you're doing better. Thank God! We were really worried. Matthew hasn't been himself since he took you to the ER."

Matthew took me to the ER?

"... just wanted to give you a word of warning for when you feel you're well enough to come back. The ice biatch is on a warpath, and really has it in for you, for some reason. She thinks you're a druggie," he whispered. "Hope you enjoyed the basket we sent you. Susan told us your favorites. Get well soon!" he ended with a loud smack of a kiss.

Basket? What basket?

"Hi Kelly, it's Jacqui Ashton. Vicky says not to worry; recovery time from a Soberrup-type pill is minimal. See you soon!"

Define minimal.

"It's Vicky! Call me. Bye-eee!"

Hi Vicky! Sorry I've been unable to call you. Been too busy screwing yer dad!

"Hi hen, it's Evan! I just heard about Sean. Serves him right, that cheating Muppet!"

What?!

"No, sorry. I didn't mean that. Sorry. Don't hold it against me fer knowing. Dublin really is a small town, if you think about it. Anyway, if you ever need a friend, I'm here fer you. Do you miss me as much as I miss you? Luv ya, babes!"

Ooow. Luv ya too, Evan!

"Good morning, Miss McCoy, this is Betty, Mr. MacIntyre's housekeeper."

Nurse Betty? Yikes!

"As I haven't seen much of you lately, I'm assuming you're feeling better. A basket was delivered for you this morning."

Aaah...

"... as it contained nothing but what in my professional opinion is rich foods, and since you're not yet well enough to take in solids, I took the liberty of storing the basket in Mr. MacIntyre's pantry. Have a good day."

She should be like that with Vicky, not me!

"Hi Kelly! It's Matthew Bradshaw from the J again. I hope you're feeling better. They called from EUSA and want to see you on June 18th. That's next Monday. I don't

know why they wouldn't call you directly, but … anyway …
Take your time recuperating. If there's ever anything I can
do for you, please just give me a call. Day or night. Hope
you're feeling better. Oh, I already said that… Well, I mean
it. Bye."

*Ooow! He's sweet! Hmmm? He's right, though. Why would
they not call me? Uh-oh, me voicemail still plays condolence message. Must change that.*

"Kelly, it's Susan. Parker says you're fully recovered.
Please call me. Bye."

*God! What a guilt-trip! Must lay off shagging fer a while and
catch up with friends who care.*

Kelly reached the hotel and decided to save listening to
the rest of the messages for later. She entered the hotel.

Whatta fock?! Have the aliens landed?!

The lobby was covered with white dust. The marble,
carpet and all furniture had been removed, and at the far
wall two figures in white, hooded coveralls, hard hats, safety
goggles and dust masks were sledge hammering the wall
between the bar and the lobby. Another five people in the
same attire arrived, carrying empty white buckets. Kelly felt
unable to move or form a coherent thought.

How long was I out?

"Kelleeey!"

She heard a bodiless voice and a small coveralled person
threw herself around her neck and immediately another
four followed. Kelly was engulfed in a dusty alien-abduc-
tion-type group hug.

"I'm so glad you're feeling better!" The bearer of the voice stood at arms length from Kelly and removed her dust mask.

"Susan! Oh, my God! Look at you! What *are* you wearing? You look like a Space alien!"

"We're rebuilding the lobby!" another enthusiastic voice said.

Kelly looked around the group as they were all removing their goggles and dust masks.

"Jacqui?" she said in astonishment.

Doing physical labor? Dirty, dusty physical labor at that. Wearing what could only be described as 'off the shelf'.

"Bryce? Alen? Matthew?!" she looked around the room.

Don't tell me Willy Wonka's little helper with the sledgehammer is Gina!

"What's going on? Am I dreaming or is this some sort of sick joke?"

"How are you feeling, precious?" Bryce said. "You look fabulous. I never got to say it, but I just adore what Roberto did to your hair! That wild, maintained look is so now!"

"Thank you," Kelly said and ran her hand through her red mane.

Wild, maintained? JGF, more like.

"Ahem, so … how are you feeling?" Matthew asked uncomfortably.

"Well, I'm here, and by the looks of you lot, you could use another set of hands," she said and looked around the room again. "Oh, and thank you all for the lovely well-wishes and that beautiful basket. Meant the world to me that you care."

"We're just glad to see you back on your feet, hon," Susan said and put a protective arm around Kelly's waist. "You really gave us a royal scare."

Kelly blushed.

Back on my feet? Should I tell her that I've been stuck between a bed and a hard guy fer the past … how many days now…? Prubly not a good time, with Jacqui hovering over her.

"Yeah, sorry about that. It'll never happen again. I know my limits now, and intend to stick within them." She turned to Bryce and Alen. "I've still got a job?"

"Of course! Why would you even ask that?" Bryce said.

"Well, apparently Ms. Lombardi's sending me to a drug test," Kelly whispered, looking at the two people still sledge hammering in the corner.

"You don't have to whisper," Susan whispered, "she's not here."

"Look, princess," Bryce said and put and arm around Kelly's shoulders. "Alen and I hired you and only we can fire you. But, yes, the company does have a zero tolerance policy, and every new hire must pass the drug test prior to employment. That does include you, I'm afraid."

"And Matthew, incidentally," Alen filled in. "Still needs to leave a sam-ple," he singsonged and looked over at Matthew. He blushed and turned his eyes to the floor.

"Don't worry, though," Jacqui said. "They test for illegal drugs only. Vicky would rather, like, go clean than touch that filth. What she gave you was probably American prescription medication sold over the counter in Mexico, that's all."

That's all*?! Jaysus! Wonder what it really was that I took, then? Someone's hemorrhoid medication? Gout pills? Viagra? … Well, that would certainly explain a lot!*

"Anyway," Alen continued, "you're not officially on the payroll yet. Right now you're just a beautiful friend, who's come to help us with the lobby, right?"

Kelly nodded. "Right," she said and rolled up her sleeves. "How can I be of use, then?"

"Matthew?" Bryce said. "Get Kelly suited up!"

As they were walking to the jays' office Kelly turned to Matthew. "So, why exactly are we doing this? Don't they normally hire contractors?"

"Local 765 went on strike as of midnight Monday. We have less than a month until we open, so it's pretty much all hands on deck or postpone opening. There really was no option."

Kelly was silent for a while. "So, how will you do any hiring or training in this mess?"

"Good question!" Matthew laughed. "Luckily all applicants know that we're in the pre-opening phases, so nobody's really been bothered. Quite the opposite, actually. Everyone seems excited to have some part in the process. And Kristin's been an awesome help in pre-screening candidates. Did you see those two guys with the sledgehammers in the corner? One's the new Director of Engineering, Dan. The other's Mitchell, the Rooms Director. Stole both of them from the Drake. They've been awesome. Strong, hard working, know what they're doing. Like to run them through a Xerox."

What kinda sick, perverted mind... Oh, duplicate them ... Right ...

In the jays' office Matthew gave Kelly coveralls, a hard hat, a pair of work gloves, a dust mask and a pair of goggles.

"Sorry, they only come in white one-size-fits-all," he said awkwardly as Kelly took the hooded coveralls. "But then again, you seem to look great in anything..." Matthew was blushing again.

Is he flirting with me?

"Mr. Bradshaw, are you flirting with me?"

Matthew avoided looking directly at her. "No, just stating a fact. You sure you're well enough to do this? You don't have to, you know. I'm sure Kristin wouldn't mind someone helping her with the applications."

"Too late," Kelly said climbing into the coveralls. "My mind's made up. What, you don't think I can handle swinging a sledge hammer? Bring it on, Chief!" She was pulling her hair back into a ponytail.

"A girl like you shouldn't even know what a sledge hammer is," Matthew said quietly. "All right then, but as you're not officially employed here yet, I feel obligated to tell you that if you're injured in any way..."

"...the J Corporation cannot be held responsible," Kelly finished. "I know, I know, let's go do some damage already!"

So that's why he was being so worried about me! He thought I'd hold the company responsible fer passing out on property! Hmph. And here I thought he was just being sweet. Who was I kidding?

Kelly and Susan were hauling construction debris to the dumpster behind the hotel. They were alone in the back alley.

Kelly turned to Susan. "I've been dying to tell you something!" she whispered.

"What?!" Susan whispered, hoping for something juicy.

"I've got to tell you because you've been so worried, and I feel like I've been deceiving you. It didn't take me this long to recover from my stomach pump." Kelly felt smug. "I'm sleeping with Parker."

Susan looked like she had swallowed something sour. "Parker?" she hissed. "Parker MacIntyre?!!"

Kelly nodded, smiling happily.

"Oh, no, Kelly."

What?! He's listed on both Fortune 500 and Sexiest Man Alive! You told me so yerself!

"What? He's really good!"

"Of course he's good! He's had a lot of practice!"

Okay, the reasoning sounded much better as a thought bubble...

"He's far too old for you, Kelly. And he's a womanizer, and he moves in circles you can only dream about! He'll end up hurting you."

"I'm aware of that," Kelly said defiantly.

They stood in silence for a while.

"Are you in love with him?" Susan finally asked.

Kelly shrugged. "I don't know. I haven't really stopped long enough to think about it. I think I love him … in a way, just don't know if I like him a lot of the time."

"And that's your first problem right there. If you're just in it for the sex, then fine, you don't have to like your bed partner. But if you're hoping for something more serious, you'd better love him, be in love with him and like him."

That's not possible. Men like that don't exist. Oh, du-uh! Jonathan Russell, of course.

Susan took a long breath. "Promise me two things. Don't get your hopes up, because that man changes women as often as other men change socks. And pray that Jon never finds out."

Jacqui appeared in the alley. "Here you are!" he said nervously. "I've looking all over for you. Are you alright? Is everything alright? Do you need help? Let me get that for you!"

He was fussing about like a jaybird, dumping the last of the debris from Susan's bucket into the dumpster. Susan shook her head at Kelly behind his back. Kelly took the bucket away from him.

"I think we can manage, thank you."

"Go back inside, we'll be there before you miss us," Susan told Jacqui.

Looking morose, he started for the back door. "But I miss you already," he mumbled under his breath.

A sharp whistle interrupted the lobby crew. "Okay, Oompa Loompas!" Kristin, Gina's assistant, said, pen poised on pad. "I'm taking lunch orders. Who wants what?"

The group heaved a simultaneous sigh of relief.

"Finally!" Alen said.

Kelly turned to Susan as Kristin was taking orders. "Where you ordering from?" she said taking her gloves off.

Susan smiled. "The Grill, where else? We've had two meals a day delivered from there since Monday. The jays now have a corporate account there. Place your order," she said, as Kristin looked at her expectantly.

"I'll have the Colby burger, well-done, no onion, heavy on the ketchup. But on the side, please. Side order of grilled green beans, butter on the side, double redskins and a pickle, please," Kelly said.

"Ooo-kay, Meg Ryan," Kristin said with a smirk "Anything to drink?"

"Oh, yeah, large milk. Thanks," Kelly said and looked around the lobby.

Everyone had become quiet. They were all looking at her. Jacqui's face was filled with disgust. Matthew smiled approvingly. Bryce and Alen looked disbelieving, and Susan was trying to suppress a laugh.

"What?" Kelly said.

Susan started laughing. "Hungry? Pregnant? Or still unfamiliar with portion control?"

"I've been on a drip, fer fock's sake! I want real food, now that I've shaken nurse Ratchet off my back!"

And I'm starved from being Parker's personal sex toy for days on end.

Susan quickly grabbed Kelly and spun her around. "Keep working, and don't look up," she whispered.

Jacqui appeared by Kelly's side and started gathering debris into his bucket.

"What's going on?" Kelly whispered, annoyed, on her knees in rubble.

Jacqui placed himself between Kelly and the front door. "Gina," he whispered between clenched teeth. Kelly was about to turn around. "Don't look!" he hissed.

Gina strolled into the lobby, followed by a young Asian man in a black suit and tie. He was carrying her briefcase, and was grinning. For no apparent reason. Gina motioned for Bryce and Alen to approach.

"This is Charles Shoe. He's my new intern. He comes to us from EUSA by way of South Korea, and I think I'll start him out as a Revenue Manager," Gina said nonchalantly. "Charles, these are Bryce Hart and Alen Marshall. The owners."

The three men shook hands.

"Your name is Shoe?" Alen asked.

"Yes, Cho. Jaws Cho," Charles kept grinning.

"And just how much experience do you have in Revenue Management?" Bryce frowned.

"I have MBA hottell management flom kennel," Charles announced haughtily and virtually gleamed.

"That's not quite what I asked," Bryce said and frowned at Gina.

"We'll start him off on a trial basis," Gina huffed. "He's on a J-1 trainee salary and will not require room and board."

Ouch! That was a stab at me! Kelly peeked out from behind Susan and Jacqui.

"Charles has excellent records from Cornell, and he passed the drug test," Gina continued.

Zinger!

"And he's already got his visa, so we can get him started immediately," Gina concluded.

Man! She's just sniping at me without even reloading!

Kelly rose to her feet and was about to say something to Gina. Susan and Jacqui pulled her back down.

"Now's not the time, hon," Susan whispered.

"We already have a perfectly competent director of revenue," Bryce started.

"Who works out of an office in New York?" Gina said. "Please! What good could he possibly do from there?"

"Oh, I don't know," Bryce said. "Ever heard of a darling little invention called the computer? He's fabulous and has run both our San Fran and Phoenix revenue departments beautifully from New York. I don't see the problem."

"The problem is that you now have three properties, and just closed on a fourth. Is he going to run all the revenue departments by himself once you're a national chain? I think not. Charles will help him set things up here in Chicago." With that, Gina turned on her heel and left the hotel, Charles in tow.

At the future staff cafeteria in the basement of the soon-to-be J Hotel, the group of workers were quietly enjoying their lunches. The jays, Kelly, Susan and Kristin were sitting at one table, Jacqui, Mitchell, Dan and Matthew at the other.

Alen was eyeing the other table. "I think my theory is valid, B. Jacqui has issues."

"Told you so," Bryce singsonged.

"What theory is that?" Susan asked curiously.

"Wee-eell," Alen said. "My personal theory is, that you can tell what kind of lover your man is by his table manners," he finished nobly and wiped his mouth. He looked around the table to make sure all ears were on him.

"Take young Jacqui, here, for example," Alen said, nodding toward the other table. "He's a typical type D."

"What's a type D?" Kelly asked.

"I'm so glad you asked, precious," Alen said. "A type D is a man who picks at his own food, eats with his elbow on the table and takes food off your plate without asking. Now, as a lover he's very much the same. Uncertain of his own sexuality. Doesn't know where to put it. Doesn't know where anything is. Like our Jacqui here."

All five turned toward the other table, to watch Jacqui move food around his plate. Susan and Kristin tried to suppress a laugh.

Or he could have his elbow on the table because he was brought up without a Mum telling him not to.

"A type A will inhale his food," Alen continued, rolling his eyes. "He can't carry on a conversation during a meal, but rest assured, by the time you've buttered your bun, he will have finished his entire entree. As a lover, he takes what he wants, or needs, with no concern for yours."

Alen paused to take a sip of his mineral water. The other four at the table were mesmerized.

"Oh, and a type A will leave the table while you're still eating." Alen paused for effect, and let the group figure out his table-to-bed-manners comparison.

Parker. Type A. Of course. A for Alpha male.

"Now, a type B is the one you want. Not only will he savor every mouthful, like it's rich with an essence he hasn't experienced before. He'll enjoy it so much that he will share. He'll offer his plate for you to cut your own piece, if you wish. Your choice. Thoughtful, caring, selfless. Like our Mr. Bradshaw here. Gentle, tender, considerate of your needs." He took a deep sigh and all of them were watching Matthew enjoy his burger.

"Oh, honey! Dubya double oh why el!" Susan limp-wristed.

Kristin turned to Susan. "What?!"

"Way out of your league!" Susan whispered from the corner of her mouth.

"You think so?" Alen huffed. "I could have Matthew if I wanted and if he *played* in my league."

God, I wish I hadn't let Vicky talk me into buying this damn thong underwear! And why am I wearing them today? Wish moo-moos would come back in fashion. Hmmm? Wonder what me pulling out butt floss at the table says about my bedside manner?... Oooh, what did I miss of the conversation? ... Parker's an A, Jon's a B, Jacqui's a D ... and then what?

"… brings me to type C" Alen continued. "He'll order for you in a restaurant, decide the menu at home and then have you cook it. He'll decide when, how much and what you eat. He's as demanding and abusive in the bedroom as he is in the kitchen, be it emotionally, physically or verbally, and you should run before you get too involved."

The table sat silently for a while.

"And on what do you base this theory?" Susan asked.

"Personal observations. So far, excluding young Jacqui here, it has a seventy-five percent statistical probability …"

"You've actually tried this theory out in practice?" Susan gasped.

"Of course!" Alen hissed back. "But no, I haven't slept with a hundred men, and I know that's what you're thinking. In the past week I've had four business dinners, and the wives seemed ever so comfortable with confiding in me. Three out of four of those wives confirmed my theory."

16

"Daddy, can I have the plane this weekend?" Vicky said with her sweetest, most innocent voice. She ran a finger along the edge of Parker's desk. "Pretty please?"

Parker looked up from his laptop. "What?!" he bellowed. "What do you need it for?"

"Ohmygosh! I just got dibs on this totally awesome crib in Palo Alto, and, you know, if I don't see it, like, right now, I might not get it," Vicky ranted, eyes gleaming.

Parker removed his reading glasses and pinched the bridge of his nose. "Remind me again why you need an apartment in Palo Alto?" he said patiently.

"Oh, Daddy-yy! You never *listen* to me! I told you no one in grad school lives on campus!"

"Campus? What the hell are you talking about, Victoria?"

"Hello-oo?! Like, I'm going to Stanford? In the fall?!"

"What?!"

"I told you!"

"I think I'd remember something like that! When did you tell me?"

"Like, a year ago? When I got accepted? Gawd, you're really getting old!"

"Drop the attitude, young lady," Parker waved a finger in her face.

"Sorry, Daddy," Vicky said miserably, and peeked at him from under her brow. "May I pleeease have the plane?"

Parker studied her in silence for a while. "You're still grounded, you know."

"For what?!"

"For slipping Kelly a mickey!"

"You never told me I was grounded!"

"I sure did! Why don't you ever listen to me?" Parker was mocking Vicky.

"I'm almost twenty-one! You can't keep grounding me!"

"Wanna bet?"

They sat silent for a while, eyeing each other like two bulls about to charge. The air in the office was electric. Vicky's lower lip started to pout and finally Parker relented.

"You're not going unchaperoned," he said sternly.

"I'll take Kelly!"

"I think Kelly'll be busy this weekend," Parker mused. "Ahem, ... heard Jon say something. Take Jack."

"Thanks Daddy!" Vicky rushed around Parker's desk and gave him a big kiss. "Tell Candi to get ready!"

"When are you leaving?"

"Du-uh! Right now!" Vicky left the office, already dialing Jacqui's number.

"I'm too shattered to think straight, Parker, let alone perform any physical acts," Kelly yawned into her cell phone.

It was late Friday night and they had finally finished tearing down the dividing walls in the lobby and cleaning up the debris. The weather had become increasingly more hot and humid, and the air conditioning in the lobby had been disabled because of the dust they were generating. After two weeks there were no break-throughs in the contract negotiations with the union, so the group had decided to start laying the floor tile themselves first thing Monday. Dan found a group of non-union painters who were coming in over the weekend.

Kelly's body was aching all over from swinging a sledgehammer and carrying cinder blocks to the dumpster. Dan finally arrived on Tuesday morning with four new wheelbarrows, which had been an enormous help. After finishing on Friday the rest of the group went to the Jim spa, to relax in the hot tub. Kelly was too exhausted to join them, so she just went upstairs to her suite and crashed on her bed.

"I don't need you to perform any physical acts," Parker said huskily. "I just want you to be there when I do."

"I can't, Parker. I'm hot and dusty and sore all over."

"So come on over, we'll get in the Jacuzzi and I'll give you a nice massage."

Mmmm-yeaaah …

"I'll rub your back if you'll rub my front," he whispered suggestively.

…and he's back to Arsehole!

"Look," Kelly said patiently. "As appealing as that offer sounds…" *Not!* "…I think I'd just much rather go to bed. Alone. I'll see you Sunday night."

"Sunday? Why not until Sunday?"

"Remember? I told you? Emma Russell's birthday. Plus, I need to move my things out of the Russells' house. They've hired a new au pair, and they need my room…"

"Listen, if you won't give me what I need, I'll find someone who will."

"Yeah, you do that, Parker." Kelly hung up and tossed her phone on the bed.

Arrogant bastard!

The phone rang immediately. Kelly looked at the display. It read 'Parker office'.

Oh, God. I don't think I have energy fer this.

"Kelly Mc…"

"Don't you ever hang up on me!" Parker interrupted her. "Who do you think you are?"

Kelly hung up.

Who do you think you are? I'm not yer bloody beck and call girl!

Her cell phone rang again. Parker. Kelly switched the phone off.

Please, just give me one night off. You're a great lay, but a horrible person.

Suddenly the phone in her suite rang.

He's gonna keep bothering me until I answer, isn't he? God! Men really are from Mars, women … are not.

Kelly straightened her aching back, reached for her key and left the suite to join her friends at the spa.

"So, I'm to baby-sit the heiress this weekend, am I?" Candi's voice was acid over the phone.

Parker had called her to prepare the plane for his children. "God, what's with women today? Is there a full moon, or something?"

"What the hell are you talking about? Oh, never mind. I get it. Your little Shamrock won't put out. Am I right?"

"Candi, need I remind you that you are first and foremost my pilot? The fact that we have a history in the bedroom doesn't give you the right to act like the jealous little wife. Cause you're not. Just remember that. We will never get married. Now you get your tight little ass to the airport and prep the plane and take my children to wherever they want to go! And be nice to them! Do I make myself clear?"

"Yes, sir…"

"Be back Sunday night and prep for early departure Monday morning." Parker hung up, sat back in his chair and sighed deeply. "Women!" he said to himself. "Can't live with 'em and can't *live* with 'em!"

Opening the front entrance door to Jim the gym, Kelly was nearly run over by Jacqui exiting. He looked flustered and excited.

"Ohmygosh, Kelly!" he said. "Vicky and I are flying to California tonight. Wanna go with?"

Are ya friggin kidding me? I don't have the energy to go across town let alone across the country.

She shook her head. "I have neither the energy, nor the money for a last-minute ticket."

"We're taking Daddy's jet."

Daddy's jet? Oh, right! Daddy does have a jet! Penis extension fer a middle aged man.

"You'll be back by Monday, I hope. Vicky and I were supposed to go to North Carolina for my interview," Kelly said.

"Don't worry, angel," Jacqui air-kissed Kelly on both sides of her face. "Susan and I are meeting the jays in Asheville on Monday, so we'll be back! Have a great weekend! Maybe we'll meet up for drinks in Charlotte?!" he said as he hailed a taxi.

So, that just leaves Matthew, Dan and Mitchell to do the tiling. Doesn't seem fair. Maybe Gina and that Charles could lend a hand? Hah-haa... More likely to get Parker to wear tights and

*bunny ears than to get Gina to do anything. ... Oooh, bunny
ears ... must talk to him about that! ... Oh, no! Am mad at him!
Right...*

Through the glass wall in the gym, Kelly could see Susan
engaged in deep conversation with another woman. Kelly
tapped on the glass and Susan waved her in.

"I'm so glad you're here, hon," Susan said. "I tried to
call your room..."

*So that was you just then, not Parker. Thank God! Almost lost
all respect fer him.*

"...look who I ran into!" Susan continued and pulled
Kelly over to the lady she had been talking to. "Oh, that's
right! You've never actually met. Kelly, this is Kate!"

*Kate? Too knackered to think Kate who. ... Oh, Kate! My im-
migration lawyer, Kate Fleming! Is she just Kate now?*

"Nice to finally meet you in person, Kate," Kelly said
and shook her hand. "I've been meaning to thank you for
trying to ..."

"Yeah, yeah, yeah," Susan interrupted impatiently, flick-
ing her hand. "Kelly, Kate's just told me something really
disturbing. Tell her, Kate."

"Well, I understand from Susan that you're about to
apply for a J-1 visa," she said looking at Kelly for acknowl-
edgement. She nodded. "I should tell you right off the bat,
that it's not likely to be approved. J-1's are rarely, if ever,
renewed."

"I'm not trying to get it renewed yet. I'm just trying to
get it," Kelly said.

"And what type of visa are you on right now?"

"Au Pair."

"In government terms, J-1."

Nooooo!

"S-so what do I do?"

"You could try to go for it, but in my experience it will most likely be a waste of time and money. They tend to look at the average immigration rate from your country of citizenship over the past five years before issuing any more visas. And as we're almost in the third quarter, my guess is that the quota for this year has been filled."

Irish immigrants! Why don't they just bloody stay home! Ireland's a nice place to live now! ... What am I thinking? I'm trying to leave!

"Kelly, darling, you decided to join us!" Alen's elated voice echoed behind Kelly. He was wearing swim trunks and had draped a towel around his neck. "You must try the hot tub! I don't know what they put in the water here, but whatever it is, it's absolutely fabulous!"

Yum! Very 'my body is my temple'. Just as I suspected. Fake tan, but who cares! Wow! What a body to fake a tan! ... Wish he weren't gay ...

Matthew appeared next to Alen, also in swim trunks. "What's going on?" he was looking at Kelly.

Yuuummmyyy!

Kelly was taking in the package that was Matthew. Very lean. No bulging muscles, but also no fat. Very fit. Skin lightly freckled. Abs just as rippled as Alen's.

So I guess the old adage is true, then. All the best men are either married or gay. ... Hail to the Chief! Boy-next-door, my arse! If the boy next door had looked anything like him, I'da stayed home! Wow! He really is like a life-size, anatomically correct, Ken-doll! ... Oh, yes, and charming and intelligent and funny. Mustn't become shallow and empty and focus only on physical appear ... Holy Mother of God! What is that?

Kelly's gaze fell on a scar the size of a golf ball on Matthew's forearm.

Gross!

"War wound," Matthew said with a smile, as if reading Kelly's mind. "Took a piece of shrapnel in the first Gulf War." He put a hand on the scar, and rubbed it with a painful expression on his face. "Yup, ah feel rain's a-comin'."

Everyone was looking at him. Susan broke the silence. "Aren't you a bit too young to have served in the first Gulf War?"

Matthew chuckled. "Damn! Forgot you knew my age, Suze."

Suze? Since when are they so chummy? Not even Jon calls her that!

"So, what is that, then?" Kelly asked.

"Had some pre-cancerous cells removed," he said matter-of-factly. "Totally benign. So what's the big pow-wow about?"

Kelly bit her lower lip. Suddenly she felt even more exhausted. "I don't qualify for a J-1 visa."

"What?!" Matthew said. "Are you serious? Why?"

Kelly introduced Matthew and Alen to Kate and asked her to explain it to them.

"So, is there another visa we could try for?" Alen asked when Kate had finished. "What's that one called, where the employer has to prove that he couldn't find a suitable American applicant to fill the position? You know the one I'm talking about?"

"Temporary skilled worker," Kate said. "Or H-1B, if you wish."

"That's the one! Would she qualify for that?"

"Possibly. Would you be willing to sponsor her?"

"Absolutely! Whatever it takes," Alen said enthusiastically.

"The burden of proof is intensely arduous and entirely on your shoulders, obviously. Since nine eleven the government doesn't issue H-1B's very generously," Kate said thoughtfully. "Her odds would probably be better applying for the H-3, which is another training visa, similar to the J-1, but good for two years. Let me think about this. Who should I contact?"

"Me!" Kelly and Matthew answered in unison. Kelly laughed. "E-mail me, and cc Matthew." She gave Kate the contact information and excused herself to go to bed.

Back in her room, Kelly turned her phone on again and listened to Parker's message.

"Look, Red, I'm sorry. I haven't seen much of you lately, and, ... well, I miss you. I hope you'll still let me fly you and Vicky to Charlotte on Monday. I'd like to enroll you in the mile-high club ... Is there anything I can do to help you finish that damn lobby faster, so you can spend more time with me? What do you need? Supplies? Cash? Labor? Let me know what I can do. Again, I'm sorry. I miss you. Now go get some rest. Good night."

Ooow! That's so sweet! And he's back to Adonis!

She started dialing his number.

Hmmm? Better not. Don't want to seem needy. Although he did call me first, so it would be more like politely returning a call. Also, he might know of experienced, non-union tilers and electricians. Besides, he needs to know that there's not going to be a trip to Charlotte fer me now. Good! More than plenty of reasons to call!

She hesitated.

Maybe I should just e-mail him. Where from, though? Fingerprint locks on all office doors... I wish they'd program my wi-fi already ... Shouldn't be so greedy ... Got a grand set-up here ...

She looked around her room.

Wonder what I did with that PDA Matthew gave me?

With her back still aching, she was agonizingly turning her suite upside down in search for the PDA box. She realized that she had never received any instruction in the use of it.

How hard can it be? Surely it comes with a manual? Ah-haa! Found it!

Eagerly she opened the box.

Where is it?

As she suspected, the box did contain a manual, but also an instruction booklet to InnTime, and a nametag.

Kelly McCoy, Public Image Manager. Public Image Manager?? Whatta fock's that, and when did I agree to be one? Mental note to self, must talk to jays re title Monday. Oy! Maybe I can program a reminder to meself in me PDA? … If I could find it…

She emptied the rest of the contents of the box on her bed. It contained a charger for the PDA, a USB cord, a silver and a leather business card holder and a small instruction booklet to Aaria, but no PDA.

Huh? I know I didn't take it out. Only time I ever opened this box was to remove the key. Maybe Matthew forgot to put it back in the box after he programmed it.

She reached for the phone and dialed Matthew's office number.

Hope he's back from the tub.

"I thought you were going to bed," Matthew answered after the second ring.

"How'd you know it was me?"

"Display on my phone. What can I do for you?"

"Do you have my PDA?"

"I'm pretty sure I gave it to you. In a little box with your key and other pertinent information."

"Yeah, I've got the box…"

"What's in it?"

"Well, the only things relating to the PDA are the charger, the USB and the manual."

"What else's in the box?"

"Something about Aaria and InnTime, two business card holders …"

"One of them silver, the other leather?"

"Yeah."

"Open the silver one," Matthew said patiently.

They've already printed business cards fer me? That was quick. Kelly McCoy, Public Image Manager. Starting to like that …

"Whatta fock?!" She was staring at a miniature computer screen.

"And now you've found your PDA."

Focketyfockfock!

"And the leather one's the case! I'm really not an eejit, you know?" Kelly insisted.

"I never thought you were, Kelly. Good night. Call me if you need help with it," Matthew said, and they hung up.

Okay. So that was embarrassing.

Kelly made herself comfortable on her bed and pulled up the PDA and its manual.

Let's see.

She thumbed through the manual.

'How to send e-mail'. *Perfect. Nice color pictures. Oooh! Look! I've got a pointy thingy! Way cool!*

She laughed to herself as she turned the plastic pen between her fingers like a baton.

I'm sounding more like Vicky every day! Now, then, let's concentrate.

She kept looking at the graphs in the manual.

Looks really straightforward. Much like regular email, only smaller. 'Select 'E-Mail' icon from Desktop'. *Okay, let's get to business. … Desktop is blank. Oooh, should probably turn it on. Where's 'On' button?*

She kept turning the PDA in her hands.

Why do they have to make everything so tiny? This is really aggravating! I can see Mum's point now! Aaargh! … Oooh! 'On' button! Found it!

She was hitting it with her thumb.

Why is this thing not working? Do I now have me Mum's fat fingers?!

She tried turning it on with the 'pointy thingy'. Nothing happened.

Maybe I don't have reception in this room. Don't you need that fer these multi-functional apparatus?

She got up and went to the window seat and hit the on button again. Nothing.

This thing is broken. They gave me a defective PDA.

The phone in her room rang and startled her. She leapt for it, hoping it would be Parker.

"Hi, Kelly, it's Matthew. I don't think you're an idiot, I just think that maybe you're not used to PDA's," he said. "They use up a lot of battery, and need to be charged all the time. Just thought I'd give you a heads-up."

Charged!

Kelly laughed nervously. "That's grand, Chief. Thanks a mil! Good night."

I'm an eejit!

17

To: kmccoy@jhotels.com
From: Parker MacIntyre
Subject: Re: J-1 no-go
Good morning, sexy!
I suggest you go to Charlotte, as planned.
Have that company apply for the J-1 for you
and simultaneously have Kate Fleming work
on this H-3. Play the odds. Kate is good. She'll
come up with something else, if neither of the
above works out.
Don't worry about the cost. You have good
credit with me. I'm sending a crew of tile in-
stallers over on Monday, and the electricians
will be there Tuesday morning. Who should
they ask for?
PMI

"Hiya Chief!" Kelly said as she poked her head in
Matthew's office. "Sooo glad to see you here this bright and

early on a Saturday morning. I've got two things...," she caught herself and looked at his unshaven face and crumpled outfit. It was the same outfit he had worn the day before. "Why are you here this bright and early on a Saturday morning?"

Matthew nodded and pointed toward the connecting doors. Kelly looked inside. A cot had been placed there. Matthew raised a hand in resignation. "Please, don't ask. Did you get your PDA working?" She blushed and nodded. "Now, what can I do for you today?" he said taking a long sip of his coffee.

"Ask not, Mr. B., what you can do for me, ask what you can do for your company!" she started ceremoniously. She sat down and with a wide smile opened that morning's newspaper on Matthew's desk. "Read the Trib this morning?

"Sure..." Matthew said hesitantly. "What'd I miss?"

Kelly pointed at an article about a local girl-scout troop sending cookies to American forces in Iraq. Matthew looked at the article, then at Kelly. He was dumbfounded.

"Yeah? So?"

"Don't you see?"

"Ahem. I'm not sure I know where you're going with this..." Matthew started, trying hard not to look at her outfit.

Kelly had awoken to the newspaper being delivered and was now sitting in Matthew's office wearing nothing but her robe over a pair of boy briefs and a tank top. She was barefoot and her hair was pulled into a loose bun on top of her head. She hadn't thought twice of it. Matthew was visibly uncomfortable.

"These are young, fit men and women in the prime of their lives, protecting world freedom, millions of miles from their homes and loved ones," Kelly started. "They face death every day. They're homesick. Once they return, you can bet they'll look up those girl scouts."

Matthew's face was perplexed.

He can't really be that thick?!

"Don't you get it?" Kelly nearly yelled. "Send them a care package! 'Thank you for your efforts.' Signed the J Hotel Chicago! Once they come home and want to have an intimate weekend with their significant other, who're they gonna call? Us!"

Matthew's eyes started gleaming. "Oh, I get it! We can send them something really cool! Oh, and if we buy in bulk, I bet we can get the same deal those girl scouts got. Or, better yet, get sponsorship!"

He got up from behind his desk and walked to Kelly's side of it. He sat down on the desk. "Imagine the publicity! We have to find a Midwest unit. Dan's a former Navy guy. He'd know! Oh, Bryce and Alen will love this idea!"

"And," Kelly continued excitedly, "I spoke to a British friend of me Dad's, who just got back from over there, and asked him what his troops would've appreciated the most, and here's a list," Kelly said, pulling a slip of paper from the pocket of her robe.

Matthew skimmed the list. "… decent sunglasses … uh-huh … cotton socks … doable … what?…mail?" he looked incredulously at Kelly.

"Yup! That's what he said. Now, they love getting American candy bars, but it's so hot, that by the time it reaches the desert stations, it's become chocolate syrup. And most troops do have access to the Internet, but what they really miss is hearing from real people, he says. It could be anyone. It could be their neighbor, or Donna-Mae, a fifth-grade teacher from Pigeon Butt, Alabama, or … well … Vicky!"

"Ahem, … actually, it's Pigeon *Butte*, Alabama," Matthew said, holding back a smile.

"Oh, sorry. Everything was done by IM… And how was I supposed to know, anyway? You've got such bizarre names for places in this country!"

"Such as?" Matthew looked quizzically at Kelly.

"Well … such as … Normal, Illinois, or … Gas City, Indiana, … or …,"

Why can't I think of any more? This was such a fun car game with Abby and Emma, driving down to Florida.

Matthew was looking down at her, smiling.

"Or Buffalo!" Kelly exclaimed.

Matthew held up a hand, his smile widened. "Okay, I'll give you Gas City, but what's wrong with Buffalo?"

Yeah, what is wrong with Buffalo? Maybe this game is best left to children.

"I'll let you know, once I think of something clever. So whaddya think of this idea?"

"I think it's excellent. Good work, girl wonder." He reached to hug her, and suddenly became aware of her being nearly naked. He stretched out his hand and she shook it. Then he hesitated. "Gina might not like it, though," he said chewing his bottom lip.

"Why not? Free publicity? Increased revenue? What's not to like?"

"The company is supposed to be religiously and politically independent."

"What's religious or political about sending the troops some cotton socks? It's not like we're taking sides either for or against the war! I mean, the troops are already there, fer fock's sake! We're just trying to make life a little less difficult, so that they can come home and come spend some money with J. What's wrong with that?"

Matthew smiled. "Tell you what. I'll talk to the jays and you to Gina," he said with a wink.

Yeah, that's as likely to happen as Finland winning the Eurovision Song contest! No, wait - that actually did eventually happen. Okay, then, it's as unlikely to happen as the Sox winning the World Series! ... Didn't that just happen, too? What's wrong with my brain this morning?

"I have a better idea. You talk to Gina and I'll take care of the jays."

Matthew laughed. "I'll fight you for it. Winner tells the jays."

"You're on, Chief! Name your game!"

"Bryce tells me you're an ace in tennis."

"I don't know about ace, but I do play. Do you?"

"Haven't for a long time. I used to play some when I lived in Boca."

"What's a boca?"

"Boca Raton, Florida."

Well, no wonder he's got skin cancer. Complexion like his belongs in … Reykjavik, not Boca.

Matthew was smiling at her. "Spanish for Mouth of the Rat."

"Well, there ya have it! I rest my case! Winner of the bizarre place name game; Mouth of the Rat!" Kelly laughed. "You free today? I'm going to the Russells anyway. They've got a court. And a pool, so bring your trunks!"

"You're on! How soon can you be ready?" he looked awkwardly at her outfit.

"Let me make the necessary phone calls, and I'll let you know. Got a car?"

Matthew nodded. Kelly was heading toward the door. "What's the second thing?" he said.

"What?"

"You came in and said you had two things."

"Oh, yeah. Pha … um …Vicky's Dad will send professional tilers and electricians to help with the lobby. No charge."

Actually I don't know that, but somehow I'll make it up to him. Mmmm... Will I ever!

"Anyway, they need a contact person. Should I tell them you?"

Matthew laughed. "I'm not even gonna ask how the two of you cooked that up, but thank you. And yes, please, give them my name. And also, please let everyone know about this."

"Everyone who?"

"The jays, Susan, Mitch and Dan," Matthew said. "And I'll let Gina know," he continued smiling.

Kelly pulled out her PDA from her robe pocket and started for the door again.

"Just one more thing, Kelly," Matthew said, face slightly crimson. "Did anyone see you walking the hallways in that ... um ... getup?"

Kelly looked down at her outfit. Blushing profusely, she pulled the robe tighter around her.

To: kdf@alienimport.com
CC: mbradshaw@jhotels.com
From: kmccoy@jhotels.com
Subject: Visa expires
Kate-I'm getting a bit worried. My visa is
about to expire SOON. Do I have to leave the
country? How long do you foresee this H-3
taking?-Kelly

"Like your new toy?" Matthew turned to Kelly.

They were driving down the interstate toward the Russells' house for tennis. It was late morning, and the clouds loomed dark over Lake Michigan.

"Luv it!" Kelly said and kept playing with it.

Matthew's PDA beeped. "Did you just send me an e-mail? You couldn't just talk to me? What? My breath bad?"

"I cc'd you on an e-mail to Kate Fleming, my immigration lawyer." Kelly said. "I love this little gadget. Isn't it amazing how much information fits into this little thing? Although, I don't understand why the jays see the need for me to have one. I mean, I can see you needing one, they need to keep tabs on you at all times…"

"Careful, Ms. McCoy," Matthew said, sounding serious, but smiled.

"No, what I meant was that if there's an emergency, you need to be contacted no matter where you are, right? But what could they possibly need me for in a hurry? … 'Help! We've no hot babes in the bar! Throw on something slutty and get down here quick!'."

"You're underestimating yourself."

"Am I? That's my job description, you know? Look hot and appear strategically in the hotel." Kelly sighed.

Both PDA's beeped. Kelly opened hers. "That was quick," she said. "What a sad little life poor Kate must lead."

"What do you mean?"

"Well, late last night she's at the gym, and Saturday morning she's at work."

"And where were you late last night? And you're typing away on your work e-mail. Sad little life you're leading."

"Oh, I see your point."

Game, set and match: Mr. Bradshaw.

> To: kmccoy@jhotels.com
> CC: mbradshaw@jhotels.com, glombardi@
> jhotels.com
> From: kdf@alienimport.com
> Subject: Re: Visa expires
> Kelly-
> You have the opportunity to stay in the coun-
> try for an additional 30 days after the expira-
> tion date on your visa. This month is granted
> to you to do some traveling, and you may
> not work. In fact, you shouldn't even be on
> the hotel premises, except as a paying guest.
> Moreover, I suggest you not leave the country
> at all until you have your status changed. If
> you do, it will be more difficult for you to
> re-enter.
> If you pay for Premium Processing, the USCIS
> is normally very prompt, and you should
> expect a response in 10–15 business days after
> submitting the application.
> Please feel free to call if you have any further
> queries.
> -Kate

"Yay!" Kelly shrieked and read the e-mail to Matthew. "I'll be here for the opening! And Vicky's party!"

"Wonder why she'd cc Gina, though?" Matthew asked. He was worried, and didn't hide it.

"I didn't know they knew each other. Must put a stop to that right now," Kelly said resolutely.

> To: kdf@alienimport.com
> From: kmccoy@jhotels.com
> Subject: Re: Visa expires
> Kate-please don't include Gina Lombardi in
> future correspondence. My manager is
> Matthew Bradshaw, please cc him always. I'm
> the one paying your fee. Don't be intimidated
> by Ms Lombardi. Thank you.-Kelly

"When will you be back from North Carolina?" Matthew asked.

"Monday night or Tuesday morning. We haven't decided yet whether or not we're staying the night. Why?"

"Well, with the gas prices being what they are, I thought we'd kill two birds with one stone and go pee in a cup together," he said winking.

What kinda sick, perverted mind …

"For the drug test, right? Sure…" Kelly blushed and was about to put her PDA away, when it beeped again.

> To: kmccoy@jhotels.com
> CC: mbradshaw@jhotels.com
> From: glombardi@jhotels.com
> Subject: Re: Visa expires
> I sincerely wish that you will take notice of your
> attorney's advice and stay away from the hotel.
> Matthew; I expect you to endorse this
> decision.

Gina Lombardi
Managing Director
Pre-opening Director of Operations
Acting Director of Human Resources
J Hotel Chicago

"Bitch!" Kelly shot at the tiny screen, after reading the message for Matthew.

"I didn't expect anything less," Matthew sighed. "She is the Managing Director after all, and wouldn't want the company to get into trouble. Hiring an illegal alien could cause us serious financial problems, if discovered. Of course, you're not really on the payroll yet. Officially, anyway."

He drove in silence for a while.

"You know what we'll do? We rate your room. How much can you afford? A dollar a day? You'll be a paying guest!" Matthew said enthusiastically.

"Brilliant! Although, won't that affect our ADR negatively?"

"ADR?! Someone's been doing some studying!" Matthew said impressed. "Everything can be adjusted. She'll never know. Do yourself a favor and forward that message to the jays."

"Is it really fitting to go behind the manager's back like this?"

"Of course it isn't. We'll think of something better further along the line."

The traffic slowed down to stop-and-go and patiently Matthew stopped and went.

He's the most patient driver I've ever shared a car with. Even Parker would have shouted racist profanities from the back of the limo by now. … Parker really can be an arse a lot of the time … Why am I with him? Oh, yeah! The other times … when he's not an arse …

"So, what's your story, Chief? How did you end up in the hospitality industry?" Kelly asked.

"It's a long story."

"So, give me the two-cent tour."

It's not like we're going bugger-all else in a hurry.

"All I know about you is that you used to play tennis in the rat's mouth!"

"Okay, … " Matthew chuckled. "I grew up in Florida and started working in the local Crest hotel while still in high school. My Dad was the GM there and got me a job as a weekend bellman. Well … bellboy, more like. This was a time before nepotism became a four-letter word. I loved the action! Never a boring moment in that hotel! Then I got a weekend housekeeping supervisor's position. By then I was a senior in high school. The Crest chain posted this scholarship for college. I applied and got it. While in college I was a front desk shift leader. By the time I turned twenty-one I was promoted to F&B supervisor…"

FNB?

"What's FNB?" Kelly asked.

"Oh, sorry. It's a restaurant term …"

… Fork Near Bowl? Fried Not Baked? Fish…

"...Food and Beverage. Anyway, after I graduated from college the head housekeeper was going on maternity leave and I was offered the job as a temp. Turned out, she never returned. Then, about four years ago there was an opening for a Front Office Manager's job at the Drake in Chicago. I relocated. Met Linda. Got engaged. Eventually got promoted to Rooms Division Manager. Met the jays, and the rest is history to be written." He shrugged at looked at Kelly. "The two-cent tour."

"Tell me about Linda. What does she do?"

"She works for the Chicago Convention and Tourism Bureau. That's how we met. The Drake takes in a lot of convention delegates. On any given night, half the house would be some convention."

"Will the J be a convention hotel?"

Matthew laughed. "Not likely!"

They arrived at the Russells', and as they were getting out of the car they saw Emma running down the hill from the pool toward them.

"Kelly! I missed you!" she yelled and jumped into a big bear hug.

"I missed you too, pet," Kelly said and kissed Emma on the head.

Emma burrowed her head into Kelly's shoulder and looked at Matthew.

"Is that your bwoda?" she said, pointing at Matthew.

Kelly laughed. "No, pet, it's not my brother. This is my friend, Mr. Bradshaw," she said as she set Emma down.

Matthew kneeled. "Aren't you pretty with your Springy water wings."

Emma's eyes widened. "You like Spwingy?!"

"Of course! Who doesn't?" Matthew said, astonished. Emma pointed accusingly at Kelly. "Can you give me a Springy shake?" Matthew said and held up his hand.

Together they went through a routine of elaborate hand movements.

"Alright! And what's your name?"

"Emma Elizabeth Wussell, but you can call me Emma. What's yo name?"

"Matthew Bradshaw, but you can call me Matt."

Matt? There's a first. ... Ohmygod! They're bonding over a cartoon! I didn't know there was a secret handshake fer mattress springs! Look at him being all natural with Emma. He'll make a great dad one day. ... Oy! Emma's pronouncing her l's now!? Man! Really need to get me priorities straight!

Emma was looking at Matthew's arm, and put a finger on his scar.

"You have an owie?" she said and pouted her lower lip.

"Yes, from being in the sun without sunscreen."

"I got sunscween! Smew!" She extended her arm to him.

Okay, so the l's were a fluke.

Matthew took a whiff. "Mmmm! Coconut."

"I get you some. Come. I hep you," Emma said and wrapped her little fingers around Matthew's index and pulled him into the house.

They met Susan in the door and greeted. Susan joined Kelly. "He's cute. The two of you would have gorgeous children," she said to Kelly.

Why does everyone keep saying that? Do I have a sign on me forehead reading 'To tick me off – tell me I'll have gorgeous children by married boss'?

"He's married," Kelly muttered impatiently.

"Right.... So, how's Parker?" Susan asked politely.

Arrogant, pompous, bossy. Great lay. Great lay. Great lay!!!

"Fine, I guess. Nobody knows about us. And he wants to keep it that way."

"Why are you still with him?" Susan sighed. Kelly raised an eyebrow. "Okay, okay. None of my business! Just ... you could do so much better!"

I know, and I'm using Parker as target practice!

"Are you going to Vicky's party?" Susan asked, changing the subject.

"Aye. Just not as a couple. You and Jon going?"

"Doubt it. Jon might. Jacqui and I are starting on the Asheville property on Monday. I doubt I'll be back by then."

"Speaking of Jacqui, was it just me, or did he act really strange last night at the Jim?"

Susan pulled her away from the house and looked around quickly. "He came on to me," she whispered.

"What?!" Kelly shouted. Susan shushed her. "But I thought he was gay?" Kelly whispered in disbelief.

"So did I," Susan laughed quietly. "He tells me that it's all an act. To attract more clients."

"Why? Because straight men can't be interior designers? Jaysus, what a yoke!"

Who does that?! Well, no wonder he was acting strange. He had just come out of the closet. ... Went in the closet? ... Hmmm? Wonder what the term is when a straight man pretends to be gay and then hits on an older, married woman? An older married woman, who's his boss! ... I don't think there's a closet at all in that scenario ...

"So, how'd he do it?" Kelly asked curiously.

"Oh, it was so awkward. Poor child. He and I were the first ones in the hot tub, and were just talking about nothing, you know, the lobby and I noticed that he was looking at me funny. I didn't think twice about it. I mean - it's Jack! I've known him forever! But then he moved in closer to me, and sort of ... you know ... brushed up against me ... and ..."

"Nooo!" Kelly exhaled. "Was it ...?" She made a lewd gesture with her arm.

Seeing Jon walk down the hill toward them, Susan nodded and quickly took Kelly's arm. "Oh, yeah! Flag Day!" she laughed. She was wiping her eyes, laughing at the thought. "Thank God he carries that cell phone of his everywhere. Had it not been for Vicky's call, things might have gotten really awkward."

Jon joined them. "What's so funny?"

Susan flicked her hand, but continued laughing. "Oh, just something young Jack MacIntyre did. You had to be there," she said.

"So, Kel, how're things with you?" Jon said, turning to Kelly.

"Grand. Susan told you about the J-1 not being an option? Well, we're working on it. The jays and Matthew are very supportive, and I'm at the hotel all the time. I love it! The anticipation and the countdown to opening day! But the ice bitch is really getting on my nerves! Although I've successfully avoided her this past week. … I'm not sure I'll want to work for her."

"You wouldn't be working for her directly, you'd be working for Matthew, and he's cute!" Susan said.

"Will you quit teasing me!?" Kelly hissed, and gazed anxiously at the house. "Okay, so I had a bit of a crush on him when we first met, but I'm over it now. I respect the sanctity of marriage. I would never do anything to hurt another woman the way I was hurt."

"And is that why you're wearing this skinny-mini tennis outfit?" Susan smiled smugly.

Kelly blushed. "Well, I don't know how good he is. I need something to distract him."

"You do realize that you've got to let him win, don't you?" Susan said sternly.

"Why?!"

Fer fock's sake?!

"Oh, Kelly, you really are naïve! Back me up here, Jon. First of all, he's a man!"

"But we've got a big bet riding on this game!" Kelly argued.

"So you'll lose the bet."

"Second, he's your boss. Two reasons his ego probably can't handle losing to a girl!" Jon filled in.

"Okay," Kelly said reluctantly. "I'll turn it down a notch." She looked around the yard. "Where's everyone else?"

"Get this," Susan said. "We asked Emma what she wanted for her birthday, and she said a 'day without Abby and Eddie'! So, Eddie's with Tammy and Abby's at Haley's."

Emma and Matthew came out of the house, smelling like coconuts. "Kelly, can I be yo ballgial?" Emma asked excited.

"Sure, if it's okay by Matthew," Kelly said.

"Look, Matt!" Emma said, still holding on to Matthew's hand with one hand, and with the other she lifted the hem of Kelly's tennis skirt. "You can see Kelly's undewea! But it's not weally hea undewea, it's hea dwess. See?"

He might as well see me arse, we'll be peeing in a cup together on Tuesday.

Matthew bent over. "Interesting," he said examining Kelly's face as he stood up.

He smiled at her. They both blushed.

Keep flirting with the married boss, and be shot in the head by the wife or promoted by Thanksgiving. Good plan!

"So, Chief," Kelly said, grabbing their gear. "You ready to get your butt whipped?"

Matthew took the gear from her. "Sure, but right after that we're playing tennis!"

Old joke!

"I'm sorry, that's such a bad pun, but I just couldn't help it!" Matthew said.

The Russells watched them walk up the hill toward the tennis court. Emma was walking between Kelly and Matthew, holding their hands.

"That's that guy from the hospital, right?" Jon said. "I thought he looked familiar, just couldn't place him." They stood as if they were glued, watching the handsome threesome in silence. "What an attractive picture they make," Jon said quietly. "Kelly still doesn't know that he saved her life, does she?"

"No, and don't you dare tell her! It's not our place."

"Hmmm? Wonder if he'll be available for dinner," Jon said and went back in the house.

Susan stood watching them. Suddenly Kelly and Matthew both reached for their PDA's and burst out laughing and high-fiving each other.

To: kmccoy@jhotels.com
CC: sbradshaw@jhotels.com
From: bhart@jhotels.com
Subject: Re: Fwd: Re: Visa expires

K-Precious, don't let her get to you.
Remember, you're OUR guest and we adore
you.
M-Could you create a dummy rate code for
her room? Say one cent per night?

Bryce Hart

Co-Founder, Co-Owner, CEO J Hotels
Chicago, Phoenix, San Francisco, Asheville,
(and another 5 properties to follow in the
next 3 years)
Co-Founder, Co-Owner, CEO Jim the Gym
Co-Owner Second City Models, Ltd
Handsomest Man on the Planet as voted by
himself.

did I forget a "title"?

B

* * *

"Can you fly up to the U.P. first thing tomorrow morning?" Parker asked Jon over the phone.

"Why?"

"Numb-nuts Delaney won't evacuate his cabin on the land we now legally own. Our guys and their equipment are just sitting there ready to level the building, but he's refusing to leave. I'm losing money here!" Parker barked.

"Why's he not leaving?" Jon felt the all-too-familiar pain in his abdomen.

"His wife threw him out. Claims he didn't get a good enough deal from us," Parker said. "Women! No pleasing 'em!"

"He's trespassing. There are laws against that. Have your Michigan attorney file an eviction notice and have the local sheriff enforce it."

"I was hoping to avoid that. You have a history negotiating with that man. I'd rather you talk him into leaving voluntarily and peacefully."

"I'll give him a call, but I can't go tomorrow. It's my daughter's birthday," Jon said sternly.

"How old is she?"

"She'll be four."

"There'll be more important birthdays coming up. She won't even notice you're not there."

"Sorry, Parker, I won't do it. No offence, but I'd like to be here for my children on important events in their lives," Jon said, trying to hold his ground. "And besides, Delaney's a freaking fruitcake. He's got guns and ammo in that shack. Imagine what he'll do if I show up, and he's already not happy about our deal. I say let the law handle it."

The line was silent for a while.

"You're right. See if you can't call him tonight, and if he doesn't offer to leave, let him know he'll be evicted," Parker said. "And Terry? Enjoy your children while they're young. They grow up so fast."

Jon laughed. "Tell me about it! … It's not too late for you, though, Commander."

"I don't know," Parker grunted. "Is Susan available? I need a few words with her."

"Sure," Jon said. "Hold on a sec."

Susan was just arriving in the house from having watched Kelly and Matthew with Emma. She was still smiling at the picture they made together. Jon thrust the phone at her.

"Parker," he whispered.

"Parker? How are you?" Susan chirped.

"Fine. How's my boy working out for you?"

"Jack's fabulous! Everyone loves him! And he's exceedingly talented! You should be proud! You'll see his work at Vicky's party next week. He's responsible for the lobby."

"Okay,… um, … glad to hear that, I guess. Listen - I'm sitting here going through some paperwork, and I notice that you've never sent me a bill for Jack. You've had him for weeks now."

"Oh, gosh, I'm so sorry," Susan was flustered. "I've been meaning to tell you that he's turned out so terrific, that I've put him on my payroll."

"Not very good business practice, Susan, forgetting something like that," Parker reprimanded. "But all the better for me."

Susan felt small. "Sorry. … Oh, hey! Thanks for all your help! Really appreciate it! Couldn't have timed it better!"

"Well, it seems that both my kids are now involved with that damn hotel of yours. Least I could do."

Susan looked around, making sure Jon was out of ear-shot. "Parker?" she said quietly. "Can I talk to you as a private person? I mean, can you for a minute shed the role of my husband's boss, one of the wealthiest people on earth and all that?"

Parker laughed. "Shoot."

"Please don't hurt Kelly."

"I don't know what you're talking about."

"Cut the crap, Parker! I know you're sleeping with Kelly! And if you hurt her in any way, I'll..."

"You'll what? Reason with me?" Parker interrupted patronizingly. "Don't worry, Susan. Kelly's a big girl."

He's horrible! There's no way I can lose to him and not lose me self-esteem. Look at him, fer fock's sake! He looks like a court jester!

"Kelly! I'm tiwed, and you play weally, weally bad! Can we go swim now?" Emma was whining.

"Yes, pet, I think that'd be best," Kelly said and tussled Emma's hair. "Call it a tie, Chief?"

Matthew was panting as he met Kelly by the net on the tennis court. "You win. You're really good."

He was leaning against the net, with sweat dripping off his brow. He mustered up enough energy to shake Kelly's hand. Emma looked at him with wide eyes. Quietly she took his hand and led him to the benches lining the entrance wall. She handed him a towel and a sports drink, which he took gratefully. The she pressed her forehead to his and started whispering to him.

That's my thing! She's never done that with anyone but me! … I'm a little jealous now.

Susan entered the court. "Matthew, the wind has really started to pick up, and I think the storm is headed this way. You'll stay for dinner, I hope. Emma?" she continued, without waiting for Matthew's response. "If you want to swim some more, we'd better go now. It's about to rain."

"But I wanna swim with Kelly and Matt!" Emma whined.

"We'll be right there, Emma. We've got a score to settle," Matthew said and looked at Kelly with a grim expression.

Kelly walked over to the benches and grabbed a towel.

"So, you 'let me win', huh?" he said and did the air-quotation marks. "Didn't think my fragile male ego could handle losing to a girl?" He was still panting.

"Is that what Emma told you? Come on, she's four!"

"Nope, she asked me to come to her party tomorrow. Told me she's having Downunder Brownie Wonder for dessert. I take it you got that new Australian place on 63rd catering."

Downunder Brownie Wonder? Sounds more like diarrhea than dessert to me.

Matthew got up with a groan and shook her hand. "I knew you were throwing the game. You win. But I demand a re-match. And for future reference I want you to know that I'm secure enough in my masculinity for you to play like you normally would."

"You sure you're ready for that, Chief?" Kelly winked as she picked up their gear and headed toward the pool.

"Ask me again in about a week," Matthew said and limped after her.

"So, how does your wife feel about you spending the entire Saturday here?" Kelly said as she and Matthew were sitting by the pool by themselves.

They had a nice swim with Emma, changed into regular clothes, and were now sitting on the edge of the pool, dipping their feet in the water. The dark clouds had started rolling in, and Matthew had happily accepted Susan's invitation to dinner.

"My what?" he frowned at Kelly. "Oh, I'm not married."

What?!

"But the jays told me you were."

"That's a misunderstanding. I mean, I was engaged when they hired me, but we broke up very shortly thereafter."

He was looking up at the leaden clouds rapidly moving in above them. "We were planning an August wedding. My parents asked Linda what she wanted for a wedding present and she said 'a hysterectomy'. That was pretty much it.

I always wanted a big family. ... Still do. But she doesn't. She's about to turn thirty-five this fall and was afraid of the risks involved."

She's thirty-four? How old does that make him?

"She's older than me. I just turned thirty-one two weeks ago," Matthew said.

Thank you. So, he's a Gemini too. No wonder we get along so well. We're kindred spirits. ... Oh, can't tell him that, though, he'll think me nuts, or coming on to him.

"Please, don't think I'm a head-case or anything for believing in zodiac signs, but Gemini and Scorpio just aren't compatible," Matthew said, eyes on the dark clouds above.

What?!

"It's like I'm looking for my soul mate and Linda just wasn't it," Matthew said and sounded both sad and relieved.

"So, instead of correcting the misunderstanding, you just pretend to be married?"

Who does that? Really not buying it!

Matthew shrugged and shook his head. "I know it's shallow, but I liked the image. I noticed that I get more respect..."

"You're respected because you're a great guy, whether you're married or not. Pretend or real."

"It's stupid, I know. I just feel like people find me less threatening and more approachable if they think I'm hitched. Still hope to be one day."

"How's that ever gonna happen? You're at the hotel twenty-four-seven!"

"Yeah, well, that was just last night. Linda decided she wanted to move back into the house we built, and live there by herself."

Oh, that's so sad! What a bitch, though! Makes him a bit of a doormat, too, fer letting her. … Or possibly quite chivalrous …

"Seriously, though, how are you ever gonna find anyone working the hours you do?" Kelly argued.

"Found you, didn't I?" Matthew said, but his words were muffled by a loud thunderclap.

Gigantic raindrops started pouring on them. They quickly got on their feet and, laughing like children, started running down the hill toward the house. The thought of taking cover in the poolhouse never crossed either's mind. By the time they reached the house, they were soaked.

Susan was arranging for Matthew to borrow some of Jon's clothes while his were in the dryer. Kelly quickly slipped into the first available dry piece of clothing and went in search of Jon.

So now Matthew pretends to be married. Or pretends not to be? Why does everyone have to pretend they're something they're not? Parker's not an arse. Vicky's not an airhead. Jacqui's not gay! And what does that make the jays? They're too stereotypically gay to actually be homosexuals! With fake names at that! And possibly Gina, too. ... *The only real people I know are the Russells. ... Well, fer all I know they may turn into flesh-eating mutant alien pumpkins at midnight...*

She found Jon by the grill on the back deck. The covered portion of the deck was quite small for two people and a grill to stay dry in the rain, so Kelly grabbed a golf umbrella and stood under the gutter.

"What's up, Kel?" Jon said as he flipped a burger in the air. "Well done, I take it? How does your Matthew like his burger?"

"He's not *my* Matthew!" Kelly shouted in the rain. Then sighed "medium rare, no blood."

"Never thought I'd say this, but I'm so glad it's finally raining," Jon said, looking at the sheets of rain hitting the pond on the west side of his property. "We sure needed it."

Okay farmer Jack.

"I need your help," Kelly said quickly.

"Uh-oh... . Is this one of those conversations, where you'd rather talk to Susan, but can't find her, or one of the ones where I need another cold one?"

"I need a man's opinion on something."

"Oh, dear God! Grab me another cold one! Quick!"

Kelly sighed and opened the cooler. She looked up at Jon. "Since when do you drink Heinies?"

"Since never. I bought 'em 'cause Matthew likes 'em."

"How do you know?"

"Susan told me."

"How does she know?" Kelly tossed Jon a can of his regular brand of beer.

"After you were released to the MacIntyre nurse, they went out for a drink."

What!!?

"But I was told that I was in the ICU for a night and a day!"

"You were. Long twenty-four hours in the waiting room for both Susan and Matthew. Neither, of course, was allowed in to see you since they're not next-of-kin."

"But how does Parker fit into all of this?"

"Parker?" Jon frowned at Kelly. "He doesn't. Oh, I guess Jack and Vicky convinced him to take you in. I don't know," he shrugged.

"S-so Matthew was there the whole time?"

"Yup. Cares about you a great deal, you know."

"Yeah, well, because I work for him and he didn't want me to slap him with a lawsuit. Say, if your assistant passed out at work, wouldn't you take her to the hospital and stay there until you knew she was better?"

"Sure. For insurance purposes, I'd have to, of course."

Ah-huh! I knew it! … I rest my case.

"But I wouldn't stick my hand down her throat to induce vomiting."

"Yeah, gross, who'd do that!" Kelly said with a grimace. Jon raised his eyebrows at her. "Matthew did that?!" she whispered in astonishment.

Jon pressed an index to his lips. "I know nooothing."

... I don't know what to do with this information ...

Jon took a sip of his beer and stuck a thumb in his belt loop. "So, what's it you need a man's opinion on?"

What? Oh, right...

"Why would a guy tell you he's not married and then pretend that he is with everyone else?"

"How'd you know he's pretending?"

"Well, I don't, but ... okay, why would a guy tell you he's not married, if you think he is?"

"I imagine you're hoping for a more noble response than 'to get you to sleep with him'?"

"Guys really do that?"

"Oh, honey, it's the oldest lie in the book. Right up there with 'My wife doesn't understand me', 'I'm about to get a divorce', and let's see... oh, yeah, 'The check's in the mail' and 'Would I ever lie to you?'."

Kelly pondered this information for a while. "Why does everyone pretend to be something they're not?"

"Oh, we all wear a mask at some point or other in life, for various reasons," Jon said seriously.

"Well, I've never pretended to be anything I'm not, in my life. What you see is what you get. I'm the real thing. The real McCoy, if you'll pardon the pun."

Jon raised his eyebrows at her and eyed her slinky dress. "Wrreally? So, the wanna-be Victoria MacIntyre, drinking her breakfast, getting her stomach pumped in the middle of the afternoon on a weekday, and wearing revealing clothing for her boss, is the *real* Kelly McCoy?"

Aw, come on! Just once I'd like to win an argument with you, Jon! Why do you always have to be so bloody rational?

"Right, thanks a million, Jon," Kelly muttered and turned to go back in the house.

"Hey, Kel!" Jon shouted after her. "If you're going back in, could you bring me a coupla plates?"

"Sure."

I am man! I bring fire! But very little else.

18

Late Sunday afternoon Matthew was driving Kelly back to the hotel in silence. She felt awkward around him, and had tried to avoid him throughout the previous night and all Sunday morning during Emma's party. The storm had become so intense Saturday night that with little persuasion Matthew had agreed to spend the night in the basement guest room, much to Emma's delight.

Kelly begged both Susan and Jon to drive her back downtown, but after hearing both chapter and verse, twice, about the rise of gas prices, she conceded. She cleaned out her room and packed her belongings in Matthew's car. They left their tennis gear at the Russells' with a promise to use the court the next available weekend. Again, much to Emma's delight.

"You okay?" Matthew finally asked, after miles of driving in silence.

Kelly heaved a deep sigh.

I guess there's no way around it.

"Did you make me hurl?"

"Who told you?"

"So, it's true, then. I owe you my life," Kelly whispered and looked at Matthew. He was trying hard not to look at her. "Thank you."

"Nothing anyone else wouldn't have done," Matthew said matter-of-factly.

Parker wouldn't. He'd have taken credit for it, though. In fact, he kinda did already...

"But you sat with Susan in the waiting room all night," Kelly insisted.

"I was worried," Matthew said, without taking his eyes off the road ahead.

"But you barely know me."

"Yeah, well..."

"I thought it was sweet," Kelly said, mostly to herself.

"Yeah, well..." Matthew said again as he steered his car onto the express lane.

Oh, this is awkward! Awkward! I need a change of subject quickly!

"So, what do you think of Gina's little intern?" Matthew asked abruptly.

Thank you!

"Charles? I really don't know him enough to have formed an opinion. He's an obvious kiss-arse, but also apparently quite the wiz with computers, according to Dan," Kelly said. "I don't think he's Korean, though."

"What makes you think that?"

"Well, I had a friend print my name in Korean, and I had a purse made, with those characters on it, and last Thursday this Charles was programming the sales computer, where I'd been checking my e-mail that morning, and left my purse there, and he threw a fit."

"What do you mean?"

"Well, he was all 'who been here?', 'who leave their stuff my area?' and when I picked up my purse I pointed out that my name was right there, he got all flustered and he said he couldn't read it, because it was in rhinestone," Kelly ranted. "Don't you find that strange at all? *And* - I don't think Cho is a Korean name. Plus, he looks more Chinese to me than Korean."

"I wouldn't be able to tell the difference," Matthew snorted. "But, why do you think he'd say he's Korean?"

"My guess is that he wants the job as the revenue manager."

"He's basically got it."

"But don't you see? What could a person who grew up under extreme Communism possibly know about maximizing revenue? They never learned anything about profit or loss!"

"I see your point. He could actually end up hurting us quite badly."

"And," Kelly was all wound up now. "I don't think he got his visa through EUSA, if in fact he has a visa at all."

"What!?"

"You have to be an EU or American citizen to qualify. This is, after all, an exchange program between the EU and the US. It's right there on their website…"

"Website! Damn! I meant to have him help Ryan shoot the pictures for our new website for me!" Matthew hit the steering wheel. "Totally forgot!"

"Would he know how to do something like that?"

"I have no idea! Gina told me to set it up. I guess she's just trying to keep him busy."

Sure beats 'looking hot and appearing at events'.

"I also forgot to tell you that you're to model for those pictures," he added with a wink.

"What!? Why me, when the jays own a modeling agency?"

"Because you've got the *look*, whatever that means, and those models were requesting five grand a day…"

"…whereas, I'm free, right? Got it."

This is getting more and more bizarre. So now I'm a model, then. Nanny to corporate hot chic to public image manager to model in 3.5 seconds. Things are happening a bit too fast for comfort. One moment I'm changing poopy nappies, and the next I'm the look of a new company! … Wonder what's next? Neurosurgeon? Space Cadet?

"If it's any consolation," Matthew said, "I am also to model for those pictures. Apparently I too have the look."

Boy! Do you ever!

"Wonder what else he's lying about?" Kelly said thoughtfully. "Charles, I mean. If he can get a fake Korean … or EU passport, he could just as easily get a fake Cornell diploma. Maybe he's a spy for the competition! Or a saboteur!"

Matthew laughed. "Easy, Nancy Drew! Let's not get carried away!"

Both their PDA's beeped. Kelly read hers aloud for Matthew.

> To: [Exec]
> From: bhart@jhotels.com
> Subject: Executive Committee
> Dear All,
> If you've received this e-mail, you are considered a valued member of the Executive Committee to meet every Monday morning in the Study at 9am sharp (No exceptions!) starting Monday, July 2nd.
> B
> P.S. Could someone please come up with a catchier name for the Executive Committee than just that?

"What's an executive committee, and why am I a member of it?" Kelly asked.

"It's basically a meeting of the minds at the beginning of the week, to go through the events of the upcoming week, and go over the numbers for the previous week."

"Why am I a member?"

"They value your input."

"Who else is in it?"

"All the heads of department and Kristin to take the minutes," Matthew said. "The jays and the directors of sales and revenue either physically present or by phone. Oh, and Gina and me." Matthew's PDA beeped again. "Read that for me, would you, please?" he asked Kelly, as he got on the exit ramp.

> To: bhart@jhotels.com;
> mbradshaw@jhotels.com
> From: glombardi@jhotels.com
> Subject: Re: Executive Committee
> Bryce; Add my intern, Charles Cho, to the
> Executive Committee.
> Matthew; make sure that all paperwork for Ms
> McCoy is in order prior to this meeting.
>
> Gina Lombardi
> Managing Director
> Pre-opening Director of Operations
> Acting Director of Human Resources
> J Hotel Chicago

"How would she have known that Charles wasn't on the list?" Kelly said.

"No idea. I guess since my intern was with me as we read the message, maybe hers was with her?"

"Oh, du-uh! … On a Sunday, though?"

"Maybe the gruesome twosome is having a secret, sordid affair?" Matthew winked.

Oh, God! Now that image will be burnt on me mind!

"There's no way that I'll have my visa by the second."

"You don't know that!" Matthew said optimistically. "Keep your chin up, it might still happen!"

Back at the hotel, Matthew helped Kelly with her luggage. They found the door to her suite ajar. Kelly stopped cold with her key in her hand.

Did I not close it when I left yesterday? I'm sure I did. It's designed to close shut when you leave anyway. ... Who'd rob an empty hotel? And who'd know that this was the only occupied suite in the empty hotel?

They could hear movement inside the room. Suddenly Kelly was scared. All blood drained from her face. She turned to Matthew. He gently pushed her aside, and kicked the door in.

Charles was sitting at Kelly's workstation, typing away on the keyboard. He jumped out of his chair when the door flew open. He cursed in a foreign language. "You scale me! Why you do that?" he said, and exited the program he had been working on.

"What the bloody fuck are you doing in my room?!" Kelly demanded.

"I ploglam wi-fi to you," Charles said nervously, speaking to Kelly's chest. "See?"

He hit a button on the keyboard and the plasma-screen TV became a computer screen. It showed the J Hotels' current website.

"Cool! Thanks a mil, Charles," Kelly said.

"Who gave you authorization to do this?" Matthew asked harshly.

"Miss Gina."

"How'd you get in?"

"Miss Gina key," Charles said and showed Matthew Gina's master key.

"And why are you doing this on a Sunday?"

"I star way kay shung. Only times."

Waykayshung? Star? Hawaiian musical, maybe? Wai khai…

"Vacation?!" Matthew shot out disbelievingly.

Thank you!

"You only just started two weeks ago! Who approved that? … No, wait, never mind, I got it," Matthew raised his hands in resignation.

Charles was grinning and got out of his seat. "You betta pack. We sell loom opened day," he said to Kelly's chest.

"You can't do that!" Kelly shouted. "I have a contract giving me a room for the duration of my training!"

"You don hawa wisa yet. No wisa, no contlat, no loom. Inclease levenue." Charles was about to leave, still grinning.

I hope he knows that mentally I'm giving him the finger right now!

Matthew caught him at the door. "Hey, Charles, just so you know, in this country it's considered rude to carry on a conversation with a woman's chest. Next time, try eye-contact!" He closed the door in Charles' face. Matthew was frustrated and got his PDA out. "We'll get to the bottom of this, don't worry. Oh, damn! Battery's dead. Can I use yours, please?" He dialed Bryce's number on Kelly's PDA. "Bryce, hey, it's Matthew Bradshaw from ... Right! Hey, sorry to be calling you on a Sunday, but something's come up, can I put you on speakerphone? ... Just Kelly and me." He switched the phone to speaker mode and laid it on the coffee table.

"Hello gorgeous!" Bryce said.

Wonder if that was meant fer Matthew or me?

"Kelly? You there?" Bryce asked.

Okay, me then.

"Hi handsome!"

"Okay," Matthew cleared his throat. "Bryce, have you approved of Kelly's suite being sold for opening?"

"No."

"Well, apparently she's been made to move." He explained what had happened.

"I hate to be all technical, Kelly, but I have to agree with Gina on this. No visa – no room," Bryce said. There was a long silence on the line.

"Matthew, is that office next to yours still vacant? We could put a cot in there for Kelly! It's got a bathroom!" he continued eagerly.

Matthew and Kelly exchanged a nervous glance. "Um, ... sure, Bryce, good idea. The shower was removed, though, to make room for filing cabinets," Matthew said uncomfortably.

"Your office still has one, right?" Bryce said. "You could shower in there, couldn't you, Kelly? Or the Jim just for now? Let's do that until you get your visa."

"Ahem, okay," Matthew said. "Sorry again to be calling you behind Gina's back."

"Yeah, the two of you really should start getting your acts together. Like it or not, she's the Managing Director. Sorry I can't talk longer. I'm about to implode a parking structure."

"Beg your pardon?" Matthew said.

"Ah-huh! See, we bought this entire block, and now we're expanding! You both simply must come visit, once the J Asheville's all done. It's going to be our flagship property. Oh, no offence to Chicago, of course."

"None taken," Matthew said.

"Over and out. TV crew's here. Turn on Fox. Alen and I are the cute ones in baby blue hard hats. Fitting, no? Gotta run." With that, Bryce hung up.

Kelly looked nervously at Matthew. "So, what do we do?"

"I guess you'll sleep in the cot in the office next to mine." He smiled at her being so uncomfortable. "And I'll sleep on the sofa in my office. The connecting doors have locks on both sides."

"Thank you. Can I have my suite until opening, then?" Kelly asked anxiously.

"Of course," Matthew said and got up to leave. "See you next Tuesday," he said from the door.

What did he just call me? The nerve!

"Mr. B. do you realize what you just said?!"

"What? See you next Tuesday? Oh, you mean see you *this* Tuesday?"

Kelly walked over to the workstation and grabbed a pad of paper and a pen. "Now, imagine you were texting what you just said," she said patiently. She wrote the message on the pad and showed it to Matthew. He blushed to the roots of his hair.

"See you when you return from North Carolina. Now try and make that dirty," he said as he was leaving.

"See ya next Tuesday, Chief."

19

The early morning sun made Parker's silver Lear jet glisten like a jewel on the tarmac, as his company car unloaded outside the hangar at Midway Airport.

Parker was already on his cell phone.

"Uh-huh … I see. … Good! Level it before he changes his mind!" He hung up and turned to Jon. "Delaney's out."

"Hmmm? I'd still stand by with an eviction notice, just in case," Jon said. "Nothing with regard to Delaney has been easy, so why would this be?"

Parker started dialing again.

Captain Jones was in the cockpit together with her copilot, going over the flight plan. She saw Parker, Jon, Vicky and Kelly walk from the car to the plane and got out to greet them. She was wearing a form-fitting navy blue pilot's uniform that accentuated her curvaceous body. Her long blonde hair was pulled back into a tight knot at her neck.

Vicky was barely awake, and was carrying a pillow and a small overnight bag. She spotted Candi and poked Kelly in the side. "That's Daddy's girlfriend," she whispered.

What!?

"I hate her. Jacqui calls her Daddy's Camilla, because he always goes back to her bed between wives. And sometimes during. Except Mom, of course," she said and lit a cigarette.

If Camilla had looked anything like her, Charles wouldn't ever have bothered with Diana ... What's wrong with me? I should hate her too! Fer fock's sake! We're rivals fer the same man!

"Put that out, Victoria!" Candi said as Vicky and Kelly got on the plane. "There's no smoking on the tarmac or on this plane, and you know it!"

"Well, then you better tell your stewardess to quit leaving ashtrays lying around," Vicky yawned and waved a crystal bowl in Candi's face.

"That's a peanut bowl, and there are no stewardesses on this plane, Victoria."

"Well, there ought to be," Vicky said sassily and took her seat. "Champagne was lukewarm last night flying back from California and there are no peanuts in the peanut bowl."

Candi leaned over Vicky. "Don't make me take that away from you," she hissed.

"You can't tell me what to do! You're not my mother. Nor will you ever be my stepmother."

"It's a nasty habit and I wish you'd quit."

"*You* smoke!"

"Never on the tarmac or on the plane."

"Leave me alone!"

"Put that cig out, Victoria!" Parker bellowed from the back of the plane.

"Yes, Daddy," Vicky said and obediently stubbed out her cigarette.

"You really shouldn't be smoking . It's not good for you," Candi said, sounding genuinely concerned.

"Why? It'll stunt my growth?" Vicky laughed sarcastically and stretched her long, gaunt legs on the seat facing hers. "Puh-lease!"

She watched Candi leave to go prep the plane for take-off and turned in her seat. "Daddy?"

"Yes, dear?" Parker said absent-mindedly without looking up from the papers he and Jon had laid out on the table between them.

Vicky stopped, astonished, and turned toward Kelly. Her eyes were wide and her lower lip was quivering. Unable to regain the power of speech, Vicky looked like a deer caught in headlights.

I bet he's never called her anything but Victoria or young lady before. Look at her! Ooow, it's so sweet. Kinda sad, really. Big step fer Parker. Maybe this will narrow the gap between them.

"What is it, Victoria? We're busy!" Parker yelled.

And the Grand Canyon has never been wider! Or deeper...

Vicky rolled her eyes at Kelly. "On our way back from Charlotte, could we cruise by Vegas?"

Parker took off his reading glasses. "You in sin city? Not on my watch! It's hardly on the flight plan anyway. Why do you want to go to Vegas all of a sudden?"

"So you can marry Kelly."

"What!?" Parker, Jon and Kelly exclaimed in unison.

"Oh, come on! It's like so simple, you know. She's going through all this visa crap for nothing, really, when you could just marry her, and she'd, you know, be in the country for good, right?"

Ohmygodohmygodohmygod! I hope he doesn't think I made her say that!

Parker sucked on the stem of his reading glasses and smiled suggestively at Kelly. "I don't think foreigners can get married in Vegas," he said pensively.

"Oh, sure they can! How do you think Smilax got in the country?" Vicky insisted.

"You didn't marry Smilax, did you?!" Parker snapped.

"Of course not! I've never been married! Who do you think I am? You?" Vicky sassed. Parker raised a warning eyebrow at her. "Sawreee."

"I got him out of your life once, I'll have no problem doing it again."

"Yeah, yeah, yeah," Vicky said, rolling her eyes. "So, about Vegas?"

"Sorry, Victoria, I know you'd really like that, but I couldn't even if I wanted to. I'm not legally divorced from Verna-Jean yet."

I've committed adultery? I hope they have tennis courts in hell 'cause it looks like I'll be spending lots of time there. Fersure. No, wait - is it adultery if I'm not married? Oh, who cares, I'm going to hell for not paying attention in church.

"Oh, well, just a thought," Vicky said and pulled her eye mask over her eyes. "Wake me up when we land."

"Okay, we've just reached our planned altitude of thirty-nine thousand feet," Candi's voice came over the loudspeakers, "and it looks like it's going to be a good ride. I've turned the *fasten seat belt* sign off. We're going to start our descent in about thirty-five minutes," she concluded mechanically. "Jon?"

Jon hit the intercom button on the panel by his seat. "Yes?"

"If you're still interested in getting some flying time in, now would be a golden opportunity for a lesson."

Jon looked anxiously at Parker.

"Oh, go ahead, you know you want to," Parker laughed.

"Thanks, Commander!" Jon smiled like a schoolboy. "Be right there, Captain Jones." He rushed up the aisle to the cockpit. "You're alright, Candi," Jon said in astonishment as he entered the cockpit. The co-pilot vacated his seat for Jon and took the jump seat. "Thanks, man," Jon said to him and turned back to Candi. "Sorry about that little jab in Marquette back in May ..."

"Water under the bridge," Candi waved away his apology. "Anyway, I'm the one to apologize. I was way outta line."

"I'm just sick of gay-bashing," Jon continued. "Especially when it's directed toward Jack, who's like a little brother to me."

"I know, I know, he's turning out alright. You should know that he and I had a long talk last night flying in from California. He's really funny, actually," Candi smiled. "You know what he said to me? He goes 'I know how difficult it is to be in a gender minority in your chosen profession. You don't need to play tough with me. I respect you just as you are.' I didn't get it at first, but thinking about it later, he's absolutely right. Now, sit down and put your headphones on. Buckle up..."

Back in the cabin, Parker walked over to Kelly and sat down in the vacant seat opposite her. He looked at his daughter, sound asleep in the seat next to Kelly.

"She on anything?" he asked, worried.

Vicky was snoring quietly. "Not to my knowledge."

Parker leaned forward, and started rubbing Kelly's knees. "She's told you about this low-life Smilax, right? He lives in the south now. They met in rehab three years ago and I really don't like her to associate with him. He's bad news. See what I'm saying?"

See what you're saying? Not unless you're using sign language. Or you're in a comic strip.

"I hear you," Kelly whispered.

You want me to spy on yer daughter? Didn't we already have this conversation?

"She's doing much better. She's eating. She's drinking more moderately. And I found no drugs in my last raid of her room. I owe it all to you." Parker gave Kelly a suggestive smile. He leaned in. His hands were moving up Kelly's thighs. "You're a great influence."

Okay, this is sick. He's feeling me up in front of his daughter! What's this? Cocktail hour in Appalachia? ... Kinda exciting actually.

"You want to enroll in the mile-high club?" Parker whispered, his breath heavy on her cheek. He took her hand and pulled her with him toward the plane lavatory. "Don't worry, no one will hear. I'll be quiet. I promise."

His daughter's asleep just a few feet away, his number one man's in the cockpit, behind just a flimsy curtain and his other girlfriend's piloting the plane!?! I swear there's a wee Willy Clinton in every man!

Kelly couldn't help but giggle.

This is madness! Imagine if the plane went down just now, how would they find us? Naked? Burnt to a crisp, but smiling satisfied?

Parker opened the lavatory door and ushered Kelly inside.

Jaysus! There isn't room to swing a cat in here, much less copulate. Although, why would anyone want to swing a cat? ... Huh? Never thought of it, that's a really perverted saying. Oooh, hands on me bosom, better concentrate on making rich guy happy.

"I love your tits," Parker whispered into Kelly's hair, while cupping her chest.

Thank you. I've grown quite attached to them meself.

"Are we there yet?" Vicky said sleepily, peeking from under her eye mask. The change in cabin pressure had woken her up.

"Just coming in for landing," Kelly said, applying her make-up. She had changed into a skirt and jacket over a light T-shirt.

Vicky stretched and yawned. "You look nice," she said smiling. "You've got that whole professional yet freshly sexed up- look about you."

Kelly poked herself in the eye with mascara.

She knows?!

"W-what?"

Vicky laughed. "You know! It's sooo the look for this season. Looking all professional, but still sexy, like you're about to screw your boss's brains out. Or just did."

Kelly was wiping her eye.

Son of a bitch this stings!

"And to imagine that I did this! I guess it's like watching your child take its first steps. I feel so proud."

You didn't do it. Yer dad did. Just then. In the loo. Twice.

"I took a catholic school girl and turned her into a high-powered sex kitten slash hotel executive. Yay me!" Vicky hugged herself, and turned toward the back of the cabin. "Hey, Daddy?"

"Yes, dear?"

This time Vicky didn't let his choice of words bother her. "Do we have a car waiting in Charlotte?"

"Victoria, you're almost twenty-one. I thought it high time you arranged for transportation yourself."

"Ooo-kay," Vicky said sulkily and got her cell phone. She pulled a number out of her phone's memory and dialed it. "Whossit we like here?"

"Mark," Parker replied absent-mindedly.

"Hi, this is Victoria MacIntyre. Is Mark available, please?" she spoke quickly to the phone.

"We're about to land, Victoria, turn that damn thing off," Candi's irritated voice boomed over the loudspeaker.

"I'm on the phone!" Vicky yelled toward the ceiling. "Hey, Mark! I'm about to land at Douglas with a girl friend. How soon can you pick us up? ... Oh, you know, just around downtown all day and night today and tomorrow morning ..."

"Turn it off now! You're interfering with my GPS approach!"

"Anna Victoria MacIntyre! Turn your damn cell phone off! Do you want us to crash?" Parker bellowed from the back of the plane.

"No, I don't want a stretch… Town car would be fab! … Twenty minutes? You're a doll!" Vicky hung up. "I'm off the phone now, Candi, you can go ahead and land!" She laughed and winked at Kelly. Kelly couldn't help but smile.

"Why do you always have to be so difficult with Candi?" Parker reprimanded Vicky.

"Why do you always have to take her side?"

"Because she's trying to navigate a highly technical, extremely expensive piece of machinery, and letting her do her job in peace could mean the difference between life and death! Do you understand me, Victoria?"

Vicky didn't reply. She sank down in her seat and pouted.

Parker and Jon arrived without incident in Georgetown, South Carolina. They'd dropped the girls off in Charlotte and were now driving a rental car toward Don Duncan's new home.

"Man, I hope he's there!" Parker muttered. "Why in God's name would anyone willingly move *here* in the first place?"

"Best dawg-gone seafood on land, no skeeters and lotsa good ol' Southern charm. An greets."

Parker laughed. "Drop the drawl, Terry, y'all ain't doin' it right."

"Ah reckon."

"Prepare to turn right in. Two. Hundred. Yards," an automated voice announced from the dashboard. "In. One. Hundred. Yards. Turn right. Turn…"

"Will you please shut that damn thing off and read me the directions!" Parker barked.

"Turn right here," Jon said with a smirk, muting the GPS.

"Smartass."

They drove silently for a while.

"Sorry about Verna-Jean," Jon broke the silence. "Did she just take off on you, or is she demanding alimony?"

"Neither," Parker grinned. "I made it up. We are divorced. I just said that so Victoria would get off my back. I don't want my daughter to think that I'll just off and marry any foreign friend she wants to keep in the country. Nope, Kelly will have to get her green card some other way."

"I don't think Kelly'd marry for a green card, she's not that eager to stay here anyway. And even if she were, she'd want to do it on her own merits. Next left. And she's the first to tell you."

"That's what I like about her. No bull," Parker laughed and turned the rental car into a residential neighborhood. "The other night, for instance, she was spending the night at my condo … girls' night out, I don't know … anyway, she asked me if she could have a word about Victoria! She accused me of neglecting my daughter, ignoring her pleas for attention and blaming me for all that's wrong with her!"

"She's right."

"What!? How dare you?"

"No offense, boss, but it's true. Vicky's screaming for attention, and you keep brushing her off. Sending her to the Rock again isn't going to help, she'll just pick up new habits, and worse boyfriends. Turn right at the stop-sign."

"What the hell is this? 'Gang up on Parker' week?"

"Truth hurts, I know. Wow, would you look at these gorgeous live oaks!" Jon whistled.

"Fuck the oaks! What about my daughter?"

"I don't know, I'm no psychiatrist," Jon shrugged. "But how much do you think she remembers of her mother?"

Parker laughed. "I've spent two hundred dollars an hour, two sessions per week for God knows how many years, to have my daughter tell the best shrinks in Chicago that she doesn't want to talk about Sara!"

"Bingo!"

"What?"

"Turn right up ahead. That's just it! Do you think she remembers the accident?"

"Christ! She was only three!" Parker argued.

Jon raised his eyebrows.

"It's possible, I suppose," Parker sighed, and turned the car. "Where the hell is this place anyway? We're nearly in the damn ocean!"

"I know you don't want my opinion, but I'm going to offer it anyway. That's his drive up there by the white mailbox," Jon said and turned off the GPS. "Don't ignore her because she's a carbon copy of Sara. You'll never get Sara back, and if you don't straighten up about Vicky, you'll lose her, too."

Parker turned the car onto an unpaved, tree-lined drive way. "That's it?"

"Yup. Simple, ain't it?"

"You're. Not. List-e-ning. To. Me." Vicky was saying patiently on her cell phone when Kelly returned from the office building after her interview.

Vicky had changed into a bikini and lay sprawled on her stomach on a picnic table outside the EUSA office. She saw Kelly and waved her over.

"Hey, buddy! I said no themes! You would know that had you bothered to meet with me to outline my party!" She rolled her eyes at Kelly as she listened to the party planner on the other end. "Bumper to bumper my ass! Every Chicagoan with half a brain knows to leave early and allow time for traffic. You're not the only party planner in Chicago, you know! ... No! I said three hundred! You got a problem with that? ... Oh, but there'd better be! ... So, a few friends called and invited themselves, big deal. ... Okay, listen. I'll compromise. I'll make your grand entrance, smile and wave for the media, but I'm not wearing a stupid tiara! Got it? ... Well, work harder! And don't bother me with these puny details again!" Vicky snapped her phone shut and let out a guttural groan.

"You and your Dad may not have a lot in common, but being rude on the phone seems to be a family trait," Kelly said and sat down on the picnic table.

"That wasn't rude. That was getting what I pay for," Vicky said and sat up. "Everyone and their mother will try and take advantage of you, if they know you have money. If you're young, female and have money, that is. Thank God I'm not blonde! I wouldn't have a nickel to my name!" she giggled. "So? How'd it go?"

"What a waste of time!"

"Whaddya mean?"

"Well, I already have a property lined up, just waiting for me to get started, so that was one thing they needn't bother with. I had all the paperwork with me, signed, sealed and hand delivered, all they need to do is to file it with immigration. That could've been done by FedEx. They asked me nothing important, or interview-like, because, again, I already have a property! Basically they just wanted to see what I looked like, and I could've just as easily have sent them a bloody photo! Oh, and hear that I speak English! Hello?!" Kelly pointed at her mouth.

"Well, maybe they needed to know that you're not, like, grossly deformed, or obese or … or, like, in a wheel-chair or anything."

"None of which are legal grounds for not hiring someone!"

"Girl! You really are pissed off, aren't you?"

"I hate waste! And that's all this has been! A bloody waste of time!"

"So, did they at least say anything constructive? Like, will you be getting your visa any time soon?"

"Two to three weeks, they *reckon*, if all goes well. Oh, and Mawrriss turned out to be Morris."

"That means nothing to me," Vicky said, looking baffled.

"Never mind." Kelly started peeling her jacket off.

It wasn't even noon yet, but the heat and humidity were getting to her.

"Is it always this hot here?" she asked, utterly uncomfortable.

"It's June in the South! Du-uh! You do the math!"

The air is thicker than Guinness! Which in itself is like liquid bread. Only time the humidity is this high in Ireland is when it's raining!

"Ready to go?" Vicky got off the table.

"Where to?"

"To see if we can't rattle that snake Smilax out of a hole."

"You really think that's such a good idea?"

"Sure, he's totally harmless. I need a little something-something, you know, Happy Birthday to me!"

They were walking toward the car.

"So, what would you like for your birthday?" Kelly asked.

What does one get a multi-millionairess heiress with everything? And then some.

"The invitations say to donate to your favorite charity…" Vicky started mechanically. She stopped suddenly and faced Kelly, smiling from ear to ear. "You know what I really want, though? I want to publicly fire the executors of my mother's trust fund! I want to tell them in front of God and everyone to take a royal hike up their own butts! I'll be twenty-one, and I finally get to do what I want with my money! That's what I really want for my birthday!" She was so excited she was shouting.

"Oh-kaaay," Kelly said slowly. "How about something from, say, Michigan Avenue? Something in single digits?"

Vicky looked deep into Kelly's eyes. She turned very serious. "There's one thing you can do for me, Kel."

"Yeah? What's that?"

"Keep doing what you're doing with Daddy."

She knows!? … She's bluffing! Ohmygod!

"Wh-what are you talking about?"

"Oh, come on! I know you're sleeping with my father!"

Kelly tried to read her expression, but couldn't. "I'm not…"

"Don't lie to me! I hate it when people lie to me! Makes me think they think I'm just some sorta airhead bimbo, or something!"

"How'd you find out?"

"Oh, puh-leease, Kelly, it's like sooo obvious! A blind bat could see how uncomfortable the two of you are together, trying to avoid looking at each other, or touching each other! But then sneaking off…"

"And how do you feel about that?" Kelly interrupted. "I mean,… you know,… me and your Dad …?"

"No details, please! It's gross enough to think that he's having sex at all, let alone with a friend!" Vicky snorted in disgust. "But, like I said. Please keep doing it. You've been good to him. Good *for* him. I've, like, never seen him this happy. Ever! And he's suddenly taken an interest in *me*! Okay, like, one morning last week, when you spent the night at the hotel, he wakes me up, you know, and has breakfast brought to my room! And we, you know, talked! That's the first time, since, like, ever! You're like the catalyst or whatever in Daddy and me getting along better," Vicky's eyes became moist. "That's the best birthday present anyone could give me. Thank you," she whispered and hugged Kelly.

"Well, … um, Happy Birthday, then," Kelly said, utterly uncomfortable.

She's really being a good sport about this. Wonder how I'd feel if I found out me Dad's doing someone my age? Eeeuw! Gross!

Vicky stood back and looked at Kelly seriously. "Just promise me two things."

"I know, don't get my hopes up and don't tell Jacqui."

"Okay, three things," Vicky said and held up three fingers. "One. Don't get your hopes up. You know what he said on the plane about Verna? So not true. And even if it were, he could have Candi fly him to the Dominican Republic, like, today, get a divorce over doughnuts and do Candi on the flight back."

Kelly gasped.

"Sorry to be so blunt, but that's, you know, … Daddy. Don't think he won't drop you like yesterday's garbage when something better comes along. And don't think you're anything special. You're the current just-for-now-girl." She counted off her fingers. "Two. Don't tell Jacqui. And three. Please still be my friend when you and Daddy break up."

Kelly huffed. "Of course I'll still be your friend. Your Dad's only my just-for-now-guy, anyway."

"Yeah, keep reminding yourself of that." Vicky pointed a finger in Kelly's face. "You ready?"

They got in the car.

"So, has it been decided yet? Are we spending the night or not?" Kelly asked, blissful in the air-conditioning.

"You better believe we're spending the night! If I know Daddy, and I think I do, his business will take about two seconds. The rest of the day is spent drinking, swapping 'dodged the bullet' stories and, I don't know, slapping each other on the back, and boasting about their successes. Likely ending the night at the local strip club."

Haven't had a drink since my stomach pump, but sure could use one now. Wonder if this Smilax might have a 'Don't get yer hopes up about hot billionaire'-pill? … Better not trust anything coming from a man who goes by 'Smilax' again.

* * *

Don Duncan's house was what one could only describe as an oceanfront fixer-upper. Parker and Jon were looking in all windows, as there was no answer to the doorbell. They heard a skill-saw start in the distance, and walked toward the sound. Inside the garage was a beer-bellied, salt-n-pepper haired, middle-aged man, dressed in cut-off jeans and sweating profusely. He was cutting a piece of plywood.

Parker let out a long catcall. The saw was turned off and Duncan looked up. The initial surprised look on his face was quickly turned into sheer delight, as only one old friend seeing another can be delighted.

"Parky Mac?!" Duncan shouted. "Haven't seen you since … what …? The oh-four Exploration Roundup!? How the hell are ya, bubba?" He walked over to Parker and gave him a brotherly hug. Terry!? I'll be dawg-goned!" he shook Jon's hand. "What the devil y'all doin' 'ere?"

"Cut the drawl, Duncan, you're a damn Yankee just like Terry and me," Parker snided.

"You know what the definition of a Yankee is, don't you? It's the same as a quickie, but you can do it by yourself," Duncan punched Parker's shoulder. "Come on, let's go in the house and have a brewski. Time for a break anyway."

The air-conditioning made the house feel like a different world from the hot, humid South Carolina climate outside. Duncan pulled out three bottles of beer from the refrigerator and the men sat down on empty crates in his living room.

"Sorry, the furniture hasn't been delivered yet," Duncan said apologetically. "So, why are you here? Don't tell me it's to congratulate me on my early retirement."

Parker laughed and took a long sip of his beer. He loosened his tie. "You're right. We're here because I want you to join MacIntyre and I won't take no for an answer again."

"Again? When did I ever turn you down before?"

"Right after we graduated."

"Right…," Duncan laughed and turned toward Jon. "I spent most of grad school sharing a room with this loser, never getting a decent night's sleep, listening to him snore and talk in his sleep all night every night! And he never had anything even remotely interesting to say! I was hoping for something juicy, just once. Thank God for Sara agreeing to marry him when she did! And then he wants me to join his Dad's company?! Hell, no! I was done with him!" He took a sip of his beer, his eyes still on Jon. "Look at you, Ter! All grown up. Shaving, and everything! Haven't seen you since Campo Verde."

"I was at the oh-four Roundup," Jon said.

"You were? How'd I miss you?"

"Terry actually goes to all the meetings, and all the field trips, but none of the strip clubs," Parker said, slapping Jon on the shoulder.

"No wonder I didn't see you! Glad this loser did hire you, though. Needs someone like you to keep him straight. Best damn thing I ever did, sending him your thesis."

"Hah! I knew it was you!" Parker barked. "All these years I've been wondering."

"All you needed to do was ask, man, I woulda told you. Shit, everyone else knew. Nearly lost my job at Kensington because of it, once Terry got a reputation established."

"So, what's it going to take to get you to come to MacIntyre?" Parker switched back to business.

"What you got lined up?"

"Emeralds in Argentina. I need a savvy geologist and a good negotiator, among other things."

"And among others?"

"Someone who speaks the language and understands the locals."

"I'm not cheap," Duncan said, peeling the label off his beer bottle.

"I'll give you fifty on top of what you were making at Kensington. And you know that I have a pretty good idea of what it really was, so don't try anything," Parker smirked.

"I need a generous budget and a solid support team."

"That goes without saying. You got Mendoza and Nordin, and their crews."

"Those losers still with you?" Duncan laughed. "I want Terry, too."

"Not negotiable."

"Then we have no deal," Duncan snapped, finished his beer and started toward the kitchen.

Parker sighed. "It can be discussed."

At the kitchen door Duncan turned and smiled. "Okay, then. But I don't want to be on the payroll or the board. I'll take the projects that I can pick and choose at will. I don't mind spending the summer in Argentina, but at the end of hurricane season I want to be right back here. And I want stock options."

Parker roared. "You haven't changed one bit, Double-D! Do we have a deal?"

"I'll let you know. You fellas hungry? Got some fresh crab. They wuz swimmin' this mornin'."

In the girls' hotel suite in downtown Charlotte, Kelly got out of the shower, to find that Vicky was gone. She didn't think twice about it, and started getting ready for a night on town. Startling her, the door burst open and Vicky rushed in.

"Oh, you're here, good!" she said. "Did you know that your cell phone's not working?"

"Yeah, it's because I had to get one of those pre-paid plans with zero coverage, because I'm a foreigner, ergo have no credit history in this country, ergo can't get a proper plan. And the battery's dead on my PDA."

Ergo? Bizarre time to use that word fer the first time. ... Twice.

Vicky was carrying a large brown paper bag, and emptied its contents on her bed. "Been shopping! Want some?"

On her bed lay an array of pill bottles, of various sizes, shapes and shades.

"You met with that Smilax, didn't you?"

"Yeah, baby! What're you in the mood for?" Vicky said as she opened a white bottle, shook two small brownish pills out and swallowed them. "Getting ready for a night on the town!" She chased the pills down with a mini bottle of vodka.

Kelly sat down on Vicky's bed, took the bottle and read the label.

Caffeine ... ephedrine ... peyote ... amphetamine ... Whatta fock?!

"Vicky, are you outta your mind!? Look at this!"

"Oh, I've read the label. Totally harmless."

"Really? Is that why they put a red triangle with a skull and cross-bones next to a caption stating 'Do not take with alcohol'?! Don't mix alcohol with a pill you take to sober up?! What kinda quacks are these people you're dealing with?! And look at this! 'Side effects: nausea, diarrhea, dizziness, constipation, kidney disease, liver malfunction, birth defects, ... death!' "

"God, you're starting to sound like Daddy! Chill out! I have a downer here for you..." she was rummaging through her pile of bottles.

Kelly grabbed them all and shoved them back in the paper bag. She rushed to the bathroom and locked the door behind her, before Vicky had time to react. In the bathroom she started pouring the pills down the toilet.

Vicky was hammering on the door with both fists. "What're you doing?! Lemme in!" she shouted desperately.

When the last bottle was empty, Kelly opened the door. Vicky was hysterical and crying. Kelly flushed the toilet.

"Nooo!" Vicky screamed and lunged for the bowl. She turned to face Kelly. "How dare you?! You had no right to do that! I hate you! Have you any idea what that stash cost me?"

"Yer life?" Kelly tried to appear calm, although her adrenaline was pumping.

Vicky fell to her knees on the cold bathroom floor and started crying hysterically.

"I hate you…" she sobbed.

Kelly put her arms around her, helped her up and led her to bed. "How am I gonna get through grad school…? " Vicky mumbled through sobs.

"You'll get through school because you're an intelligent, hard-working, dedicated student, not because you're popping uppers," Kelly said, stroking Vicky's hair. "You hate when people treat you like some rich little heiress bimbo, right? Well, quit acting like one, then, fer fock's sake!"

"What?"

"How's yer Dad ever gonna take you seriously, give you a job, put you on the board of directors, if he thinks you're wasted all the time? Is that the person you want yer Dad to leave his company to? You know, he doesn't even know what a passion ya have fer precious gems! Ya know why?"

Vicky hiccupped. "Because he doesn't know I exist!"

Kelly flicked her lightly over the head.

"Aow! Did you just hit me, you bitch?!"

"I need to get through that thick skull of yers! It's time the kid gloves came off! Yer Dad dinna ken bugger-all about you, because you act like a spoiled brat and he treats you accordingly! High time you started acting like the future president of his company that you hope to be one day! You kenny just expect people to respect you because of who yer Dad is! Respect has to be earned, ya yoke! Grow up!" Kelly was upset and her accent was getting thick.

Vicky was sobbing hard and looked at Kelly with wide eyes. "No one's ever talked to me like that before."

"Well, I'm sorry," Kelly said. "Ya had to hear it."

They sat on the bed staring at each other for a while.

"You're really beautiful, you know?" Vicky said while drawing a figure eight in the air. "I love you. Will you be my step-mom?"

Oh, God! She's high as a kite! Now what do I do?

"Vicky, where's yer phone?"

Vicky pointed to the ceiling, still doing the figure eight. "Hey! What's English for Ursa Major?" she said.

"Big Dipper."

Kelly found Vicky's cell phone on the floor, and was texting Jacqui. Vicky was jumping up and down on her bed, giggling like a little girl.

"What's so funny?"

"You sa-id dip-per!" Vicky singsonged.

> To: Jack Cell
> Come quick! V hi! RC ste 1471.
> K

"Why isn't it Big Bear?" Vicky pondered, again look-ing at the ceiling, her finger compulsively doing the figure eight.

"Because it was named by a man!" Kelly said, staring at Vicky's phone in her hand, willing it to ring. She was hop-ing that Jacqui had received her message. She kept having flashbacks of the day her stomach was pumped, and real-ized she wouldn't know what to do if Vicky passed out.

Makes what Matthew did all the more special ... and gross, really...

"Vicky, what's yer zip code?"

"...'Ground control to Major Tom...'," Vicky started singing.

Okay, ladies and gents, Victoria MacIntyre has left the build-ing. ... High as a ... Higher than a kite really. She's in bloody outer space.

Suddenly the phone in Kelly's hand rang.

"Kel? It's Jacqui. How is she? What's she on?" he shot out like a type-writer.

"Vodka and amphetamines among many. Totally incoherent."

"Uh-oh."

Don't say uh-oh! What uh-oh!?

"Keep her awake. Make her barf. Don't let her pass out until she has. We're just leaving Asheville now. We'll be there in, like, an hour, maybe two!"

"Two hours!? I can't keep her on the bed, let alone alive fer that long! She's bouncing off the walls, I'll have ya know, and I don't mean that figuratively! I'm no nurse! I don't know what to do! And how d'ya make a person *barf*, anyway? Shouldn't I just call nine-one-one?"

"NO! Please, just trust me. Talk to her. Keep her awake, and preferably alive. We'll be right there."

"…'take your protein pills and put your helmet on…'." Vicky was singing and using two pillows for cymbals. "Phroesshh!"

"Jacqui," Kelly whispered. "I'm really scared."

"Don't be. You'll be fine. And so will she." He hung up.

Kelly looked at Vicky standing on her bed, doing the air-guitar.

" …'take your protein pills …'." Mid-verse she slumped down on the bed. "I'll jes take a lil nap an' 'en we'll go par-tay!"

"Nononono!" Kelly shouted and hurried to her side. "Sing me another song! Talk to me. Tell me a story," Kelly said, stroking her hair. "I'll start one for you. Once upon a time…"

Please hurl, please hurl, please hurl…

"Onsh upin atm, thurz two gals Collie an' Mickey …" Vicky slurred. "Howsa song go? 'Mickey Maawse…'." She started singing again.

I wish Parker were here.

The sun had set, and Duncan skillfully navigated his Grady White back into shore. His cooler was empty, and although the men had been unsuccessful in catching any fish, they had nonetheless had a productive day on the ocean. Duncan was joining MacIntyre Industries.

Parker got off the boat with unsteady legs and pulled out his cell phone. Duncan made the sound of a whiplash.

"Checking in with the ball and chain?"

"I'm between wives," Parker grunted. "Checking in with an alcoholic daughter. Hoping to catch her alive."

He was dialing Vicky's number. Kelly was still holding the phone in her hand when it rang. She jumped when she saw the display read 'Daddy cell'.

Ohmygod! What do I do?

She reached for a piece of paper on the nightstand and crumbled it to the receiver.

"Hi, Daddy!" Kelly answered, in what she hoped would pass as Vicky's voice. Vicky was sitting on the bed, singing quietly. Kelly went into the sitting room and closed the door behind her. "I'm alive. I'm sober. I'm with Kelly," she continued.

"Damn awful connection," Parker said on his end. "What you been up to?"

"Nothing, Daddy!"

Oooh, 'Daddy'... naughty...

"You don't sound right. What's going on?"

"I'm fine, Daddy! Ask Kelly if you don't believe me! Bye Daddy," Kelly said quietly, still crumbling the piece of paper to the receiver. "Love you!"

That's okay, no?

Parker let out a roar of laughter. "Now I know you're drunk! Let me talk to Kelly!"

Man! Leave it to me to find a dysfunctional family! Every other American uses that expression ad nauseam!

"Mr. MacIntyre? How may I be of service?" Kelly said in her own voice.

"So, it's Mr. MacIntyre today, is it? Okay, I can play that game," Parker said quietly and looked around to make sure he wasn't overheard. "Miss McCoy, you were a very, very bad girl on the plane this morning," he said in a husky voice, "you've made it damn near impossible for me to concentrate on anything else all day..."

"...M-I-C... K-E-Y ... M-O-U-S-E ... Mickey Mouse, Mickey Mouse...Donald Duck!" Vicky was standing in the door to the bedroom, singing at the top of her lungs.

At least she can still spell. Not totally out, then. Just please hurl already!

"What the hell is that?" Parker demanded.

"Our pizza's here," Kelly said hastily, partially covering the mouthpiece. She was trying to signal to Vicky to shut up and go back into the bedroom. She turned her back to

Vicky. "Sorry, Mr. MacIntyre. Please hold that thought and we'll pick it up from there tomorrow…"

She heard a gurgling sound behind her. She quickly hung up with Parker and turned around just in time to be spewed with Vicky's vomit.

Eeeuw! Careful what ya wish fer, Kelly McCoy! Ya just got it!

Parker stared at his dead receiver and laughed. Duncan walked up to him with a fresh, cold beer. "Whatcha grinnin' 'bout? Good news?"

"I think my daughter's pizza was delivered by a Mouseketeer!" Parker laughed. "Well, at least she's eating!"

"Ohmygosh, Kelly, I'm so sorry," Vicky was saying, trying to wipe her vomit off Kelly's face.

Gross! Gross! GROSS!!

Vicky started giggling, then laughing uncontrollably.

Hilarious. Really funny. Watch me shut you up.

"That was yer Dad on the phone just then."

Vicky sobered up. "Whatcha tell 'im?"

"Pretended I was you." Kelly took Vicky by the hand. She pulled her into the bathroom. "I'm going to shower, and you're going to sit right there on the commode and talk to me! And then you're going to bed!"

"Yes, mother!"

"Vicky?" Susan whispered. She and Jacqui had arrived at the girls' suite.

After cleaning herself up, Kelly put Vicky to bed. She passed out immediately. Kelly's initial anger had changed into genuine worry and she watched Vicky like a hawk until Susan and Jacqui arrived. Jacqui took one look at his sister and determined that she was fine. Kelly wasn't convinced.

"Hmm...wha?" Vicky mumbled without opening her eyes.

"Honey, what's the difference between Tertiary and Paleozoic?"

"Geologic time's divided into five major epochs, each having several sub-epochs," Vicky mumbled sleepily from under her covers, without moving or opening her eyes. "Pre-Cambrian, ... Paleozoic, ... Mesozoic, ... Tertiary ... and Quaternary. Tertiary's from about sixty-five to one million years ago. Paleozoic's about five-sixty to two hundred and fifty million years ago. Mesozoic between." Vicky yawned. "Why? D'I miss my exam?"

"No, hon, you aced it. Now go back to sleep," Susan said and kissed Vicky on the forehead.

"Yay me!" Vicky mumbled. "Luv ya, Susan."

"Love you, too, hon." Susan turned to Kelly and smiled. "She's fine."

"What was all that zoic stuff, and how do you know she's right?!" Kelly hissed.

"I've been married to a geologist for twelve years. Sometimes I listen!" Susan laughed quietly and closed the door to the girls' bedroom.

Jacqui cleaned up Vicky's vomit on the living room floor and made them some coffee. They sat on the sofas sipping it quietly.

"So that's the stuff I took and got so sick?" Kelly asked.

"Most likely," Jacqui said.

"So, there's no way I can pass this drug test I'm meant to take tomorrow, then?"

"You might," Jacqui said. "See, this stuff is manufactured in some garage in, I don't know, Guadalajara, and smuggled into the US. Each batch is different, which kids like Vicky find exciting, because they never know what the effects may be. Those labels mean nothing. It could just as easily contain meth as Midol."

I can't believe he's being so nonchalant about this. Am I overreacting or is he underreacting?

"Well, what about all those warning signs, then?"

Jacqui laughed. "It's not like they're under FDA regulation to post them, you know! Who puts down *death* as a side effect, anyway? I mean, it's pretty terminal, don't you think? They mean nothing, they're just there to hype the kids."

"Not much help, considering how sick I was."

"You'd had a rough day," Susan said. "You had a few drinks on an empty stomach, running around all day and then you get really horrible news. It could've happened to anyone. Besides, it's been weeks, your stomach was pumped, and you're not a habitual user. It's probably out of your system by now."

I want to go home. My biggest concern on the party scene used to be whether the beer was poured right.

20

The flight from Charlotte to Chicago early the following morning was downright unpleasant. Kelly hadn't slept a wink the previous night. She was too worried about Vicky, and on the plane she was still watching her sleep.

"Will you quit staring at me!" Vicky hissed from under her eye mask. "I mean, I appreciate your concern and all, but I'm okay, really." She removed her eye mask, smiling. "Really."

Kelly smiled and tried to make herself comfortable in her seat. They had encountered an awful lot of turbulence, and Kelly couldn't wait to feel solid ground under her feet again. She was trying to get Parker's attention, but he was avoiding her like the plague, pretending to be in deep conversation with Jon the entire flight.

Bet he did Candi last night! ... So what? We never said this was exclusive. We never said this was anything, really, we just started doing it... Or maybe Candi wanted to do it, but he didn't, and now she's flying through rough weather to make us all air sick? Yeah, that's better ...

Parker was still pretending to avoid her.

It's a universal guy thing! Even Sean did it! Why do men avoid eye-contact with the woman they're with? If Parker looked up at me now, my skin would start prickling and shockwaves would start running up and down my spine ... theoretically. Don't guys want that? What's the male equivalent to ... Du-uh! Wouldn't want that reaction sitting right next to his number one guy!

She fell asleep.

When they arrived at Midway, they had two company cars waiting for them. One for Parker and Jon to go back to the office and the other to take the girls to the hotel. Vicky had decided that she needed to pay a surprise visit to her party planner. As Kelly was getting off the plane Parker lightly touched her arm.

"What did you do to my daughter?" he whispered.

"What do you mean?"

Uh-oh...

"While you were sleeping on the plane, she asked me for a summer internship," he laughed. "Can you believe that?"

Kelly frowned at him. "Yes."

"I thought she was on something."

Ya really need setting straight, but now's not the time.

"Will I see you tonight?" he whispered throatily as they were walking down the tarmac toward the cars.

Kelly stifled a giggle. "Count on it," she whispered from the side of her mouth as they separated.

"Do you have a hard time following the simplest instructions?" Gina was reprimanding Matthew in his office.

Charles was standing at the door, grinning.

"Does he have to be here?" Matthew asked, nodding at Charles. "I thought he was meant to go on vacation."

"He leaves tonight, after the web site pictures are shot," Gina snapped quickly. "As do I. I'm going to Asheville for a few days. Dan's switching mine and Bryce's offices while I'm gone. I'm leaving you in charge. Need I remind you that when I return, I expect Ms. McCoy to not be on property, or you will answer with your job? Is that clear?"

"What if her visa comes through in the meantime?"

"Well, then she's expected to start working, obviously. Assuming, of course, that she passes the drug test. Although, I wouldn't count on either." She turned to leave. "I know that you and Bryce are very close, but since he's not here, I run this show. You need to learn not to second-guess my every decision and go running to Bryce. And incidentally, this room," she knocked on the connecting doors, "will also be sold for opening. And it had better be a three digit rate!"

"But there's no shower in there anymore!"

"Make there be one by opening," Gina said coldly and was about to leave.

"So, is Kelly still to pose for those pictures for the web site?" Matthew asked.

Gina heaved a deep sigh. "Not my decision, obviously."

"So she's still allowed on property for that?"

"You're splitting hairs, Mr. Bradshaw," Gina's face became pruny. "She may pose for the pictures, and appear at the Milk Bar, which I'm told is out of my jurisdiction, but that's it! Do I make myself clear?"

"Crystal," Matthew said and watched Gina and Charles leave his office.

He hung his head and ran his fingers through his hair. He jerked up, and reached for the phone.

"Hi, Kelly, it's Matthew Bradshaw. Whatever you do, don't use your PDA. For anything. Just come directly to see me when you return from Charlotte. Bye." Kelly stared astonished at her cell phone in the car. She had just turned it on, and that was the only message she had.

Why can't I use me PDA? Oh, I bet they've decided that I don't need one, and they're gonna give mine to that Charles instead. Oh, well. … Hmmm? Wonder why Matthew always introduces himself as Matthew Bradshaw? Like I know any other Matthews? … Oh, no way he could know that …

"Kelly, sorry to be such an airhead, but is it M-a-c Coy or M-c Coy?" Vicky said.

"M-c-C-o-y. Irish. Why?"

343

"Writing you a check," Vicky said without looking up. "You were really cool last night. I sooo appreciate you not calling the EMS. The media would have had a field day with that one, you know. And Daddy would have put me under house arrest till I was, like, his age!" she giggled. "And what you said about me and Daddy, you know? So true. I'm gonna try and stay off that stuff from now on."

"You remember last night?"

"Oh, totally! I never black out. I might not always be in control of what I say or do, but I never black out," she said, and tore off the check. She handed it to Kelly. "Thanks for being so cool."

Kelly looked at the check.

Ten grand. Seems to be the going rate fer being Victoria MacIntyre's friend.

She handed it back. "I don't want it."

"You're insulting me."

"When will you realize that I'm not your friend because you've got dosh? I care about you, and I want to see you alive."

"Just take it, will ya?" She handed the check back to Kelly. "My way of saying thanks."

"You trying to stay off drugs is thanks enough."

Vicky sat back, check in hand and studied Kelly for a long while. "I don't think I've ever known anyone like you, Kel. You're weird."

"Reflects the company I keep, I'm sure."

* * *

They arrived at the J as the electricians were finishing up. Neither had seen the finished lobby and stopped dead in their tracks as they entered it.

"Wow!" Kelly let out a whisper.

The new lobby was vast and bright. It extended from the bar in the far corner, past the reception desk and into the hallway leading to the ground floor offices, the staff entrance and the Study all the way to the restaurant in the other corner. The color scheme carried throughout the space and it looked warm and welcoming. The tan granite floor was shining and laid out in a pattern that subconsciously beckoned them to the bar.

"My brother did this?" Vicky said quietly. "It's too cool! Go Jack! ...eee..." she added hesitantly and looked at Kelly.

Kelly smiled. "It's okay, Vicky. I know he's straight," she whispered.

"How do you know?"

"It doesn't take *gaydar* to figure that out. I worked two weeks with him. The way he swings a sledgehammer versus the way Bryce and Alen do it, is the difference between straight and gay."

Huh? Didn't realize that I knew until I just said it!

Vicky sighed. "Thank God! It's getting more and more difficult keeping *that* little secret." She looked around the lobby. "So, where do you suppose the party planner's office is?"

Kelly pointed toward the grand staircase in the corner. "Basement. First door off the stairs. I'll see you after!"

Kelly took the stairs to the second floor. At the top of the staircase she could hear voices from Matthew's office. The door was open.

"She won't do it," Kelly heard Matthew say sternly.

Curiosity got the better of her and she stayed outside his door, eavesdropping.

"That caption on that girl? Come on! It's a given!" a voice Kelly didn't recognize insisted.

"You can ask her, but I doubt she'll do it," Matthew's voice said.

"The whole Milk Bar concept was her idea in the first place!" the other voice argued.

They're talking about ME!?

Kelly entered the office. "Morning, Chief!" she tried to sound casual and dropped her overnight bag and purse on the floor.

"Kelly, meet Ryan, our IT manager. Here today to do our new web site. With Charles," Matthew added with dismay.

"To-today?"

I haven't slept or washed me hair. I'm not wearing any make-up. I look horrid. No one will recognize…

"Grand! Let's get started!"

"Guys, could you give Kelly and me a moment? We'll meet you in the lobby in a few minutes," Matthew said ushering Ryan and Charles out the door and closed it behind them.

"You'd better sit down for this." He pulled out a chair for Kelly. His face was grim. "First of all, I think your PDA is bugged."

Bugged? Like in a virus? PDA's get those? Oh, du-uh, it's a computer... But it's so tiny! Maybe it's got a smaller virus, like just a sniffle ... or a cough ...

"I don't know whether it's a physical bug or if someone has access to your j-mail account. But somehow people seem to know everything you send and receive."

What?! Why? How? Who? Why? ... Why?!!

Matthew pulled out a long slip of carbon paper from his pocket. It looked like a store receipt. "We ran an audit on the lock to your suite. Seems that Gina's key has been used daily since you moved in. Again, let me just emphasize, I don't know why she's been in your room, if that has anything to do with your PDA being bugged or even if she's involved at all. Charles being at your computer the other day certainly raises the flag. We're investigating, of course, but for now, please just keep this to yourself."

Ohmygodohmygodohmygod! That first night when I was playing with my PDA I sent some really raunchy e-mails to Parker! And received some worse ones from him! Oh, I'm dead! Fersure.

"They can't find anything that's been deleted, can they?" she asked nervously.

"Nothing's ever really deleted. A knowledgeable computer guy can find anything that's ever been there."

"Knowledgeable? Like Charles?"

"Possibly."

Shite! He's probably already sold those e-mails to some sleazy magazine and made a huge profit ... No, wait! He grew up Commie. He wouldn't think in those terms. And what's it to anyone anyway, if I send a few dirty messages. I got the tilers and electricians out of that. Surely Gina should be pleased. Hah! Who am I kidding? Kelly's mind was racing.

"I'm afraid that it's not just your e-mails," Matthew said. "Your phone's probably tapped, too. Would you mind if I took a look at your PDA? I might also have to disable your j-mail account for now."

"Was there a 'second of all'?" Kelly asked handing her PDA to Matthew.

"You have to move. Today. After the shoot, and the drug test."

Kelly sighed and shook her head. "Why does she hate me?"

"She doesn't hate you. She's intimidated by you!"

"Why?! I'm no threat to her!"

"Really? Let's see. You're young and hot. She's old and cold. You get along with everyone. She gets along with no one. The jays love you and hate her. You're a hard worker. She's lazy. Need I go on?"

Kelly shook her head quietly.

"Do you have anywhere you can stay?" Matthew asked, worried.

Kelly nodded. Matthew went to his closet, but before opening the doors he turned to Kelly.

"Are you ready for this?" he said, smiling.

"Oh, God," Kelly felt deflated. "Is there going to be a 'third of all'?"

Matthew opened the closet doors and pulled out a front desk clerk's uniform. "You're to wear this in one of the pictures," he said, trying not to laugh. "With my condolences."

He can't be serious!

Kelly took the outfit. It consisted of baby-blue cotton slacks, a baby-blue and lime pinstriped waist coat, a lime green long-sleeved blouse and a baby-blue and lime polka-dotted, ruffled bow.

Someone was actually paid to design this shite?!

Kelly looked up at Matthew, expecting him to yell 'Gotcha!'. He didn't.

"If it's any consolation," Matthew said, "I'll be wearing the same thing."

"Bet you'll look absolutely adorable in a ruffled bow!" Kelly teased, playing with the bow in her hands.

Watch him blush! Three, two ... oops! Beat me to it!

"Bow-*tie* for men, wise guy!" Matthew turned back to the closet and pulled out the other clothes they were meant to wear.

"You have a choice of T-shirts. The rest of the pictures you can wear civilian clothing." He handed her the stack of T's. "You can change in there, if you want," he said pointing to the connecting doors. "Or in your suite if you need time to prepare. All pictures will be retouched, so you don't need to bother with make-up and stuff. Meet us in the lobby when you're ready."

Kelly took her stack of clothes and went to the connecting office, disbelievingly eyeing the uniform.

The reception staff is actually meant to wear this fer work? How will we ever hire anyone?!?

Ryan turned out to be quite good with the camera. He had a vision and gave excellent directions. He shot Kelly checking Matthew into the hotel. Kelly then changed into casual clothing, Matthew into the uniform and he checked her in. After Vicky finished with the party planner she joined the shoot, and agreed to having her picture taken in the bar. She also turned out to be a wonderful assistant, where hair, make-up and wardrobe were concerned. Kelly blatantly refused to wear the 'I got milked' T-shirt, but agreed to the 'got milk?' one. In one shot, Ryan got her and Matthew a milk moustache. Vicky stood behind Charles, making obscene gestures, and Kelly and Matthew were unable to contain themselves. Those pictures became instant classics. Charles had not been of any assistance to anyone. His presence was a mystery to Kelly. All he did was stand next to Ryan, grinning.

"Okay, folks," Ryan said. "Last one! Kelly, babe, get into a robe. Matthew, lose the tie and jacket. Chuck, find me a national newspaper. We're going to shoot in Kelly's room!"

Charles didn't like being bossed around or being called Chuck, but conceded. Ryan had Kelly sitting by the vanity, with her back toward him, brushing her hair. He shot her through the mirror, catching Matthew lying across the bed behind her, reading the newspaper.

This is stupid and I'm shattered and hungry. If I keep smiling like this, my cheekbones will crack and my gums will dry out!

They had only one break all day, for lunch, and Matthew and Kelly used that opportunity to go take their drug tests.

"Kelly!" Ryan said. "Turn your head toward me, babe. Not so much! … Good. Right there! Now raise your left hand just a tad … Beautiful!" He kept shooting. "Bend your right middle finger a bit more around the brush, would'ya, babe? It looks like you're flipping me the bird!"

I AM!

"I think I'm gonna make you a brunette in this one, okay, babe?"

"Whatever, just please quit calling me babe!"

"Okay, babe…" Ryan smirked. "Sorry…"

Kelly rose. "I think we're done here." She sat on the bed next to Matthew. "I'd like copies of everything, please."

"For personal use?" Ryan had had everyone sign waivers that the J Corporation had the sole right to the pictures.

"Of course. When do you think you'll be done?"

"The pictures will be done later this afternoon. Hoping to have the website running Friday prior to the MacIntyre party."

He was gathering all his stuff and was about to leave. He took one last look at Kelly and Matthew on the bed. Matthew was absorbed in an article in the newspaper and Kelly was looking at it over his shoulder. Ryan took a quick shot.

"You know, Kelly, I'm not a professional photographer, but you photograph really well. Have you ever thought of a career in modeling?" Ryan sounded sincere.

Kelly laughed. "Not likely!"

"Why not? You have surprisingly good teeth."

"Bad teeth is the stereotype for Brits! I'm *Irish*," Kelly huffed.

No need to tell him I wore braces for two years.

"Besides, I like food."

Kelly started packing, while Vicky was napping on her bed. Matthew appeared at her door.

"The results from our drug tests came," he said. "All clear!"

Phheeew!

"Did you see the pictures?" he continued excitedly and produced four poster-size prints of the shots that Ryan had taken earlier that day. One was of Kelly and Matthew laughing in the Milk Bar, one was of her checking in to the hotel, one was of her by the vanity brushing her hair, and the last one was of her and Matthew reading the paper together.

"They're good. What're you going to do with them?" Kelly asked.

"Hang them in the lobby. Could you come up with some catchy phrases to post under them?"

Kelly looked at each of them for a long time.

'I don't belong here, and it shows.' ' I smile, because I have no idea what's going on.' 'I smile because yer uniforms are a joke.' 'I smile because I'm imagining you without yer uniform...' 'Not Milk.' 'If I keep brushing my hair like this I'll be bald. ... And have carpal tunnel.' 'The secret to my shiny, shiny hair? Re-touching.' ... Hmmm? This one's really good. We do make a handsome couple. Too bad he's married.

"Let me think about that, okay?" she told Matthew.

"Fair enough. Call me as soon as you hear anything about your visa. I'll do the same, should they contact me."

"Matthew?" Kelly said, feeling slightly uncomfortable. "Any chance I could stash some of my stuff here, somewhere? I mean, I'll be back soon, I hope. No point in hauling everything back and forth."

"Give me a call, once you're ready to leave. I'll come up and give you a hand. There's an old closet in my office you can store stuff in. Been meaning to make that into a file cabinet, but haven't quite got around to it yet."

Matthew stood at the door, with his hand on the doorknob. He looked as though he wanted to say something. Just then Vicky walked yawning into the sitting room. She looked in awe at Kelly's bags.

"Why're you packing?"

"Long story," Kelly said, folding her clothing neatly into a suitcase. "Bottom line is, I've been shunned until I get my visa."

"So, come and stay at our place in the country! We have a pool!" Vicky said excitedly.

"So do the Russells. But I'd really rather stay at your flat," Kelly whispered so Matthew wouldn't hear.

"Oh, didn't Daddy tell you? He's getting ready to fly to Argentina," Vicky said quietly. She could read the disappointment on Kelly's face. "We have horses! I bet you haven't been horse-back riding since you left Ireland?"

Why is it always 'horse back riding' in this country? Back home it's just 'riding'. The horse and the back are a given. I mean, what else would it be? Cow head riding? Goat butt riding? ... Wait ...

"How do you know I ride?"

"Oh, puh-leease! You can't get a tight little tush like yours from just tennis!" she slapped Kelly on the butt. "Right, Matthew?"

As expected, Matthew's face turned crimson. "See you later, ladies," he said and left.

"See you next Tuesday, Mr. B.!" Kelly shouted behind him, uncertain whether he'd heard or not.

"So? Whaddya say?"

"Help me pack?"

"Sure. By the way. Been meaning to ask you. Who's your 'and guest' at the party?"

"Everyone I know is already invited …" Kelly said. "Could I bring Patrick, Susan's assistant?"

"That Korean guy? He's invited."

"You know him?"

"Yeah, sorta. I met him at a Russell barbeque once. He's hot!"

Really? Huh? He is rather attractive, actually. Never thought of him in those terms. Never could get past the computer geek of him.

"Anyone else?" Vicky asked.

Hmmm, let's see here. Freddie Couples, Pierce Brosnan, Mel Gibson, Dan Marino, … probably all already invited. … Whoa! I really am into older men!

"Oy! Any chance I could keep someone out?" Kelly asked excitedly.

"Someone not already on any of my lists? Sure. We have bouncers. Give them the names. No prob."

21

"Just got cc'd on an e-mail from EUSA. I'm so sorry, Kelly. It's a no-go on the J-1," Matthew said on the phone, sounding utterly disappointed.

Focketyfockfock!

It was early morning and Kelly had just returned from a misty morning ride around the MacIntyre estate.

"Did they give a reason?" she said, peeling off her boots.

"They said that since you already had an application in for an H-3, you couldn't apply for this one. You'll get a copy of the original USCIS refusal."

"Any news from Kate Fleming, my immigration lawyer?"

Matthew laughed. "Yeah, just got my head chewed off by her. I called and told her about this decision. She made me feel like a damn fool for not knowing that you can only apply for one visa at the time."

"I didn't know either! What do I know about immigration laws? That's why I hired a lawyer!"

"Exactly! Anyway, she says that we should have a decision on the H-3 within a matter of days. Either way."

The line was silent for a while.

"I'm just sitting here looking at the government website, and you know that there's another visa you might want to look into," Matthew finally said.

"Yeah, what's that?"

"A celebrity visa. You know those web site pictures we shot? You're a model!"

"Yeah, right!"

"Oh, no wait," Matthew read on. "You have to be internationally famous prior to applying. Hey! Did you see a copy of yesterday's *Smile!* magazine?"

"No! Surprised you have."

"The jays made me buy one," Matthew said. "Ryan sold them a copy of that picture of you and Vicky in the Milk Bar. The caption isn't the greatest, but hey! It's free publicity, right? The jays are elated."

"What's the caption say?"

Do I really want to know?

"B-bosom buddies," Matthew stuttered uncomfortably.

Kelly laughed. "Let me guess! It's a bit *nipular?*"

"Yeah, well…"

Ooow! I can almost hear the blood rushing to his cheeks! … No, wait! That's the sound of my blood rushing to my cheeks! … Hold on a sec! Ryan gave me a CD with those photos … there's nothing dirty on them! … Well, suppose that wouldn't be the first thing I'd look at … or look for…

"Have you ever won anything?" Matthew was still reading the website, dying to change the subject.

"For modeling? Hardly."

"No, I meant tennis? There's a visa for athletes."

"Well, I did win the fifth ring championship," Kelly announced proudly.

"Is that an international event?"

"Sure! Between Northern Ireland and the Republic of."

Matthew laughed. "I think they're after a title at like Wimbledon or the US Open…"

I'm still proud of my win. It's a big deal fer a twelve-year-old!

"Hey! Listen to this! You could invest a million bucks in a new company, hire seven non-relatives and be set for life!"

Kelly couldn't help but laugh. "Sure, Matthew."

If I had a million bucks, I would be set fer life!

"Lend me a million bucks, will ya, and we'll go into business together!" She sighed. "I appreciate what you're trying to do, Matthew, but it seems like you're grasping at straws here. If it's gonna happen, it's gonna happen. If it's not, it's not. And although I'd love to work at the J, there's a big world out there. Lots of places I haven't been to yet."

"I like your attitude," Matthew said. "Will I see you at the MacIntyre party tomorrow?"

"Wouldn't miss it for the world!" Kelly smiled as they hung up.

She showered and changed, and walked into the living room. Jacqui was sitting on the sofa. The muted big screen TV was broadcasting the second round of the British Open from St. Andrew's in Scotland.

Look at that! Even in wide-screen those fairways are narrow.

Jacqui was frantically sketching on the coffee table, occasionally glancing up at the TV. The coffee table was covered with drawings, and the floor with crumpled papers. He looked haggard and frustrated.

"Who's leading?" Kelly asked.

Jacqui looked exhausted, as he looked up at Kelly.

"Huh? Oh, it's a tie between some South African and that cute Spanish guy."

"Ernie or Goose?"

"Huh? Oh, I don't know. Garcia, I think."

Okay, he's getting really inconsistent with this pretend gay thing. Like pretending he doesn't know sports, and yet, here he is, following it!

"I need a theme!" Jacqui whined melodramatically. "Why can't I think of anything? My brain is like … I don't know … melting, or something."

"Try sleeping," Kelly said, taking a seat on the opposite side of the coffee table. "And showering. What are you working on?"

"The Asheville lobby!" Jacqui said shooting a glance at the TV. "Wow! What a fox!"

I rest my case!

The TV showed the current leader's wife.

Why do they always show the athletes' wives at sporting events, but they never show the models' husbands at Victoria's Secret fashion shows? ... God! I'm really becoming a feminist!

"Why aren't you at work?" she said.

Jacqui looked at his watch. "Oh, no! Why didn't you tell me how late it was! Susan's going to kill me!" He started gathering his drawings.

"Where's Vicky?" Kelly shouted after him.

"Roberto Leon's for everything," Jacqui said and ran out the door.

Kelly had spent over a week at the MacIntyre mansion, and hadn't seen Parker once since returning from Charlotte. She now had the house to herself, and left him a message stating just that fact. She was tempted to go to Parker's study and e-mail him a copy of the Milk Bar picture.

It made Matthew stutter ... wonder what it'll do to Parker!?

She got comfortable by the computer in the study and tried to connect to the Internet.

How can a rich billionaire like Parker MacIntyre have dial-up? Homing pigeons would be faster!

She looked out the window and saw two pick-up trucks, with men in green polo shirts sitting in the back, drive up the driveway. Betty, the housekeeper, walked up to them and gave one of them a wad of cash.

Whatta fock?!

Parker, Jon and Duncan were meant to leave for Argentina the previous week, but Emmett, a category four hurricane, was brewing in the Caribbean. Although not affecting the Southern Atlantic coast with anything worse than gale-force winds and heavy downpours, Candi had refused to fly to South Carolina to pick Duncan up before the storm moved out or died out. Parker wanted to leave on Friday, but had been guilt-tripped by Jon to stay for his daughter's birthday.

He pulled up the driveway of his mansion an hour after he'd received Kelly's message. As he was driving toward the house, he could see her on the front lawn. She was mowing it. Parker stopped his car and got out.

"Hey Red!" he shouted at her.

She heard him, but kept mowing. Parker walked up to her. He could see that she was upset. She was muttering in Gaelic. He put his hand on the handle, and killed the engine.

"Why are you doing this? I have landscapers, you know," he smiled. "Come on, let's go upstairs, I don't have much time." He took her by the hand, and started pulling her toward the car.

Kelly tore herself away from his grip. "Ya two-faced hypocrite!" she yelled. "Yer so full of it! Trying to appear all caring, and ATM-like and helpful, and then you do this!" Kelly waved her hand across the lawn.

"You've lost me," Parker frowned.

"You were just creating a smoke screen, weren't ya, to get into me knickers!"

"What are you talking about?"

"Yer landscapers!"

"What about 'em? Jimmy Joe is the best in the business. He's been on my payroll for years!"

"Yeah? And do you know who's on his? Illegals! They showed up this morning. None of them speaking English, fer fock's sake!"

"And?"

"Are ya bloody kiddin' me?! They're the reason it's so difficult fer someone like me to get into this country! Someone like me, who's trying to do things right! To do things legally! And you're fighting it by hiring illegals."

"How?"

"How?! Because there's so bloody many of them, the laws are tightened. And that affects anyone trying to get in legally! And they don't pay taxes! This Jimmy Joe of yers certainly doesn't withhold any fer them! None of the money they make stays in this country! Don't you know that there's people here who are just as capable of mowing yer lawn, and are legal!? And because you keep hiring illegals, they go unemployed!"

"Do you want to do my lawns now?"

Kelly hesitated. "Well, no. It needed doing. And I sent Jimmy Joe's crew home…"

"You what?! What did they say?"

"Guess what, Parker? I don't speak Spanish!"

"Who do you think you are, anyway? The little missus? You have absolutely no right to dismiss my hired help!"

"Fine," Kelly said and started walking toward the house. "Nice screwing ya, Parker. Not so nice being screwed by ya."

Parker ran his hands through his hair in frustration. "Wait!" He went after her. "I'm sorry, sugar, I didn't mean that. Trust me, I never knew that they were illegal, or else I wouldn't have hired them."

Kelly looked into his eyes for a long time. "Seriously?"

Parker took both her hands in his. "Would I lie to you?"

"Bye Parker!" Kelly started toward the house again.

Parker grabbed her by the elbow. "What the hell's your problem?"

"You! Yer me problem. Do yerself a favor and book an appointment with yer proctologist and see if he can't locate yer head!"

"You little bitch…!"

"Yer so full of yerself! Ya think ya know everything and are better than everyone else. Well, guess what? Yer not. Quite the opposite, in fact. One day yer going to wake up dying and alone, because you've alienated everyone else!"

Kelly started to walk away, but turned around quickly. She was on a roll, and intended not to lose momentum. "And that includes yer kids!"

Parker smiled self-righteously. "You've known my kids for, what? Two months? And you have the balls to tell me I've alienated them?"

Kelly studied his eyes intently for a moment. "Where's Vicky going to school in the autumn?"

"Stanford! Hah!"

"What's her major?" Kelly kept staring at Parker. "Economic geology! Didn't know that, did ya? That's right. Yer daughter is passionate about geology, and is frankly brilliant at it!"

She saw a glimmer of surprise in his eyes. "And yer son! What's his sexual preference?"

"Men in tights, I don't know," Parker was getting more and more frustrated.

"Try soccer mums!"

"You know, Irish, I'm getting really fed up with your bitching! You can't change the world, and certainly not me. My family has functioned perfectly well before you entered our lives, and will keep doing so long after you leave!" With that he got back in his car and drove up to the house.

* * *

"Can you come pick me up?" Kelly asked Vicky on the phone, trying to stay calm.

She had picked up her purse and her cell phone and was hiding in the kitchen. She knew that if she saw Parker again, she might start throwing things.

Too many beautiful, expensive things in this house. Gotta get out. … Must enroll in anger management class …

"When?" Vicky heard the anxiety in Kelly's voice.

"Right now. Had a huge row with your Dad. Gotta get away fast."

"I can't. I'm having my hair done, and it'll take me forever to get there anyway. Take one of the cars. The keys are in a box on the kitchen wall. Can you drive an automatic?"

"No prob."

How hard can it be? It's automatic! What worries me is driving on the right side of the road! Wrong side? Aaarrghh!!

Kelly located the box in the kitchen and took out a key under a nail marked 'Jack's Jeep'.

"Just make sure not to get one scratch on the car or Daddy'll have your ass for lunch!" Vicky warned.

"I promise I'll be careful," Kelly was already rushing toward the garage.

"Oh, Gawd!"

"Whatwhatwhatwhat?"

"I just pictured my Dad having your ass for lunch!" Vicky whined and hung up.

Kelly sped from the house and found her way toward the Interstate cursing Parker under her breath. The traffic was heavy and she had no idea where she was going. As she entered the Interstate she passed a sign for O'Hare.

Maybe I should just go to the airport and start begging. I could have enough for a ticket in ... ten years or so. By then I'll be deported. ... Oy! Free trip home!

Her cell phone rang. Had the display not read 'Susan office', she wouldn't have answered.

"Hi, darling, it's Jacqui. I need to pick your brain."

"Now's not a good time, Jacqui," Kelly said between clenched teeth.

"Yeah, but this'll only take a sec. When I say Asheville, what do you think?"

... ??? ...

"Nothing."

"Aw, come on, Kell-yyy! You must think of something. I need a theme. Come on! You were spewing out ideas like a gumball machine on the Chicago property! Can't you do the same for Asheville?"

"Like I said, Jacqui, now's not a good time!" Kelly said, irritated, as she barely had time to avoid another car cutting her off, switching lanes in front of her without signaling. She leaned on the horn.

"Just a little something, to get me in the mood. Toss me a bone. Asheville! What comes to mind?"

"Nothing, Jacqui! I told you! I've never been there!"

"God, chill out, girl! What are you, on the rag, or something?"

"Screw you Jacqui!" Kelly hung up.

Y tu papa tambien! … Oy! I do speak Spanish!

She had barely hung up on Jacqui when the phone rang again.

"Hiya, pet!" her mother's voice brought tears to her eyes. "How are you?"

"Grand, Mum. You?"

I wish you were here right now telling me everything will be alright!

"We're all grand. A letter came in the post fer you today. It's from Uni. It looked official, so I opened it. Hope you don't mind…"

"What's it say?"

This can't be good. You're supposed to say everything will be alright, Mum!!

"I'll read it to you. Let me just find me glasses…"

Was that my exit? Doesn't really matter, since I have nowhere to go. Wonder where I'll end up just following this road? Wisconsin? Huh? Nothing in Wisconsin but … Oh, yeah, there's that football team that Vicky likes, and that every Chicagoan feel obligated to hate. The… What? … Cheeseheads…?

"… year ago to date you asked for, and were granted, a year's extension on your thesis…" her mother was back on the line. "As we have not heard back from you, we are compelled to give your place on the Masters' Programme to another student…"

When it rains, it pours. … What's with the traffic around here? Where did all these people learn to drive? … Du-uh! Right here!

Kelly leaned on the horn again.

"…cannot be appealed," her mother concluded. "I'm sorry, pet. What will you do?"

"A dinna ken, Mum."

"Why don't you jest come home? We miss you dreadfully."

There was a static silence on the line.

"You've found some nice young American boy, haven't you, hen?" her mother teased.

Parker? Nice? Hardly. Young? Boy? Not in years. American? … Okay, I'll grant him that.

"That's good, dear. Don't be getting too attached, now. Remember, you're only there visiting," her mother continued. "Well, at least you're over Sean."

"Ya think?!" Kelly said sarcastically.

Aw, f-f-f…

"Mind yer sassy mouth, Kelly McCoy! Yer neither too old nor too far away fer me to bend you over me knee! Don't think fer a minute I won't be on the next plane!"

"I'm sorry, Mum. I've just had a really rotten day, and I feel miserable. I'm sorry."

"Well, you know what yer Dad would say – the only way is up," her mother sounded cheerful again. "Keep yer chin up, pet, and the rest of you will follow. And remember – the night is always coldest jest before dawn."

"Well, yer jest full of clever clichés today, Mum! Got a third?"

"Ya bet, Miss sassy-arse! Sarcasm from a pretty girl is like the thorn of a precious rose," her Mother rebutted.

Kelly bit her lip hard. "Sorry," she said quietly. She could hear the digital double-beep on her phone, indicating another call. "I'm sorry, Mum, I'm going to have to cut off now, I'm driving. Luv to Dad!"

"Please be careful, hen!"

The traffic came to a dead halt.

Where could all these people possibly be going?

Kelly hung up with her mother and answered the call waiting.

"I'm sorry, Red," Parker started. "I agree with you. After all, this country was founded by immigrants. We need more people like you. And fewer damn illegal immigrants. I knew Jimmy Joe hired Latinos, but I didn't know they weren't legal."

Yeah, right! So what's yer housekeeper doing paying them cash? Fer other services rendered? ... Hmmm? Maybe I did jump to conclusions. They could've had a bet on the Cubs-Sox game fer all I know!

"I got your e-mail. I must say, you've got guts!" Parker laughed. "Love that T-shirt. Picture was taken in an air-conditioned room, I take it?"

Shallow, empty, single-minded creature!

"What do you say? Quickie at my condo?"

"You know, Parker, you can't just insult me like you did, and expect me to drop my knickers for you just because you're now in the mood! I'm not a light switch!"

"You always turn me on," he said in a low voice. "Look, Red, I was wrong when I said you couldn't change me. You have. I haven't been with anyone else since I started sleeping with you. That's huge for me! You're the best piece of ass I've ever had!"

I suppose fer a guy like him, that's meant as a compliment. He's really good, too. And he can be sweet when he wants to. And he's really been good to me. And that little thing he does...

"So, what do you say?" Parker asked.

Kelly sighed. "Where are you?"

"Kennedy. Driving back to the office. Where are you?"

"I-90. Driving back to the city."

"What? The I-90 is the ... Always the little smart ass, aren't ya?"

"Race you to your flat!"

Mmmm! Make-up sex! Kelly thought and leaned on the horn.

They decided to meet in the parking structure below Sears Tower.

> To: Jacqui mobile
> Sorry a/b B4. Send Ashv info. C what I can
> do. XK

Kelly was just sending the message, when she saw Parker walking toward her, smiling broadly. He looked around to make sure he wasn't seen and made an obscene gesture.

This isn't right. The mere sight of him should make me skin prickle. Send shock waves up and down me spine. That's it then … I don't love him. Focketyfock! … Am I in love with him? … Not so much … Really don't even like him half the time! What am I doing with him, then?! … Oh, Christ! Me Mum's right! Parker's me rebound-guy! … Aaarrghh! I hate when she's right!

"We need to talk," Kelly said calmly when Parker reached her.

"Oh, no! *The talk.* This can't be good. Why do women always feel the need to analyze everything? 'Where's this relationship going?', 'Do you love me?' 'Why don't you ever talk about your feelings with me?'. Come on, Red! Why can't we just enjoy what we have?"

That's sad, really. Kinda pathetic, and nothing more than I would have expected from him, but sad, that he feels like he has to pretend to be macho…

"Parker, I don't love you," Kelly said quietly, and fought the lump in her throat. "I think it's unfair to both of us to carry our non-relationship any further."

Parker looked at her for a long time in silence. A car drove by and parked close to where they were standing. Parker put an arm around her and led her toward the elevators. "I think we should talk upstairs," he said.

The elevator ride was awkward. Kelly could feel the tension between them, and tried hard to focus on the little elevator TV. In his condo, they sat on opposite sides of the living room.

"So, what's this really about? You're not having a good time?" Parker said.

"No, it's…"

"There's someone else, isn't there?"

"No, I…"

"What? You want to get married? You want a baby? Not happening."

Wow, Parker! It would be nice if you'd get just one of these right once.

Kelly shook her head slowly. "No. I just … I just don't like the person I am when I'm with you …" she said quietly. She was trying to read his eyes. They gave away no emotion. "You're a wonderful lover and you've been a great help to me in many ways, and I'll always be grateful to you for that … but … I think I want more than what we have. I think I want what Jon and Susan have … I'm so sorry."

"Don't be," Parker said and moved over to her. He leaned her head against his chest, and kissed her hair softly. "I, too, envy the Russells. You should want more. And I'm not the guy to give you that. You're still so young. You're much too young for me. Or maybe I'm too old for you? You were vulnerable and I think I might have taken advantage of that. I'm sorry," he said and kissed her hair again.

Damn, damn, damn! Why does he have to be so sweet now? Now I just want to jump up and scream 'just kidding!' and tear his clothes off!

Kelly looked up at him. "Can we still be friends?"

"I hope so. You're friends with my kids, and it would be pretty awkward otherwise."

Kelly sat up and took his hand. "Thank you."

See? He can be a good guy. I do like him …

Parker held her hand, and leaned in. "How about one for the road, huh?"

Crash! Boom! Bang! Back to Arsehole!

Kelly laughed. "You're right! No changing you!"

They stood up and hugged for a long time.

"Friends?" Parker whispered.

"Friends."

"What's going on?" Vicky walked into the room. "I thought you were fighting! Are you making up? Should I leave the room?"

Parker looked at Kelly. "She knows?"

"I keep telling you, she's much smarter than you give her credit for," she said quietly.

They were still holding each other, and turned to face Vicky.

"We just broke up," Kelly said.

Bizarre. This is the most comfortable I've ever felt around him.

Vicky pouted. "Too bad, Kel. I'da loved having a step-mother I actually like. But you'll find that he makes a way better friend, than lover or husband. Or father."

"I heard that, Victoria!"

"Good! You were supposed to!" Vicky huffed. "Kelly, I have, like, nothing to wear for the party tomorrow. Wanna go shopping?"

"Luv to," Kelly said. She turned to look at Parker for one last time. "So, we're good, then?"

He nodded. "I'm gonna miss you, Red. I wasn't lying when I told you you're the best I've ever had," he said, smiling sadly. "But I think this'll be better. For both of us." He let out a roaring laughter. "I think this is the most functional breakup ever!"

Kelly pecked a quick kiss on his cheek. "Be good to Vicky," she said, grabbed her purse and left the room. Her cell phone beeped.

> Sender: Jacqui mobile
> Ur t best!
> XOX

Aren't I just!? Oooh, reminds me. Must ring Patrick!

22

All of Chicago was abuzz about Victoria MacIntyre's birthday party. The guest list read like a *Who's Who* of Reagan Generation wealth. You knew you were a nobody if you didn't receive an invitation. Nearly four hundred of Vicky's 'closest' friends showed up. The party had expanded so much that it now took over the entire ground floor and the ballroom across the hall from Matthew's office on the second floor. The two party scenes were connected by the grand staircase, covered in a red carpet for the evening.

The jays had offered Vicky a deal which she found impossible to turn down. In exchange for a few words in favor of the hotel and bar, they would carry all costs for the party, except the liquor. Vicky agreed to make a grand entrance down the staircase, greet the media and pose for a photo-op. Matthew lent them his office for last minute preparations.

"Are you sure you're comfortable with what you're saying, then?" Kelly asked, while fastening Vicky's mother's pearls around her gaunt neck.

"For the millionth time, Kelly!" Vicky said impatiently. "I know it by heart! Backwards! Yadda-yadda-yadda thank you for being here. Blah-blah-blah J Hotel, Milk Bar. Let's party!" She turned around. "How do I look?" She was wearing a simple black cocktail dress. Classy and expensive.

They heard a soft wailing from the sofa. Jacqui reached for a Kleenex. "Like Mom," he wailed.

"Kelly?" Vicky said, ignoring her brother.

"I'm thinking Holly Golightly, but I don't know why."

It's disturbing that she's skinnier than Audrey Hepburn even!

"That's exactly the look I was going for!" Vicky shrieked and stuck her tongue out at her brother.

"Now, go! I'm just about fashionably late. My party planner wants the two of you and Daddy front and center. You know, … just behind the reporters, obviously." She ushered them out the door. "I'll be making my entrance in one minute exactly. That's sixty Mississippies, Jacqui. Kelly will help you when you run out of fingers."

Jacqui gave her the finger, and led Kelly down the stairs.

Okay, so that's one *Mississippi…*

Vicky made her grand entrance to rousing applause. She had a glow about her. She was smiling and waving gracefully to the media. Halfway down the staircase was a landing and a microphone had been set there for Vicky to give her speech, as written by her party planner. Vicky took her place by the microphone and waited for the applause to die down.

"Wow! You'd think I just won an Oscar or something! Thank you all for coming tonight. I especially wish to thank my father for being here. Mr. Parker MacIntyre, everyone!" she pointed him out in the crowd.

The reporters spun around quickly and shot a few pictures of him, while he blew a kiss to his daughter.

"I know there are some emeralds somewhere with his name on them, but they've been there for thirty million years, so what's another weekend gonna matter?" Vicky continued.

This wasn't in the original speech. Oh, God! She's drunk!

"How does everyone like the new J Hotel Chicago?!" Vicky shrieked and the crowd exploded in whistles and catcalls. She was in her element and loving every minute of it. "I'm gonna start calling the J my new home, and expect all of you to do the same! Just remember," she added quickly before the applause could start again, "that I know where you live and I know your net worth, so don't go doing anything I wouldn't do!"

"That pretty much leaves 'em with free hands, Vicky!" a young male reporter cried out.

"Someone's finally catching on!" Vicky said and the laughter continued. "I'd like everyone to meet my best pal in the world …"

Uh-oh! Please just stick to the script, Vicky…

"… Kelly McCoy from Ireland! There she is, standing between my Dad and my brother! Isn't she gorgeous?! I want to thank her …" Vicky started sincerely.

Kelly quickly slashed her hand across her throat and tilted her head toward Parker.

"… for being such a great friend. Kelly McCoy, everyone! Guys, she's hot, she's single and you can meet her right here in the fabulous Milk Bar every night!"

The whistles and catcalls were deafening by now.

Somebody get her down from there! She's worse than Cilla in the Dating Game. She's making me sound like a bloody alky!

The photographers quickly found Kelly and were fighting to get her picture. She was blinded by the flashes exploding in her face. She could feel a strong arm around her waist, and the scent of a familiar cologne filled her nostrils. She felt safe in Parker's arms and smiled at the reporters. Jacqui hugged her from the other side and both men kissed her on the cheek.

Okay, so this is bizarre. I'm the corned beef in a MacIntyre sandwich.

"Smile, while it's all still good," Parker said huskily from the corner of his mouth.

What's that supposed to mean?

"What do you mean?"

"Hope you'll never have to find out."

"Alright, everyone! Are you ready to par-TAY?!" Vicky ended her speech.

The bands started playing. Vicky joined her family at the bottom of the staircase.

"Miss MacIntyre!", "Vicky!", "Over here!", "Look this way, Vicky!" The reporters were all over her.

"I've said all I intend to say to the media tonight," Vicky said calmly. She took her father's elbow and made her way to the bar.

Parker got up on stage and was given the microphone from the bandleader in the Milk Bar. "Victoria? Could I see you up here for a moment?" he smiled over the crowd, which was teasingly murmuring 'uh-oh' and 'you're in trouble' as it parted to let Vicky up on stage.

Jacqui escorted her. Kelly and the Russells were standing at the bottom of the stage stairs.

"Happy birthday, sweetheart," Parker said, smiling, handing Vicky a large, square box.

Ooow!

Vicky shook the box to her ear. "Too big to be Harry Winston's," she said, face glowing. "Too small to be Brett Favre..."

"Yeah, like you even know who Brett Favre is!" Jacqui huffed.

"Like *you* know!?"

"Oh, just open it, will ya?"

Vicky tore into the wrapping. She pulled out a yellow hard hat. It sported the MacIntyre Industries logo.

Okay, so I don't subscribe to Cosmo, but I'm sure that *isn't this season's top accessory.*

Vicky's eyes were moist. Her lower lip was quivering, and she looked at her father with big eyes. He was smiling widely.

"I'm offering you the same deal your brother got. No special treatment. You report directly to Mr. Russell. You leave for the field with us first thing Monday morning. If you don't screw up this summer and if, after you finish your freshman year at Stanford, you're still interested, you're welcome back for another summer. After that, we'll see," he said, still speaking into the microphone.

Vicky let out a shriek and threw herself around Parker's neck. "I love you, Daddy! Thank you!"

The crowd burst into spontaneous applause. Susan was wiping her eyes.

"I love you, too, sweetheart," Parker said and kissed her cheek. "Now, you notice that it's yellow…"

"I know, I know," Vicky waved her hand. "White for management, blue for foremen, yellow for peons. I'm so totally cool with that!" She put the hard hat on and turned to Kelly. "How do I look?"

Like a mushroom.

"Like a million bucks!" Kelly shouted up to her.

"Which reminds me!" Vicky said and grabbed the microphone from her father. Parker and Jacqui joined Kelly. "Could the executors of my mother's trust fund please come up to the stage?" she said, squinting her eyes in the spotlights, trying to look over the crowd. Two men in suits appeared. "Thank you for coming tonight," Vicky started politely. "I'm sure my mother is looking down from her little cloud and is proud of the job you've done. How about a round of applause, everyone?" The crowd clapped awkwardly. "But today I'm twenty-one! No more having you looking over my shoulder every time I write a check. No more scrutinizing every credit card statement …" .

"Should I get her down from there?" Jacqui turned to Parker.

"What's wrong?" Kelly whispered.

"Don't worry," Parker said. "She'll come down alright. Soon enough. Just both of you be there to pick her up when she does."

"…please know, gentlemen," Vicky continued. "that you're hereby most cordially dismissed. So, take a hike," she said and jerked her thumb like a referee in a baseball game, "and *do* let the door hit your tight-wad asses on your way out!"

The crowd roared with laughter. The applause was overwhelming.

Is she on anything? She can't be! I've been with her all day. Prubly just high on life.

"This could get really ugly," Jacqui said. "I can't believe she doesn't know."

"Know what? What are you doing to her?" Kelly was worried.

"You're about to find out," Parker said solemnly.

The laughter was dying out. Neither of the executors had moved. One of them leaned toward Vicky and whispered something in her ear.

"What?! You son of a bitch! You can't do that!" Vicky said into the microphone.

She started crying, got off the stage and rushed to her dad. "Daddy! That man just told me I don't get my money until after grad school!"

"Or your twenty-fifth birthday, whichever comes last," Parker said calmly.

The crowd started to murmur. Kelly grabbed the mike Vicky was still holding and ran to the bandleader.

"Play something!" she hissed giving him the mike.

"What?" he said and looked perplexed.

"Play something, anything, just do it!"

"What do you want us to play?"

"I don't care, so long as it's loud and it's NOW!"

The music started and the crowds began mingling again. Kelly made her way back to Vicky. She looked ridiculously small in her hard hat, crying and looking pleadingly at her father.

"They can't do that, can they, Daddy?"

"They're not the ones doing it, dear. Your mother is," he said calmly, and put a protective arm around her frail shoulders. "Actually your mother and I are. You're probably too young to remember her sister. She couldn't handle money worth shit. She died in an institution. Broke and addicted to everything. Your mother didn't want that to happen to you. Jack got the same deal."

Vicky looked teary-eyed at her brother. "Jacqui?" He nodded. "But Mom and her brothers turned out alright... Why didn't anyone TELL me?!"

One of the gorilla-sized bouncers appeared by Parker's side and whispered something in his ear. Parker nodded. He smiled at Vicky. "I know nothing will make you feel better after your disappointment ..."

"...and public humiliation," Vicky hiccupped.

"...and public humiliation just now, but I think this might be a good start," Parker said with a wink.

He turned Vicky toward the front doors of the hotel. Jacqui motioned to the bandleader. The band started playing Stars and Stripes Forever. The crowds parted. In the door stood a middle-aged man, in an immaculate Army uniform. He was smiling from ear to ear and extended his arms toward Vicky.

"Bobbyyy!" Vicky shrieked and ran toward him. She jumped in his arms and he picked her up light as a feather. "You're back! You're alive! You're all in one piece!"

God, her life's like a continuous bungee jump. With these types of natural highs and lows, who needs drugs?

Kelly turned to Jacqui. "Who's that? Old boyfriend?"

"Oh, yuck! Old is right, boyfriend would be sick! That's our Uncle Bobby."

Kinda old to still go by Bobby! I mean, he's no Kennedy. ... Hmmm? Wonder if Bobby Kennedy hadn't been killed, and had been elected, would he still have been 'Bobby' in the White House? President Bobby? … Sounds more like the president of a tree house club than the leader of the free world. … I can hear the conversation on The Hotline now. 'Yo! Bro Comrade Chairman Lenny? Bobby here…' … Way to stay cool in the cold war… I'da nuked him! … Wait … Jimmy Carter went to the White House as 'Jimmy'. … Well, it could've been worse. He could've been 'Jimbo'!

"Hey! Everyone! Come meet my uncle, Colonel Ashton!" Vicky yelled to the crowd. "He's just come back from the war!"

People were gathering around them, everyone eager to shake his hand or pat his back. Kelly saw the jays fluttering about him.

What is it about a man in uniform? If I met this guy under other circumstances, I probably wouldn't look twice. Nor would the jays. … And look at this crowd. Statistically half of them should be anti-war anyway, but they're all pro uniform …

"So, you and Parker are officially a couple now?" Susan interrupted Kelly's thoughts. "Kinda risky, don't you think?"

Kelly turned to face her. "We broke up yesterday."

"Thank God!" Susan sighed. "Sorry… How do you feel?"

"Much better about him, quite frankly!" Kelly laughed. "It was just a summer fling, anyway…"

Susan took Kelly by the elbow and they elbowed their way through the crowd to the bar. "Well, summer's only just begun!" she said with a wink. "Hey, Matthew! How about a couple of drinks over here?"

Matthew was tending the bar, wearing a white shirt, a bow-tie and black waistcoat. His hair was slicked back. He smiled as he approached Susan and Kelly.

Holy Bat, Shiteman! It's Cary Grant!

"I'm going to pay you a compliment, now, Matthew, so be prepared to blush," Kelly said. Matthew diverted his eyes. "You look like you walked out of a black and white movie!"

"How's that a compliment?"

"Look around! Nothing but women at the bar!"

Matthew looked around and blushed. "Yeah, well … that's just because all the men are hovering over G.I. Joe, over there. So, what'll it be, ladies? Suze – champagne? Kelly?"

"Milk," she said and burst out laughing. "Sorry, I don't know why, but suddenly I found that tremendously humorous!"

Oh, Parker! You shallow, empty creature! I'll never be able to think of milk the same way again…

"Ooo-kay," Matthew looked at her curiously. "Shot of rum in it?"

"Really, really not. Haven't touched liquor in weeks," Kelly said. "So, what's new with the Russell clan?" she shouted at Susan.

It was difficult to carry on a conversation in the bar. The music was loud, and the place was packed. Kelly could see Vicky and her uncle on the dance floor. Her eyes were scanning for Parker.

Susan grasped Kelly's hand quickly. "Abigail reached her target weight this morning!" She was beaming, as only a proud parent can beam.

"That's brilliant! I'm so proud of her! Please tell her I said that!"

"She went jogging with Jon this morning, and she's pushing your diet on Tammy…"

Kelly saw Parker on the dance floor, cutting in to dance with Vicky.

Ooow! He's really been sweet today. And scorching hot in that tux! Maybe I was too hasty. Maybe I should give him another chance. He's leaving for Argentina soon … Maybe a bon voyage romp wouldn't be out of the question … Good plan!

"Patrick, you made it!" Susan's exclamation interrupted Kelly's thoughts.

She swung around in her bar stool and saw Patrick's smiling face. "Do you have it?" she whispered excited.

Tapping at his chest, Patrick nodded and smiled.

"Are you ready?" Kelly said looking up at him from under her brow.

He nodded again, his smile widening.

"Do I want to know what the two of you are up to?" Susan sounded worried.

"Or I?" Matthew leaned across the bar.

Aw, come on! I had a detective story moment going! Don't spoil it fer me!

"Matthew, Patrick. Patrick, Matthew," she introduced them quickly. "It's not like it's anything illegal! I'm trying to help the hotel, here! We're just about to bust some Charlie Cho butt! You seen him?"

"Last I saw him, he was scampering after Gina like a pup," Matthew tried to suppress a smile. "The gruesome twosome was not pleased about having been denied entry to the party. Try Gina's office."

Kelly got out of her chair. "Let's roll!"

"Not without me!" Matthew said, and joined them.

"Or me …" Susan sighed. "I'm too old for this, but welcome the idea of putting the gruesome twosome in place."

The lights were on in Gina's glass-enclosed office just off the lobby. The door was closed and blinds were pulled down.

"When did she put blinds up?" Kelly asked Matthew.

"What? Oh, that's right. You haven't been here for a while," Matthew said. "She had Dan do it first thing after she took over this office."

So she could have just as easily stayed in her second floor office, if she doesn't want to be seen. I'll never understand how that woman thinks.

They tiptoed to the windows. There was a small gap in the blinds, and they peeked in. They could only see the back of Gina's head and Charles on the opposite side of her desk, nodding like a bobble-head.

"I can tell just by looking at him, that's he's not Korean," Patrick whispered, pulling out a sheet of paper from his breast pocket.

He went to the office door and knocked on it. Gina motioned to Charles to open it. As he did, Patrick held up the sheet of paper. Instinctively, Charles' hands went to his crotch. Matthew and Susan were still around the corner, peeking through the gap in the blinds, and before they had time to react, Kelly jumped up behind Patrick.

"Busted!" she laughed and pointed at Charles.

"Ms. McCoy!" Gina appeared next to Charles. "What are you doing here? I thought I made it perfectly clear that you're not to set foot on hotel property!"

"But … " Kelly was so taken aback, that she was at an uncharacteristic loss for words.

Matthew appeared next to Kelly and put a hand on her shoulder. "Kelly is here for the MacIntyre party, especially invited by Victoria MacIntyre herself," he said calmly. He ushered Gina back into her office. "We need to talk. Please, excuse us, Charles."

Charles looked perplexed. Gina nodded at him and he quickly disappeared out the back entrance. Matthew closed the office door.

"I'm sorry she was such a bitch to you, Kelly!" Susan was laughing. "But seeing that weasel scurry outta here must have been worth it!"

They started walking back to the bar.

"What's on that piece of paper, anyway?" Susan asked Patrick.

Patrick handed it to her. " 'Your fly is open'. In Mandarin," he said. "Okay, so I took a chance. It worked!"

Susan was laughing harder now. "So, now what?"

"Well, now hopefully Matthew will be able to convince Gina that Charles may have forged his documents," Kelly said. "And, with a bit of luck, she'll see the light."

"Gina?" Susan said, raising her eyebrows. "Get rid of her little personal slave? I wouldn't put my money on it!"

"May I have this dance, ma'am?" Out of nowhere Jacqui appeared and was leaning over Susan's shoulder. He appeared slightly intoxicated, but nevertheless acted chivalrous.

"I'd be delighted, young man." She mouthed 'Help!' to Kelly behind Jacqui's back. Kelly flicked her hand at her.

What's he going to try in a room full of people, and yer husband just a few feet away! ... He's not exactly like his dad in every way! Jest don't slow dance with him.

"Are you enjoying yourself?" Patrick asked.

Kelly nodded and turned to face him. "I wonder if I can I expect this every night after we open!"

"I would assume at least on weekends," Patrick said. "I think ..."

He was abruptly interrupted by a journalist wedging his robust body between them.

"So, I understand you're the MacIntyre flavor of the month?" he said, licking his lips.

He was clad in a trench coat, and sported a shirt underneath, that may have been white when purchased. Decades ago.

I know the invitations read 'black tie optional' but this is pushing it a bit... Who does he think he is anyway? Spencer Tracy?

"I beg your pardon?"

"Vicky says you're best buds. Care to elaborate?"

"Is this man bothering you?" Matthew asked sternly.

He had re-appeared behind the bar. Kelly leaned toward him. Her eyes were gleaming with anticipation. "What happened with Gina?" she whispered.

Matthew leaned across the bar. "She'll – and I quote her verbatim – look into it. Meaning …"

"Hey man! I was talking to her! Trying to do my job here!" the journalist interrupted. "Just gimme two minutes with the current 'It' girl, okay?" He pulled out a small tape recorder from his pocket.

"You'd be disappointed, sir," Kelly said. "I know you expect me to dish the dirt on Vicky, but there's nothing to dish."

God, I hope I got my jargon right.

"Vicky, as you know, is leaving for the field on Monday and I suspect the media will miss her as much as I will," Kelly said haughtily.

"Yeah, yeah, yeah," the journalist said impatiently. "I have all I need on Vicky. I want to know more about *you!*"

"I really have nothing of interest to tell you," she said politely.

"You can give me something or nothing," the reporter shrugged. "Don't matter to me either way. I'm gonna write about you anyway."

Kelly got off her barstool and leaned toward the recorder. "I'm an Irish hot-head who hates Riverdance and enjoys a good stout. I work at the new and fabulous Milk Bar, in the state-of-the-art J Hotel Chicago, due officially to open on Wednesday. If your paper will hit the stands by then, please tell your readers that if they want the dirt on Kelly McCoy, that's M-c-C-o-y, then they'd better come see for themselves. Just like Vicky said," she winked at Matthew and Patrick. "If you'll excuse me, gentlemen, I'll just pop into the wee lassies'."

She left the journalist gaping, Matthew smiling and Patrick watching her walk away.

I'd better work on me statements. Just then I sounded like I do nothing but drink beer and yell profanities at Michael Flatley all day.

The jays found Parker on the dance floor. They tried to whisper something to him, but the music was too loud. They pulled him with them to the lobby.

"There's a fireman here," Bryce said. "He says we can't shoot the fireworks off the roof."

"Whose crazy-ass idea was that, anyway?!" Parker bellowed.

"Well... your son wanted to surprise his sister..." Bryce offered. "But you see, we have people up there already, setting it all up!"

They reached the fireman. He stretched out a hand and introduced himself.

"What's this about you not letting us shoot some fireworks?" Parker barked at him, shaking his hand.

"City ordinance, sir," the fireman said calmly. "Extremely dangerous."

"What if we clear the street?" Parker offered.

"Wouldn't make much difference, sir. The only place you can shoot off fireworks is over the lake, and you'll need a permit for that."

Parker sighed and went for his checkbook. "Oh, I see where this is going," he smirked. "How much is a permit going to cost me?"

The fireman looked genuinely shocked. "Are you trying to bribe me, sir?"

"Oh, no, not at all. I just want one of those permits, so my people can move the fireworks and all these guests to the DAMN LAKE!" Parker's pitch was rising.

"What's going on?" Jacqui appeared next to the jays.

"Well," Alen whispered excitedly. "The man in uniform has just informed the man in the tux that he needs a permit for the fireworks, and hot papa is trying to buy one. But the hunk in the helmet thinks the stud with the check book is trying to bribe him," he whispered as if explaining the plot of a soap opera. "I think this is all just a dreadful misunderstanding."

"Got that right," Jacqui said, and stepped up to the fireman. "Officer, I'm sorry about the misunderstanding. I'm Jack MacIntyre and I spoke to someone in your office weeks ago," he said and pulled out a slip of paper from his inside pocket. "Is this what you're looking for?"

The fireman studied it. "Okay, see here where it says 'Not within one hundred yards of buildings, commercial, residential or otherwise.' That includes firing them off the roof of this building, sir."

"Okay, fine," Jack said hastily. "Ohio Street Beach okay with you?"

"Fine. Who's going to be the one shooting them off? You?"

"Oh, good heavens, no!" Jack slipped inadvertently into Jacqui. He cleared his throat. "I mean, … we've hired professional pyromaniacs."

"I hope you mean pyrotechnics, son," the fireman looked grimly at Jacqui. "Fire safety is no joke."

"Yes, sir. I'm sorry, sir," Jacqui said, feeling small. "Will you be there to watch? Midnight sharp on Ohio Street Beach?"

"You better believe it," the fireman said.

"Will you bring your truck?"

The fireman started chuckling and walked out the front doors.

Parker smiled and put an arm around his son. "Come on, son, I'll buy you a drink."

"How on earth are we going to get all these people to Ohio Street Beach?" Jacqui said as they were surrounded by Vicky's party again.

"We'll think of something, don't worry."

"Let's open up the roof!" Alen exclaimed excitedly.

"What?" Parker stopped in his tracks.

"Yes, there's a gorgeous little terrace on the roof," Alen said. "We haven't decided what to do with it yet, except shoot off fireworks tonight, but it's safe for at least fifty people, and has a wonderful view of … guess what? Ohio Street Beach!"

"And the other three hundred and fifty people?" Parker said suspiciously.

"Will enjoy music and dancing and read about it in the papers tomorrow," Jacqui filled in. "Fabulous idea, Alen, let's do that!"

It was getting close to midnight and Kelly's feet were aching. Second only to Vicky she had been the most popular girl on the dance floor. She dodged another reporter and ducked into the ladies room again.

Okay, I'm getting better. At least I didn't diss me own countrymen just then. Although just then I sounded like some movie buff. Nothing wrong with that? I am a movie buff! They're going to twist every word anyway, so I really shouldn't be arsed.

She studied herself in the mirror and adjusted her cleavage.

One more dance. I'm going to dance with Parker and tell him I made a mistake. Right… Good plan!

She left the ladies' room and nearly bumped into Jacqui picking at a cuticle, leaning on the doorframe. "Hi Jacqui," she teased. "Looking for a date?"

"There you are! The Russells are leaving, and want to say goodbye," he said and ushered her toward the front doors. "They're waiting for the valet."

"Thanks a million, Jacqui."

Thank God fer that! Didn't want Jon to leave fer South America fer months without saying goodbye!

She stopped in the vestibule, between the two sets of doors. The noise from the party was muffled by the inner door and the street noise by the outer. She saw Susan and Jon standing under the canopied entrance, his arm around her shoulders, her head in his armpit.

Ooow! I want that!

It started drizzling. Suddenly Matthew appeared from around the corner. He shook Jon's hand and kissed Susan's cheek. Curiosity got the better of Kelly and she slipped quietly through the door.

"...just adores you," Susan was saying. "According to her you can do no wrong."

"Oh, and I love her right back," Matthew said, without blushing. "She's so genuine. So open. So straightforward. Just the kind of girl I want."

What? … Who? … Not me, surely? Inappropriate fer a married man to say, anyway!

"She feels comfortable around you. She used to be very shy, I'll have you know," Susan said. "Especially around men. "

I never!

Susan kissed Matthew on the cheek. "That's from her to you. She keeps asking about Misterrr Brrradshaw."

"So she got her R's figured, huh?" Matthew said, smiling.

Emma! Phheeew!

"Will you and Kelly please come over for lunch tomorrow?" Jon said abruptly. "Maybe even put in a game of tennis?"

"I'd love to," Matthew said.

Kelly joined them. "Me too!"

They turned around to face Kelly. "Kelly! Good! So, we're just saying good night, then, not good bye, just now," Susan said. She leaned toward Kelly and whispered "Where are you spending the night?"

"At Pha ... um, Vicky's," Kelly said, hiding her face in Jon's neck, hugging him goodnight.

Their car was brought around.

"We'll see you tomorrow," Susan waved as she was getting into the car.

Kelly turned to Matthew. "Break time?"

"Actually I'm done," he said. "I'm just hanging around because it's so loud in the ballroom that I couldn't sleep anyway." He tilted his head and looked at Kelly. "You are really beautiful tonight," he said. "If I didn't know any better

I'd think it was your party. I hope you don't think this inappropriate, but … would you like to dance?"

"Hey there, Red!" Parker walked through the front doors. "Don't want to miss the fireworks, do ya?"

"You're leaving?" Kelly asked, discouraged.

"Just taking my brother-in-law home. I might be back later. Scurry along up to the roof. Jack says it'll be worth it."

"Parker, I'd like you to meet … " Kelly turned around, but Matthew was gone. "Never mind."

Parker, I'd like you to meet the new and improved Kelly McCoy, the one who'd like you to take her to bed tonight, just as a friend!

Kelly faked a yawn. "I think I'll turn in soon." She looked at him, in what she hoped was a suggestive way.

"Got something in your eye?" Parker said and lit a cigar.

Focketyfock!

"Just shattered, that's all."

"Got someone to drive you home?"

That was yer opener to offer me a ride and do it in the back of the limo!

"Kelly? Dad?" Jacqui poked his head through the front door. "You coming? It's T minus two!"

Kelly looked up at Parker.

Last chance.

"Hurry along, Red. Have fun!"

Damn, damn, damn, damn, damn!

There were easily a hundred guests on the roof. They were huddling under baby-blue J umbrellas distributed generously by the jays themselves. It wasn't more than a drizzle, but everyone knew that it would turn either very cold very soon or the drizzle would turn into a five-day downpour. Or, it being Chicago, they might break a heat record.

The jays had arranged an impromptu bar by the door. Vicky was handing out champagne. Her teeth were chattering. "Jacqui, this is really a good idea. Too bad about the weather. We'd better go back in soon."

"You think I just brought you here to enjoy the *view?*" Jacqui said, flabbergasted. He turned Vicky around. "Look!"

Just then the fireworks started. They were spectacular. The crowd was 'ooh'-ing and 'aah'-ing in chorus, and starting not to mind the rain so much. Vicky was moved to tears, as she stood watching the multi colored display in the sky, huddling under an umbrella with her brother.

Jacqui kissed her on the forehead. "Happy birthday, sis!"

"I wish Mom were here."

"I'm sure she can see it from where she is."

Family moment … better let them be Kelly thought, and found a spot by the west side railing.

She looked down at the street below. It was surprisingly quiet for a Saturday night. She could see people hurrying in the rain. Couples walking hand-in-hand, oblivious to the elements. She could see a white limo pull up at the entrance to the J and a man with a cigar walk up to it.

Parker!

Kelly was about to yell out his name, when she saw him holding out his hand, and assisting a curvaceous blonde get into the limo.

Candi! … I thought she was blacklisted? Did they just wait fer Vicky to disappear? … Or me? … Ohmygod, I'm an eejit!

Kelly darted through the fire escape and hurried down the stairs, all twenty-four floors of them, cursing herself out.

How could I have been such a fool? I'm a double-eejit! He's been doing her on the side all along! Arsehole! I knew it! Everyone kept warning me! FocketyfockFOOO-OCK!

She made it to the ground floor and elbowed her way through the crowd. Tears were streaming down her cheeks. She got to the bar and grabbed the first available bottle. She ran through the bar exit nearly crashing into Matthew carrying a tray of clean glasses to the bar. He tried to stop her.

"What's wrong?"

"Leave me alone…" Kelly pushed past him.

"Where are you going?!"

"To make a hole in the lake!"

In the back alley Kelly leaned heavily against the garbage compactor. It was raining slightly heavier now. She slumped to her knees and started crying hysterically.

I'm such an eejit! I have the worst luck with men! It's official. I'm a loser-magnet. Why didn't I just let it lie! We were good yesterday! Even after Charlotte I was fine about him and Candi. What's changed? I always had him pegged fer an arse. Why should I care?

She pressed the cool bottle against her hot forehead.

I've hit rock bottom and started digging. Maybe I should become a nun… Nothing worse than a sexually dissatisfied woman with a cause, Parker says. … Bet Gina was a nun in a former life!

Matthew found her. "What's going on?"

"You don't want to know," Kelly sobbed without looking up.

"So, why did I ask?"

"What's wrong with you?"

"Me? What did I do?"

"I mean men! Why can't you keep it in your pants? Why is it so hard for you to stick to the truth?! Why does a guy having a date the day after a break up make him a stud, but a girl doing the same is a slut? Why is it necessary to be so mean to your woman? Why do I always fall for the wrong men? Why … " Kelly's voice broke and she hung her head in her arms.

This sucks! Everyone warned me. God, at least fer once I kept me big fat mouth shut! It could have turned really embarrassing had I tried to verbally seduce him … I don't care! He's an arse, she's a bitch. They deserve each other! I'm better off without … … So why am I crying?

Matthew sat down next to her. "I'm sorry, Kelly," he said sincerely and gently put an arm around her. "But, … Well… Not all men cheat or lie."

Yeah, just the ones I end up with!

Matthew took the bottle away from her. "And alcohol's never the answer."

"What am I gonna do now?" Kelly hiccupped. "I've got nowhere to live."

Matthew rose and offered Kelly a hand. "Let's go," he said sternly.

"Where to?" she took his hand, but didn't rise.

"Back inside."

Kelly shook her head violently. "He's coming back. To the party. I don't want to see him."

"Let's go to my office. We can talk."

"I can't. I'm not allowed on hotel property."

"Listen to me, Kelly," Matthew kneeled and took her face in his hands. The look in his eyes commanded attention. "You can't stay out here. The place is crawling with paparazzi. Apparently you're the current *it* girl. Do you really want your cheating boyfriend to see you in the papers like this? Crying in the rain in the back alley of a hotel?" He dried her tears gently with his thumbs.

Aw, come on! Why do you always have to be so bloody sensible?! You're just like Jon! Can't I just have one minute of self-pity?

"Gina's still here. She's already mad at me for that Charles stunt and for having banned her from the party of the year!"

Matthew helped Kelly on her feet. "She left right after I spoke to her. Come on. Let's go." He cracked a smile. "And it's supposed to be the party of the *century*."

* * *

Matthew and Kelly were sitting on the sofa in his office. Kelly felt comfortable after having talked to Matthew for a good hour. He made her realize that she wasn't upset about Parker, because she just didn't care enough about him, but she was upset about her choice in men in general.

Matthew was a wonderful conversationalist. He never offered his own opinion. He asked all the right questions at all the right times, to let Kelly arrive at her own conclusions. He never asked for the name of Kelly's boyfriend, nor did Kelly offer.

"How did you get to be so sensitive, anyway?" Kelly asked.

Betcha the wife's a feminist.

"Did you take women's studies in college?"

"Worse," Matthew chuckled. "I have four older sisters!"

While Kelly cleaned up and changed into a J T-shirt and her favorite pair of jeans, stashed in Matthew's closet, Matthew confiscated a tray of finger food for them. He was now watching, amused, as Kelly meticulously picked out the finely chopped bits of onion on top of a salmon-sour cream cracker.

"You never eat onion," Matthew said, smiling. "I've seen you order things 'hold the onion' or pick it out. Don't like it? Allergic? What?"

"Makes me breath stink," Kelly said matter-of-factly and shoved the cracker, minus onion, in her mouth.

Not that it matters. Won't be kissing anyone tonight. Besides, salmon-breath isn't very attractive either.

She stifled a yawn.

"You should go to bed," Matthew said, sounding concerned. "Your eyelids look heavy."

There was a loud bang at the door followed by some scraping noises and a few muffled grunts. "What the ..." Matthew sprang to his feet and opened the door.

Kelly was right behind him. A young couple stumbled into the office. "Dude!" the young man said, wobbled to his feet and helped the young lady up. "Get a room, will ya?" he huffed and walked away with his date.

What a bizarre thing to say to someone already in a room!

Matthew closed the door, laughing.

"Matthew," Kelly said, eyes gleaming. "Has the hotel cleared all its permits?"

"Sure. All systems go. We're ready to open Wednesday, right on schedule. Why?"

"Why not open tonight? I mean, look at that," Kelly said and pointed at the door indicating the young couple. "Those are MacIntyre friends. Their combined net worth could buy you..."

What? Bolivia? ... Man! Why can't I think of anything clever here. I've got a point to make!

"A mid-sized South American country?" Matthew offered.

"Exactly! And they're too drunk and horny to leave. Open the rooms up! Tell them the rate is, ... I don't know, a hundred over rack. They won't think twice of it! Have Vicky make an announcement," Kelly said excitedly.

Matthew frowned and chewed on his lower lip.

"Do you have the staff?"

"Sure. Both night managers are on duty tonight. And heavy security, of course," Matthew said, but looked thoughtful. "It's just..."

"Gina won't like it? You don't have enough housekeeping staff to clean the rooms for opening? What?" Kelly interrupted him.

"Nothing. Get some sleep. Good night."

"Oy! Don't exclude me now!" Kelly insisted. "You've already broken enough rules, why stop now? What? You afraid Gina will find me?"

"At one thirty Sunday morning? Gimme a break!"

"Okay, then. Let's get this show on the road!"

Matthew burst out laughing.

"What now?!" Kelly said impatiently.

"I just had a Gina moment! I was jealous of you! I was cursing myself out for not having thought of selling the rooms tonight myself!" He went to his closet. "This is the uniform you wore for the photo shoot. You can change in here. I'll meet you in the lobby," he said, eyes sparkling.

He was pulling on his suit jacket. He smiled as he was about to leave. "See you next Tuesday, Gina!" he said and closed the door behind him leaving Kelly alone, laughing heartily.

* * *

"You can have the cot in here. The bathroom is being built, but tomorrow's Sunday, so no one's gonna bother you."

He was programming Kelly's fingerprint on the lock to the connecting office to his. It was nearly five a.m. Sunday morning, and they had finally cleared the last of the MacIntyre guests.

"Thanks. Where are you going to sleep?" Kelly asked.

"The sofa in my office."

Opening the door, Kelly yawned. "I know this sounds ridiculous, but I think I'm too tired to sleep."

Matthew laughed. "Want some light bedtime reading?" he said and walked through the connecting doors.

He picked up a stack of file folders from his desk.

"Applications for weekend manager. The sooner we find a suitable candidate, the better. You take half, I'll take half."

"I thought you said these doors were locked?" Kelly said pointing to the connecting doors.

"I unlocked them for easier access when I used to sleep here," he said, while making the cot with fresh sheets. "I can easily lock them again."

"That's okay," she yawned again. "If you really wanted to jump my bones, you had ample opportunity already."

Matthew turned to her. "What's it going to take to prove to you that not all men think about is sex?"

That's about as lame as 'nice guys finish last' eh, Mr. Ambiguous marital status.

"You're right. Sorry. Good night."

"You still have two of your bags in my closet, you know. Do you need anything? Contact lens solution? Make up remover? …"

A work visa? An apartment? A non-cheating, non- lying boyfriend?

"I'm good, thanks a million, Matthew," she said through a yawn.

Later Sunday morning Kelly pressed her ear to the connecting doors and tried to listen for any sounds from Matthew's office.

I can't just walk in? What if he's still sleeping? If he is, he's not a snorer, anyway. Hmmm… maybe these doors are soundproof.

Just then she could hear the phone ring in his office and the muffled sound of Matthew's voice answering. She pressed her ear closer to the door.

I'm being very naughty…

"I can't right now, Linda. How about this evening?" she heard Matthew's voice say.

Linda? Isn't that the supposed ex-fiancée? Possible current wife? … I really shouldn't be listening to this … she thought, but didn't move.

"No, I'm playing tennis," Matthew's voice said. "… Kelly … Irish, Linda! … It's a whole different country! … Well, how would you feel if someone called you Canadian? … Exactly! … People keep saying that. How's Sebastian? …

I'm not changing the subject! ... Okay, see you tonight. ...
Love you, too."

Yeah, right! They're all the same. 'Not all men lie or cheat', me
arse! I knew it!

Kelly could hear Matthew moving around in his office,
and she knocked on the connecting door. "Matthew? You
decent?"

"Yes, but I can get indecent in a matter of seconds!"

That's a bit rich! He just got off the phone with Linda! Men!
'Not all men think about is sex' yeah, right! Another cheating liar!

She entered his office, waving a file folder. She ignored
his flirt. "I think I've found your weekend manager," she
announced and took a seat. She started going through the
file. "Age forty-six. Going on thirty years experience. Last
seventeen as a manager. All luxury, full-service hotels. Name
Hank. Cornell graduate. MBA in hotel management..."
Kelly paused and looked up at Matthew. He was grinning
at her.

What? Do I have something on me face? I'm dressed appropri-
ately. What's so funny?

"Bottom line," she continued, "you'll want to meet with
him." She laid the application on his desk.

"Did you sleep at all?" Matthew said and was looking at
the crumpled uniform she had worn the night before.

Kelly pointed at the sofa, which bore no signs of having
been slept on. "Did you?"

Suddenly there was a sharp knock on the door to
the other office. The connecting doors were open, and

Matthew and Kelly tiptoed to the other room. Matthew looked through the peephole. 'Gina' he mouthed. They could hear the digital beeping of the lock. Matthew grabbed Kelly's hand and together they leapt through the connecting doors. He closed the door just as Gina entered.

They could hear her enter the room. She rummaged about for a while, and they heard her close the door behind her. Matthew looked through the peephole in the door to his office and was expecting to see her walk away. Quickly he grabbed Kelly by the arm again, and ushered her through the connecting doors, closing them behind her just as Gina entered his office.

"Matthew?" she said, surprised. "Is someone sleeping in that connecting room?"

"I'm house hunting, as you know," Matthew offered.

"Fine. And the rest of the hotel? Who authorized it to be sold last night?"

"I made an executive decision. Bryce approved it. ADR went through the roof. I just sent you an e-mail about it. I didn't expect you to be here today."

"Officially I'm not. Bryce, Alen and I are meeting for breakfast. I was told that Ms. McCoy spent the night here," Gina said, studying Matthew's face.

"Kelly? Haven't seen her in a while."

"You need to keep it that way!" She reached for the connecting door. "I'm just going to have a quick look at the progress of the shower in there."

Oh, no! She's coming back in!

Kelly rushed through the office door and closed it behind her as Gina entered.

Now, what?

The door to Matthew's office opened. Kelly rushed in. Matthew pointed at his bathroom. Kelly ran there and was barely in when Gina entered Matthew's office again.

"It's not looking good," she said.

All color vanished from Matthew's face. "What?"

Ohmygod! She's found something of mine in there? ... Wait! There's nothing of mine in there!

"Tell Dan he needs to turn it up a notch. I need that room sold for opening! And you need to find somewhere else to spend the night."

Gina handed Matthew Kelly's purse. A Machiavellian smile spread across her face. "This had better be Linda's! But from now on you need to keep your personal life away from the hotel!"

Matthew blushed and laughed nervously. Gina left the office. Matthew was looking through the peephole at her walking away. He motioned for Kelly to come out. They burst out laughing.

"We're so bad!" Kelly laughed.

What a Blake Edwards moment!

"Man! That was like straight out of a Blake Edwards movie!" Matthew said, leaning against the door.

What?! Do I now have a bug in me brain?! Or does he have what Mel Gibson had in 'What Women Want'?

"Fellow fan, I take it?" Kelly said. "Not all men lie, huh?"

"I didn't," Matthew insisted. "Just withheld the truth a bit."

Big diff.

"Oy!" Kelly stopped cold. "How'd she get in? You programmed my fingerprints on that lock last night!"

Matthew tried to divert his eyes. "Hers overrides everyone else's. As do Dan's and Mitchell's ... and mine."

So much fer privacy! At any given moment three men and a bitch could've walked in on me!

"For emergencies," Matthew continued quickly.

23

"Hiya!" Kelly poked her head in the jays' office. "There are two things that I'd like to run by you, gentlemen. If you have a moment to spare."

It was late Monday afternoon and Kelly had just confirmed with Kristin that Gina had left for the day. The jays were going over the revenue for the MacIntyre party that weekend.

Bryce signaled for her to take a seat. "For you, sweet-ums, any time."

"Thank you. First," she started and placed her folder on the desk between her and the jays. "Most Chicago mid or high rises now have elevator televisions with ads and news and weather. And if I understand your demographic correctly, the people who can actually afford to live in these buildings are, or know, the sort of people the J wants to attract. In a word - wealthy," she paused and looked at Alen and Bryce's blank faces. "Am I right?"

The jays nodded.

"I had Ryan, your IT guru, design this for me," she continued as she pulled out a CD. "May I?" She inserted the CD into Bryce's computer. "Did either of you ever see the original movie *Scream*? It's this really scary movie, with the killer wearing this mask … It kinda looks like that Munch painting, like a melted face," she added as neither partner's face gave any inkling of confirmation.

Man! I never realized!! That's where they got the mask from! … And the title! Du-uh! I'm an eejit!

"Anyway," Kelly continued. "At the end of the movie, you think all's well, the killer's dead and the survivors will live happily ever after. But then," she lowered her voice for effect, "just before the credits start to roll, you see the mask again, really quickly, just for a frame or two. It really makes a chilling effect." Kelly paused and looked at the jays' perplexed faces. "So here's what would be playing in elevators downtown."

Kelly played the CD. A baby-blue letter J appeared on a black screen for two seconds. The jays did not look impressed.

"I don't think we've budgeted…" Bryce started.

"I met with the marketing managers of both Sears and Hancock," Kelly interrupted, "and they both agree to two flashes like you just saw every thirty seconds. Imagine it! In a ride to the top you get the J flash two or three times!" Kelly exclaimed enthusiastically. "Do you know how many people you could reach in one day?"

The jays still didn't look impressed.

"How did you get them to agree?" Bryce finally asked.

Kelly shrugged. "Oldest trick in the book," she said. "Told each that the other had already agreed."

At this the jays finally cracked a smile.

"There's still the matter of cost," Bryce said.

Kelly held up her hand. "They'll agree to run our flashes for free, if we advertise them in our elevator TV's."

"Minor, insignificant, little detail," Alen said. "We have no TV's in our elevators."

Kelly reached for her folder, pulled out three sheets of paper and handed them to Bryce. "That brings me to my second thing. Here are three quotes for Chicago companies that install them. Cost estimates include installation, software, tech support and warranty. Please consider it. You could run weather, a bit of news and … say… concierge's weekly picks. I'd be happy to set it up. I mean, it's hardly rocket surgery!"

It's not like I have bugger-all else to do. Just spent all day riding up and down in elevators.

Bryce and Alen were looking over Kelly's proposal in silence. They looked at each other, nodded and smiled.

"We'll look into it," Bryce said, and extended his hand to her. "Remind me to give you a bonus."

Kelly shook his hand and smiled. "Bryce?"

"Yes, doll?"

"Give me a bonus."

All of a sudden Matthew burst into the office. "You're here!" he said, looking at Kelly. He was red-faced and panting.

Kelly held up a hand. "Okay, okay, I'm leaving, I'm leaving…" she said, grabbed her folder and headed for the door.

Blocking the door with his body, Matthew smiled at her. "Why would you leave?" he said with a mischievous smirk. "When it's still office hours, and you're now legal!"

He held up an official looking letter with a government seal on it. It took Kelly a moment to digest what he just said.

"I'm in?" she whispered. "I'M IN!?!"

Matthew smiled and nodded. Kelly threw her arms around his neck and hugged him fiercely. Bryce and Alen joined the group hug.

"We have to celebrate!" Bryce said. "Drinks are on me!"

"You're legal to start as of immediately," Matthew said, eyes dancing. "And you don't have to go back to Dublin!" He shook her hand.

Her eyes were welling. "Does this mean I can have my old suite back?!"

Smiling widely, Matthew nodded. "They're cleaning it for you now. Welcome to the J Hotel, Chicago, Ms. McCoy!"

24

En route to Argentina, the MacIntyre Industries Learjet was preparing to descend toward Bogota, Colombia for a brief fuel stop. Back in the cabin, Vicky was gathering all the information that had been dumped on her at take-off. She felt she was fully up to speed with the outlines of the proposed venture and spread a map on the table. She sat down next to Parker, gleaming. Thrilled to be part of the business. Jon and Duncan smiled in anticipation at her from across the table.

"Okay, gentlemen, here's how I see it, and feel free to interrupt at any time. The Aussies are probing La Martha, which Kensington found resulted in nothing way back in ninety-seven or eight. So, I say we forget that. Terry's made a valid point about this area." She pointed at the map. "Kensington found some very promising rutile and cassiterite in the Rio Gaucho gravels, but the locals started giving them a hard time, so they pulled out."

Parker turned to Vicky. "Why would we care about rutile and cassiterite, Sparky?"

Vicky rolled her eyes. "Du-uh, Daddy. That's like Geology 101. They're indicator minerals to emeralds. Everyone knows that! And if all else fails, we might get titanium."

Parker put an arm around his daughter. "A plus," he said and kissed her forehead.

Vicky was beaming.

"We're now on our final approach to Bogota," Candi's voice came over the speakers. "Please double check that your seatbelts are securely ... SHIT!"

Something came flying through the right windshield, hitting the co-pilot. Candi quickly turned around and saw the curtain torn, Jon injured, hands over his face, blood streaming. The plane was shaking. Candi realized that the elevator was jammed. And had been jammed since impact. The aircraft was in a steep dive. The altimeter was spinning. She pulled back on the yoke to get out of the dive but couldn't make it move.

"Shii-IT!"

The realization of the dilemma hit her like a truck. She looked back and hoped to get Jon to come help her, but he was still down. He was bleeding profusely from a gouge on his forehead. Parker looked up and Candi gestured to him to get into the cockpit. She pointed to the co-pilot, indicating that he needed to be taken out. Parker released the harness, and yanked the co-pilot out of his seat like a piece of meat. He was bleeding copiously and his face was pierced with shards of Plexiglas. Vicky and Duncan scrambled to buckle him down and tend to his and Jon's injuries.

The roar of the wind was overpowering. It sounded like a tornado in a small space. All verbal communication was impossible. Maps, papers and feathers were flying everywhere and the foul smell of blood and gore filled the cabin.

Candi motioned to Parker to take the co-pilot seat. She reached over and grabbed the quick-donning oxygen mask, motioning to Parker to do the same. He did. His eyes were the size of saucers and were watering from the air-stream flowing in from the broken windshield. Candi pointed at Parker's sunglasses hanging from the top of his shirt and motioned for him to put them on.

Candi pushed the intercom button, and shouted at him "Help me pull!"

Parker looked over at Candi, and pulled at the yoke, as she was doing. Nothing happened.

"Harder!" Candi yelled.

The buildings below were getting bigger. Suddenly the airframe gave a loud bang and shutter. The nose started coming up. As they bottomed out they could see the faces of people on the ground looking up at them. Suddenly the nose was well above the horizon.

"Rat shit!" Candi yelled. "Can't get the nose down!"

"What do you need me to do?" Parker said panicking, but straining to sound strong and helpful.

"Push!"

"Push what?"

"The yoke!"

The elevator was sticking. Candi realized that there was a serious flight control problem, and that they were going to have to make stuck flight control approach and landing.

"The biggest pain in the ass in all of aviation, and I get to do it!" she cursed.

"What?"

"Just follow my lead. Don't fuck up!"

Parker shut up. He was breathing quickly and small droplets of sweat were forming on his upper lip. Candi picked up the microphone and called the Bogota flight tower. "This is Lear two-five-two Juliet. We have a serious flight control problem here. We need you to clear the pattern until we land."

"Si, Capitan! We see jew have bird strike," a voice answered.

Mentally Candi was going through the emergency checklist.

"Just so you know, Parker, this thing's gonna heave around like a bronco, so don't go soft on me!" She pointed to the gyro. "Keep it steady at minus five!"

"What does that mean?!" Parker said, panic clear in his voice.

"That's the gyro, that's the yoke. The yoke controls the gyro. Keep it at minus five," Candi sounded cool and professional.

She could see the sheer panic in Parker's eyes. She smiled at him in what she hoped would pass for reassurance. She lowered the landing gear to reduce speed. The plane started buffeting. She looked over at Parker. He was staring at the gyro. His knuckles where white from struggling to hold the yoke.

"Lear two-five-two Huliet," the voice from Bogota tower came across the headset. "All runway clear. Jew are clear to land."

Candi got on the intercom again. "Assume crash positions!" she yelled.

She turned around to look at the passengers in the cabin. The only one looking up was Vicky. Candi motioned to her to get down. Vicky nodded and threw her body over Jon's. Duncan followed her lead and pinned down the co-pilot. The plane was shaking violently. Candi lowered the flaps. "I think I've got her now!" she said. "Stand by to back me up!"

Feeling the mushiness of the controls, she knew she had to carry extra power and land hot. "Push the throttle forward and hold it when I tell you!" she instructed Parker. Candi quickly reached over and placed Parker's hand on the throttle. "Right there! Good!"

Parker dropped the throttle like a hot potato.

"No! Keep your hand on it!" Candi shouted.

The end of the runway was rapidly approaching. Candi was grateful it was a long runway. Longer than a Lear would normally need.

"We're not gonna land on the numbers here. But I'll be happy with concrete," she said and shot a quick look at the orange windsock on the field.

The noise of the wind coming through the broken windshield diminished and they could hear an increasing whine from the engines.

"Stand by to reverse those throttles when I tell you!" The wheels briefly touched down on the runway with a sharp sound of peeling rubber. "Damn!" Candi said, knowing that her initial contact with the runway had been too hard.

As the plane porpoised briefly back into the air she fought the yoke further into her lap. "Ease up on the throttles!" she shouted at Parker.

He did. The plane settled on the runway. Candi frantically manipulated the rudder pedals and yanked the yoke further back into her stomach.

"Max reverse NOW!"

Parker instinctively did as instructed. The nose wheel settled onto the pavement and Candi began braking as the reverse thrusters started to take effect and slowed the plane down. While Candi taxied toward the terminal, she radioed Ground Control, and was going to ask for an ambulance, but saw that one was already arriving on the tarmac, together with a fire truck. She successfully parked the plane by the terminal, turned toward Parker and took off her mask.

"You okay?"

"I need a drink," he said, breathing heavily. He turned to face her and pointed at her cheek. "You're bleeding."

Candi brushed the blood off her cheek and undid her harness. "Not mine." As she rose from her seat she patted the dashboard. "Good job. We'll use you again."

She walked into the cabin. "Everyone okay?" she asked, and bent over to look at Jon and her co-pilot. "Don't move them yet. Let me get the paramedics in here."

"You were awesome," Vicky whispered.

Her upper torso was covered with Jon's blood. She was shaking slightly and her eyes were moist. She got out of her seat and put her arms around Candi.

"Thank you," she said, her voice quivering.

Candi shrugged. "Just another day in paradise," she said and opened the passenger stairway for the paramedics. She surveyed the scene. Duncan was shirtless. Vicky was only wearing a bra and jeans, both having used their shirts to stop the bleeding of the injured men. "You didn't do half bad yourself, kid. What the hell was that, anyway?" Candi said.

Duncan was assisting the paramedics in getting Jon and the co-pilot off the plane. He looked at what was left of the carcass. "Condor," he said.

"An endangered species!? Aw, shit! How much paperwork is *that* gonna be?"

* * *

In the Milk Bar Kelly was sharing the news of her visa. She had already talked to her parents and was now on the phone with Susan. Kelly hadn't had a drink since her stomach was pumped, and the champagne was quickly going to her head.

Matthew turned to Bryce. "Okay, I know you want her to appear at events, but until we hire a Guest Services Manager, I wouldn't mind having her."

Bryce poked him in the side. "We know you wouldn't mind having her!"

Matthew blushed. "Having her help me with some of the dailies," he said.

The dailies were the daily reports, a mind-numbingly boring chore that had to be done daily by the director of revenue and another person on property. The dailies consisted of cross-referencing the Internet sites that the J had contracts with and the arrivals for any given date at the hotel. Also, included in the dailies were double-checking for duplicate bookings, VIP's, special requests and overbooked dates. A tedious job, but it had to be done. And done twice. Daily.

The TV in the corner of the bar was on CNN. It was muted, but Kelly recognized the plane in the background. "Ohmygod! Susan, turn on CNN! I'll call you later!" She hung up. "Turn that up!" she yelled at the bartender. "That's ... That's Vicky's Dad's plane!"

"... Intyre, the mining mogul, who narrowly escaped death today," the female reporter was saying. "Your thoughts, Mr. MacIntyre?" she turned toward Parker.

Parker smiled at the camera. His shirt was stained. "Well, we had some hair-raising moments for awhile. But I have full confidence in our pilot, Candace Jones, through whose heroism and calmness I, my daughter and two right-hand men are here today to tell the story," he said, appearing calm and professional.

"We understand that you yourself were assisting your pilot in the emergency landing," the reported said.

Parker laughed. "Again, my hat's off to our pilot, for guiding me through that. All I know about planes is how fast they get me to where I need to be and how much they cost to maintain."

"Have you sought medical assistance?"

"Our co-pilot's in the hospital. None of the rest of us were seriously injured," Parker said looking down at his shirt. "This is blood and gore from the bird that caused this whole mess. Now, if you'll excuse me, I'd like to go tend to my crew," Parker said and flashed a quick smile at the camera.

Well, there ya have it! It's a pattern. You screw with Kelly McCoy and bad things happen to you. ... Gotta ring Vicky! Wonder if her mobile works in ... Kelly looked at the TV screen. *Bogota? That's what? Colombia? Maybe I should just e-mail her ...*

She leaned toward Matthew. "Did you have me PDA unbugged?"

He smiled. "De-bugged. We found nothing. So, it may be a coincidence, or someone may have access to your j-mail account, or be tapped to your PDA from the main line. Either way, we don't know how to put an end to it. Go see Ryan, and he'll reprogram your PDA for you," he whispered.

Kelly tried to contain her giggle. "Why are we whispering?" she whispered.

"Because I don't know how serious this is yet, and I don't want the jays to get worried," Matthew whispered back.

"It's a bit rude," Kelly whispered, giggling quietly.

"What are we whispering about here?" Bryce whispered.

Kelly and Matthew burst out laughing. "I just told Matthew what Parker MacIntyre looks like naked!" Kelly said.

Jaysus! That's the best I could come up with? What a load of dung! Now they'll think I know what he looks like naked ... or that Matthew's gay!

"Would I ever love to see him naked!" Alen sighed, drooling over the TV showing an eyewitness' video of the MacIntyre Learjet making its landing.

There's always some sicko with a camcorder! Kelly thought, watching the Lear porpoise on the runway. *Betcha they're miffed nobody died!*

"You'd be disappointed, honey," Kelly said, staring at the screen. "He's like a high-dollar facial cream. You pay for the packaging." All six eyes were on her. She blushed. "Spent the night at Vicky's once. Saw him get out of the pool."

25

The J Hotel had been operational for five days when Kelly was sitting in Matthew's office, yawning. The previous week and been the longest in Kelly's memory. Although she had stuck to soft drinks, she felt as exhausted as she would have been after a week's drinking binge. Appearing and looking hot turned out to be far more laborious than Kelly had anticipated. She opened and closed the bar every night. It was tremendously successful. Adding to the success was the news on Vicky being involved in the accident, which had sent journalists to interview Kelly. The publicity was overwhelming.

Kelly closed the bar at two that morning and had hardly slept after that. She was too pumped up on adrenaline.

It was now eight thirty Monday morning. Matthew was going through the websites that the J had contracts with. Kelly found it impossible to concentrate.

" … and every morning I'd like for you to print these out. You can use my computer, until we get you an office," he said and showed her the pages he had printed. "Go through the numbers and cross-reference them with this printout from Aaria…"

God, I'm shattered. I should get out of these contacts and just wear me glasses. And out of these clothes and into bed.

"… look for any discrepancies," Matthew continued. "Once you're done with that," he printed another wad of paper off Aaria, "I'd like for you to go over the numbers for the next ninety days. Look for discrepancies and especially for uncommitted rooms on sold out dates…"

I could really use some 400-count Egyptian cotton sheets right now. … 300-count would be okay, too. … A pile of newspapers would do, frankly … What did he just say?

"Wait. Next ninety days? Every day? Isn't that a bit redundant? I mean, we have a supposed revenue manager after all…"

"Yeah, a revenue manager who's not worthy of the title, and whom we can't seem get rid of!" Matthew huffed. "So, you were listening. 'Cause it looked like you were dozing off."

"Sorry," Kelly said and sat up straight. "Long night last night." She tried to stifle a yawn.

"I know, I've seen the numbers," Matthew showed her the F&B revenue report. "Good job! And you're getting better at handling the media, too, I hear. Everyone wants to come see the hot redhead."

Kelly blushed. "Team effort. Okay, so check the dot-coms and run the occupancy report daily, make the schedules on InnTime every Thursday ... Wait! Schedules for everybody?"

"Yes," Matthew said smiling. "Everybody clocks in."

"Everybody? Including Gina?"

That schedule will take me about a second to do, because that's how long she's here every day.

"Including the jays," Matthew said. "They call it equal treatment."

I'd call it 'Big Brother'.

"Is that it?" Kelly said, stifling another yawn.

Anything even remotely interesting to keep me awake?

"That's it for now. Let's go. Time for Exec," Matthew said, pulling on his suit jacket.

Time for a nap, Kelly thought, but gathered the printouts and followed Matthew to the Study.

She looked over the reports.

This'll put me to sleep! Fersure.

"Today one hunda pessent. Tuesday one hunda pessent. Wednesday one hunda pessent..." Charles was reading the occupancy report for the coming week.

Can't he just say 'sold out all week'?! He must really love the sound of his own voice! This is dumb anyway! Everyone here can read the stupid occupancy report. What a waste of time! If I weren't knackered coming into this meeting, him reading that report will certainly put me under … six feet under … And could someone please pay fer some English lessons fer him?! 'Hound and Pissant' sounds like a rural English pub, not the occupancy of an upscale, luxury, Chicago hotel!

The Executive Committee was gathered in the Study, a small conference room, seating twelve, just off the lobby. Everyone had showed up, except the jays who were in Asheville, the sales and revenue directors, who worked out of New York and Gina, who claimed she was stuck in traffic. They joined the meeting by phone.

"Thank you, Charles. And lastly," Bryce's voice came over the speaker phone, "I'd like to congratulate everyone on a successful first week."

"Matthew and Kelly?" Alen added. "Fabulous job on the MacIntyre party! Great idea opening the rooms up! We broke rack rate that night! Keep up the good work!"

"I wish you wouldn't let minors check in, Mr. Bradshaw," Gina's acid voice said. "We have honor bars in the rooms, and cannot be liable for someone pulling a Kelly McCoy-like stunt on property."

That little bitch! She still on that?!

Kelly was suddenly wide-awake.

"With all due respect, Gina," Matthew said, "we carded everyone, and if there wasn't an accompanying adult in the suite we emptied the bars. Turned out there weren't that many rooms we had to do it in. What was it, Kelly? Three? Four?"

"Three."

"Good thinking, dynamic duo!" Bryce trilled happily. "Kelly, I would officially like to offer my congrats on getting your visa! How long is it good for?"

"Two years."

"Fabulous! I suggest we get started straight away on the H-1B sponsorship, if you're still interested. Who knows how long that'll take…"

"What's this about a sponsorship? No one's cleared this with me!" Gina interrupted him.

"Right…" Bryce started. "See, we sponsored our Guest Relations Manager at our San Fran property. That visa gave us another three years with that gorgeous creature. … Where's he from again, Alen?"

"Scandinavia somewhere. Denmark I think."

"Well, that explains his burly, rugged good looks…"

"The point, gentlemen?" Gina interrupted impatiently.

"Right," Bryce turned professional again. "We've decided to offer this sponsorship to one qualified candidate on each property. And in Chicago, we've chosen Kelly!"

Yay!

"This needs to be a vote," Gina said. "Ms. McCoy's not the only foreigner at the Chicago property. I'd like to nominate Charles for this sponsorship."

Ya would, wouldn't ya, ya bitch! Three more years of having yer own little Muppet do yer dirty work.

Everyone in the Study was silent, staring uncomfortably at the phone in the center of the table.

Charles was grinning. "Thank you, Miss Gina. I assep."

Big surprise!

An abrupt noise shattered the silence across the phone lines. It sounded very much like a dog barking.

… That lying skiver! She's not stuck in traffic! She's still at home! … Well, she can't be all bad, then, if she has a pet … Although, what does that say about the dog?

Matthew cleared his throat, trying to cover the barking sound. "Now, in all fairness, and following your line of thought, Gina. Kelly and Charles aren't the only foreigners here. Every J-1 who's interested should have a fair shot," he said.

"I agree," Bryce said. "How many do you have?"

"Six including Kelly and Charles."

"Okay, let's post a memo. The sponsorship is available to every qualified non-American currently on the payroll. The Execs will vote. Well, not Kelly and Charles, of course. Kristin, could you type something up, please, doll?"

"Consider it done," Kristin said.

"Charles and Kelly, could you please leave the room for a mo, while we discuss this further?" Bryce concluded.

Kelly and Charles were standing at the end of the hallway, away from the busy morning check-out rush in the lobby while the rest of the Execs were finishing the meeting. Kelly started looking over the ninety-day report, fighting to stay awake. Charles looked at her, grinning. He coughed without covering his mouth.

Oh, gross! He just spat on me! I don't care where he's from! That's gross in any country!

She decided to ignore him. Her eyes scanned the occupancy report and cross-referenced it to the dot-coms. She was almost at the end of it.

Whatta fock?!

"You're holding out rooms for the marathon, aren't you, Charles? No wonder we're not sold out yet. You're sitting on them!"

"You don undestan," he said, trying to grab the reports from her. "Go way. Go palty. Palty plincess."

"Listen, you little freak! I was in the marathon last year, and I know that the city was packed! You couldn't get a hotel room after July! And if you did, you'd be sure to pay rack rate. At least!" she was growing more and more upset, trying to keep him away from the reports.

"I don hawa lissa you!" Charles said turning to leave.

"I'm not done yet!"

Abruptly, Charles swung around. Kelly stepped back and his hand caught her necklace and tore it. In shock, Kelly watched her priceless necklace fly across the hallway. Charles was grinning widely.

"That impotant fo you? That nothing," he said and started laughing and pointing.

Kelly planted a fist across his face. Charles was sent hurling backwards, crashing against the Study door. He let out a scream and charged at her, like a cat, nails poised. He wrapped his hands around her throat and they tumbled down on the floor together. Just then the Study door was jerked open and Matthew, Mitch and Dan entered the hallway. Charles was sitting on top of Kelly, his hands around her neck, his nose bleeding profusely on her, squealing like a pig. Matthew leapt toward them and jerked Charles off Kelly. He pushed both of them into the staff entranceway, away from the guests.

"What's going on here?" he demanded, holding Charles and Kelly apart.

Charles was pointing at Kelly, holding his nose. "She clazy! She hit me in face!"

"He started it!" Kelly pointed back, coughing.

"'He started it?' What are you? Four?" Matthew was straining to stay calm. "I don't care. This is a luxury hotel, not a motorcycle bar. And you both work here. Charles, in this country it's not okay to hit women. And Kelly? He's half your size. Have mercy!"

Kelly pulled herself free from Matthew's hold and went looking for her necklace.

"You're both suspended, pending investigation. Dan, Mitch, can I call on you as witnesses, if need be? Charles, gather your things, and have that nose checked out. Mitch, go with him. Stay with him the whole time. I need a copy of his injury records. And Charles? Don't you dare show yourself on this property, until I say you can," Matthew continued. "And Kelly," he stopped short, as he saw her face was flooded by tears. "Will you be filing charges?"

"Why you ahways take hel side?" Charles asked irritated.

"Didn't I just tell you to go?!"

Charles was about to grab Kelly's reports with him.

"Leave 'em!" Matthew hissed.

Charles left with Mitch through the back entrance muttering under his breath. Matthew went to Kelly's side. She was sitting on the floor, hugging her broken necklace and crying softly. "You alright?" Matthew said, his voice emotionless. "Let's get you cleaned up. Dan? A hand, please?"

"No, wait!" Kelly said. "He's holding out a block of rooms for the marathon. Look!" she picked up the reports. "I don't know what this means exactly, but it can't be good, right?"

Matthew took the reports and studied them quietly. He was frowning. "Oh, my God," he said softly, and ran into Kristin's office, Kelly and Dan in tow. He opened the website.

"Looks like we caught him in the nick of time. Wonder why he'd do something as stupid as this? And under Gina's code at that? Look at this, guys," he said and pointed to the screen. "He was about to give away most of our inventory for less than a third of what we should have made for that weekend!" Matthew was typing away on the computer. "Go clean up, Kelly. Meet me in my office. I think it's time for a conference call to the jays."

* * *

Kelly was sitting in Matthew's office, shuddering. She took a long cold shower, convinced that germs can handle heat better than cold. She scrubbed herself raw and afterward gave Dan her top to throw in the incinerator. She wore a light turtle neck to cover her bruised throat.

Matthew was dialing Bryce's number. Kelly hung her head, and studied Matthew from under her brow. He avoided eye contact. His expression was dark.

This is so embarrassing. First time I meet Matthew I'm hung over. Then I'm drinking before noon. Then I'm drunk and high and pass out, probably hurling all over him. Then I'm crying in an alley. And now I'm fighting. And I've only been legally employed a week! Wonder what he thinks of me? … Oh, God! I can't believe I just thought that! How shallow am I?

Dan turned to Kelly. "You sure you'll be okay? You won't need to go the ER?"

"I'm fine," Kelly muttered. She was holding an ice pack to her knuckles, which were starting to bruise.

I was hurt worse wrestling with Emma, and she fights clean! … And she was only three at the time! … And she's a girl!

They were watching the footage of the fight, as caught by one of the security cameras.

"Whoa! Lotta shoulder in that punch, girl! Remind me never to tick you off!" Dan was impressed and rewound the tape.

Don't tick me off, Dan.

Matthew finally got through to Bryce. He turned the speaker toward Kelly and Dan. "Bryce, it's Matthew.

Something's just happened, I think you should know about. It's related to that crash we heard at Exec. You're on speakerphone. Kelly's here with me, as is Dan, our eyewitness." Matthew paused and frowned at Kelly. She looked at him, feeling small. "Kelly's been in what I can only classify as a catfight."

"Kelly, precious, are you alright?" Bryce gasped over the line.

"I'm fine," Kelly smiled to the speakerphone. "You should see *him*!"

"There was a him in a catfight? Someone, please visualize, don't verbalize!"

Okay, let's see … Cruella deVil meets Godzilla meets Humpty-Dumpty attacks Irish … who am I this week? … Irish …

"Kelly was assaulted by Gina's intern, Charles Cho," Matthew said abruptly.

Hmmph! My visualization was better!

"I hope you kicked his tushie!"

"Ahem, … that's not quite the point," Matthew said. "We need to set some standards here."

"You're right, I'm sure," Bryce said. "What did you do?"

"I suspended them both. Someone needs to conduct an investigation. Although some very expensive personal property of hers was damaged, Kelly has declined pressing charges, so we can keep this on the QT. Luckily all of this took place under a security camera. We're just going over the footage now. Charles looks guilty as sin. We're lucky Kelly's not pressing charges. I'll revoke her suspension."

"That's a good start. How did this whole thing start, anyway?" Bryce asked.

"As far as I understand," Matthew was looking at Kelly, still frowning, "they were in disagreement about rates for marathon weekend."

"Rack rate would be what my money's on," Bryce snorted.

"That'd be Kelly."

"You go girl! Does Gina know of any of this?" Bryce asked.

"Well, that's just it. We're not sure how, if at all, she's involved. That's how you'll notice she's not part of this conference call. More investigating is needed."

"We'll take it from here," Bryce said

"So, I've done all I need to do? It's in your hands now?"

"Oh, totally!" Bryce said. "Just keep him off the property. And Kelly? Next time you're in a catfight, please make sure it's staged, the media's there, and it's with someone that *matters*!"

26

After the harrowing landing in Bogota, Parker and his crew chartered a jet for northern Argentina. Candi stayed with the plane in Colombia, as spare parts needed to be ordered. She wished to oversee every step of the repairs. Also, she was buried in paperwork.

Jon's injuries only required some stitches, and he was released the same day. The co-pilot, however, was airlifted to Miami. He had suffered a severe concussion, lost a lot of blood, and required serious reconstructive surgery on his face. The Colombian doctors had commended Vicky and Duncan for assisting the injured men. The co-pilot might not have made it otherwise.

Jon's initial hunch about the Rio Gaucho indicators was being followed-up on and so far turned out to be quite promising. Vicky was intrigued by every aspect of the project. She was thrilled to be treated like one of the guys, working side-by-side with the best in the industry and for finally being validated for being a person in her own right. The fresh air and strenuous physical labor brought color to her cheeks and her appetite back, and she looked healthier than she had in years. She quit all her bad habits. Because of her charm, beauty and command of the language she was able to assist Duncan persuade local officials who initially resisted his proposal.

Parker enjoyed being out of the office and back in the field. He was enormously impressed by his daughter. He saw a younger, more eager, female version of himself in her as he was now watching her knee deep in the stream, panning. He knew that the company was going to be in good hands after he retired. Between Jon and Vicky the management succession of MacIntyre Industries was in place. He motioned Jon over to him.

"I'm leaving tomorrow," he told Jon quietly. "Just got word on the plane. It's ready. You seem to have everything under control here. See if you can't wrap things up by the end of this field season. Anything you need from me?"

"I think we're all set here," Jon said overlooking his crew. "I should be back in Chicago by early October. Just, if you could, please, leave your windbreaker for me, I'd appreciate it. I can't believe I didn't bring mine!"

Parker smirked. "Been a long time since you were in the field, huh?"

"Yeah… So, what's next for you, boss?"

Parker's eyes were focused on the horizon. His voice was low, and full of sorrow. "I've recently discovered what an ass I've been all my life. Since I lost Sara, anyway. That little nanny of yours made me see that. I tell you, it was a painful eye-opener. I never realized how close I came to losing everything..." his voice was breaking. He looked at Vicky panning in the stream. "Everything... Kelly's right. I'm an ass! Damn! It's a miracle no one's put a bullet through my brain years ago! I've been too proud to listen to anyone, including Kelly, who was basically spelling it out for me. This close call with the plane just put all the pieces together."

"So, what are you going to do?"

"I'm gonna do the right thing for once in my life! I'm gonna ask that girl to marry me! I've treated her like dirt, and I'll be lucky if she doesn't kick me in the nuts while I'm down on one knee!"

"You're gonna ask who? ... Kelly!?"

"Daddyyy!" A shrill shriek from the stream interrupted them. Vicky was rushing up the steep bank. Her cheeks were red from excitement. Her waders looked ridiculously big and heavy on her. Her hair was streaky from the drizzle. She was muddy and wet, but to Parker she had never looked more beautiful. "I got one! I got one!" Vicky reached her father and Jon on the bank and ceremoniously held up her pan to them.

"Alright, Sparky! Way to go! Let's see!" Parker said.

Glistening in the water, at the bottom of the pan was an emerald the size of a buckshot. Vicky was smiling from ear to ear.

"I know this is nothing to you guys, but it's a good indicator that we're on the right track, right? I say we move further upstream, and I bet we find something bigger, you know, closer to the source. Am I right?"

Parker smiled at her. "You've been a good student. Do you want to keep it as a souvenir? It has no commercial value."

Vicky shook her head decidedly. "Can't. It's prospecting evidence. Good data wins, eh, Terry? This goes in a bag and the site on a map. Right? I'm just so excited, Daddy! My first emerald! Yay!"

Parker took the pan from Vicky and handed it to Jon. "Bag-tag-map, would you, Terry? I need a word alone with Vicky." He took her hand and they went to his tent, to find shelter from the cold wind.

"*Vicky?*" Vicky said, disappointment obvious in her voice. "You've never called me that before in my life. I thought it was gonna be Sparky from now on, anyway, eh, Commander?" she teased.

"This is private," Parker said and motioned for her to take a seat.

All color vanished from Vicky's face as she sat down. "I'm clean, Daddy, I swear! I quit smoking cold turkey and I haven't had a drink since my birthday party, and then only …"

Parker put up an hand and silenced her. "I know, and I couldn't be more proud of you," he sat down, facing her. "This is about me. The plane is repaired. Candi's flying down as we speak, and I'm going home tomorrow morning."

Vicky looked deep into her father's eyes. "Waaait a minute! I know that look! We've had this talk before!" her voice was defiant. "I'm getting a new stepmother, aren't I?!"

"Would you mind?"

"It'd better be Candi!"

"You knew?"

"Well, du-uuh! And it's about time, too! I mean, Charles finally married *his* Camilla!"

"You've lost me..." Parker said, confused. Vicky dismissed him with a wave of her hand. "Well, I just wanted to see that you were alright with this. And also, how do you think Kelly will take it?"

"Kelly's a big girl," Vicky shrugged. "She was never that much into you, anyway. You guys were awful together but good to everyone else, you know. And you got her off moping for that cheating bastard ex-fiancé of hers. But now she needs to wake up and have a taste of the Irish coffee that's brewing right under her damn nose!"

27

To: ccho@jhotels.com
BCC: mbradshaw@jhotels.com
From: kmccoy@jhotels.com
Subject: Yooper Runners
Mr. Cho,
It may have escaped your notice that the above-mentioned group has not yet posted payment, nor do they have a valid credit card as a backup. If neither occurs by noon today, the group will be denied entry, and your head will be on the plate.
Please don't insult my intelligence again by saying that 'you trust this group'. It doesn't work that way.
Kelly McCoy

It was early October. The long-dreaded marathon weekend. The hotel was filled to capacity with pumped up athletes. Due to a 'computer error' they had been oversold for weeks, causing Matthew much stress and overtime cleaning up after Charles. Matthew suspected that Charles had found a way to circumvent the passcodes needed for the dotcoms. And without that evidence the mistakes could not be held against him.

The proverbial 'tree falling in the forest'- theory, Kelly had thought. *Translated into 21st century techno-geekyness.*

The complaints file on Charles was already as thick as a phone book, and Kelly started every morning wondering how he could still have a job at the J.

She was sitting in Matthew's office on Friday for their afternoon meeting. They were going over the numbers. She was unable to tear her eyes from the pictures of them leaning against the wall.

We do make a cute couple. Too bad we're such great friends now.

Over the past few months Kelly and Matthew had formed a very close friendship. They often played tennis together, had most of their meals together, since both of them still lived in the hotel, and even went house-hunting for Matthew together. Still, Kelly had on numerous occasions walked in on phone conversations between Matthew and Linda, and found herself oddly disturbed by her uncertainty about his marital status.

She was now pretending to play with her PDA, but was in fact fanatically typing an e-mail to Susan, about something that had been on her mind for months.

To: Susan.Russell@Byrne-Russell.com
From: kmccoy@jhotels.com
Subject: Matthew
s-real quick, pls. i kno i can trust u. u spent all
that time in the hospital w/ him and u have
the best judgmnt of character of any1 i kno.
so – is matthew or is he not married?-k

"Why are these still here? I thought they were meant to go in the lobby," Kelly pointed at the pictures and hit 'send'.

"They were. But the powers that be didn't think they fit with the design."

"I have a hard time imagining Susan saying that! She saw mine, and asked for copies!" Kelly argued.

"It's not Susan."

"Who then? Jacqui?"

Matthew shook his head.

Surely it can't be the jays! It was their idea in the first place.... Oh, du-uh! They were meant to hang outside Gina's office...

"Never mind. So, how're we looking for this weekend, then? Will the jays still be in town?" Kelly said excitedly.

"Yup. They just got in. Dying to see you," Matthew said, and leaned back with a sigh. "Can't wait 'till we're through this weekend, it'll be a lot easier after that, until Thanksgiving. You still running on Sunday?"

"Plan to anyway," Kelly said. "Jon just got back, and he's determined we're breaking four hours this year. Although

I don't see how that'll be possible, as we've hardly had time to train. Will you come watch?"

Matthew was rocking slowly in his chair and looked at Kelly. He seemed to be deep in thought. "What'll it take for you to wear one of our T-shirts?" he asked.

A paper bag over me head!

"I'll wear the baby-blue one, with the J logo, but nothing else!" she said.

"Then I'll definitely be there to watch!" Matthew winked.

What... ?!

"None of the other shirts, wise guy!" Kelly said blushing. "So, how're we looking, then? Even zero?" she tried to sound professional.

"Yes, finally, as of this morning," Matthew rubbed his eyes. "It'll still be mad, though. Between the runners wanting to have the rooms late for showering, and the Sunday check-ins arriving early... Marathon Sunday is always a madhouse! Thank God, I got Dan to take this weekend! I can't wait until Gina's approved of one of our candidates."

"You're not Manager on Duty this weekend? There's a first!"

"I know!" Matthew smiled. "I closed on that old Tudor we looked at in September. Hoping to move in this weekend."

"So, they finally accepted your offer, then?"

"In this market, they would've been foolish not to."

Oh, just say it, Kelly! 'Are you or aren't you married?' I've never been this shy before! All … well, most the signs point to not married. I've got to start trusting men eventually. What's the worst that could happen? He'll find out that I fancy him? Me head will explode from all the blood rushing to it? … Better not risk it…

"This may be way out in the left field, but would you consider training me for MOD shifts? I mean, I'm here all the time anyway. It's not like I'm drinking while in the bar…" Kelly said carefully.

And I would get to wear something less slutty and constricting.

"I was hoping you'd say that," Matthew jumped up. "I was afraid to ask, because … well … we can only pay you trainee wages. But if you get your H-1B, you'd be considered management, and it would be expected of you to do at least one shift per month. And you'd qualify for bonuses."

Well, don't count yer chickens. That sponsorship has been Charles' since the day Gina heard about it!

"When's that going to be decided, anyway?" Kelly asked impatiently.

"Monday at Exec, I hope, seeing as the jays are in town." Matthew leaned forward and smiled conspiratorially. "You didn't hear this from me, but it's now between just you and Charles."

So, really just Charles, then.

Leaning back in his chair, Matthew picked up the reports again. "What happened in the bar last night?"

"I have no idea. I wasn't here. I was at the Russells. Jon got home from Argentina... I told you about it ages ago! You approved it!"

Holding up a hand, Matthew smiled. "Easy, easy," he said. "I was just wondering if you saw something when you got back."

Kelly squirmed. "The bar was closed when I got back..."

"What?! What time was that?"

"Around ten."

"Well, that explains it, then. This is the first night since opening, that we haven't broken budget." Matthew held up the F&B report. "Seen the numbers from the bar from last night? They suck!" Kelly took the report from him and studied it. "You know, if you're not married to the idea of going into marketing, I would strongly suggest you consider a career in hospitality. You've got what it takes," Matthew said.

Well, that's just from good upbringing. All it really takes is smiling a lot, being polite and a good listener.

"I had a brilliant mentor," Kelly winked.

"There you go again, underestimating yourself." He picked up a stack of guest comment cards. "These are September's."

"How'd we do?"

"Ninety-eight overall."

"That'll be hard to beat..." Kelly said, biting her lower lip.

"But not impossible."

"Is that normal? For a new property, I mean."

"Good question. There are two things that can happen when a new hotel first opens. Either the guests are overwhelmed by the newness of it all, and that seems to be happening here. Or, the property still has some serious kinks to unravel, and the comment cards come back fiercely negative. We won't really know until a year from now, when we have a basis for comparison," he said and separated a stack of comment cards, held together with a rubber band.

"These are your personal positives," he said, handing her the stack. "A hundred and four, in all. And these," he handed her three more, "are your negatives."

Kelly laughed. "Let me guess. All in the same hand-writing, and really bad English?"

"You really want to know?"

"Fire away."

"You're inhospitable in one, a whore without the 'w' in another and a militant lesbian in the third."

"I've been called worse," Kelly shrugged.

The phone on Matthew's desk rang. He looked at the display. "Uh-oh, what did you do now, Ms. McCoy?"

"What?"

Matthew pressed the button for the speakerphone. "Matthew Bradshaw," he answered and leaned back in his chair.

"I need to see you and Ms. McCoy in my office immediately," Gina's voice came across the line.

"On our way," Matthew said and hung up. He looked at Kelly. "Told you so," he singsonged.

Ohmygod!

"Charles showed her that e-mail from me!" Kelly gasped.

"Most likely. Well, forwarded it anyway," Matthew said while getting into his suit jacket. "It wasn't the most diplomatic way to address the issue…"

"But I was right! … Right …?"

"Yes, but I wish you'd consulted with me before sending it. The gist was correct, the wording extremely rude," Matthew said, as they left his office and started walking down the grand staircase.

"Don't worry, though, I sent Charles on an errand that will take him all day."

"You wanted him out of the hotel for marathon, huh?"

"You better believe it!" Matthew chuckled as Kelly's PDA beeped. "Read that, then please mute it. You know how Gina hates interruptions during her one-on-ones."

To: kmccoy@jhotels.com
From: ccho@jhotels.com
Subject: Re: Yooper Runners
Patry prinses,
The group leader say check in mail. Why you
all ways so mean for me? Best interests you
are nice for me.

Charles Cho
Revenue Manager
J Hotel Chicago

"Is this some kind of a joke? It's in extremely poor taste," Gina said, pushing a folder across her desk to Kelly and Matthew.

She looks different today. Did she do something to her hair?

Kelly took the folder and she and Matthew glanced at it. "An application for weekend manager. I remember meeting with this guy. Perfect for the job," Matthew said.

"Right!" Kelly agreed. "Shateed Johnson. Great guy."

"Oh, is that how you pronounce his name? Odd. Because when I look at it I read Shithead," Gina said, whispering the last word. "Please tell me this is a typo."

Matthew and Kelly both shook their heads. "Nope," Kelly said.

She sounds angry, but looks … Ohmygod! She got Botoxed! … Better concentrate on her mouth, not her forehead! Good plan!

"Mr. B.? You're needed in the lobby," a voice came across Matthew's walkie-talkie.

Gina looked angry. "Turn that off, Mr. Bradshaw!"

"On my way," Matthew responded on the radio halfway out the door. "I'll be right back, ladies."

Gina sighed. "We can't hire him," she said curtly.

"He's the best candidate we've met with."

"Well, if that's the case, then you need to meet with more suitable candidates. We simply cannot have a manager with a name like Shithead."

"Shateed," Kelly corrected her irritated.

Concentrate on the mouth! ... Impossible! She might as well have a red beacon on that immobile forehead of hers!

"Whatever. This is extremely ghetto and doesn't reflect well on the J image," Gina continued.

That is IT!

Kelly jumped to her feet and leaned over Gina's desk. She felt the hairs in the back of her neck rising. "And just what is that image, Gina? Racists? Prejudiced? Bigoted? This poor guy can't help where he was born or what his parents named him!" she shot out. "Did you even read the entire application or did you decide to dismiss him based on the spelling of his name? Did you even get to the part where he mentions that he goes by Hank? This guy is funny, he's smart, he's articulate and he's well educated. Plus he's got tons of experience. We'd be lucky to have him. He's perfect for the job, and if you want to reject him based on his background, then I've a good mind to tell him just that and enjoy watching him drag yer sorry arse to court! Besides, I'm the Public Image Manager around here, and if anything doesn't reflect well on the J image it's yer saggin flesh!"

"You're way out of line, young lady. You need to get your priorities straight," Gina said ashen-faced.

"No! What I need is for you to quit telling me what I need! You need to listen to me and listen good! Have you any idea how hated, disrespected and despised you are? Do you have a death wish?"

"Are you threatening me?" Gina rose to her feet and stared Kelly square in the eye.

"No, I'm trying to help you!" Kelly shouted and straightened her back. She was towering over Gina.

"Don't you know that everyone here calls you 'the Ice Bitch' behind yer back? You have the worst people skills of anyone I've ever known! You never have a kind word to offer anyone! You wouldn't recognize a good thing if it sat on yer nose! Like Shateed here! Or Matthew! Never so much as a 'thank you' or an 'atta boy', although he puts in eighty hour weeks! And you! You show up for an hour, then take two hours for lunch! And then have yer nails done during business hours! And you take ten-minute smoke breaks every hour! And yer double standards! I was banned from property until my visa cleared, but Charles is still here, with forged documents!"

"You can't prove that."

"Wanna bet?"

Call my bluff, ice bitch! I dare you! ... Impossible to stay mad at someone who looks like she just ran through Saran Wrap at seventy miles an hour!

"I've heard quite enough, Miss McCoy."

"I've only just begun, Ms. Lombardi!" Kelly hissed. "You think I don't know InnTime? I know you salt yer hours, and I can't wait for Bryce and Alen to find out! And by the way - it's still illegal to tap someone's PDA's. Even under the Patriot Act you have to have reasonable doubt and a court order! I could sue you for invasion of privacy!"

"And I could sue you for slander! I don't know what you're talking about," Gina said nonchalantly.

"Yeah, right, you don't! You don't think I don't know how to read a lock audit? You don't know of half the good things yer staff does to pay for yer manicures, but I can guarantee that you're involved in most of the foul play. And then you have the nerve to scold Matthew for exceeding the August budget by *only* eleven percent! And you do it at Exec! How dare you!? And then you praise Charles, who has no idea what he's doing, who's illegal and you know it and whose tongue is so far up yer arse, he can lick yer eyeballs from the inside!"

Huh? I can stay mad at Saran Wrap face!!

Gina slammed the top of her desk with her hand. Kelly shut up abruptly. "That's enough, Miss McCoy! You're being insubordinate! I don't have to sit here and take this from the corporate pin-up girl! And how dare you insult Charles? He's just as capable to do the job as I am!"

Hardly a yardstick!

"...and he will get my vote for sponsorship!"

"Oh! Big surprise!"

"He went to Cornell!" Gina yelled, her voice rising an octave.

"So did Shateed!" Kelly retorted. "And furthermore – I don't want that sponsorship that badly. Because I don't think I can stand working for a conniving, back-stabbing, two-faced bigot like you any more!"

"That'll suit me just fine, because I have a good mind to terminate your employment!"

"For speaking me mind? For being honest?!"

"I can do it for a lot less than that!"

"No, you can't! Bryce and Alen hired me and only they can fire me!" Kelly stared at Gina and felt the electricity in the air between them. "But you know what? They needn't bother, because I quit!"

"You do know that your visa only allows you to work at this property. You have a lot to lose," Gina said calmly and sat down again.

"No, I've got everything to gain by walking out right now! Bryce and Alen had a beautiful dream and you had to turn it into a nightmare!"

"How dare you?! The J has made a profit every day since opening!"

"Yes, and no thanks to you! You've done diddly squat but take credit for other people's hard labor! The concept is a winner! I generate revenue for the Milk Bar! Me! The corporate pin-up! Matthew works his arse off, and keeps meeting or exceeding budget! You … you're nothing but a burden! And you better shape up before they find out what a lying skiver you are!" Kelly stormed out of Gina's office.

She was fuming as she nearly ran into Matthew and Bryce. Matthew saw Kelly's expression as she slid into the elevator. "You okay?" he said.

"Leave me alone!" Kelly replied just as the elevator doors were closing.

What a bitch! I was right from the start, I should never have taken this job. It has brought me nothing but premature gray hairs and ulcers working with that bitch.

Kelly's PDA received an e-mail as she burst through the door to her suite, but it was still on mute, so she didn't see it.

> To: kmccoy@jhotels.com
> From: Susan.Russell@Byrne-Russell.com
> Subject: Re: Matthew
> Not. ☺

She started throwing her belongings into bags.

So I didn't know that my visa only allowed me to work here. That's a bit like glorified slavery isn't it? No wonder people do it illegally! Why spend the time, money and effort when it's so much easier not to. No wonder Charles is such a kiss-arse. ... Bu that still doesn't justify Gina treating people like she does. I regret nothing. She had much worse coming her way. ... I really should start looking into anger management classes ... Or just go home where I'm allowed, expected even, to speak me mind!

In the closet, she discarded all her party clothes.

Corporate pin-up girl! Well, no more! Bye-bye sluttiness, hello torn jeans and T-shirts.

She threw a pair of high-heeled sandals in the corner of the closet.

Bye-bye constricting torture devices.

She paused, then pulled them back out and put them on her feet.

Actually, I'm going to keep these, they do something for my posture.

She was in the bathroom throwing toiletries into plastic bags.

Now what do I do? Start all over? So not worth going through all that again. Go back to Dublin? … I could so easily go over the deep end right now. I've things here, I've things at Vicky's and I've things at the Russells', and I've nowhere to live. Again.

Kelly collected all her bags and placed them by the door. With a heavy sigh she sat down on the sofa and looked around the sitting room.

Might as well go out with a bang, she thought as she went to the honor bar.

She poured a minibottle of rum in a glass and topped it off with a Coke.

Maybe I could ask Jon or Susan to come and pick me up. I could stay in their guest room and become another one of many undocumented aliens who does odd jobs for cash under the table. Good plan! Maybe Parker's Jimmy Joe will hire me. … Hmmm? Better not. Not after that song-and-dance I keep giving everyone about illegals.

Her cell phone rang, startling her. She looked at the display. 'Matthew mobile'.

"What do you want?" she answered angrily.

"I heard what happened between you and Gina," he said, sounding sincerely worried. "Do you want to talk about it?"

"Nothing to talk about," Kelly said and finished her drink in one big gulp. "Why don't you talk to Gina, get her version."

"I'd rather get yours. Please let me in?"

"Where are you?"

"Outside your door."

Kelly tiptoed to the door and looked through the peephole. She could see Matthew looking right at her, his expression sad. Kelly hung up the phone and opened the door for him. "Drink?" she said and tossed him a can of Heineken. "I'm emptying the minibar, and won't mind some help."

Matthew opened the can. "Might as well," he said, and took a sip. "After all, it's past six o'clock and I just clocked out."

"You clocked out at six? That's a first!"

"It is," Matthew said, and sat down on the window seat. "I wanted to talk to you uninterrupted. See that you were okay."

He's so sweet. Is he for real?

"So, do you want to talk about what happened?" Matthew said.

Kelly was pacing up and down the room, gesticulating wildly. "She's such a bitch! She's such a horrid, evil, lying, conniving, despicable, … back-stabbing, … vile, two-faced, bigoted, criminal, … skiving bitch!"

"I agree." Matthew said calmly.

Kelly was still pacing. She stopped and looked at Matthew. "Another Heinie?"

Matthew looked at his full can and shook his head. Kelly poured herself another rum and Coke, and started pacing again.

"I just feel like going straight to Bryce and telling him to keep her under surveillance. Not only is she dead weight to this operation, but she's also into some really bad … stuff, … and he should know it."

"He does know it," Matthew said, placing his beer can on the windowsill. "He heard everything you said to Gina.

Kelly stopped pacing. "What?"

Matthew was smiling. "Remember that call I got while in her office? Well, that turned out to be a guest compliment. When I got back, you were already up in arms over Gina, so I called Bryce over to have a listen."

"You heard everything?"

Ohmygod!

"Well, why didn't you stop me? Why did you let me carry on like that?" Kelly was fighting a lump in her throat.

"Seemed inappropriate," Matthew said calmly. "You were really laying it all out, and we wanted to hear it. I especially wanted to thank you for standing up for me. You didn't have to do that."

"I know, I'm sorry. Heat of the moment."

"No, what I meant was, it was really decent what you did. No one's ever done that for me. Normally I fight my own battles. Nice to know I have you in my corner."

"You've always had me in your corner, Matthew, you know that."

A silence fell over them, and the room was glowing in the last rays of the setting sun. Kelly walked to the window and pressed her forehead against it. The glass felt cool. She looked down on the busy street below them.

"I'm sorry I snapped at you before. It wasn't you I was mad at," Kelly whispered without looking at Matthew.

"I know."

They were both quiet for a long while. Kelly was looking at the traffic. Matthew was looking at Kelly.

"I'm really going to miss this place," Kelly finally broke the silence, her eyes welling up. "I mean, I've hated it, and I've loved it, but for better or for worse, it's never been boring."

A small tear ran down her cheek. She brushed it away quickly. She turned to Matthew and extended a hand, trying to sound brave. "It's been a true pleasure working with you, Chief. You're by far the best thing that ever happened to this place."

Or to me.

Matthew took her hand and held it for a long time. "What about you?"

"What about me?" Shocked, she pulled her hand away.

"You quit," he said softly. "Is there anything I can do to convince you to stay?"

He placed his hand on her elbow and gently pulled her closer to him.

Tell me you're not really married.

"I've felt something for you ever since the moment I first met you," Matthew said softly.

Huh?

"I tried to fight it at first, because I was told you were on the rebound, then because you were dating someone else and then you were on my staff," he said, while slowly pulling her closer.

Screwing, not dating.

"My feelings for you were so strong that at one point I felt like resigning, because I thought it would be too difficult to work with you on a daily basis."

Kelly inched closer to him, and took his hands in hers. "Thank you for not resigning," she said quietly.

"I couldn't," Matthew said, and rose from the window seat.

Softly he stroked his thumb over her cheek, where a tear had just fallen. "I couldn't stand the thought of not seeing you every day. Not being close to you. Not talking to you. You're the best thing that ever happened to me," he said sincerely. "Kelly, I think I love you. And I can only hope that there might be a shadow of a possibility that you feel even remotely the same way about me."

Kelly put her hands on his waist and gently pressed her body against his. Their faces were close. "So you're not married, then?" she said looking deep into his eyes.

Matthew smiled and shook his head. "Nope."

Please, please, don't say 'dodged that bullet'.

"Never been so lucky," Matthew said, smiling, holding Kelly tight.

"And you really are the kind and caring creature you appear to be?" Kelly whispered, her mouth nearly brushing his.

"So it would seem."

"No more pretending?"

"Deal," Matthew said, and gently planted his lips on hers.

Those are the softest lips …mmmm ….

28

He's the gentlest, most considerate lover I've ever had.

Matthew and Kelly were lying in her bed, long limbs entangled. It was still dark outside. Neither had slept all night. Matthew pressed Kelly closer and kissed her neck. "Are you sleeping?" he whispered.

"No, you?" Kelly said, then realized the idiocy of her words and they both giggled.

"You are the most exciting, witty, intriguing, fascinating person I've ever met," Matthew mumbled to her neck.

"What? Not hot, sexy, beautiful, great fuck?"

Matthew's PDA started beeping. Kelly's was still on mute, but vibrated.

"Ignore 'em," Matthew said trying to kiss her.

Kelly rose, and reached for his PDA. "I quit yesterday. I'm under no obligation to anyone here. Unless they're asking me to return the noisemaker. Or throw me outta here. But you still work here," Kelly said.

Matthew smiled, and pulled her back into bed. "It can wait," he said, and kissed her passionately.

Mmmmm… He's a really great kisser. Ohmygod! How's me breath?! … He doesn't seem to care…

Matthew's PDA beeped again.

"You've got to see what it is," Kelly said. "Could be urgent."

Matthew resigned. He read the first message, and his face turned ashen. Silently he showed it to Kelly.

> To: mbradshaw@jhotels.com,
> kmccoy@jhotels.com
> From: bhart@jhotels.com
> Subject: Emergency meeting
> Must see both of you in Gina's office immedi-
> ately.
> Bryce Hart

Kelly read it and gasped. "What is it? You're fired? They know you spent the night here?! What do you think it is?"

"I don't know," Matthew said, biting his lower lip. "But it can't be good. Bryce always signs his messages just 'B'. Here's the second one."

> To: mbradshaw@jhotels.com
> From: bhart@jhotels.com
> Subject: [none]
> NOW!!!
> B

"Okay, so now I'm confused," Matthew said and got out of bed. "We'd better get going," he said, and started searching for his clothes.

Kelly was stretching like a cat on the bed.

"Don't do that!" Matthew said, looking at her naked body on top of the covers. "We'll get into more trouble than we're already in. Come on, let's get dressed."

"I don't work here any more, remember?"

"Aren't you even curious?" Matthew said, pulling his pants on.

Kelly sat up in bed. "I know what this is about. They've heard Gina's side of the story. They bought it, and now I'm to be publicly humiliated." She got out of bed, and walked to Matthew. "I'm not going," she said determined and rubbed her bare chest against his.

Matthew moaned softly, then quickly pulled away from her. "We can't do this right now!" he said hastily. "Let's just go see what they want. Who knows, we may both be fired, and then we'll have all the time in the world for lovemaking."

Lovemaking? I've finally found a man who's not afraid to use that term, and mean it too! I love him.

Kelly pecked a quick kiss on his lips and started dressing. She looked at Matthew and smiled. "They're going to wonder if you show up wearing the same clothes you wore yesterday," she said.

"Who's gonna notice?"

"Hello? They're gay!"

"You're right. Of course. Do you have anything I could borrow?" he said. "Nothing too revealing, or high-cut, I'm not too proud of my calves, and lilac really doesn't do justice to my bone structure," Matthew limp-wristed.

Kelly laughed and threw a polo shirt at him. "You're so bad! I love you!"

Oh, holy fock!

Matthew caught the shirt, and walked over to Kelly. He took her in his arms and looked deep into her eyes. "I love you, too, Kelly McCoy," he said and pressed a soft kiss on her lips. He dropped her like a sack of potatoes. "Now get dressed!"

"What's this? Casual Saturday?" Alen said as Matthew and Kelly appeared in Gina's office moments later. "Have a seat," he said pointing at the chairs across Gina's desk.

I know these chairs were Susan's idea. Uncomfortable. Hard wood and straight backs. Like sitting on a church bench. Keep you awake during meetings with the ice b... Where is she, anyway?

Kelly looked around the office. Bryce got up slowly from behind the desk and sat on it facing them. Alen closed the door and leaned against it.

I feel like a third grader caught smoking and being disciplined by the Mother Superior.

"Coffee?" Bryce offered looking down at both Matthew and Kelly.

Both shook their heads.

Please, just get to the point.

Bryce cleared his throat. "Kelly, you really are just a tad too outspoken," he started. "I understand that you and Gina have never seen eye-to-eye on ... well ... anything, but nevertheless, she is your Managing Director, and with that position comes some respect."

"But..."

Bryce held up a hand. "That respect, however, in this case is not deserved, and you'll both be pleased to know that Gina Lombardi no longer works with the J Corporation."

Kelly tried to read his expression, but couldn't.

"Nor does Charles Cho," Alen added from the door.

"After having heard your accusations, we started investigating," Bryce continued. "And you were right, Kelly. On every count. We've been blind, or too busy, or too intimidated to bother before, but once you stormed out of this office last night, your point so blatantly made, we could no longer afford to ignore it. As per our property covenant we could only fire her for good cause. You gave us that cause. I'm not going to bore you with the legal details right now, but just know that they're gone. For good."

Kelly looked at Matthew, dumbstruck. 'You knew?' she mouthed. Matthew shook his head. Suddenly Alen started giggling at the door. His giggle was contagious and Bryce joined him, and suddenly they were both laughing out loud.

They were kidding! Gina's not gone! Some sick joke!

"'Ding-dong, the bitch is gone! Which old bitch? The icy bitch!'," Alen was singing to the tune from *The Wizard of Oz.*

"So, she's really gone, then?" Kelly asked carefully.

The jays smiled and nodded. "Thanks to you, Kelly McCoy! She tried to argue her case, obviously, but the evidence against her was stronger," Alen said.

Kelly let a sigh of relief. "Phheeew! And here I thought you were going to fire Matthew..." Matthew's hand on hers stopped her cold.

Right. They don't know about us. Oh, God! Am I stuck in another secret non-relationship? ... Right ... Nepotism and all that. This is a relationship that should stay secret. Kinda exciting, actually...

"Why in the world would we ever fire Matthew? He's the best thing that ever happened to J!" Alen said, awestruck.

That's what I said!!

Bryce cleared his throat. "Mr. Bradshaw, the position for Managing Director has unexpectedly been vacated. Until it's filled, I'd like you to assume the position," he said in mock seriousness. "Of course, don't ever expect it to be filled by anyone else!"

"Thank you," Matthew said. "Under one condition."

"Name it," Bryce said.

"Kelly resigned last night. I'd like her reinstated."

"Ms. McCoy," Bryce said. "You pointed out to Gina that only Alen or I can fire you. Well, we're also the only ones who will accept your resignation."

"And, we've decided to sponsor you," Alen added.

"Really? But I thought it was a vote?"

"It was, but seeing as the only ones voting were the Execs, and you always carried all but one vote anyway, we really didn't see a point," Bryce smiled.

"And we suggest that you start looking into a Masters Program," Alen said.

"Since you just saved the company a quarter mil in fines for hiring an illegal alien, we'll be happy to sponsor you with school as well," Bryce added.

Kelly rushed to her feet and kissed both Bryce and Alen. Her eyes were welling up. She was speechless.

"There's just one more thing," Matthew added. "It's become increasingly difficult for Kelly and me to work long hours and weekends in the near future."

Ohmygod! He's outing us!

"What!?" Bryce and Alen said in unison while Kelly took her seat again.

"We're in love, and intend to make no secret about it. We would like some spare time to explore that emotion," Matthew said kissing Kelly's hand softly.

"Finally! Do you realize that we've had a pool going since the two of you met, when you'd end up together!" Alen exclaimed.

"I'm so happy for you! Just don't let it interfere with work, is all I care about!" Bryce continued. "Now then, it's Saturday! Go out, have fun, make beautiful love all weekend. We'll see you Monday at Exec!"

Kelly and Matthew walked smiling, hand-in-hand out of the office. They snuck quickly and quietly through the lobby, where the night manager was busy giving his report to the early shift behind the reception desk. They hurried into the elevator.

"Where to, dear?" Matthew said as the doors were closing.

Kelly crossed her arms behind his neck, and kissed him, long and hard. "Only way is up."

The Beginning

Made in the USA